Music for

a

Pandemic

Quartet

MICHAEL SCHUVAL

Epigraph

SCALE AFTER SCALE OF YOU,
TRUTH AFTER TRUTH OF YOU PEEL
TO THE CORE OF TRUTH,
THE WHITE, HARD CENTER
OF REALEST LIFE.

Edgar Lee Masters, *The New Spoon River (Joseph Revell)*

I

Enter the Players, Masked

Paul exits his car in the almost-filled lot of East Nook Beach. He'd been there several times in recent weeks. Today it was different. Unlike the previous visits, it was packed with people who had streamed there because of the eighty degree temperature and high humidity, unusual for the second week in May 2020. Also a draw was the bright cloudless sky stretching over the still waters of the harbor. The other—more prominent difference—was the *masks*.

There were masks everywhere. Attached, of course, *to faces*. Mostly paper surgical type masks, with a few cloth ones. Atop the faces of those who'd come to lie or roam on the pebbly sand of this early May beach. The masks were fixed to middle-aged faces, geriatric faces, twenty-something faces, mother-father faces, not-so-rebellious teenage faces. And—yes, children's faces.

Paul hadn't seen these masked people before, during the eight previous weeks of the Corona Virus Pandemic. He had gone out every single day in this period of "Self-Quarantine" or "Lockdown" and hardly anyone wore masks; then by late

April all of the grocery and drugstore employees were required to wear them. Only a rare few of the shoppers had used them. He couldn't recall seeing a single pedestrian in a mask, whether those walking in town or those whom he'd come to recognize on his daily stroll in Fensher Park. And that was the putative *height* of the Covid-19 outbreak, as the "novel" virus had been named. Nor were they advised, in those early panicky days, to wear them by the CDC (Centers for Disease Control and Prevention). Had that changed – suddenly? He didn't know.

He walked down towards the water which was still, glinting with pearly sunshine. The people were energized, though masked, and full of buoyancy. They talked and joked, through the face-coverings, and ate (around them) on the blankets they'd brought. Kids chased each other in sand-splashing circles. Some wore bathing suits as if summer had actually arrived. Down the shore men had dropped fishing lines trying their luck in the harbor. Paul understood. This was not your usual manifestation of spring fever. This was the expression of people who had been, in effect, locked in their homes for months. Many of them had hardly stepped past their front doors. The children hadn't attended school or played together, the adults hadn't worked (unless from home) and social interactions had all taken place electronically on a new video platform called "Zoom." Q-U-A-R-A-N-T-I-N-E.... That was the watchword of the day, usually with "Self" preceding it. The word had always been applied to highly contagious people whose presence in a room signaled latent doom, a state of affairs that said—"This is for the patient's own good—and for the public's. It'll be as brief as possible." The last resort, the only possible way to handle the situation of this *particular* person or several people.

Americans were not used to that; these people had never experienced such a thing. Now *all* were quarantined, all suspected of carrying the contagion which could wipe the rest of us out. All of us were potential serial killers, from Grandma to little Sally and everyone in between. Now they were out—prematurely according to health authorities—temporarily. They were out, breathing diminished, voices muffled. All for their "own safety" of course. They had followed the authorities' guidelines all these weeks—STAY HOME, STOP THE SPREAD—now the masks—grinding their lives to a halt—SELF QUARANTINE.

Paul sat on a rock by the jetty. He took out his phone, tapped on the photos app. Scrolling down he came to the March pics. There it was—March 22. Eight pictures from this same beach. About a week after the "shelter in place" quarantine had begun. The pictures were mostly long-view shots down the curving coastline, similar bright blue sky as today's, blanched with clouds here and there. That day it was twenty-five degrees colder and a crisp breeze occasionally tore in from the south. He zooms in on the digital images in his hand. Yes, they're there—people. There's a small group playing with a frolicking dog. Others are standing on the rocks of the jetty Paul sat on at that moment. Some had brought folding chairs to plant in the sand and steal a bit of fresh air. What were their masks like? They weren't—there were none. They had, for the most part, "obeyed," the social distancing that had been imposed—they'd been told early on to stay SIX FEET AWAY from each other. That day, people didn't shy away from fairly close conversation, talking about their dogs, their kids, closed schools and online learning. There weren't many out. He'd stopped and spoken, exchanging opinions on "the situation," with others. In those early days when you met others a prominent topic was—the Immune System. *What are you taking? Vitamin C, yeah, I picked up some myself, a thousand milligrams. Have you heard Vitamin D is imperative?—Oh, you have... I started taking this Oil of Oregano stuff, really terrific, great natural anti-viral/anti-bacterial. Good tip, thanks. Elderberry, huh? I'll check it out...* Paul had a couple of those on his March excursion, sharing information. He met two people who'd been laid off, two others had been furloughed. Uncertainty flickered in their eyes, hand-shielded from the sun. We need to be out here in the sun, they'd all agreed.

Most wouldn't heed that common sense. They'd stay in or duck out mouse-like to grab provisions and dart back behind doors. It would go on...and on.

He put the phone down, tried to read a book, feeling the heat permeate his back, neck and face. Concentration wavering, he scanned up and down the yellow-shimmering beach. They were all acting as if it were a typical, lovely Saturday in May. He closed his eyes, drifted for a time, numbed and drowsed by the heat and hard light. A phrase—**The New Normal**—appeared before him. The slogan the media and government officials had been spewing out for weeks into months—they were now apparently living in. In that state of drifting somnolence on the jetty he could see, without effort or analysis, the psychological conditioning involved in repeated use of the phrase. Normal, new... Normal plus new. That's *not* normal. That's not a "new" normal. It's Ab-normal.

Paul shakes himself out of the torpor. He stands, steadies, turns, walks towards the parking lot. A bench near the bathrooms offered shade and he sat. He takes a long gulp from his water bottle. Something felt off—*was* off—felt even more strange to him than all the recent repertoire of outlandish events. Just then a large family passes, jabbering in Spanish. All the kids, three, five, seven years old, had masks on. He notices a man nearby, snapping photos on an expensive looking camera, long lens protruding. He has to speak immediately—or he might start running—*shouting*—and get locked *further* up. They would call it "Covid-19."

"Can I make a suggestion?"

"Sure," the man lowers his equipment to his chest. He doesn't care what Paul's about to say.

"You should do a photo essay on all the masks. The mask wearers."

He could see it: The new normal. The new mask-faces, one after another, in a line, accepting. Not hiding but hiding. Out in front. Obeying. Wearing. Appearing. Like mute witnesses, thousands lined up…. One after another…. Exposing their concealment….

"Well, yeah," the photographer replies, examining his lens, "there are lots of photos already out there of, you know…people wearing the masks."

The man with the camera starts to move. People wearing the masks. That's not what I meant, Paul thinks. No—he says it aloud, surprising himself. Not what I meant at all. The photographer is gone, down the beach.

It's time for him to go, too.

II

Genealogies

They were from an island. Nothing exotic, forty miles east of a city "that never sleeps." Yeah, okay. Nice beaches. They lived on the south shore of the island in families typical of those who resided there in those early '70s years. Eager, nervous living in an actual house (and what does that mean), enthusiastic, awed, anxious, upwardly mobile (without the designation), mortgaged to the hilt, Dad making pretty good money, maybe Mom worked part time (or would have to). At least two kids, one on the way, also anxious, trying *hard* to hide it, behind Italian Ice stains and pizza-sauce smears. It was all pizza it seemed… endless white carboard boxes with crusts left inside… and Burger King… McDonald's… Oily crumpled french-fried bags…burp…billions sold…. Dental offices, block parties, fireworks, baseball cards, greasy bicycle chains, board games, little hands holding transistor radios, big hands placing big records on spinning players, pediatricians jabbing who-knows-what needles in your shoulder. Pool parties, Hamburger Helper, Betty Crocker. Wonderama on Sunday morning TV. Bugs Bunny and that duck. Archie Bunker and Arthur Fonzarelli. Sufferin' Succotash. Sunrise Highway. Paved toward the paradise of new residential developments, right off the bay, in fact stuck between canals, paradise winding round and round, skirting cul-de-sacs, high shrub lines, sweeping past new Cadillacs and Chryslers, indistinguishable brother-sister homes except for those with cheesy-luxury facades, debts curling up in the corner by the fireplace near the stack of overdue bills, one pretty identical street after another, glowing green cut lawns, barbecue smoke melting snowmen, the dog ate my homework. Paradise winding all the way around till it meets itself. There in the hiss of cicadas and the strange sense of "now what?" "what's next?" Summer camp. Tensions in the classrooms of September. Passive aggressive teachers. Buzzed-out bus drivers. A new teacher. New clothes, new shoes. Too tight—everything. Smiles through anxious faces. Everything's too tight. Shaping up. Proving yourself. Report cards. Dodgeball. Prove yourself. Does she like me? Don't chicken out—fight. Shame. Bravery come from nowhere. Notebooks, half-done assignments. Dad coming home from work. Sweaty, tired. Fed up. Wants a beer, a shot and maybe an argument with Mom. Don't talk to him now. Go upstairs. The staircase, our best friend. Holding the banister. Listening, peeking down. Laugher from the TV, Carol Burnett. They couldn't hold it in. Belly laughter. "Go to sleep," Mom yells. Dad is watching Carson. Smoking. Sitting up in bed. " 'Night." Heeerrre's Johnnnyyy. Fade-out.

Mary Wellner's family lived on one of those south shore streets. In one of the newly-decorated houses with the modern-gadgeted kitchen. Paul Wilmer's family lived on one of those streets, ten blocks away. They won't study together till junior high school. When Paul moved in the local elementary school was already filled. He had to be bussed to the school on the other side of the canal. They met in the local park when the new playground equipment came and everyone went wild jumping over shining monkey bars, diving through neon-colored tubes! He saw her she saw him, they didn't say much, they played, pushed and pulled now and then on cool days after school, rough, but play. They knew they were neighbors, had to be, and each other's names sort of, mixed in the other's games. He was "Pauly," she Mary Well-something. Cute girl and tough didn't mind tumbling with the boys. She was a girl in the background who came into focus occasionally. He couldn't forget her. Collier Avenue Junior High. Paul was class-clownish, a pretty good student. Mary was proper, a very good student. They ran in circles which often intersected. Paul thought Mary didn't like him. Mary felt Paul thought she was prissy. Their peers would joke about how close their last names sounded—were they *maaarried*? Dumb. Uncomfortable too, for kids. Paul was magnetized by her – he didn't quite realize.

Something happened when they met again at Theodore Roosevelt High School. They were drawn together. Not immediately, not directly. There was a party they attended where they realized they had mutual friends. New friends. Paul wondered, what's going on with this girl, has she changed? Yeah, she had. Mary saw Paul around school, laughing, looking confident, with people she wanted to get to know too. And looking stoned. Often. She kept appearing where he appeared. After school at the pizza place. Or the park—in the next town, where they shouldn't have been. Parties on the weekends. A concert. They were both present. Music was always there. The music. Mary started dating a boy whom Paul partied with. Paul was there the first time Mary got high. He kept an eye on her. Her nerves or anxiety kicked in. He saw her falter and talked her through it gently, mixing joking with serious. He told her "no biggie, first time can be shaky," and got her giggling. Their friendship deepened from there. From there it was – Mary looking out for Paul – Paul for Mary.

She comes from a cold place, autumn was a name for early winter and she had to figure it out on her own. Most of it. Way upstate. Not far from the border. A little girl in a little house in a tiny town near a small city you wouldn't notice. A place with big spaces and small relations. Alone in that house mostly, since Mom was working and Dad was—somewhere. Jill made friends with the furniture. She loved a certain dresser. Old, dark blue—smooth. In secret she ran her hands over it. Pressed herself to it. She had a few dolls. They always disappointed her. Her name was Jill Merigeli. Italian all sides and in between, she didn't "look Italian." Everyone wanted to tell her. As a girl even, she knew it was a ridiculous statement. She didn't look anything, she thought, as she stared into a faded mirror above her mother's make-up table in the empty bedroom after school. Hair too bright, face too...too nothing. She felt she looked as faded as the glass she faced. She couldn't locate herself and stopped trying. In school she found if she cared for others—they would care back. As she had learned to become proficient at building fires at home, her intuition told her where to find a bit of warmth, if not security.

He's younger than the other three, beyond years. Born and raised north of the city "that doesn't sleep." His streets and childhood resembled his older neighbors on the island. Except there was more. More square footage. More spread out lawns. Higher trees. Higher taxes. Space in general. Money specifically.

His name is Dan. Daniel Fox.

As a kid they called him Danny which he got used to. When he went to college suddenly it felt like a kid's name. He couldn't stop others from calling it—especially his girlfriends. He tolerated it. When someone called him Dan, that sounded at twenty or twenty-three, like a man in his forties. Only his mother and teachers called him Daniel. It made him sit up as if being reproved. When he met Mary and she addressed him as Daniel—it gave him a different feeling. She gave him a difference about everything.

Daniel never lacked anything growing up, he thought, but he was wrong. Outwardly, he had gorgeous swimming pools, well-stocked refrigerators, well-equipped playgrounds. The "best" schools and tutors. Inwardly, rifts, gaps. Danny didn't examine those.

Paul meets Mary. Daniel meets Mary. Jill meets Mary. Daniel meets Jill. Paul meets Daniel. Paul meets Jill.

Mary is the hub, the others will revolve around her ways of moving. Of being. Something she has. She knows it...doesn't know what it is.

Daniel saw her in a bar on the upper east side of Manhattan. Happy hour. A year before the towers fell. Mary was laughing, doing shots of alabama slammers with her colleagues. A pair of eyes caught hers, greenish, she paused—a quick second. That was the one she saw on the street. She joins the fun, doesn't turn again to the young man standing against the wall. In the mirror behind the bar she sees him peeping at her. Why me, I'm the oldest one here, why not these twenty-three year olds. She returns from the bathroom, there they were, the green eyes in front of her. He makes a joke, not very funny, she's already half gone, she stops and giggles. Cute boy...too young. Right? She's sitting near him now, with a shot he's bought her. They're lifting them, he's toasting. She doesn't get the words clear. She's forgotten her friends at the other end. He's forgotten almost everything.

Mary moves back to the island she started from. With a husband whose name is Daniel Fox. Soon she has a daughter. This time she's on the north side of the island.

Years go by in the blur that years—and having children—make on human memory. Her circle of friends includes locals and others from a neighborhood many were half living in now—the world-wide Web. She had a Facebook page, other faces were drawn to hers. One was Jill Chambers, née Merigeli. Very same town, Worthington. Mary noticed Jill's posts. A dry wit, intelligence. Notes to herself, Jill Chambers—different?

It happened. Mary, pushing her toddler Tobias, into the playground. Other mothers there on a brisk late-winter morning with children. Toby crouches in the sand hard from the cold, digs with a shovel. Mary takes out a book, on a bench alone. A novel a friend recommended. She had a picture of him she used as a bookmark. She stared at his candid eyes, tried to read what he was thinking, now, at that moment. A woman, alone, sits near her, hands in thick coat pockets, gazing out at the day. Mary feels she knows her. "Finally a break, huh— sunshine?" The woman turns, glad to talk. "Yes, about time we had some." No, alone, no kid here, she says. They exchange names. Mary... Jill... Are you—Jill from Facebook? Yes. That's me. You're funny. I mean, I enjoy your sense of... Oh, thanks.. She seems sad. Yes, one here, Mary tells her, of Tobias, banging his shovel into the earth. And a twelve-year-old. Girl. Next year, junior high. Numbers exchanged. She lives only minutes away. Mary had known, somehow, they'd meet.

Jill came to dinner with her soon to be ex-husband, Phillip. They were living apart. Maybe if they met new people, made new friends...? No. Pleasant dinner though. Jill's first impression of Daniel—very handsome. *Very* confident. But—detached? A cool customer, doesn't reveal much. Daniel thinks—attractive. Became sad—or always was. Missing something. A good person.

Dan had heard about Paul for a long time. "My best friend, Paul," she told him. A bunch of times. "Brilliant writer." Had seen his letters. Poems. Mary had them in a box, decorated with magic markers. Who *was* this guy? The box was all Paul.

Daniel tried not to think about him. He and Mary had never had sex, according to her. He was back from Europe, eastern Europe was it? Staying with his folks. Paul was there when they arrived. Watching TV news over the bar. He puts his smoke down, shakes Daniel's hand. Dan registers the lack of firmness in his hand. "Heard a lot about you, great to finally..." Paul saw in the first two minutes he had already decided something about him. He decides not to decide. It's Mary's husband. Wait and see.

A couple of drinks, an appetizer. Paul searches Mary, she looks—happy, giddy, he can understand that. He doesn't get her choice in Daniel. He doesn't get many things. He's her total opposite—young, materialistic, immature. He does have a sense of humor, Paul has to give him that. Daniel warms to him as the second scotch goes down. Promises they'll get together soon. Sorry you couldn't make it to the wedding. Yeah, me too... Paul goes away again.

He never loses touch with Mary. A walk in the city. A drink on the island. Their meetings are their meetings. Paul is going or coming from somewhere. "Won't be here long." He imagines he can hear Mary speaking to him— "Hey, you. Come back." The letters and emails flow with nary a break. Poems. Visions of life, shared, changing. Connection between, adamantine.

Jill is curious about Paul. Keeps hearing Mary speak of him. His drifting presence evades an encounter. Until he's there again near Mary, in Worthington. She finds him a place, and if Paul could be said to decorate, she helps him with it. Paul is home. Says he'll stay awhile. Is tired of... Just tired.

Jill meets Paul. A coffee shop with Mary. He's... nice. But—what? Blank. Open—and *closed*. Struggling with something and... already surrendered. Later it came into her mind; a documentary she once saw on amnesia. Amnesiacs. He's balding too. When he bent to pick up his bag she saw it. A teacup size atop his head. The bag was all books, he cradled it. He smiled at her, took a last gulp of coffee. And left.

Paul observed her plain appealing face. Slender well-kept body. Envisions what could happen. She feels to him a hundred miles away. He listens to Jill—hears the words, can't gather them.

Paul doesn't wonder much about Jill. There's nothing so charismatic about him, for Jill. Mary had painted him as... exceptional? Luminous? Not there, anyway. Then why is Mary so... why does she... She ponders. What is his life? What was that last glance he gave her—after he drank a sip of coffee?

This is how they met, these four. There are roots in common, geographical ones. What of the roots of their coming together? Wanting to be together? What, who, they mean to one another?

Underground. Like all other roots. Deep within like so many other connective pathways. Divergent, deviating. Colliding, joining. Snagging. Moving away. Moving, touching.

III

Initial Impressions, Possible Prognoses

No one's really going to remember when it began. For each of them it was different.

Of course it was China.... China was the word on everyone's lips, in everyone's minds. Who knows what to believe about China? Anything and everything is possible as regards that "place." Is it a place or a state...of what? Mind? Reality? Un-reality? China. Where everything's made and comes from. China, who finances the world, who eats up all its debt. China, who pilfers all technology and sells it back with cheap parts and one-year warranties. China with the thousand year plan, China with the rationale for *everything*. For concentration camps; facial recognition cameras; social credit scores. Rationales for child labor, for random imprisonment, for diurnal disappearances. China of Confucius and Lao Tzu. China of Mao. China of the Art of War and Little Red Book. Revolution, blood, confession, humiliation...renewal. History gone! China of the constant renewal. China of inscrutable faces and manifold intentions. China, ancient, modern, nothing, everything. China, mirror for the world which chooses the features it likes, pretending it can refrain from taking all of them, deluding itself as China deludes itself, knowing its own delusion, using its own delusion, clothed in delusion, proud of it as it marches through history, seeing blindly, counting everything, hive mind logic, towering above the world a cruel dissembling older brother who's learned his lessons well, biding his time, waiting, watching, for the siblings to stumble so he can pick up their pieces, unaware of the gulf he stands near, even when falling feigning knowledge of each plunging moment, plundering the air he passes, gathering stones as they crumble and evaporate. China, face of the world who can never figure itself out, in the meantime here's a watch, here's a phone, here's a blouse, here's a roomful of things that don't cease to multiply, here in a factory that doesn't end. Blurry video to prove it.

It was early February (or was it late January?) wasn't it, when word came West that something stranger than usual was occurring in China. News on television and the internet, an outbreak of a virus, people getting ill and the name of a city that would come to be synonymous with sickness, death and tyranny: **Wuhan**. Apparently hundreds, thousands were sick, untold numbers having already died. Escalating cases every day. They said. The pretty news anchors described a "Wet Market" in Wuhan where exotic animals were offered—slaughtered—for the appetites and medical applications of the local population. That's where, this thing, this "Corona Virus," originated. Blame it on the *bats*, they all said. The bats of Wuhan. Also...the *pangolins*. They put a new word out on the waves—Zoonotic: a disease which originates in animals and jumps over to humans. That one would never stick, too many new words and ideas for people to manage. Words don't start with Z. The basic idea now was—somehow *it* leapt from a bat into a scaly heavily-poached poor pangolin. In the market, wet, in Wuhan. When? November? December? 2019? Somewhere in there. And from the quirky-looking pangolin, boom—or…h*ssss*… Coronavirus lands in human territory. There it is. By late January the situation was dire. Almost overnight, China locked down eleven million people in Wuhan and millions in surrounding towns and cities. Unlike the "lockdowns" yet to happen in western nations, China meant the word literally. Nobody could leave their houses or apartments. Unless they were sick—or dead. And the latter was an open question. Those who left without permission were dragged off by police. There were reports of entire hospitals being constructed in a week. Was it possible? Well, it *was* China, where anything is…

Yes, it was China, then Wuhan Wuhan Wuhan, bat bat bat, it was and would be Virus, Virus, Virus. Oh, *would it be.* Virus. Injected into the world's veins, the V-word, into its dreams and hard-waking hours. Spilling like unremovable paint across wall after wall. A blanket tossed over the world's body, heavy, wet, energy-draining. Sort of like a virus. Then… Corona, Corona, Corona… Coronavirus, a common virus causing "mild to moderate upper respiratory symptoms." The common cold, yes, old friend ah-choo, is wait for it—a "coronavirus." This one however, bat-delivered and pangolin-transmitted, was different. Much more "severe." Corona, corona. A neighborhood in Queens. The queen of Corona. A city in southern California. Corona, a *white or colored circle or set of concentric circles of light seen around a luminous* body, *especially around the sun or moon.* Corona, *any part or structure suggestive of a crown or curved crown shape.* A royal virus, with crown-like spikes, drawing one into its poisoned circles. Names of this thing proliferated as wildly as did, purportedly, its transmission. Coronavirus... 2019-nCoV (2019 novel coronavirus)... SARS-CoV-2... and finally... TA-DA!... Behind curtain number twenty, we give you, ladies and gentlemen: COVID-19. This was *"the disease"* the previous name (virus itself) engenders. Yeah, okay. This last would stick—like a bat pinned to a factory wall. Covid-19, or just—"Covid." Later—"the Covid thing." A spellbound public tangled up in medical-media induced name-fatigue and complete confusion. Corona Virus disease, year 2019. They were moving forwards backwards. Whatever, pass me the remote. Oh, look, coronavirus on the news. What's on Netflix?

Will it spread, that's the question. Has it already spread, that's the answer. By mid-February twenty-five countries report coronavirus cases. Iran and Italy are "blowing up" with cases. It's an epidemic, of course it is – is it a *pan*demic? The World Health Organization has taken that under advisement. Cruise ships are docked in harbors whose countries will not accept their passengers. They linger...waiting... By the first week of March ninety countries confirm cases. By the second week of March—the WHO declares the outbreak—a Pandemic. That's the *new* word, the one that splats into billions of minds, locks in right between Mama-Papa Coronavirus and Covid-19, forevermore entwined. Was it coming—to us? The—pan-dem-ic? To—Mom? Dad? The kids? No one wanted to phrase the most personal of pronouns, as they bathed and shaved in morning mirrors, still allowed to go to work, to feel they could move around...freely. They say it's spreading, it can't be—contained. Extremely...contagious. All over Italy now. Really? Yes, the whole country is locking down. TV. YouTube. CNN. NBC. Browser tabs multiply. Hands sweaty, honey did you see, did you hear, did... Eyes scanning. Information. Far worse than seasonal flu. That's what they say. Who? Fauci, head of CDC. Centers For Disease Control. Or is it National Institute of...something. He's been on TV a lot. What do *you* think? I don't know *what* to think.

Flights stop. Borders close. Things are cancelled—sports, concerts, meetings. First, five hundred people only can gather. Then, one hundred. Then... Country by country, schools close... Offices shut... Government buildings lock. Restaurants, bars, barbershops, salons. Life is changing, closing. Hourly. March hits, late winter is late freeze setting in. Trapping everything in yesterday. A killer is on the road. Bugs in amber. Apes in cages. Humans, this time. At windows. The virus. Silent, invisible. Sans papers, sans I.D. (Cov-ID), without voice or scent or form detectable. All the doors close. Getting ready, the killer out there, unseen. They need "more ventilators," it's a respiratory virus, you see. Breath and breathing. Daily they proclaim it's approaching, they don't know where, when or how. Can't hear a thing, no bombs in this war, no explosions. Each night they recite the latest numbers—new cases. On the screen. New mortalities. Numbers across the screen.

They stand at windows, watching what, holding, cups of tea, coffee. Whiskey. Watching a world re-form itself into a crown-like image, spiked edges. Coming down slowly... inexorably. Over the space they had once, a day or two ago, called life.

For many it began... one man or woman, alone in a room, staring at a screen. Whether a television screen looming on a wall, a laptop screen sitting meekly on a desk or a phone in a hand—this is fast becoming the predominant way interactions with the world transpire for human beings. For some it already is.

Paul Wilmer wasn't, quite, one of the latter. He often mixed in, sharing opinions and insights in the flesh, open to ideas contrary to his own. Paul though, had to be careful *his* engagements with the online world didn't usurp the majority of his free time. By February 2020, his time could be said to be wholly free. Six months before, he'd given notice at his job, having been there two years. He'd done well in this position in which he worked with drawings and specifications, estimating budgets for multi-million dollar projects. His boss valued his work and what he called Paul's "tenacity." He didn't let go when information he required was missing, or ignore when he spotted an error. He called it out, sometimes with a lack of tact and temperance. Just when he was beginning to refine this skill, he decided to pull the plug on his presence in the firm and in that industry. No one could understand. "You're doing so well. You're contributing and you *will* be rewarded." *When* will I be rewarded? He kept his mouth shut, laconically expressing it was "time to move on." They tried to elicit reasons – was it money, because eventually *there will* be more money. Wasn't it always money in some form? For the work he did—his attitude to the work—yeah, he wanted a lot more goddamn money.

Why didn't he voice his financial concerns? He would have listened if his boss had put a number on the table. He didn't put a number down. Merely words. How much everyone appreciated his "contributions." If they wanted him to stay why not name a figure? That's not why he remained silent. The truth was—in his mind he was out the door. For at least six months he'd been planning to do it, pacing his small apartment at night. Freedom was not a word to Paul, an empty ideal. Freedom meant being able to use his time, *all* of it, as he desired. It meant being a creator of something which comes from within. For him, it's words... transformed into poems and stories. He was captured by the magic of the Word. He couldn't affirm why or trace when it arose. In his early thirties, with the help of his girlfriend, he patched together a bunch of his poems that sort of might be a book. Paul wasn't so sure... Did they really go together, these disparate pieces written over ten years? Lizzie assured him they were a good representation of his work. She chose some publishers, and out the manuscripts went, courtesy of U.S. mail. Months pass. He either heard nothing at all or polite form letter rejections. His patience—and interest—departed. Liz did too, to another state and another writer. Or was it a painter? One wintry day he received a registered letter from a prestigious University Press. Here we go, begging for money and I ain't an alumni. Why would they send a registered letter...he sloppily opens it tearing a corner of the page... "Dear Mr. Wilmer, we haven't got a clue who you are or where you've honed your poetic skills. It's obvious you've done it somewhere, somehow. We want to introduce your work to the world. Call us at your earliest..." He flipped the envelope. Was this real? He called the number. Yes, Mr. Wilmer, we wish to publish your book, *Significant Forgettings*. He felt he'd dropped the phone. But he had it.

Six months later he was holding his book of poems. It looked okay even though the font was small. Yup, those are my poems. Hm, no typos. He sent one to Liz and it came back— address unknown. Thanks, Liz. The publisher's connections enabled him to be reviewed in a smattering of journals and newspapers around the country. Most were cursory but a couple of critics tried to understand what Paul was going for. One, in the New Yorker, spoke of him as a "not-so-young-anymore poet, albeit one with guts, lyricism and lots of promise."

The book didn't do much. They sold four hundred copies which was higher than usual for poetry, they told him. Paul waited – offers...invitations... Chances. A decade passes. Two decades. He never stopped. In his forties, after long, brutal attempts he broke into composing short stories from inside out, not by hobbling the Iowa Workshop trail. He placed some things in lit journals. Without an agent his options were limited. No one knew his name or his efforts.

It was the freedom thing. Why he went on when going on felt against his will. Against common sense. Freedom and creating. They were conjoined in him. That's what made it almost impossible for him to hold a job longer than two or three years. On a sunny morning in July 2019 he hands his boss the resignation letter. Was Paul Wilmer crazy for walking out of a good job—with no prospects for his future? "Man, you're fifty-two years old! *What* are you intending to do?"

His sole answer—in his mind—was—"Try to be free. Create something every day."

And he was, in February, free, awhile. No great explosions, literary or otherwise, had occurred in his life since his resignation. He tended to stay up late listening to music. Drinking brandy or toking the pot grown too potent for him. Waking late in the morning he'd make his way from his rooms out into the world. Towards one of the libraries in the area to work. Books, notebook, laptop, coffee. By that time it was well into afternoon.

During the autumn and winter he worked on poems, trawling for inspiration to initiate a fiction piece. Something – wasn't there – creatively. Things in his life, in general, weren't what he'd envisioned last summer on taking the leap—his rhythm was off. I should change my sleeping habits. Exercise more. Balance, mentally and physically. He hadn't really been diving into the depths. Was he resisting fully immersing?

Another thing he felt weakened by. His internet use, his relationship to the "thing" called Internet. The internet was his window into news, music, videos, and information – "what was going on." It was entertainment, it was research, it was goofing off, it was jerking off, it was learning. And it was avoiding.

Paul had come late to computers, not jumping in until post 9-11-01. He knew he wasn't alone in experiencing the internet almost like a seductive woman, calling siren songs to provoke him into "her" world; an endless one of information, videos, audio, articles on any topic imaginable. He had called others out for their "addiction to gadgets and technology." He was now caught. Not by gadgets. By the *networks* themselves, that promised—freedom? transcendence?—through information and Knowing, but ultimately trapped you as you lost sleep, quashed creativity and forgot which path you'd set out on hours before.

Paul saw it, knew it, couldn't forswear, his addiction. At what point was knowing what you knew enough – beyond it only additional futile ideas and uselessness? He'd burned a lot of time the last fifteen or so years, clicking one link after another, listening/watching/reading the next thing he felt obliged to...explore. Is that what it was, Paul? Exploration? He prided himself on his "dedication" to seeking the truth. Was it spiritual, ultimate truth? Was it this-world, who's running the world truth? He was confused by the two kinds of truth, often contemplated where they conflated—*if* they conflated—if they were reconcilable. He couldn't remember when this all started, perhaps it was his readings of Noam Chomsky and Michael Parenti. When he saw through their eyes how power was abused in the world by his government—and most others—something cracked in him. The world was more ugly and unfair than he could have dreamed. He doesn't recall either when he first came across the term "conspiracy theorist." He himself admitted he was obsessed. With what, Paul? Finding out the truth? About what? Events in the world which most people accepted as simply events that unfolded without manipulation by overt agents, covert agents, or any agents? By those who *join in a secret agreement to do an unlawful or wrongful act or an act which becomes unlawful as a result of the secret agreement* – despite what appearances might show the public?

That was the key—*appearances* were deceptive. In the wake of September 11, the Twin Towers, the Pentagon and all that followed, Paul—and myriad others—found themselves slipping, inadvertently, down the Rabbit Hole. By 2002 the Internet had begun to expand in terms of websites and information but also millions of people had acquired broadband access. No waiting for web pages to slowly appear across the screen. Now those "pages" danced across your bulging CRT monitor—no longer was it a struggle to read text on a page or stand by for a video which took longer to load than to view. For researchers it was a flight into "hyperspace."

You name it. Political assassination. Freemasonry. Illuminati. Occult groups. Gladio. Agenda 21. How it all connects, how it doesn't. Club of Rome. Mind control. Chemtrails. Bilderberg Group. ETs. Social engineering. For years it was text, "articles" appearing on the screen and you scrolled the mouse—down—down. These screeds were frequently accompanied by photos, drawings or diagrams to augment the ideas. Or to further muddle you. This kind of exposition reminded Paul of the pamphlets he used to get in the mail in the '90s. YouTube didn't emerge till 2005. In those post 9/11 days it was text and images with hyperlinks that led you to other sites. Similar to plucking out Russian dolls, it went on and on. Several years forward podcasts kick off, radio on the internet. Those skilled enough with the tech created audio presentations that evolved into discussions. A crucial aspect of the conspiracy research was Chat Forums. Like the Usenet forums of the '80s and '90s, the concept was people talking, through a network, on a screen—lines of nested text, dipping endlessly, disjointedly. Layout and formatting improved. Several of these better organized Forums became very popular, had divisions and subdivisions of categories, facets of "hidden" history, all things concealed from the plebs who go to work, get drunk on weekends and die in debt. Paul joined a few of those, posted semi-regularly to one in particular, Project NSight. This is how ideas were exchanged. At first YouTube was a terrain of cats, dogs, pranks and music videos; a couple of years in, what had been talked about on podcasts and chat forums began to appear there in video form. While most of these video makers were unskilled, it was fascinating to witness the ideas bloom into weird video flowers in front of your eyes. In those days 9/11 was the lodestone. *Loose Change*, a documentary, drew a large viewership. It challenged the official story of that horrifically momentous day and opened a good deal of minds to the lies of governments and their mouthpieces in mainstream media. From there it flooded... Videos on every possible subject associated with how this planet is manipulated, steered to agendas dictated far beyond the rulers we (assume we) have elected. By 2012 some of the producers had become not only adept at making impressive videos, but knowledgeable on a wide array of topics and interconnections between them.

Paul watched all of it developing. He fell deep, surrendering hours to the glowing screen in front of him, as he had as a boy with television. The screens sending images, audio, voices, words, telling him what was *REALLY* going on in the world outside his window. He realized it was too much. He would pull away, for a week or two. As events in the world got crazier he found himself involved in what he called "digging in" – with a goading need to understand, to find out. What though, Paul? What was really going on. And then? Wake people up? Prevent the evil? How would you do that? He didn't know. He knew he had to know. Was it the *information itself* you needed to see? To keep seeing.

Did it affect his creative work? Sure it did. It was occluding his full fruition. He lambasted himself to himself. Shouldn't he be living a balanced, joyous life? A recognized author with a loving family? He didn't give up on giving up the "addiction." Was it addiction to information? Or was it to technology that rendered the information to him? He couldn't differentiate anymore.

Paul wasn't the only one, far from it. What troubled him most: There *was* value in discerning, in seeing into causes, power structures, lies behind situations in our collective lives. Yet—how valuable? How much time was it worth to devote to? What ultimately was the reason for such commitment? It had to do with love, as in all devotion. Devotees are aflame with yearning. He had faith in it bearing him forth out of the hole—into deeper skies, light and some joy.

By mid-February Paul was aware of the "China virus" as President Donald Trump had labeled it. It was hard *not* to be aware of it, all over of the news. He noted what got posted online from mainstream sources and those questioning "official narratives." He'd heard about the wet market—the bats. Discovery of a new virus, a Corona Virus, whatever that was. Lots of Chinese with pneumonia and flu-like symptoms ramped way up. Crazy shit was always happening in China. Paul knew that for years the Chinese overlords had been tightening the screws, putting facial-recognition cameras everywhere, setting up a "social credit score" system, biometric identification. Who knows what else. An Orwellian nightmare. He watches as they lock down sixty million people.

On January 21 the U.S. government confirmed its first coronavirus case, a man in Washington state who'd been in Wuhan, China. When the cruise ship Diamond Princess unexpectedly docked in Japan due to passengers testing positive for this virus, the response was subdued. Cruise ships are notorious for illness-spreading. Nothing to freak out about. On February 15, the U.S. government evacuated over three hundred of its citizens from the Diamond Princess, flew them stateside where they were quarantined for fourteen days. On February 24, President Trump tweeted, "Coronavirus very much under control in the USA." On February 29, the U.S. reports its first coronavirus death, at a nursing home, also in Washington state.

Paul continued his routine. What caught his eye—and quickened his heart rate—were videos allegedly leaked out of Wuhan. People being dragged from the doorways of their apartments by police as they struggled for a grip on the door frame. Who were they? Had they tested positive for this virus and were being taken—forcedly—to a hospital? People being snatched right off the street, jammed into vans that sped away leaving astonished onlookers. Who were they? What had they done? Some were even more troubling—people seemingly collapsing—as they sat at a desk working or walking down a street, their belongings tumbling from their splayed-out bodies. Paul asked himself: *What the hell was happening in China? Was it going to happen elsewhere?*

The Fox household hadn't seen those alarming videos from China but they were, like most Americans, aware—one of them very aware—of the "coronavirus" developments in China. In February 2020, it was on a small portion of their radar. Mary Fox saw her son Tobias off to school in the morning, packing his brown bag lunch, his figure fading as it drifted towards the bus stop and into the yellow exhaust-spewing hulk. She surreptitiously stood on the porch until it drove away. Her daughter Jessica was a freshman at Northwestern University outside Chicago. She was helping her make preparations for the spring break vacation. She and her friends had picked Panama City Beach, Florida. Mary had the urge to stop the whole thing, tell her it was off but the girl was nineteen years old, as stubborn as she herself had been. Talking to her about normal things was a chore. Anything controversial was a burden. She couldn't deny her dependence on her mother, mostly organizational, and on her father, mostly financial. Mary had been to one of these Florida spring breaks and hadn't enjoyed it. By the time she was in college she felt "partied-out" from all her high school extracurricular activities. What so excited her new friends she had already lived—drinking games, puking, drug experiments, fake comradery, dare-you-to… She either came home during her breaks or went somewhere alone to chill. She was a serious student, majoring in Art History. Jessica was *not* a serious student. Her decent grades were attained through her "native intelligence" as her guidance counselor had phrased it. She had pushed her parents to let her take a year off before entering college. Dan was neutral, Mary was against it. Jessica convinced her father to persuade her mother. She insisted Jessica do something productive and was pleasantly surprised when she came to them with a plan. She would reside with a host family in Barcelona for six months, attend Spanish classes in the morning and work in a restaurant evenings. There were conditions: Jessica was to call twice a week and not protest if she and Dan visited. They never made it, ostensibly because of Dan's work schedule. Jessica made a success of it, was well-liked by the family and at the restaurant. She returned possessing conversational Spanish and a modicum of maturity. Mary still felt the gap between her and her daughter.

As her responsibilities lessened at home, she shifted attention to her own life and her relationship with her husband Daniel. Did she *have* a relationship with Danny, the version of his name she rarely used? When he wasn't away, he arrived after she and Toby had eaten. She was no longer insulted that Daniel seldom ate the meals she made. Mary hadn't worked in twenty years, since giving birth to Jessie and moving back to the island. Sporadically she'd done volunteering—in the library, a local museum, a church food bank. Daniel was very clear as to his preference that she "be around" for the children, for *him*, although the latter was never explicitly expressed. "More time for us all to spend together," had been the refrain. Twenty years of marriage and the phrase sounded absurd when she remembered. Dan invented ways to avoid her, taking Toby to his games, meeting with his old friends. Working on his cases. They still had sex, weekly if he was there. Why sacrifice orgasms? Mary had quit rising when he did, a habit she'd stuck to for years. She knows the morning. She asked herself, "What am I getting up for?" He never mentioned her absence in the morning. Toby was a year old. Nine years ago.

The coronavirus was background noise for Mary in February. Yes, she heard it on TV, saw them pumping up the coverage, talking to the so-called experts, the WHO, the CDC. Mary perceived it as a tactic to ensure the hypnotic spells of pharmaceutical commercials would be viewed. There had been previous "epidemics" as she recalled. She kept an eye on it out of curiosity, had more important things to focus on. She was trying to recover what she called – in the diary she'd begun – **Who I really am**. The dropping off of her periods had increased her feeling of lostness. She felt herself slipping. Danny doesn't realize I'm not the same person he married? Clueless. If not for Toby she'd have been gone long ago. Or would she?

He was the "Southeast Asia-Australia" guy at the firm. For ten years he'd been with Nicholson Maxwell Levi. He received the moniker upon joining and taking to the skies to go across the world. His first ten years as a lawyer were spent at Roxwell Hearns Somers. After three moderately successful years he began to feel unappreciated. At year five, having put in many hours to finalize a huge merger (oil) he was given a corner office, a raise, a double end of year bonus. At seven, when Scott Werner was made partner, Dan acknowledged it—he was another over-educated suit pushing expensive paper. He was confident that he had untapped talent to employ elsewhere. Well-versed in international law, trade, tax policies (including World Trade Organization statutes), he'd become the go-to guy for the latest rulings in intellectual property. At year nine he reached out to headhunters. He had to stay local—his daughter was in school—his wife was pregnant. Would you be willing to travel? He talked to Mary. How often, she asked. Where to? He shrugged. Far. How far? Asia. Australia. She frowns. That's at least two day's travel round trip. Daniel looks at his bagel on a Sunday morning and at his middle-aged wife's belly expanding with their son. Her drawn, tired face. She's too old for this, maybe we shouldn't have gone forward... Mary, I love you. He doesn't speak it. Yes, she's strong, but at forty-two? The flying, she's saying, how often will it be? She leans on the table, dipping then nibbling crackers in cream cheese. I'm not sure. The recruiter said... every five or six weeks. Not so bad, Mary tells him, taking his hand across the round wood table. They've barely kissed or touched in weeks. It turns him on, he wants to have sex. You need to think about it, Danny. You'll be exhausted after traveling for – twenty-four hours or whatever it'll be. The jet lag will be – intense. She was right, he hadn't considered the *jet lag*. What's the time difference? I'm not sure, he mumbles, hesitant to learn. His hard-on is forgotten. She taps on her keyboard. Singapore is... twelve hours. Australia... *fourteen hours*. Wow, Mary sighs, eyes on the white-lit screen. Yeah, wow, Daniel doesn't say. Why do I have to get on and off all these airplanes?

The money couldn't be passed by.

Because, said the recruiter, Nicholson Maxwell Levi is all about maintaining *personal* relations with their clientele. That means—in-person. When he met the founders on his final interview Darren Maxwell made it clear – "We would not have arrived where we are absent a *personal* connection. The technology is incredible. It's bridged distances, but nothing can substitute for breathing the same air. Or for— clinking glasses of fifteen-year-old single malt"—everyone titters—"after signing on a new deal." Daniel smiles, the three figures on the clean white paper they'd slid across to him moments before whirling in his head: base salary, yearly increase and bonus. Those figures were beyond, substantially, his market value. And were "subject to aggrandizement depending on performance." "What do you think of our concept, Mr. Fox?" corpulent Larry Nicholson assays Daniel, referring to the in-person ideal. He didn't know what he thought. It was something new. An adventure. Perhaps.

Hadn't he wanted adventure in his life? He glances at the figures. All of them had thrown numbers in the air. Narrowed them down, agreed. A secretary—someone—had typed them and printed the page. Those figures—they'll change their lives. His growing family. He sees a jet airliner pass through the window, crack the walls apart, and cross the room. No one else notices. He smiles like a sphinx at the three older men who smell of cigars, cunning, cupidity. "When do I begin." They stand and extend their arms across the table to Daniel. Who also stands.

The question now, waking and sleeping with him— When does it end? Ten years of airports, marathon moving through skies, he'd lost count, reclining his seat, Beethoven in his ears, inhaling the recycled business class air, stretching out his legs yet again, hardly touching the meals that pile. Waking, waiting, bags round the carousel, chilled, it's torrid in Singapore. Drop me at the hotel. Waiting, the car, the plane, the meeting to commence. To close. Ten years missed birthdays, games, recitals (ballet?), anniversaries. Singapore, Sydney, stops in Manila, Kuala Lumpur. Sprints to San Francisco. Being home an interval till the next runway. A year or two ago, when was it—coming home from JFK, an Uber, eyes heavy drifting in and out, he saw in piercing clarity his wife Mary had become a stranger. No, no—he had become the stranger. That's who he was now.

"Give it a year, Dan, the travel will ebb," turned into "A few more contracts, my boy." My boy was a forty-five-year-old man, alternately too thin or belly-bloated and he couldn't figure out why in either case. The sides of his hair were silver and he didn't bother hiding it. "Six more months," they kept telling him. He hadn't made partner, once again. He didn't care anymore. The money grew yearly, all that mattered, yes? He didn't need the partnership bullshit, the meetings and functions. Let me keep – what? Going? Nothing. He wasn't tired anymore. He just wanted the Beethoven. You keep all the rest. Let me off the carousel.

Daniel was cognizant of the virus before most Americans. His firm did business in China. He heard in mid-December something was going on in Hubei province, specifically the city of Wuhan. It was discussed at team meetings. Contacts in the region report "mysterious pneumonia cases" in Wuhan. The following weeks brought additional information—a wet market in the city was suspected of being the origin of a new kind of virus. There was talk of quarantine, border closings. For now it was speculation. Travel was still unrestricted. In January 2020, company trips were being made to Beijing.

Daniel had a flight to Singapore scheduled for the first week in February. As he packed Mary came in and out from her bathroom.

"Do you really have to make this trip, Dan?"

"Yeah, Mary, if I didn't I wouldn't be going."

"You have no idea what's happening."

"In terms of what?"

"What do you mean, 'what'? The *virus thing* in China."

"Oh, that. We don't know if it's anything."

"Trump stopped Chinese foreign nationals from coming in. Are your colleagues traveling there?"

He pauses, folding a pressed white shirt. "No one's scheduled this month."

"You see? Stay home, Dan. You don't need to be in—"

"Mary, there's no problem. Singapore is two thousand miles away. China always has crap like this going on. Wet markets with all kinds of health hazards. Exotic beasts chopped up in front of you. Didn't we visit one?"

"Maybe. You don't need to be over there risking your – you don't need to be ... in Asia. Right now."

He embraces and kisses her. She looks up into his eyes. Why doesn't he hold me more often?

"It's a two day trip. I'll be home in four days."

"I'm quite familiar with the math, Mr. Fox."

He laughs. "Oh, you're good at math?" Smacks her bottom. "You studied art history."

"What makes you think you can spank my ass like I'm a schoolgirl?"

"Because you're a very good student. Never forgot a lesson. You can identify by title and year any painting you come—"

"That's not remotely—"

"Across. And I want to reward you. If you allow me."

"Warning you: You had better not bring any wet-market disease back to us, Fox."

"I'm the only disease you'll receive." He tests the bag's capacity, zipping and unzipping, compressing his clothes. "Why do I feel I'm an amateur at this game?"

"Which game?" Mary has her back to him, searching for a book on her shelf. She's unavoidably attractive he thinks, fifty-two and she's still got it.

"This—" he smacks the suitcase.

"Oh. Maybe you forgot how to smack it."

Was that an invitation? A yielding?

"Can you give me a refresher course? Tonight?"

"Sorry, Dan, I have some reading to do." She clutches a book to her chest.

"Which one?"

A long haired girl on the cover, conversing with a mélange of animals.

"Alice In Wonderland? Haven't you read it a hundred times?"

"It's actually 'Alice's *Adventures* In Wonderland.' " She heads to the doorway. "Something tells me it's ripe for a re-read."

"Mar." He called her Mar for short which she didn't favor.

"Yes."

"Will I – see you later?"

She cranes her neck— "We sleep, sometimes, in the same bedroom. How shall I avoid you?" She turns and goes.

He zips open the bag—deliberates: Why did she marry me? Stuffs in his deodorant. That's the best I can do. Maybe this will be my last trip. Closes it.

Jill realized one February morning the winter had been mild. One snow so far that was gone the next afternoon. It was cold, but not gloves hats double-sweaters scarves bone-deep upstate cold. She believes, for the most part, in what they say about man-made climate change. She supports candidates and movements that advocate for reducing carbon in the atmosphere. It's hard to disclaim the earth is warming, isn't it obvious that man's activities—greedy, short-term, detached from nature—are, if not causing, than contributing to the global warming most scientists declare is going on? That's why she finally bought a new car, a Prius hybrid.

She still lived in his house, it was *their* house, given as a wedding present by Phil's parents. Jill was astonished but the more she found out about the family she saw it was "no skin off their back." The house had been under Phillip's name, which she hadn't known until he petitioned for a legal separation after ten years of marriage (having already been de facto separated two years). A four bedroom, three and a half bathrooms house made one person feel they were rattling around like a peanut in a bucket. She got that image one night when she sat in her kitchen (Phillip had given her carte blanche to design and have it built). She was incongruously present. Her lawyer devised the agreement to grant her half ownership of the house—plus a cash settlement and Phillip's assent to *pay all taxes and expenses associated with upkeep of said property for ten years forward from today's date....* Well "today's date" was coming in a matter of months. She can't afford the taxes, maintenance, etc. He was a smart businessman and knew the day would come when he'd reap the return on his investment. Is that what their marriage had been?

This island she'd been on for nearly twenty years was a blip hanging on an ocean. In the opposite direction were vast spaces, places she'd never seen. She'll put the house on the market – get his advice on the best manner to proceed – he'll take over the whole thing and she didn't care. Go ahead, take it over. With your wife and your child. Nine years old was she?

She hadn't run into them in a year—a supermarket aisle which made it impossible to avoid. She acknowledged them, mechanically, left immediately and almost puked in the parking lot. She couldn't reconcile herself to the fact that five or six miles north of her on the bay was Phillip and his...family. She let it drift up into her high ceiling living room and stick in a corner – enveloped in dust never sucked away. Another fact – a feeling-fact – she ignored was that she was an interloper in the house. It had always been Phillip's—*family's*—she was a tenant, taken care of for the moment. She'll be out soon. Maybe he'll buy the house himself – reclaim it into the Chambers' treasure chest, their "Portfolio," a word he loved to employ. This feeling also floats. It spoke to her when the TV wasn't on loud enough or the Chardonnay was doing nothing for her. "You're a passenger passing through here, Jill. You may still use the name "Chambers" but we know who you really are, dear. Enjoy what you have, for now. You know you don't belong...." She wasn't sure if she put the dear into the litany or they did. That in itself was a crazy question. The best thing is to leave this all behind, the house, the town, the memories. The ceiling.

She won't miss her job. Who would? Who likes going five days a week to do what they have no interest in doing? Not an original thought but one which struck her when she worked at the grocery store and saw her parents toiling in their basically meaningless jobs in factories and shops. How it wore them down year after year. Depleted their enthusiasm week by week. What could they do? Unless you work for yourself and build something, it *was* meaningless. Phil had helped his family business grow and derived satisfaction from it. Most people don't have a well-established family business to springboard them. Most are not going to start their own, either from lack of "capital" or absence of drive. She had neither, nor did most of the people around her. Were those people, the driven ones, happy? Satisfied? Selling what? Stocks of a company employing people who hated going every day to make what they sell in an abstract form? Money was a total unreality in her life till she met Phillip and he fell for her. For a time, anyway. Her mother swore it was her hair—"A red that was rare," she called it. He wasn't frugal—for once she had some nice things to wear. Then a closetful. He took her to restaurants that rob you graciously. Broadway anything. Hotel suites where she got lost. Then the vacations. Palm Springs. Vegas. Paris. Their honeymoon in Italy. She'd look in the mirror and ask herself who it was experiencing these places and things. One day her oasis would show itself to be made from sand and sunlight. I told you it was all a mirage the mirror will say.

Bookkeeping wasn't exactly her dream job yet she ended up doing it. She loathed that phrase—how can you "end up" doing something when you were still alive and breathing? The only thing you end up doing is being dead. Was it an oxymoron—being dead? Some days she did feel dead. A day sitting in her cubicle, staring at a QuickBooks spreadsheet, answering emails, making and taking phone calls, breaking for lunch, more figures and QuickBooks. Suddenly she "wakes up" back in the house heating a frozen dinner, waiting for the wine to cool. *What happened* to my day—she doesn't ask herself exactly... It's in the ceiling. Unexamined, since she'd be compelled to uncover what she really wants to do. For five years following their separation she had emailed...sent handwritten letters full of emotion and memories. Went into therapy, implored him to join her, "sort things out... save what was good between them." She knew the whole thing reeked of – despair. He did go to four or five sessions. Watched her cry with sympathy. They went home—her home—and had sex after two (in a row). That stopped—she could feel he was *gently* ending it—which made it worse. She had nowhere for her anger. She shouldn't have asked him to the therapy or screwed him. She felt like a fool. More so because he was telling her kindly he didn't love her. It was all gone. He had *been* gone.

She wasn't a nun. Computer dating, set-ups from friends and colleagues. She remembers their cars most of all. What they drove. Not their smells, most men didn't wear cologne anymore. Desmond was sweet. His Chevy pickup. That lasted a year. No, two. Why didn't it work out? It was probably her. She had tried to go into her childhood with therapists (three, four?), but couldn't fathom... how it applied. Leaving the house will help, she told herself.

Talk around the office. Did you hear about this virus thing in China, Jill? Internet searches. The news. Not much information. She let it slide. Cases in the U.S., CNN said, in a nursing home. Those poor people stuck on the cruise ship, what was it called Diamond something. Can you imagine!? Not being able to leave your room? What if you're in an interior cabin—my god, no window! There'd been illness breakouts on cruise ships. Not uncommon. That's one of the reasons she wouldn't take cruises. And what *was* this thing, this corona? Like a flu? Was it so dangerous? China had a lot of cases, but China was—weird. They ate outlandish things. Everybody knew that. What troubled her a little is when her cubicle neighbor Bernice told her China had "locked down" whole cities of their people. Millions. That made her pause. It stayed with her. All those people – stuck inside? Like prisoners? Yes, apparently, Bernice answered. Jill worked through lunch that day. Yogurt at her desk. No internet.

Her life went on. Work. Gym. Shop. Home. Microwave dinners. White wine. A daily chat with her best friend Mary. TV on the wall. Scrolling Match dot com for a new match. Click. A new life.

IV

Dinner Party on the Edge
(Strange Beginning)

This was a dinner party destined not to happen. By all logic it shouldn't have taken place but for some reason—later contemplated by all involved—it had. There were the usual cocktails, hors d'oeuvres, main course. A worldwide pandemic had been declared two days before. It was March 13, 2020, eight o'clock. The doorbell rings and Jill Chambers, checking her hair in the foyer mirror, smiles at herself and holding that smile turns sprightly pulling open the door: "Hello, nice to see you all, so glad, so glad you could come...."

Paul was early. He decided to wait in his car. When he saw Mary and Dan arrive he would drive up. He hated the moment of arriving at a gathering, ringing the bell, being let in—standing there alone and crossing a threshold to someone else's reality. Hello, nice to see you. Thanks, you too.

He spots a late model Audi winding the curve around which Jill's house is located. It's them. He hasn't seen Dan in months, the perpetual plane hopper. What'll he say to him? Whatever. I'll park behind them. Oh, they parked in the driveway. Figures he would do that. I'll park on the street.

The wine, remove the price sticker. They don't use them anymore. Argentina. Mary probably bought an expensive French thing. Dan picks it out. Mine cost eleven bucks. What's the difference. They heard my door close, Mary waves, Dan turns away wouldn't want to be spotted waiting for someone. I hardly know him. After all this time. This might be the last chance for a while— she's smiling at me—

"Hey there," Paul crosses the street to Jill's driveway. The lights come on, reflecting their bodies.

"Hey," Mary kisses him.

"Hi Paul."

"Daniel. Good evening." Handshake.

"Chilly, right?" she shivers. "Let me get my sweater. It's locked. Dan, did you hear me?"

He clicks open the door.

She shoulders a black sweater, grips a bottle and bag. Elbow-slams the door, he clicks it locked. "Ready?" she stage-whispers playfully. Paul makes an ambiguous gesture. They all walk toward Jill's front door.

Jill is talking on her cell phone from the conference room of her office. She leans up every so often, peeking out the glass window into the hallway. She should be at her cubicle.

"I just thought it might be pleasant to get together, break bread. No other reason, Mary."

"Mm-hm."

"I mean, I know it's a weird time, kind of—"

"Yeah Jill, it's...lot of uncertainty."

"That Chinese flu virus or whatever it is..."

"You've been following it?"

"Sort of. It's hard not to. It's—"

"Yeah, everywhere, on TV and in the—"

"It doesn't seem so bad."

"Yes, it might blow over. They're really hyping it."

"Yes, that's it, I couldn't put it into words. Of course *you* could, Em."

"I'm just a little nervous about Daniel."

"Is he scheduled to fly to—"

"Home away from home. Singapore."

"Oh, yes. How close is it—"

"Kinda far. But you hear this thing spreads...to other places."

"Yeah. Italy. Iran."

"I'm trying to make him cancel that stupid trip." Mary sighs, audibly. "Anyway," switching gears, "when were you thinking for the dinner?"

"How about – Friday, March thirteen?"

Mary lifts her mug, 'World's Coolest Mom,' contents cold, peers out her kitchen window at grey March haze.

"Friday the thirteenth, huh? Should we wear a mask? A costume?"

"Maybe we should all dress up. That'd be fun."

"Yeah, an early—or late—Halloween. Let me get my daybook. Today's the third, Tuesday...so ten days. Dan flies out on – that Monday, the sixteenth. Toby's got – oh good, nothing Friday...or the whole weekend. We'll hire a sitter for him, not a problem. What time, Jill?"

"How's eight o'clock?"

"Great. Eight it is."

"Oh, good. Mary, I have to get back to—"

"Oh, one more thing—"

"Uh-huh?"

"Mind if I ask who else you invited?"

"Right now...it's just us."

"Us – three?"

"So far. I am hoping for a fourth."

"Have you asked anyone yet?"

"No, I was – not yet."

"How about Paul?"

"Your Paul?"

"Paul Wilmer. Yes. What do you think, Jill?"

She was hoping Mary would suggest him.

"I – yeah. Paul should— be fine. I haven't seen him in quite a while."

"I'm sure he'd be happy to see you. He often mentions you."

"Oh?" She sinks into the high-backed chair, forgets the work at her desk.

"He does. Do you want me to invite him? Or do you—"

"No, it's fine. Please do."

"I'll call him today."

"Thanks, Em. I'm looking forward. It'll be...fun."

"Me too, babe."

"Okay, back to profits and losses..."

"You're *all* profit. See you soon."

Jill goes into the break room. She pops a coffee k-cup into the holder, punctures it with the lever, listens to it drip. She doesn't know what "happened" when she and Paul went out a few times, had to be at least a year now. Feeling silly that at age forty-nine she had to have a girlfriend invite a man to a dinner party she's giving. Was she still a country bumpkin? Immature? She didn't really get Paul. That she knew. His sort of artistic detachment. His elliptical manner of ... doing everything. Even being direct! Jill smiles at how accurate that thought is – she remembers them at the cinema on line for tickets – attempting to hurdle the opening small talk. Afterward she asked him in for a nightcap. They spoke about the movie, something foreign and slow. Subtitled. She barely followed it, almost nodding off repeatedly. Paul was giving his interpretation and Jill, pouring him a scotch, threw up a hand – "I have to say—I didn't glean any of that Paul. It *sounds* brilliant though!" She cackles, "Maybe I did fall asleep." The air changed a bit. He came to a stop. She filled the gap, gabbing on awhile with a work-related story and noticed Paul was tearing a napkin. She pauses— "Yes? I'm listening." "No, that was...it." He was attractive in a way complex to define. To be explored. She would have kissed him if he'd come to her. He didn't. They finished their drinks and he rose, they were at the door. He mumbles thanks for a nice evening. "Paul—could you explain the film to me – another time?" He kissed her on the cheek.

He didn't call her again. Maybe they had no common ground. Jill knew he was more simpatico with Mary than she. She saw it when they were all together. Mary had a man. Paul was free. Probably too free. She runs into him here and there. The library, Starbucks. On Main. Striding with a regal defeatedness. That's what came into her mind. Like a king in exile. He didn't know where to go. She knew the feeling. Was there somewhere they could meet, a corner they could turn, off Main Street, off some street, to find each other? She felt it was impossible but life was impossible she remembered thinking as a little girl. So why not. Why not.

March 11. Jill texts Mary in the early evening. She's sitting in her kitchen, TV on low across from her. She clicks the remote, up, down, doesn't matter, every channel, corona corona corona. Numbers going up, positives...**mortalities**. They used that word. Things were getting cancelled and shut down all over the world. Schools. Flights. The Vatican. The U.N. South By Southwest and Coachella. She smirks at those, drinking her honey-chamomile tea, where will the kids go now to rave? It wasn't that funny... China has "outlawed" eating wild animals. Better late than never she says aloud to Lester Holt on the screen. Jill wants to applaud. She would if she weren't alone. Applause needs an audience, especially ironic applause. Her refrigerator is crammed with all the things she chose for her friends on Friday night—fresh fish, veggies, delicious bread, ingredients for the hors d'oeuvres she'd planned. She took Friday afternoon off to prepare. She bought a bottle of excellent champagne. Why? To celebrate what? Friendship. Or the ending of winter. It didn't matter to her. Now it all seemed ... there was no reason. For anything.

Her thumbs tap-dance the small screen:

> Jill: Hey Em, how are u?

Three minutes:

> Mary: Hey Jill. Okay, considering...
> Jill: I know! I'm watching it now
> Crazy
> Mary: Yupsy ☹ Me too
> Jill: Listen, about the dinner party?
> Mary: We're still on ?
> Jill: Should we? With what's going on?
> Mary: I don't mind. I don't think the guys will either
> If you want to cancel I understand
> Jill: No, I don't. Just checking ho you guys feel
> Mary: How do you feel? Are you okay Jill?
> Jill: Yeah I'm ok. Physically

Mentally not so sure 😉
Mary: I hear you darlin'
We're all 📶
If you're up for it, so are we
Jill: I got all my stuff ready
🍳🍴
Mary: Nice
Don't work too hard hon
Jill: No, it's only us four
Mary: Mm. Talk tomorrow?
Jill: Sounds good. Love you
Mary: Love you mucho 😚

The next day, Thursday the twelfth, New York City bans gatherings in excess of five hundred people. No more Broadway shows, concerts, Madison Square Garden, Radio City Music Hall. Schools switching to online classes. The pro sports leagues are folding their seasons, major league baseball cancels spring training. Many states declare "a state of emergency." The World Health Organization officially declares the coronavirus outbreak a "Pandemic." Plenty of declaring.

Jill calls her mother.

At work on Friday, March 13, you can feel it—the nervous tension in the air. New, unfamiliar energy coalescing. Jill's colleagues are milling in the kitchen talking low. The bosses are in the conference room. She's at her desk waiting till ten – to text Mary. She's up in the air. What was she thinking to plan this dinner party during a virus epide—*pandemic*. She tries to focus on the screen, the numbers blur in front of her. Her co-workers whisper... "They might close the office." "So...we'll work from home?" "Could be, I guess, yeah." Jill tries to stay off the internet. New York is opening drive-through testing centers. WHAT?? What is it freakin' Burger King? Five thousand dead worldwide. Is that a lot? President Trump declares a national state of emergency. Finally she texts her. Mary doesn't respond. At noon she leaves her a voicemail.

At 1:00 p.m. anxious, sweating, she walks the long hallway to the parking lot. As she's clicking open her car door the phone rings. She plops her heavy bag on the hood, grasping for it in there—

"Hi Mary, everything oka—"

"Hi Jill, sorry 'bout that. Hectic here."

"Did you hear Trump just—"

"Yes, I heard. Are we still on tonight?"

"Well...I mean..." People are in groups, talking. By the cars and entranceway. "I was just heading home. Are you guys *sure* you – want to—do it?"

"Jill at this point, why not? I already hired a sitter. Dan'll be home early. I spoke to Paul, he's fine—of course."

"Oh, okay. I guess I'll—yeah, I'll go home and get everything ready."

"Might as well. You've been preparing. I know it's starting to get crazy—but...what can we do? We're allowed to gather and—share a meal."

"I'll see you at eight then, Em." She had fallen into calling her by her first initial. It tickled Mary.

"Anything I can bring that you're missing?"

She slides into the driver's seat, foot on the break, pushes the engine button.

"No, nothing, thanks."

"See you soon."

Jill drives away from the office park. She has a funny feeling. The office, the driving, the whole thing. As if she's not driving. But being pulled. Like everyone else. And somehow arrives there, home.

Her house was impeccable. She'd had "the girl" in that afternoon. The lighting was brighter in the hallway for any glances at the mirror, dimmer as you went into the house towards the den. She was nervous, her hands and voice fluttery as she ushered her guests into the den. When they arrived in that room with its striking combination of browns and purples, Jill requested their coats. Instead, she was given bottles of wine and a crumb cake Mary had made. Jill's lack of hands for these gifts brought an ice breaking burst of laughter and tensions eased. All three, waiting for her to return, pleasantly recognized the music playing in the den— Ella Fitzgerald and Louis Armstrong. They sang in an unexpectedly lovely mesh, à la Jill's decorating scheme. A shout from the kitchen— "Guys—red or white?" "Doesn't matter... Whichever." Jill reappeared with a Sauvignon Blanc and a Malbec.

She poured Daniel and Paul white and Mary and herself the red. "Oh, almost forgot," she runs into the kitchen. "Don't grade me on these," she lays two platters of hors d'oeuvres between the bottles and the bowls of nuts, chips, dip, sodas and ice bucket. "First time attempt so – be kind?"

"Mm, this one's sooo good, Jill. Is it – provolone?"

"You got it, Mary. Melted provolone in green pepper, diced onions and sea salt."

"Very good," Dan praises with a mouthful.

Paul held a piece of sourdough smeared with a purplish substance, marveling she really must like this color. He tastes and makes an involuntary "mm" sound, chewing and swallowing. "Wow, Jill. What do you call it?"

"That's a Greek Olive Tapenade."

"Tapping aid, huh?"

"No!" she play-chides him. "Tap*en*-ade."

"Ah... Well, however you tap it – it's inventive," he commends, as Dan and Mary dig in to slices.

"Wish I was the inventor. So it's olives with minced garlic—a little parsley—a splash of Extra Virgin olive oil."

"Great job," Mary pinches her cheek. The men sound their approvals through hors d'oeuvres filled mouths.

Ella and Louis sing April In Paris. Jill is wearing a dark blue skirt and a silvery blouse. She's got bangles on one her wrists and a subtle perfume which Paul, near her, can faintly perceive. Daniel has on a grey suit and a loose crimson tie. Paul is in stone washed blue jeans, a white sweater and a beige sport coat. Mary is in a sleek pair of black slacks and a pink blouse with a crossing of grey and orange lines. Her low-hanging necklace displays a symbolic pendant. Her hair, done that morning at the salon, is partly straightened and her usual curls stand out vividly to the changes.

"I just want to say," Jill addresses the elephant—"need to I guess—that...this is a weird time. I think it's gonna get weirder." They listen, motionless. "I know this isn't the ideal moment for a dinner party – we don't need to call it that anymore – and it's – I mean this thing is... well...it's serious. I'm not saying for us to ignore it. But for – a couple of hours tonight, we can maybe...enjoy each other's company?" Jill blushes. Blushes at having blushed—

"Hear hear," Mary lifts her glass—"To seeing dear friends. To you all."

"Cheers," Paul quietly adds.

They clink the glasses and drink.

"Here we are... Yup... Strange, huh?... Got that right... Did you see... Yes, did you hear... No, I didn't... Really... Really?... *Really*...."

After this initial mumbling of all their confusions and nervous energies a silence falls. They actually felt it fall. Mary as customary speaks out her truth:

"I don't know what the fuck is going on. Toby's school is cancelled. An email at two o'clock today. Maybe a week, maybe longer. Jessie's coming home from Northwestern on Sunday. They're *shutting down* – going online – for the rest of the semester. Everything's happening so goddamn quickly."

"Wow," Jill sighs and swallows her wine. "Closed schools. So...strange. I heard about schools closing in – other countries. You never expect it..."

"Here. Yes, true." Daniel takes a breath. "It's come on suddenly. Except it's been in Asia for months."

"So it's getting to us – now?"

"You could say that, Jill. China's been locked down—a big chunk of it—since late January. South Korea since February."

"And Singapore?" Paul asks.

"He was scheduled to be there this week!" Mary blurts.

"Singapore—hasn't locked down—or closed borders. They will. Possibly next week." He gulps his wine, refills his and Paul's glasses.

"His firm cancelled all Asia travel this week."

"They had no choice. But—yeah." He shrugs at no one, grins at everyone.

"I tell you," Paul says, "that whole getting stuck on a cruise ship seems like a nightmare to me."

Jill raps the table, "Awful!"

"Can you imagine," he continues, "being confined to your room for days on end—not knowing what's going on? Fucking nuts!"

Silence again. Mary pours red for herself and Jill. Ella and Satchmo sing of a lovely day in the rain. Paul feels he started off wrong. Jill just feels wrong.

"I'll turn it off—"

"No, it's fine," Mary stops her, hand on her waist. "It's...soothing."

Paul and Daniel reach into the nuts bowl—"You first," they both say.

"Twenty-one hundred U.S. cases." Jill's dismayed. "Gosh, I'm going to ruin... Let's change the subject."

"Hon," Mary allays, "what else can we talk about now?"

"Yeah. I don't know," she plucks a tissue. "Figured I'd..."

"Don't worry," Danny speaks. "To tell you the truth – we're all out of sorts. As Mar said, what else can we do. This thing is staring us in the face."

"Do they even know what this thing is?" They all turn to Paul.

"What do you mean, Paul?" Jill voices. "It's a virus, a coronavirus. I admit, it's the first I ever heard – that term."

"What I mean is...what do I mean?"

"Yeah, what *do* you mean, Paul?" Daniel mocks.

"I feel like there's something...something weird underway. I can't quite..."

"Epidemics do happen," Jill states. "That Mers thing. Others."

"Of course they do," Daniel backs her. "Sars. Swine flu also not long ago. They do happen. There *are* outbreaks. But let's hear the conspiracy."

"Let's try to keep an open mind—and listen to what Paul has to offer."

Paul's both embarrassed and enlivened by Mary's defense. He's not ready to put it into words yet.

"I think...that it's not – as they're telling us. Or showing us."

"They're shutting borders around the world," Jill says sternly. "Schools, businesses. We're probably next."

"Not probably. Definitely." Daniel is confident. Mary notices the hardness she's accustomed to. She recoils inside. "Within a week or two we'll...follow the same path."

"What do you mean 'the same path'?" his wife challenges.

"I mean—shutdown. Quarantine."

"They'll actually shut down cities in the U.S.? New York City?"

"Yes, Mar." The wine is making inroads. "New York. And many others."

"My god." Jill's head sinks. It's hitting her, it's *hitting* all of them. "That's...millions...and millions...of people." In the low lamplight their faces are turned from each other. "Trump declared a state of emergency today. Whatever that means."

"It means we're screwed," Paul remarks. "It means— businesses closing, millions unemployed, it means financial ruin and – ruin...in general. I'll ask again. What is it? A virus that came from where? A city named Wuhan in China? Am I right?"

"That's what they're saying," Jill confirms. "For now, at least."

"Okay, for now. Are you aware Wuhan has some of the worst air pollution in the world?"

They look at him blankly.

"I'm aware," Dan opines, "there is a serious pollution problem in numerous regions of China, that's not a secret."

"I'm talking horrific levels of pollution—the old sources, coal plants, industrial wastes, dumping, etc., and the new ones—the toxic gunk from computers and printers taken apart, soaked in lead by workers in unprotected circumstances...."

Again, blank—now more concerned—looks.

Paul sticks— "Approximately three hundred thousand people die every year in China from pneumonia. What have many people been presenting with that led to this covid-19 diagnosis?"

"Pneumonia?"

"Correct, Jill."

"That doesn't reveal much," Daniel contends. "So they have pneumonia, it's a – it's an eventuality of this virus."

"I've read that a lot of those people in China were only given CT scans, not properly tested—if you even can be. Anyway... So the origin is this—wet market in Wuhan? Where they slaughter animals? It was a *bat* that transmitted it to humans? A bat that what, bit a human? Or an old Chinese lady chopped up and made a stew of? Is this a Batman movie? Dracula redux?"

"Paul!" Jill almost shudders. "That's not really necess—"

"I mean what's the *story*, what's the *myth* developing here?"

"Yeah, that's really not..." Daniel tensely affirms... "called for."

"He has a point," Mary stands, moves to the backdoor. She pulls open the blinds a few feet. Gazes at the darkness. "They say it came from a bat. Years ago it was a pig. Remember? I learned yesterday it wasn't *just* a bat in the Wuhan market. There was another player." She swivels, eyes widening... "It was..." she stares at them—Paul silently snickers, Dan waits mindful of her dramatizing, Jill is unnerved—

"Mary please you're scaring me—"

"...A pangolin! Yes, our mammal cousin, of the order Philo—Pholi...dota, of Africa and tropical Asia, having a covering of…broad, overlapping, horny scales…feeding on ants and termites.' "

Jill relaxes, Paul releases laughter, Dan evinces reserved admiration. Mary curtsies, rejoins the group.

"So it was bats…" Paul resumes.

"Of the order Chiroptera," Mary appends, "also mammals—"

"Multiple mammals involved in this," Dan mutters.

"To panolins—"

"PanGolins," Jill corrects him. Mary gives her a thumbs up.

Paul grins, trying to hold to a train of departing thought. "Somehow it goes from bats—who meet, perhaps like us tonight for a dinner party, with their cousins, the panGolins."

"This is getting ridiculous," Dan grumbles, pouring the red over his white. "We are in the midst—beginnings—of a *pandemic*, my friends."

"Calm down, Dan," Mary leans into him.

"And, unbeknownst to the poor pangolins, their legendary fly-by-night cousins—kissing cousins perhaps?— impart to them the seeds of a… bat-shit…um…pangolin-piss…passed-on-then-to-woeful-Wuhan-humans… pandemic!"

Mary smiles at his ingenuity. Jill is overwhelmed, excuses herself.

"Is that one of your new poems, Paul?" archly inquires Dan.

"Yeah, Dan. Improvised. Like this pandemic deactivating what they call civilization."

Dan glares at him and his wife—then at the hors d'oeuvre he forgot he'd picked up. He drops it. They sip their drinks till Mary can't resist—

"But do cats eat bats I wonder?"

"What, Em?" Jill asks. "What was that about cats?"

"Nothing... Do cats eat bats? Do bats eat cats? That's all."

"What *are* you—I'm totally confu—"

"A little bit from Alice In Wonderland. Sorry, Jill."

"*Adventures* in Wonderland, you mean." Dan lays a touché on his wife.

"Dan, I'm just asking questions." Paul sends a peace offer.

"You have every right to." Dan accepts.

"You're wondering about all this too."

"Yeah Mar, I'm wondering what's happening to the country. And the economy. And my job. And – where the bathroom is."

"Follow me," Jill directs. "Three minutes and we're ready. In the dining room."

Paul crosses to Mary, sits. It's in her eyes when she leans her head, around her mouth when she tries to smile.

"It ends with Y and starts with A." He takes her hand. "I feel it also, Mare."

It's time to eat. It's March 13.

They didn't expect a room arrayed in candlelight. Daniel gapes—is this a dinner party or a wake? Mary lets the beauty of Jill's atmosphere enter her being. Paul is simply impressed.

Jill follows them all in, baking mittens on holding a tray steaming with flavors. "Sit guys, wherever you like." Daniel and Mary are one side of the long table, Paul the other. They reserve the head for Jill who sets the large platter at the end. "Okay, I'm bringing out the main course and the sides with it, they'll all go together," she chuckles, heading back into the kitchen.

"Let me help you," Mary follows.

"No, you don't have to—" she's already in.

"We forgot the wine in the other room."

"I'll get it," Paul rises.

"Boys, I'm bringing you a rosé," Jill calls. Paul does a mock moonwalk, cracking Dan up, lands in a chair with a bang. Jill bursts in carrying a tray and a bottle. Mary trails with two smaller trays.

"Lady and gentlemen," Jill instructs, "let's help ourselves. What you have here for the main is Tilapia Milanese which I'll explain if you want details. This is Glazed Carrots and that's – gee I hope you all like asparagus? ...with ginger and cashews. Dig in, everyone." They spoon the lovingly prepared food on their plates.

"Absolutely scrumptious," Mary tells her beaming across the candles. The men concur, humming and motioning. Jill taps keys on the iPad. From the speaker across the room come sounds of soft pop music.

"You cover all the bases, don't you."

"I try, Paul." He's handsome tonight, she realizes. "Oh, let me open this wine..."

There they are. Four friends having dinner on the edge of a pandemic. Their lives are changing, have changed, will be changing ...as they take their first bites of delicious fish and vegetables, mixing it with wonderful wine and though they laugh and smile they also occasionally reach for their breath to fully give themselves notice they're present in the room pondering kids and jobs, money and bodies—bodies of their own bodies of others they love. This invisible thing they're being told by world experts this invisible thing which can hurt those bodies eliminate— they push it away, momentarily. They leave it in the next room, hoping it'll go, thoughts of invisible things, outside, into the backyard. Maybe it'll go down the block, keep going, into the next town, across the bay and then... just go. They merge again into the conversation, the breaded tilapia, the talkative wine. It's invisible what can we do about it....

"Oh, Girl from Ipanema, I love this song," Mary sings along liltingly.

"Me too," Jill harmonizes.

Music helps. The wine helps.

"You must send me this tilapia recipe, I'm in heaven with each bite. Is this egg in here?"

"Sure is."

"Lemon and... pepper?"

"Freshly ground, Em, you got it!" She's sparkling in the candle glow. She and Mary share giggles and whispered words. Paul watches her. He never noticed how – alluring – her red hair is. He sees plums, coppers, burnt orange. Or is it the special light casting its glimmer?

"What?" she catches him.

"Oh, nothing, uh...your hair is – it different?"

"Yes, I had it kinda fluffed."

"It suits you."

"Thank you."

She was proud of her hair, straight from God so said her mom, rare for Italians to be graced with that color. It was the one thing she did feel graced with.

"Will you work at home, Dan? There were rumors today in my office that we might."

Dan about to lift his fork, exquisite asparagus dripping ginger, soy sauce, olive and sesame oil, pauses—*What will it be* to work from home every day?

"Yes, I suppose I will." Maybe it'll be a welcome break from the commute and all the rest of it. Mary considers having him there all the time it's been so long they've spent any real time she needs to go shopping tomorrow early stock up on things you don't know what'll be available in the stores in the coming—

"Many of us will be working at home," Dan utters as if to himself, the asparagus now less beguiling.

"Are you working now, Paul?"

"No, Jill. I finished my most recent job."

"Uh-huh. Any plans?" She pours more rosé.

Paul looks at his plate. His fish will answer for him. He imagines that – "Paul is currently on a sabbatical..." makes a mental note to use it. Has he ever had plans? Has he ever planned anything beyond days or months? "Yes, I'm working on – the great American... project."

"Oh, a novel?"

"Could be."

"Paul is too humble. He's been working on several projects. Short fiction pieces, poems – an essay for a literary website..."

The last part was a complete fabrication. Paul is touched by it. He has no supporter remotely like Mary. Daniel betrays no reaction—scoffs inside at his wife's blind boosting of Paul's writing. The guy is in his fifties with a scattering of things published, she's still gushing over his "writing projects." She's showed him his stuff now and then. Dan could see he was skilled with words. What did it add up to, did it *build* to anything, these stories? The poems forget it, he had no ear for them. Not those kind of poems. There was nothing in truth to dislike about Paul Wilmer, except his propensity to find a conspiracy in all current (and past) events. Otherwise he was a decent person. Good sense of humor. What Dan couldn't understand was his seeming lack of drive, the fact that he never really tried to enter a field and move forward in it, even his writing. He didn't, in *fact*, get him.

"That's great. I'd love to read. If you'd be willing."

"Sure Jill, I'd like that."

She's very charming tonight. She's – different. Is it the nervousness, the situation, making everything heightened? He's interested.

"Email me."

"Will do."

"Okay," Jill begins, "I have something special. I don't know if it's appropriate anymore."

"Well, let *us* decide," Mary rubs her shoulder.

"It's... I have a bottle of champagne. *Good* champagne."

"Why would it not be..."

"It's usually for celebrations. This obviously is not—"

"Jill," Dan buoys, "we've gone this far. Hors d'oeuvres, tilapia, rosé and – hey, we're laughing." They all laugh, subduedly.

"You're right—I'll grab it."

Paul excuses himself.

"Toby's...okay...right?" Mary touches Daniel's arm.

"Sarah is with him, he's—"

"Should I check if—"

"He's fine." He touches hers.

They listen to the silence. The candlelight is saying—something.

"It's French." Jill comes in. "I feel weird now."

"C'mon, Dan will pop it." Mary inspects the bottle. "We're allowed to enjoy ourselves." Dan unscrews the cork, aims it away—pow! out runs the bubbly—tilts it to the glasses as Paul reenters.

Jill raises her glass. "I want to thank you all for coming tonight. I'm sorry the timing—okay Em, I see that look," she giggles—"I'm so happy to be with two handsome men and my lovely lady here. I wish you all the best of things and –

also that we will be here—for each other... in the days to come." She stops and those last words hit everyone, setting off shivers through them. They lock eyes briefly, tap, and it's okay, a little champagne. The unique taste in the mouth on the tongue and swallowed. Strange beginning.

All three guests decline dessert – it's getting late, they're full. They share a quick coffee and assemble in the foyer for coats.

"Take care, Dan. Good luck with—work and all."

"Thanks, Paul. Keep at the writing. Something'll break sooner or later."

"I appreciate that."

"'Bye, Paul. I'm glad you came." Jill kisses him on the cheek, a little squeeze on his bicep.

"Jill, everything was super. All of it."

She blushes again. Why can't I stop that!

"Hope to see you soon." She says it fast, she means it.

He kisses Mary, leaves. Mary gives Jill a kiss and a strong hug.

They all leave. It's March 14.

Jill's alone in the big house. She has to go and blow the candles out.

V

March into Fog

The mayor of New York City announces that the largest school system in the nation will be shutting down Monday the sixteenth through April 20. He orders hospitals in the city to cancel all elective surgeries. Also on the sixteenth President Trump issues guidelines urging avoidance of social gatherings "of more than ten people" and restrictions on "discretionary travel." The Supreme Court suspends oral arguments scheduled for March and April. The Los Angeles mayor shuts down places of social gathering, limiting restaurants to take-out. On March 19 the California governor orders all forty million citizens in the state to stay at home. European countries—and numerous others—close their borders to all "non-essential" travel. When coronavirus cases exceed seven thousand in the state of New York on March 20, Governor Cuomo orders "all non-essential workers must stay at home," beginning Sunday night the twenty-second. Office buildings and retail operations throughout the state shut down with exceptions—grocery, hardware, liquor, gasoline, restaurant take-out, drugstores. By March 22, global virus cases have doubled from the previous week, to 300,000. The WHO tells the world: "The pandemic is accelerating." The term Covid-19 becomes widely used as "the disease" caused by the "novel coronavirus" which originated in China, according to authorities.

This is when the days—nights especially—begin to get blurry for Mary, Paul, Daniel, Jill, on the island jutting into the Atlantic Ocean. Their lives are changing, they're not unique in that. Households are receiving college kids prematurely. While caring for—educating—all of their younger children. How are parents to accomplish this? Easy, be forced to work from home by "executive state orders." For what, again? A deadly virus you idiot, haven't you been watching? What, like the flu? No, not like "the flu"—*far* more lethal. They have to shut down society to protect it. Isn't that excessive? No, idiot, this is a *pandemic*, how many times must you be told that by Don Lemon, Wolf Blitzer, Rachel Maddow, Anderson Cooper, Lester Holt, Nicolle Wallace, Chris Cuomo, Joy Reid, Brian Williams—the gorgeous blondes on Fox? Not to mention the ladies of The View talk show. How many times must you be told this is like no other virus including influenza, that transmission rates are increasing exponentially (what does that mean again?)? Turn on the news, it's never off, corona corona corona, Covid 19, use the numeral, *capitalize* the first letter. Covid. 19. Covid-19. A dash in between. Is it correct? Virus, virus, a "novel" virus. Practice it, no not Sars-CoV-2, that's complicated and technical, it won't catch on, it's Covid-19 you should remember. We'll do it for you. No matter the channel. The experts are here for you all the time.

Yes, things grow nebulous around that time. Moving in March into an indefinable landscape. On a road toward a goal no one can name. You should not do this. You should not do that. You should stay away from everything. Sterilize it all. Hands, hands, hands, continue washing them, at least thirty seconds at a clip, sing happy birthday, rub them together, left right, right left, in between fingers, lots of soap. Things smudging together in those last weeks of March which usually signified an exiting from a winter all are glad they left behi— not an entrance into something you can't even pronou— Did – you – was it – you – tell me I shouldn't – or did I hear – it – on the news? Who was it that said – did you – *Where did you get toilet paper*? I'll send you a link to— an article—video—to that information. We need more information. Anything to help interpret the writing on the wall. Which wall? The one in my kitchen. In the den. In the garage where I go and open the door. Look out. Forget why I'm looking. At the driveway. The lawn. Empty street.

Your livelihood up in the air. Your whole future a toss of the dice. Over what, again? An invisible germ. Lightning. It'll bring you to your knees. Stop your life. A freight train. But isn't that what this—lockdown—has done? It's not a "lockdown." No? No, *idiot*. You're not in jail. It's a shutdown. A *self*-quarantine. Writing on the wall. Behind the governor, as he, she, charmingly holds court, another informative press conference—the writing says you're doing it yourself, *to* yourself, based on our guidance. Er, guidelines. Your *own* safety. For you and your family's best way to move forward during this—uncertain time. For your own. Safety. Invisible enemies you see are often the most powerful. You mean like microwave radiation from cell phones and Wi-Fi signals? Who said that? Who was it? No, of course not, the virus, the Virus is what we're— You mean 5G? No we don't, we mean the Virus Pandemic. 5G, potentially a lot more unsafe and unhealthy than 3 or 4G? Rolling out now in locations, as we do what you've prescribed for our own safety? Who is that? Who said that? No one. Go on Governor. Please inform us about the virus. We're all ears and eyes, thank you for all the graphs. Back to the latest numbers. Cases. Mortalities. Honey, did you hear? Listen to the CDC—they control—they prevent. What? Listen to Dr. Birx, blonde-coiffed elegantly shawled matron who sounds so – very... Listen to Dr. Anthony Fauci. Dr. Fauci, short but dignified in his stylish suit, silver hair, sandpaper voice scraping clean all doubts, decades in the government health system, granting him great authority. Doubts about what? Listen to Fauci. He's imparting to us what's up, he's guiding Trump how to – proceed. The nation is listening. Watching them track the invisible thing after us. On the graphs. They're on TV, in the afternoon, routinely. Pointing at invisible...

You ever trip on a step when leaving your house or entering a building? Yes, you have. This is what days – or is it nights – begin to feel like. A stumbling over unseen obstacles. Pratfall over absent bricks or cleared away toys. Slight foolishness plus – what? Suspicion. That whatever it was, it meant to see you flailing.

Toby seems excited with the changes in his routine. Mary has to explain to him that school is not "over" for the year, it's relocated to his dining room for a while. The learning won't stop. Science, reading, math. All of it. She hopes. On Monday she accompanies him to his school's parking lot where they've set up tables with (hand sanitizers) a teacher sitting behind each one. Tobias spots his, pulls his mother in her table's direction. She resists him, he stops. What, Mom? he says. It strikes her – the patterns of her thoughts are changing. It's only March sixteenth. What else will change when it comes to – what else will change about my thoughts my approach how I the way I react to things –

Toby's getting weirded out it must be my expression. Is that changing too my facial – she looks at the ground – it's the same word they used for it when she was a kid right? Yes, of course it is. It's the ground. It's still the ground. Sorry Tobe, I was thinking … something I… let's go. He runs towards the – his hair not well combed that morning…

Ms. Lornelo passes Toby a mountain of "Information Packets"—assignments, readings, quizzes, study materials. "That should tide you over for a while," she smiles at the boy and then his mother, glancing upwards. An impulse to tousle his sandy hair—out for now.

Mary bends, "How long Ann?" quietly, as Tobias spots a friend and scampers to him.

Ann Lornelo unfolds her hands, teacher-chalked fingers in an I-wish-I-knew mime. They stare at each other's wordless worries.

"They're really not telling us much, Mary. Two – three – weeks?"

"And…more?"

The teacher nods.

"What are we in for?" Mary floats the question to the chilled air. The children nearby on the lawn they won't traverse for no one knows how long. Exchanging short tales of parents and television and the things they've heard and the things they feel.

Ann peeks around making sure no one's there. "It's not official—they may go to an online – 'platform' they're calling it."

"Online classes?"

"Yup."

"So they're planning this thing…long term."

Ann's face agrees. She likes Mary, she's different. She sometimes ponders how she ever became a parent.

"Ann—keep me posted?"

"Promise. Text you anything new."

Jessica flies in that night from Chicago. Mary waits ninety minutes in the cell phone parking lot for the delayed flight. A half hour for baggage claim. Her daughter laconic as usual. Fuming. Not about her university closing—her spring break trip getting cancelled. Her head on the passenger window. Lights of the multitude of cars picking up young adults glint and bounce off the wet roads leading eastward. She monosyllable answers her mother's queries. Mary concentrates on the traffic. The radio narrates numbers and cases. She thinks of trophies, changes to easy listening. Midnight at the oasis. Wouldn't it be nice if they played that—she flashes on another doomed spring break vacation, Toby's—week of...April 9. They too had a Florida trip planned. Disney... Oh, Toby. He loves the damn place. Lights going out everywhere. She'd booked the trip six months ago. A second sullen child in her future.

Sunday morning Mary had gone to Costco, filled her SUV. Besides the basics, including canned and frozen goods, she stocked up on paper products having heard there might be a shortage. Mary felt something, *saw it* in the faces of fellow shoppers. They were all trying to figure something out that had nothing to do with aluminum foil or wild caught salmon. She got out quickly.

Daniel spent the next few days in the office – his "final trip" was cancelled. He gathered folders, documents, made copies, scans, packed trusty law guides. Made arrangements with his secretarial and paralegal team. Wednesday the word came from the top: In anticipation of a region-wide stay-at-home order, the office will be closing on Friday, March 20, by Noon. Please clarify your assignments with your supervisor and/or colleagues..."

He told Mary when he arrived home Thursday evening. He had gotten used to not divulging to her the details of his professional life unless and until it was necessary. Which usually meant last minute. Nor did he reveal his resolve to end the travels. This was different. He wanted a moment, a good one, to share it. He saw it as a gift for her, hoping it would open things up. Start anew.

He met with Tony and the Asia crew Friday morning. They talked of the pending calendar, how they'd be proceeding, chains of command, communications. Their IT team spoke of VPNs, portals, passwords, backups. Made drawings on whiteboards, projected PowerPoint slides on the wall. Sign in here—the VPN must be on at all times. Change your password twice a week. Call us twenty-four hours a day if any issues arise. Someone will ring you within fifteen minutes. "Make it ten," Tony Levi joked. Or did he?

Tony stopped him when the meeting broke and everyone was leaving for a new life – shook his hand and held it – "Dan, if you need anything—business-wise or whatever – reach out. I wish you and Mary the best with all this." Daniel was taken aback, rather moved.

The ride out to the island was unimpeded. He tried to recall if he'd ever seen Tony express such emotions. He got lost in the radio, REM singing Shiny Happy People. Driving his Audi A6 away from a pandemic. "No, man," he said aloud to himself in the soft brown leather seat—"There is no *away* from this thing." He drove on to his house. To his wife and his children.

Paul's a diver. He gets lost sometimes when he's in the depths. He'll go down three days, no one can reach him. Not that anyone's trying to. Oddly, when he breaks the water line, sitting again in his swivel chair, he doesn't feel wet, but dried out.

Why tarry down there? He weighs it, after every journey. Drifts in his mind—the first drop, weightless letting go, initial exhilaration. Familiarity, the returning visual orientation. Then from there he loses the – in a way he loses *himself*. Vague recollections. He knows he's witnessed strange things, gleaned outlandish insights. Yet putting them into coherent form—speaking, writing—is frustratingly challenging. He focuses on the journey.

He takes shorter trips now. I can see under water, he assures himself. I know how to remain calm. Edge closer... closer... let go, trust the water to carry you, your skills of locomotion, your muscles to flex when and how they need to. He avoids, like most of us, that moment of truth. He'll do what he has to. "Moments of truth" for Paul, are the only real moments. Everything else is a sound of something ticking. A fly, a breeze on a blind, a clock he rarely minds.

So he falls back on habit as we tend to do in times of stress and confusion. He embarks on his voyage. YouTube of course. He connects with new researchers in words and video. They're popping up more and more, day by day. And his dependables, tried and true journalists, researchers well known yet marginalized, vilified for their "controversial viewpoints."

The chat forums that had attracted him were those whose participants eagerly discussed the arcane – in spirituality and conspiracy research. He'd retreated from most though he still checked out forums like Above Top Secret occasionally. He decided to apply for membership to a forum he'd lurked in for a few years. This was Project NSight. There were no fees. You wrote a letter explaining why you wanted to join, what you might add to the forum. You were supposed to disclose to the owner and administrators who you really were. Paul did and realized he could have hidden it from them. He picked a username—almost all had made-up names. Some uploaded a photo of themselves, which enhanced the confusion. Was that their real face—under their fake name?

That's how these forums were. Nobody wanted to post their actual identity discoursing on subjects ninety percent of the population had not contemplated. Would you link your name—on the forever Internet—with intimate knowledge (or experiences) of extraterrestrials, pedophilia rings, mind control techniques, secret societies, and so forth?

Irv Myre, the big enchilada of Project Nsight, was an enigmatic figure. Paul saw him in interviews. He had an accent, was it African? He was present daily on the forum, posting on various threads. He had an ongoing one in which he invited members to ask him questions, implicitly acknowledging he had answers, experiences that could illuminate aspects of the world which *you* haven't encountered—and likely would not.

Paul was not a frequent poster on Irv's forum. He never initiated a thread of his own. He signed on almost every day, reading posts about vaccines, 5G, spiritual insights, Ufos, the underlying deceptions. The regular posters on NSight were among the most knowledgeable—and civil— he'd come across. Much was tolerated. Expulsion required extremes in behavior. Irv said his career had been in "management, consulting and coaching." Those titles could mean anything. Paul had a few cordial exchanges with him in message threads, and noted his interactions with other posters—they often contained a hint of self-abasement and an attempt at rapprochement which felt manipulative. There were rumors he had an "intelligence background." He sometimes thought of Irv Myre as a diplomat.

One thing that had begun to trouble him about the NSight forum was the "thanks" below each post. All the members' names who "thanked"—*liked* you—were there. Paul noticed something disturbing —he was looking for those thanks under his posts. He was disgusted to recognize himself jonesing for digital dopamine hits. Hey, a thank you from... Why didn't they *thank* me?

Other things began to bother him. He was growing tired of his obsessiveness with its subjects. Yes, the matrix, yes, the "powers that (ought not) be." The billionaires who run the world. The new world order. Yes, "the sheeple" who will not see what's directly in front of them. Paul had been probing it for years. The loss of individual rights in the expanding worldwide Technocracy—the vanishing of freedom. He saw the circularity in the interminable discussions. He didn't perceive many people "waking up" to the real situation they all faced. New threads were being created out of the same ideas over and over. Same omelet on the same old plate. What did the talking bring? Accomplish?

Before the pandemic—or pLandemic—he had been visiting NSight every couple of days, posting infrequently. That would reverse, dramatically, for a short time.

A thread had been started in late January on the Coronavirus, having yet to receive the Covid-19 appellation. A small number of cases had been reported in the U.S. Paul kept an eye on that thread. The posts came on strong, as usual when an "urgent" event was developing.

When did it change for him? He was reading the thread and it struck him—Irv Myre, presumably clued-in to global affairs, had assumed a curious stance. He seemed to be accepting there was a virus epidemic that had come out of China, traveling from country to country, definitely not the flu, *far* more dangerous. Irv's certainty—and the *subtle levels of fear* in his posts—jostled Paul to examine things extensively. To prepare to dive.

Jill was keeping darkness at bay by means of her computer screens and TVs, including the kitchen-mini, almost always on. She set up shop in the kitchen, now and then switching to her "office" upstairs. She was acclimating to working remotely. The security and passwords. The being alone. She didn't reflect on the whole thing till the third morning, Monday the twenty-third. Monday is difficult, the transition, getting ready, leaving and arriving afresh. None of that anymore. In the morning she washed, brushed her hair, put on halfway decent duds. She had to do the minimum since there was a Monday meeting via the ubiquitous new Zoom software.

No one knew of course, how long this "shelter in place," would go on for. A week or two? A month?

Jill's boss sent an email. He asked that everyone "Continue to perform the duties you were accustomed to handling in the office." They were expected to be available for video conferencing or scheduled phone calls; to complete their tasks in a "timely manner, reaching out to supervisors for additional instructions or clarifications." However, "We are all confronting a unique situation. You may have young children at home requiring attention. We will understand if you need time to take care of these immediate matters."

Well, that's great, Jill shifts from the screen to her empty house. Let me feed the kids breakfast. Then I'll see that they bathe, dress and I'll set them up for…whatever they're doing. Schoolwork? Online class? Calisthenics? Is that still a thing? At least she wasn't being "monitored" as the V.P. implied in the email. Was it true though? Maybe she'll go to the gym. The mall? She could use some things for spring. Jill liked going to the mall. Trying stuff on. The new colors, patterns. She treasured those home goods shops, browsed them twice a week. She enjoyed the Zumba classes – even though she felt awkward doing the moves – at her gym. Everything she derived pleasure in doing was gone. It was sinking in—and being avoided. Maybe it's just a couple of weeks. She tabulated the profits and losses. Whatever they sent her. Strangely, it wasn't very cold, rainy or windy. Hardly any snow, no school closures the whole winter. Funny. Closed instead by the invisible thing which sounded similar to "covert," a word she had to look up. Concealed, secret, disguised. Yes, it could come as the mailman, the Zumba instructor, the cashier. The TV on low above her, cases increasing hourly. 330,000 worldwide. Is that a lot? Authorities in New York recommend health facilities stop testing non-hospitalized patients, in part because of a shortage of PPE (Personal Protective Equipment). What does that mean? She texts Mary, she'll call Jill later, she's busy. I'm busy also. Aren't I? That's not proper, she was scolded by a teacher once... it's *Am I not*. Yes she is busy. She's working, Mary's not. But now she's got the kids and Dan at home. Should she get tested? No, she feels fine. She needs to go shopping. Mary told her to stock up on paper products. Yes, she'll cut work short, why not, she has to fix the kids dinner or change a nappy or—. She'll stop at 3:00. No, 3:30. She washes her hands. Perhaps she'll call Paul and remind him about the hand washing thing. He's kinda out of it. The water runs in the sink. A little waterfall in the greyish light coming from the backyard. She runs it over her hands, soaping thickly, for at least thirty seconds. It's what they say on TV.

Remember how you used to string toilet paper on the trees on Halloween, drawn-out white strips hanging ghostly in the October moonlight, swaying in the cold dew of the morning? Sure you do. Running from the scene of the crime. Kids. Using what was near to create mild chaos, unrolling and draping paper meant for shit, employing it for Fun, a jolly F-you to the neighborhood.

It's always there on that rolling thing in the bathroom. Ignored. Constantly being left with one tiny unusable piece then the goddamn cardboard roll you can't do anything with except throw impotently at the shower curtain. At hand. Always there. Women use it for a quick wipe – men use it—dad to son—for the blood-blooms that form from sloppy razors. So neglected, so forgotten, omnipresent, indispensable, white strips of countless cures and cleansings!

You can't use anything else, really. Paper towels, napkins, no, too thick, clog the pipes. TP is "just right." Everyone shits. Some more than once a day. Healthy they say. That release. A reach away. No thinking. Drunk, hungover, an easy semi-conscious tear and apply. Two minutes and the operation's done. On to greater projects.

Then a pandemic appears and it hits the fan. No toilet paper to clean oneself up with. Or paper towels, which is one thing but hey, *toilet paper*? You fucking kidding me? No I'm not, my friend. What are we supposed to – you'll do what you have to. You'll listen as the TV unnerves you about "the toilet paper shortage," in the breathy, sacral words of an overpaid hack standing "live from the scene," on the sticky bacterial floor of Target or Walmart or Another Huge Store. You'll text your friends and family sharing clues and GPS signals from those with the low-down, following one truck on a lonely highway carrying a load of TP, flying dustily out of rural Ohio or is it tarburnt out of Indianapolis?

Pennsylvania...Jersey... Any word? *Anything*? You'll petition your neighbor who has a hundred and sixteen rolls of Charmin or is it Cottonelle to grant you one of their magical white rolls scrolled around that oh so wondrous cardboard!

Facebook faces the sad truth—civilization is crumbling, lines are swarming. Fathers mothers small ones loading carts with only their un-dried tears, no paper no paper to load.... Millions of otherwise non-inner-gazing citizens face their first existential crisis. Munch's famous painting—**The Scream**—is revised in the minds of millions returning home, head hanging, eyes pebble-cold, slack-jawed, empty-handed—his orange blue yellow exploding painting, now a naked American gender-neutral shape in a supermarket parking lot, face contorted in a shattering angst of pure incapacity to withstand *Reality,* arms held high in both defiance and surrender, fingers clinging to an empty cardboard roll, eyes bugging out, witnessing the final package of toilet paper being shoved into an SUV, a family fleeing the scene...

Holy, shit! Napoleon meets his Waterloo, Alexander his India. The Hendersons, Ryans, Garcias and Goldbergs meet their empty paper goods shelves. An eruption of white flags...

The National Guard has been "activated" in all fifty states of America. The United States has "reached" fifty thousand coronavirus cases. Scratch that, now it's eighty-five thousand cases, surpassing China's reported total. The Senate has compromised on an economic Stimulus Bill. Adult Americans will receive a check for twelve hundred dollars; unemployment benefits will add six hundred dollars to whatever the states usually allow; *billions* of dollars will go to businesses as "PPP (Paycheck Protection Program) loans," evidently to be returned. New York City becomes the "epicenter" of the U.S. outbreak where reported cases are doubling every three days. President Trump announces that the USNS Comfort, a Navy hospital ship, will be heading to New York to assist local hospitals.

Boris Johnson, UK Prime Minister, tests positive. Enters hospital.

China is lifting some of their lockdowns after two months.

Global deaths by Saturday, March 28, "surpass" thirty thousand.

The 2020 summer Olympics—to be held in Japan—are postponed for the first time since World War II.

The javelin throwers are something, aren't they? Holding the interminable spear—a message they're sending out into a universe which must hear it. They commence a run, a slow jog to the line, ninety-eight feet, precipitating. The throwing arm extends, the pole now angled in preparation, feet faster, one side of the torso forward, arm to the rear, feet dancing in little steps, the final propelling and then a stuttering stamping stop! one leg up – and back! whole body off the split-second ground as the arm that golden appendage which can gently touch or choke discharges the pole the infinite spear and the body comes stumblingly earthward having released an arrow sailing with the eyes that sent it onward into a space birds whisper about. He or she stands there not there but in the air in the lift that took the body with the soaring.

708 B.C. is when they started to throw the javelin in the Olympic games.

Something else there. It's like a new coating on the walls, a gloss or paint you can't see. It's as if night has mutated into day and day has…disappeared. It's too bright at night, you can't locate the sweet spot of sleep that got you through the daily parade.

Paul feels it. He sits at his window looking at the squirrels skipping along fences. Something is *off*. Not "the new normal" horseshit. He breaks to drink coffee, munch on crackers. Gaze out at the yard. He can sense it but can't pinpoint it.

Jill is trying to stay focused. Her house seems bigger than it used to. Her Facebook feeds are filled with posts regarding hand sanitizers, paper products and messages – "Stay strong," "We're all in this together." She doesn't eat much. She gets nauseous. The work has slackened. She reads books she had put aside, novels women pass around. Calls her mother, who's pleased, every night. Talks to Mary. Walks evenings at 5:00. Others are exercising on the streets. They wave, don't stop.

Dan had the idea in his head and being at home for three days clinched the decision for him. He goes to Lions Pride Inn on Thursday and makes the deal for the suite. Paid by the month, courtesy of Nicholson Maxwell Levi. Mary doesn't know, he'll wait a day or two. He tries to give his parents advice, reassurance, alone in the old house above the city. Mary sends them vitamins, funny emails. He's fatigued, wishes he could rest but must be alert. To what? She observes him at night checking the doors and windows, twice, three times. Driving in his car toward home, road desolate, he feels a prickle in his lower spine – twitches – for chrissake it's *not* panic – persuades himself. Turns up the music, Steely Dan, Hey Nineteen. In the morning he stares at the ceiling. Has he ever done that?

Mary's not smiling. Her friends often compliment her beautiful transforming smile. Dan loved it. She never had to fake. Now she can't fake it. She'll steal away to meet Jill for a walk or a brief chat with Paul. Sneak a cig on the side of the house. Keeps Toby occupied, games, reading, discussions. Teaches him about classical composers and jazz. Paul suggested it. She cooks, freezes soups, meats. Puts lotion on at night. Looks out the windows. They fucked one night last week. The night after Jill's dinner. They had a moment of connection, did it in her bathroom, and in bed. Ah, Danny— I can't feel you. Even when you're as close as you can get.

They're all lost in the supermarket.

Here they are merrily on the road manically to Stop & Shop, to Shop Rite, to King Kullen, to Wegman's, to Ralph's, to Publix. The kids, I need them to carry and help me load. Get in the car let's go!! Forget the fucking doll get her in the car we'll pay with credit I don't care how much we owe. This isn't food shopping this is stay out of my fucking way and let me live goddamn it let me survive I'm an American I'm entitled to my paper towels instant coffee Ben and Jerry's and those extra crispy ridged potato chips. It's eight in the morning shit it's already crowded it's eleven thirty in the morning damn a line out there it's six at night okay a fraction better I can't find squat old bags of rice and frozen crap you'd never eat in a million take whatever's left. No I had it first hands off that cereal my kids will freak if they don't get their rice krispies dude and don't come so close you heard what they said about social distancing. Okay lady take it take it and choke on it mutters his breath under his voice. Or vice versa. Pasta, yeah grab lots of it that's always good for yeah ten of 'em who cares get sauce ten or twelve pile it in. Bread crackers five ten fifteen pile it canned veggies dump them in ten twenty cans frozen pizzas burgers waffles who knows how long this thing could last cans of tuna in oil in water who cares pop them in there. Pretzels potato chips taco chips ice cream throw it in food we need to survive who knows how long this – yeah. Thing will last. Thing will last. Who knows. How long. Repeat. Covid Nineteen Hey Nineteen Covid Nineteen Nineteen thing will last the next election thing will covid nineteen was last year dump it all in we'll shove it into the pantry the cupboard closets drawers the freezer the fridge or whatever wherever dried soup wet soup bags of rice canned this or that yeah pasta cereal shit we need more toilet paper none to be had pile it in this isn't food shopping this is war and the enemy are these disappearing shelves the empty spaces dilating with every aisle we spin these heavy-laden tanks damn one wheel is broken thing will last thing will last Mom I'm tired a little longer honey then we'll be home again so we can learn more about this thing this coronavirus but Mom I want to play with okay that's enough don't you know it's late March and this isn't food shopping this is suburban combat get what you can while you can before the shelves fall under the weight of disappearing items we need this stuff you see because Mommy doesn't know when these shelves will again have things on them we can make nice to eat yummy in the tummy you see we need to eat at least three times a day and maybe the Walmart has hamburger meat let's go check Daddy before they close and late at night they are in the kitchens pantries looking at all the things they've compiled bug-eyed and dazed at the things they've captured stacked like a broken piñata in the pull-chain light and oh yeah there's that package of meat bits we found ———

Almost no one was wearing masks in March. Wouldn't be until late April, early May. Social distancing – 6 Feet – didn't prevent the cascade of infantrymen and women from their foray out of house into the wild virus-mine-strewn streets of the towns and cities. Into aisles where six feet shrinks to two which turns into "sorry, excuse me," twelve inches slipping by. When the news media speak the soldiers perk their ears up. Oh, they look they listen and they present for duty. They're saying there might be a food shortage. It's all about the trucks — yes, the *trucks* – they're saying so we better get to the store. We better zoom on over to one of those food purveying establishments with very large parking lots and limitless aisles where you consistently find what you're looking for.

I'm lost in the supermarket…

Mary as usual texts her friends, on Facebook people are saying you had better get to the supermarket because… Things are running out we don't know how long this thing is gonna last. Gonna last. She texts Jill, honey, go to the store. Buy canned goods bread milk eggs and whatever you can. Asap. Yes thanks I was going in a bit really looking crazy out there. She texts Paul, Hey, you should run and get some food brother. I'm not hungry right now Mary thanks. Seriously, get a bunch of stuff. I didn't know the world was ending he replies. She doesn't answer.

He knows. Paul Wilmer acts also, enacts what the media deities send down from Olympus through Mary his brother. Uh, sister, who relays it to him. He ingests the message, gets in the car, drives himself to Stop & Shop. Jill is out there and Mary has returned—still there.

Jill finds herself. Jill is shaking. Jill finds herself shaking. In the King Kullen parking lot her small upstate hands – are shaking. At her sides. From the thin wrists standing looking at them by her car door. She feels like crying. She never cried when entering a supermarket. Yes. She did. After Phillip confessed he was having a baby with… Now she's crying, she has her wool hat on it's not even cold today. Stop it, chides herself. Walk, like you always does—*do*. The automatic door will open now. It does... Dependable. Unsteady a second – whoa, no it's the floor – no, it's her. Clasps her cart tighter and pushes. Feels she's lived this already – something familiar in the space, her wobbly sensations.

Paul enters Stop & Shop. It's late afternoon. Smear of paint along the usual scene. Slightly blurry, is all. He doesn't notice it. The slight off-centeredness. The parking lot is packed. He's in Siberia—doesn't realize. There's a new mountain behind the building. It's fine. He deploys a cart. The lines at checkout are lengthening. Things are happening without undue haste. "Without undue haste" pops in his head, flashing. They're taking everything, calmly. The savannah is bloodied but orderly. He heads first to the rice and beans aisle. Obscure foreign brands scattered like orphans, written in Tagalog and Slovenian. And Covid Nineteen. He'd nabbed paper goods that morning at Target, an early truck had arrived. How lucky I am, my very own plastic-sealed multi-roll compressed packages. My fourteen rolls of Bounty, twelve rolls of Charmin. He tosses a box of rice in the cart, canned soups and vegetables and keeps moving.

Jill wants to sprint through this thing. Too many people and they're acting—acting weird, not going anywhere in circles. Looking for things that aren't there. She maneuvers around them, her heart beating faster plucks whatever she can that looks okay, pears apples nuts and raisins greens tomatoes broccoli. Keep moving she thinks. Don't get close to any of these people. You don't know who—You don't know what. Don't get close don't touch anything if you don't have to. Surfaces might what's the word... Her hands are still shaking. She feels like laughing suddenly. Even as it rises she's aware it's hysteria. Though she can't help it leaking she blocks the desperate outburst. Instead her eyes collect water jesus this is – fuck all this – canned stuff Mary said plopping soups chickpeas veggies ketchup mustard into the steel cart turning another corner apple juice and the light above is not good enough she wants to be at the house she's so lonely inside of. These people are all like her trying to escape this goddamn store *one more thing* but it's already gone ice cream she thinks please have ice cream left....

Here he was, rolling the cart, Paul looks at the shoppers. Dancers. Six feet between dancers. Averted from their dance partners. "Oh, excuse me," "No, you, go ahead." Right, thanks. Eyeing each other. Could he... Does she... Everyone ultra polite ultra possessed of absence. Even now home pressing the TV on. Anticipating the bloom of the corona flower light bordered by the black frame. Hoping tomorrow will bring a pack of toilet paper or chicken breast. Flour. No flour to be found! *Howmy gonna make...* Half the shelves are bare whatever's left sucks it's taken anyway. Paul finds himself taking. Gathering. Crackers. Olive Oil. Spaghetti, tuna, Mary said to... *Cans.* Of stuff. Arms reach for boxes of cereal—all at once in a thousand Siberian Supermarkets arms with hands out to retrieve the raisin bran wheaties lucky charms but what's on the box is something can something be – on the box? Or this can? Holding the can of soup —looking at, encountering it, as an omen. That *shelf*— it's—dirty. Holy shit should I be wearing gloves? The arms reaching stop – stop to before no they're already grasping the box the package the can the container what does the container contain is it corona contained in the container is it on in the things contained by my cart by the on the in the things we're clutching? How many Siberians are below the mountain extending fingers pausing conjecturing should I touch should I lay it in the cart where has this come from who has touched or stocked this box what may jump out of this at me like a freaked out jack in the box what's going to jump —later? At me.

Mary is calm. She's usually calm because she doesn't give a shit. Half of her has given up the other half simply wants to see Jessie and Toby graduate college—then doesn't care what happens to her. Right now she's on the moon no in the same supermarket Paul is in seven hours earlier. She can sense him navigating the craters and the barren spots where what they call food had been at one time. Don't forget the bread eggs and milk, she prompts him in her mind. No pop tarts, good, Toby shouldn't eat that crap. He can have chocolate. It's getting packed in here they're swarming. Goddamn, can't they give me an inch—*six feet*, you know, assholes? Can they pile those fucking carts any higher? They might as well pillage the place jesus leave something for Paul. Not only him! she fumes, swinging the wheels a perfect 180 and snatches the yogurt rolling. Panicked greedy little suburban spiders. Aren't these the people we ran from in the stone ages? We're both back at the end of the world with these small-minded motherfuckers? Don't be so judgmental she can hear Jill the voice of reason. She's right. Compassion. They're nabbing all the good things, the not so good things and leaving the bones on the sides of the road. Please Paul, listen to me. Get here soon. Don't wait for the bones.

I can no longer shop contentedly...

Paul looks at them all looking at the metallic shelves. Yes, Mary, I'm with you even though you've gone surrounded by home and hearth and a shiver rushes the wholeness of all their ruptured knowing suddenly it's March they remember these queen of corona dancers where they should be in that hour. Meeting clients or working out or picking up kids or making supper not here in the foothills of the Caucasus Mountains at 4 a.m. in the afternoon x-raying packages with eyes that can barely decipher the clock at the foot of the bed. They all want Mommy. "Oh, excuse me," they coo as one chorus ambling towards the check-out line no sanitary wipes no sanitizer they'll have to go home wash their hands off with cold steel rails coat leather whatever's at the bottom of where they left their memories rub out the thoughts that maybe they contacted a piece of something which will blanch their lives into a sand dune that blows away. Paul tosses stupid frozen foods into his cart.

Jill has faith she whispers a prayer her pastor taught her for times of trouble. She won't curse anymore it doesn't lead to anything productive. At that moment in time Paul and Mary get an image of Jill how cute how fragile how lovely she is. They both have a desire to protect the redheaded floating form disguised as a bookkeeper. She's staring into the mist of the meat shelves maintaining and losing her balance as the refrigeration case spills its condensation aloft entrances her in dewy splendor she can almost smell the sizzle of the lamb chops chicken wings thinks of her mother bent over miserable making her dinner another bone-freezing evening as her father snores away his budweiser life in a chair in the wall beyond them. "Miss, are you gonna take that?" Jill "Huhs?" to the cold air rising around her. "The hamburger meat? It's the last one are you gonna—" "Yes, of course. I'm *holding it*, aren't I?" she answers not looking at the man flung by the sharp iciness in her sound. She drops the meat onto the shelf, wheels ahead, wheels back, seizes the package again, thrusts it into her cart. "*Am I not holding it?*" she proclaims to no one, they don't hear, they're all steering and sniffing for any sign of Dr. Fauci's tiny friends. Maybe they're on that package. Or this potato. It's just fucked up, Jill swears, to none of them, in her redheaded head.

The shelves are vacant. He's not afraid. There'll be other trucks in the fullness of time shelves filled with microbe bearing packages products that will eventually devour everything. They will compose their own chronicles perhaps about other viruses, viruses with two legs. Paul doesn't think these things. No one does. These are normal people doing normal things. He feels an abrupt sadness at the register, noting the suppressed trembling. They have no clue what to do and nothing on these shelves is going to help them figure it out. Not even this People Magazine, Natalie Portman looking happy on page 42. Her dress is beautiful. I wish I could do something for them he thinks, *makes* himself think, hearing the words in his mind. Puts the products on the conveyor so the girl can scan them. He'll pay and go. Poor girl, he expresses silently.

Jill leaves, Paul leaves, Mary leaves. They're all three in the parking lot in the new slanted hillside of a March that while ending was only beginning. Loading bag after bag into trunks of their vehicles. Boom. Boom. Soft booms close doors. Boom. Engines click on, modernly, quietly. They've come a long way since the desert when moving was truly felt. Now it's a fairly steady glide. That's all. It's not all. They, all three, are moving, backwards, with their food.

They say Manna sustained the Israelites forty years in the desert. As they migrated in perpetual circles, maybe spirals. That God had sent it to them. Continued to do so. Sustain them as they wandered. It ceased to appear once they attained the borders of the land of Canaan. They stopped moving. They were on their own. Again.

VI

Lions

He's rehearsed it in his mind a dozen times in the past week, made notes as any skilled lawyer would do, pros and cons, potential pitfalls, counter arguments. She's too good for him, she'll trip him up, he usually gives in to her. It's already done, this thing, in his mind, now it's just the words. The inevitable resentment. The ongoing third party in their marriage, who sleeps between them. Mary's sleeping now beside him, tired out from her shopping trips, her gathering supplies. Costco, Target, Rite Aid, Home Depot. Batteries, booze, food. The last few days she was a whirl of movement, the house, the kids, the bags flying everywhere. The phone calls and texting with friends and doctors. Helping them all, even the doctors. The printer spitting out information on vitamins, minerals, immune system boosters. Mary would cover all the bases. But she was tired, had crashed last night at nine o'clock. Right after feeding the kids. He told her to go to bed early. "Please Mar," he said. "You need to take care of yourself." She listened to him. She was still sleeping. Will she listen again? Understand?

He went down, made coffee, sat drinking and reading the paper until Toby came in. "Quiet, Mom's sleeping." Toby was good, had his cereal and OJ and flew back to his room to play. Jessie flashed through, bread toaster butter, gone. After a while he made a plate of toast with cream cheese and jam on the side, and a pot of coffee with the cream she likes and took it up.

When he heard her washing he sat in one of the chairs near a window. "Morning," was her greeting. "Hey, I brought you a little someth—" "Yeah, thanks for that." She goes to the night table, pours coffee and cream, bites a bit of toast with veggie cream cheese. He's holding his mug and newspaper. She can feel him.

"Kids eat?"

"Toby had cereal and Jess had...something."

"Good. I'll get dressed and see what's on the—"

"Can we, uh—talk a minute?"

"Yeah, sure. Important?"

"Kinda. Yes."

"Okay, then." She brings the plate to the chair by the windows opposite his. "Oops, forgot my cup." She returns with it and sits Indian style on the comfortable Rhys chair. "This really hits the spot, Dan." She plucks her mug from the gulf blue carpet.

"I'm glad. Did you sleep well?"

She considers, tipping her head to the sunlight. "Long certainly. It's almost noon. Is the pandemic over?"

"Not that I've heard."

"Too bad. I'd willingly relinquish my new teaching job. And my babysit—"

"Yes, it—"

"Sucks?"

"It's not great."

"Don't be a lawyer here, Dan. It sucks. Say it."

"It sucks." She smiles. Bites and sips. She's pretty in the window light with no makeup. Still wet with her robe covering the body he never tired of. He had to focus.

"What is it?"

"I have good news, quite good, I believe."

"Oh, really?"

"Yes. And...some not-great news, perhaps, but not bad, either."

"Not bad?"

"No, it's..."

"Okay."

"First—I spoke with Tony Levi a few days ago." It was actually almost two weeks ago. Why delay when he knew it might be healthy for their marriage? Because he's a lawyer and doesn't bring in a piece of information until it's absolutely necessary.

"How is Tony? Margaret, is it? It's been a while."

"Yes, his wife Margaret. They're fine, far as I know."

Mary's waiting.

"What we discussed – it's important for both – for all of us – " he sweeps his arm, as if over their whole world – "it's – going to affect us all." He starts to get emotional, controlling it. She gives him the moment. "I met with Tony and told him it was finished. And—"

"You're quitting the firm?"

"Hm?—No, I'm not quitting the— just let me...please."

"Sorry. Go on."

"What I told him was—" he raises his hands— "I don't want to—do the traveling anymore—" he expands his arms, pauses for a reaction, the hands fall on his thighs. "That...I had to make an adjustment in my...career... The kind of traveling I've been doing – could no longer be – a part of it."

"Oh..." Mary drinks coffee looking out at a bright March afternoon. She had thought it was Sunday till she checked her phone and saw the word Monday.

"That's it? That's your response."

"When does this begin? When does this 'kind of traveling' end? Is there a time frame?"

"Yes. The cancelled trip to Singapore last week would have been my final one."

"Last trip to Singapore?"

"Last trip, period. The understanding is, any future travel will be—occasional. And domestic."

"Hm. After ten years, huh? It's over? Just like that?"

"You don't sound—aren't you glad? Isn't it—"

"Yes, yes. I am, Daniel. It's sudden is all. I remember us talking about this—what, five years ago? Then a year or two ago?"

"Yes, it's been on my—"

"What made you—"

"Pull the trigger?"

"We hadn't spoken about it in—"

"It's been on my mind, Mary—I was - I know, I waited too long..."

"I didn't say that."

"But you think it. And you're right. You're so right." The emotion again in his voice. It irks her the way he suppresses his feelings. He never shares anything cathartically with her. "I waited too long Mar, but I did it. It's finished."

She doesn't know how she feels. She's happy for him because he looks so relieved. His body language is different.

"It's - it's - wonderful, Daniel."

The feelings around his absences, his travels - she distanced them long ago. They became like a clock on a wall.

A function of your environment you ignore. Or presume you do.

"I know it's been difficult – maybe I *don't* know... how it's really been for you all these... Do you understand what I'm trying to say, Mary?"

"Perhaps. But say it. Plainly."

"I miss you. I love you."

"Mm."

He moves to her, unsure whether to lean down or kneel. He pulls his chair in front of her. They kiss, join hands.

"We'll start something new. It's been so long. I promise I'll try, we'll – we'll go back into therapy."

"Let's see, Danny."

"Yeah. Whatever you want, Mar. Something new. Between us," kissing her hands, moving up to smooch her lips, caressing her face. "All of us," again the movement of the arm that makes her twitch. What is that gesture? A control thing. Not fully letting go.

She kisses him. It's a good thing, for Toby in particular, to have his dad present. He reads her mind—

"I'll be home earlier. I want to be here for dinner. At least dessert." He smiles at his little joke and she feels affection towards him—he is trying.

"I think it's great. The kids will be delighted. I'll have to get used to your – " she laughs girlishly – "just... your being here!" They laugh, he holds and kisses her. "What else was there?"

"Hm?"

"What was the other thing?"

"Oh," his throat catches. "Right. It's not a big deal I, um—"

He loosens her hands – pauses. She notices. A swift transition. He reclines in his chair.

"I can't stop working, throughout this, however long it lasts."

"And? Don't tell me they expect you in the office? Dan, you're not commuting into the city—"

"No, no, that's not it. It's – it's just – I already see I'm going to find it hard to work – in the house."

"Why is it hard to work here? You have your office. Or take any room, I don't care."

"Mary, try to – listen. The kids, they're – on the phone, they're online, doing their lessons..."

"Right. And? They're too loud for you?"

"It's not that they're too—"

"How are they disturbing you? Jessica hardly leaves her room. Tobias is in the dining room, pretty quiet for a ten-year-old."

"Mary, I have contracts that are hundreds of pages. People I need to consult, often in different time zones."

"You can't do it in your own—"

"Hear me out a second. You've told me about the landscaping situation. The leaf blowers here."

"I *tried* to tell you about it. You mocked me when I said how bad it had gotten—"

"C'mon, I didn't mock you Mary!"

"Your attitude was full of condescension."

"You were right. It's ridiculous. It's totally out of control. I realize why you connected with that group, what's it called?"

"Worthington CALM."

"CALM, right. It stands for?"

"Clean alternative landscaping methods. The primary aim, as you finally agree with, is to get gas-powered leaf blowers banned."

"I'll help you."

"They could have used your help years ago."

"I'm sorry for my previous attitude."

"That's why you can't work here? The leaf blowers? Which by the way is totally nuts to allow during a pandemic of a respiratory illness."

"It absolutely is."

"Of course the council members are useless."

"It's not only that. It's part of it."

"And your solution is?"

"To take a room, paid for by the firm—at the Lions Pride."

"A room at—'the lions pride.' What is that a fucking tavern, what are you talking about," she rises—

"Lions Pride, the country club."

"You're taking a room at a country club? Now? In the middle of all this—"

"Mary, please listen a moment..." he rises—

"I'm listening."

"You're walking away."

"I have to get dressed. I can listen and dress at the – " She tosses off her robe, stands naked, her back to Daniel with the light from the windows configuring her body. She bends at her armoire, pulling panties, bras, blouses... "Well?"

"I— " She half-turns to him—she knows the effect her body has on him—

"Go ahead Dan," she arches her back again.

"Uh-huh. Now who's mocking whom?"

"I don't know what you mean." She faces him nude, arms akimbo. She doesn't move.

"Yes, it's a country club. They have rooms. I've seen one that's—"

"Oh, you've already rented it. Isn't that rich."

"No, I...went there. It's quiet, it's spacious and—"

"Quiet? It's a fucking golf course, Dan. You're running from leaf blowers? Are you mental, or what?"

"Yes, but, no, I don't think I am, my *dear*." He moves closer, a half dozen feet from her. She backs up, knocking against the armoire. "There's no golf going on now."

"Oh, isn't it thoughtful of the Lions Pride!"

"That means very little landscaping. I was guaranteed by the manager it would be once a week and—"

"Oh, how lovely of them. And of you Dan." Her eyes filling up. "So once more, I am left alone. With the house. The kids. With everything. While you do whatever you've—"

"No, Mary—"

"—been doing – for twenty fucking years."

"I'll be ten minutes away."

Her naked body accentuates her vulnerability; and the tears, the small moans; she sways from side to side.

"Same old thing. Alone and dealing with – all of it. How can you? During this time?"

"Mary, I promise you I'm not – *abandoning* you. I love you baby, I swear I love you so much," he reaches to touch her—she flinches, he recedes. "I have to work and sometimes I need quiet. And the space to – figure all that crap out. I'll be home for dinner. Every single night. I'll take care of Toby, whenever you need time."

"Time? For what Dan? For seeing you? For wanting to be with my husband?"

"Yes, of course." He moves to her. "A few minutes away. Home for dinner."

She lets him enfold her. He's never known what to do with her nakedness. It always overwhelmed him.

"It'll be fine. I promise."

"Okay, Dan."

"This thing might last only...a month."

"I doubt it."

He kisses her. She kissed him harder. It wouldn't be right to make love now. Would it?

"What? What is it?" she whispers. "Now you don't want me, Dan? When I'm all wet?"

She's kissing his neck, stripping his t-shirt.

"Let me close the blinds."

He does. She locks the bedroom door. He turns, sees her hair swinging, her long supple back and the ass he had no words to describe. Their bodies knew – *liked* – each other.

On a Monday afternoon Mary and Daniel are making love in their bed. As quietly as possible.

VII

The Covid Room

There's always a room. You don't want to go into. Whether it's in your house, or your mother's house or your friend's house. Or in your own mind. A room. A place of thinking, feeling. You don't like it there. A locale to pass through. You need to pass through. Nobody wants to go near it. Nobody wants to go there.

Food gotten, provisions pantried. They face themselves facing the mirror. A little-large moment of inevitability. Brought to you courtesy of Time and the earthly powers "that ought not be." Brought to you. You brought it to you too, you met it halfway even as now surrounded by paper towels and frozen potato puffs, you hide. Or pretend you're not hiding. You can't run when the ground has gone out. Standing in place itself can be the most dizzying action to take. You can only gawk at the food you can't eat. Spoils of war for spoiled appetites. At least it's there, proof we did our part.

Mary's looking into the cabinet she's set aside. Vitamin C with bioflavonoids, D3, K, A. Zinc, CoQ10 of course.

Selenium, Magnesium. Oil of Oregano on order. Colloidal Silver? Maybe. Astragalus, yes, pick up tomorrow. Echinacea, in tincture form. Goldenseal. Turmeric. She's got the little bottles lined up, her soldiers. She's the General. She's told Paul and Jill what to get, has to replace the Elderberry for Toby. She's armed. Jessie won't take them, she left a container of C by her bedroom door. Still out there. Make sure Daniel's taking C. It's all about the Immune System. Immune, exempt or protected. Isn't that what she's always done, protect? Didn't she learn to shoot on her own, didn't she teach Toby to throw a ball *and* a punch, didn't she wipe their tears and toughen them up tenderly?

After you've got your food and your vitamins, there's nowhere else. You're alone. You're with your family but you're alone. What'd I use to do? I would be in the office now. In class. Running errands. Turn off, on, off, the TV. I'll read, I'll finish the book I – are you hungry? No, we just ate. Why am I hungry again?

Something is spreading, no doubt about it. Is it a virus? A physical virus? Something in the air, is it a chemical? Is it a toxin of determinable chemical makeup? Is it ultramicroscopic? Does it have an RNA or DNA core? A protein coat? A surrounding envelope? A contagion is being communicated. Of what is it composed? Is it a code? A message transmitted digitally, a segment of self-replicating code planted in a program— propagating itself to other computers via networks...? Is it a code? Is it a text? Is it a word? Is it propagated by repetition, entering the heart and mind like a burglar setting off alarms yet remaining unmolested, familiar with all the escape routes, taking root in the mind, watching itself destroy the host containing it?

All the TVs are switched off at once. They try to sleep, everyone tries to sleep, to turn off the code, the numbers, the machines, the graphs and lines, the doctors, the reporters on the sidewalk. How do you turn it off? Should I take an Ambien, I can steal one from Dan. No Mary, that's not the way to go, she hears her mother's voice tell her. They try to turn it off but this time it doesn't go off. The picture fades into a single pixel that pops, yes, the computer screen dissolves itself into blackness, yes, the radio's sound diminishes into waves receding, yes, this time it doesn't go off—all the way.

And they know it. They can feel it. It's a very long night. It lasts for five months. Longer. It lasts because it doesn't want to end. Some*ones* don't want it to end. In itself a kind of ending. It's a long night. It's a night which takes in days, day and night, morning and evening, a long continuous...tick, tick, tick. You sit and stand and walk – listening.

Jill reaches for her cell phone, pushes out a text to Mary. It's late.

    Jill: Hey Em u up?

No response. She starts to fill the kettle from the pitcher, hears the ding of a message, splashing water as she drops them on the countertop.

    Mary: Yeah unfortunately.
    You ok?

Yes, now she'll be okay.

    Jill: Yeah
    I'm ok I guess
    Mary: It's so crappy what's
    going down right now

> Jill: Oh god it really is Em
> It's so shitty
> Mary: We have to stay positive
> hon

Jill kept tapping keys sending her next message before Mary's last came—

> Jill: I find it hard now to be alone
> Jill: Yes stay positive, I hear you
> Em
> Not always easy
> Mary: You're not alone, I promise
> you darlin
> I'm five minutes away
> Always hear for you
> Jill: Yes I know you are
> Mary: Shoot, HERE
> Jill: Everyone okay?
> Mary: Yeah, I think so 🙆 Trying
> Jill: You have a lot on your plate
> Mary: I'm concerned about you
> Jill: No don't be I'll be fine
> Mary: You want to come here?
> We have room
> Jill: No no I'm fine thanks
> Mary: You can no problem
> Are you sure?
> Jill: Yes sure
> Thank you Em
> Mary: I love you girl
> I'm here for you
> Jill: Me too Em
> Love you

> Mary:　I mean it you're not alone
> Sending you a hug
> a hundred now 😊
> Jill:　Me too 🖤
> Mary:　Sweet dreams and try
> not to worry
> Jill:　Sweet dreams

Try not to... She tries, she does. Holding her phone. Puts it – puts it down. Stares at it... shakes it off. She drinks her tea with two hands.

There is an amusement park ride called The Rotor, designed by Ernst Hoffmeister in the 1940s. You enter a spherical structure and stand against the curved surrounding wall. It begins to rotate, faster and faster picking up speed. Soon you are moving round and round the world. In actuality you're not moving. You're being moved. A machine is moving you, you're stuck to a wall, immobile, via centrifugal force. All you can do is watch.

Paul is turning off the chat forums, the videos—one last one? No, enough, quits all the browser tabs, all the sites telling him what covid-19 is, what it's developing into, what it's *not*, what it really means, who the players are behind "the narrative" they're dishing out. He'll make a cup of tea, but feeling a steady pressure in his temples, a pang in his chest, he gulps down an aspirin—supposed to be good for those kinds of pangs. Swallows a CoQ10 gel, also good they say for the heart. Alright, I'm good, I'm okay, he tells himself, I'm overheated from all this research. The information. A cup of tea—he fills the kettle, fires it. Dropping the green teabag into the stained white cup. I have to cool it with the internet for a bit. Relax. Take a break. Then I'll be good. He takes a breath, notices it's a little hard to take a deep one. Takes another, then another, slow, in...six count, out...six count, in again. His heart is rat-a-tating, rat-tat-tat, rat-tat-tat... He touches his hand to his chest. Deep breath. Another one. Okay. I'll be—I'm okay. What's hap – he doesn't want that thought. Steadies himself. I'm fi– he tries to stop it I'm o– I'm okay. Deep breath. He forgets to breathe out, the kettle is whistling, how long has it been—he lifts it from the burner – soaks the teabag in the steaming water. It'll be - it's okay. He's looking into the night in his room.

Jill covers herself with her spreadsheets. Shields herself but the work has begun to...slow. Screw it, I'll go out. She drives to a park, pulls in, idles her car. No one's in there. She doesn't want to be that only person in the park. She picks up things she doesn't need in Stop & Shop and goes home. Calls Mary, talks briefly, calls her boss, not much to discuss. Calls her mother, not much to say. Her sister has come to stay. "I'm glad, Mom. It's good Aunt Lorena is with you." "Yes, it's not good to be alone now. What about you, Jilly? How are you managing? You aren't alone—are you—all the time?" "No," she lies. "I'm not alone. I have some close friends I meet, you know, we take walks. And a man I met, we're in touch too." "Oh, that's good Jilly. I'll worry a little less." "Mom, be careful, don't... don't go out too much. Stock enough food for a...while."

There's nowhere to go. The TV seems all one program. She prepares a meal, a nice salad, pasta, the sauce her mother taught her how to make. It's all on her pretty plate on her lovely island counter. The curly rotini swimming in spicy marinara, the reds oranges greens of the salad in bubbly oil and vinegar. The plate stares at her. They both get cold.

Finishing is not a word in Daniel's vocabulary. He types one last email to his secretary. When did he ever cut his work off at five-fifteen? He's made a promise to Mary. He'd be home in time for dinner. How could he refuse, five miles away. He's in his spacious suite, clean, bright, airy. Most important—quiet. Barely anybody in the hotel, mostly long-term residents. He'd asked for and been given a room in the quietest part of the complex. He sits at the desk near a large window, accordion folders at his feet, files scattered atop it in pell-mell piles. He knows where everything is and how to locate a document, that's one of his calling cards. He's a legend for being able to sniff out a doc during a meeting with a dozen folders arrayed. To him, it's an intuitive skill. He closes his eyes... tomorrow, I'll organize all of it tomorrow... he drifts for a few moments... Huh! A knock. He's up – taut, alert – a knock again. "Yes? Who is it?" No answer. As he's peering out, the card-released lock opens, it's the maid opening – as he's opening – they both say "Oh, oh, sorry, no problem, come in, excuse me, thank you, thank...you."

Strange voice on this maid. Kinda thick and strained. She comes in, takes out her sprays and dusters, pauses— "No, no, it's fine, go ahead, I'm leaving," he tells her. Should I gather my folders? It's a lot to pack and carry. He puts small folders into his briefcase, leaves the rest. The maid – Carol? – is already spraying and swatting at the cabinets. She's got sheets out to re-make the bed. Dan catches her eye, she smiles, lifting off the blanket. "Goodnight, thank you," he says, letting the door close behind him. She doesn't respond. Whatever.

As he swings his Audi onto the Turnpike it hits him. She's deaf. The maid can't hear. He slows down and feels – for a moment – he's going backwards. He checks the clock - 5:35. It's fine. She'll be pleased. Or, at least not pissed. Caroline. It was on her name tag. The maid.

He watches his wife dishing it out—first to Tobias and Jessica, then onto his plate. She's made a quiche. When has she ever made a quiche? He's about to comment on it when he remembers he's rarely noticed what's she's cooked. She goes to the stove for the string beans. Dan tries the quiche, genuinely finds it delicious. "Mm, really good, Mar." She's by the counter, looking out at the backyard. "Hm?" "I said it's really good," a quiche chunk speared on his fork. "Oh, I'm glad you like it."

"You like quiche, Toby?" he asks his son.

"Yeah. It's okay." He winks at the boy. Toby smiles shyly, glancing at his mom. Why did he look at her? Dan reflects.

"Mar," Dan calls. "Eat with us."

Jessie takes bites between texting or checking her phone.

"Jess, please stop that."

"What, Dad?" she pulls earbuds from her ears.

"Stop – for now. Eat."

He feels stilted giving his daughter a command. No practice.

Jessie says "okay" and puts the earbuds in her ears. They eat. Mary pours wine for herself and Daniel, dishes out seconds. Dan gestures again to her and finally, when they're nearly done, she sits. She nibbles at her plate. Does she know something he should know? She always does. Now he should, too. Even that self-directive is weak.

Mary lights a cone of Frankincense, drops it in an ashtray, its brownish smoke emerges like a belly dancer from her long glass table in the den. It usually comforts her. She keeps rising, checking on the kids, Daniel, going back to try to relax on the couch. Relighting the incense. Inhaling it, hoping for it. "Mom, what's the smell?" Toby calls down. "It's nothing, incense," she says. She lets it go out. It's too dark to make out her reflection. She should light a candle.

Paul lights a stick of Palo Santo, lifts it to his nose, taking in the sweet pungency. It's a comfort. A healer. He passes it over himself, bathing his head in the smoke. It spirals in the air above the desk lamp shining in the room. It's late or it's early. He keeps lighting it.

I understand what this is, Mary says to herself. In her kitchen alone. What this is, this space that's taking us, entering us. Does she, though?

She sees a flame outside and starts towards it—it's a reflection of her candle—on the countertop.

Finally he comes home to eat—I don't want to eat with him. He wants me to sit near him and eat the food I cooked—I can't do it. Covid nineteen. Nineteen. Jessie is nineteen. I wonder if it crossed her mind. Strange. Nine and ten. Teen. Nine plus ten. Covid. Co-vid. Co and vid and nineteen. That's the Welcome mat. The name. She writes them all down on napkins. All the names and what they might mean. Is there meaning in it? What's it saying? Besides Welcome, come in ?

Paul bites his fingernails. His tea is cold and his slop bucket of information—videos, audios, articles, chat room posts and endless links—filled to the brim. He can smell it and it nauseates him—he almost wants to puke from it all. Is this whole thing a show? A phantasmagoria? In one of his last posts before withdrawing from the Project NSight forum he wrote, "It's finally happening, isn't it? This thing we've been talking about? The 'new world order' presidents and unelected mouthpieces have chirped about for decades? Is this the big leap forward in that grand design?"

Why'd I write that, why do I have to show off what I think is knowledge, what's the point, what do I have to prove?

He shuts off the radio, nothing sounds good. Or right. The classic rock. The classical. None of it is good.

They're running around themselves. Escaping nothing. Still running.

She goes from room to room. None feels right. She remembers Phillip in them. Reading his Wall Street Journal on the couch in the living room. She goes back and forth. Sits a minute—stands—forgets what she's looking at or why—then goes. Into a room. Another room.

Daniel comes to her in the kitchen. She's drinking white rum.

"You okay?" He leans in for a small peck on the lips.

"Yeah. I don't know. I guess."

He's about to take a seat – doesn't. She touches his arm, briefly caresses. They know this is not a time for touch or embracing. Nobody moves through it together. There's no suitcase to pack, no airplane waiting. She can offer him nothing. Not a bag of goodies for his long trip across oceans. Not a new book she's read. Just a clock and a room to hear it in.

She inspects for cracks in the floor. Tiptoes past them. "Baby, there's nothing there," Phillip says soothingly. No. Phillip's not there.

In his small bedroom, Paul, getting late. Tried to sleep. Impossible. He's sucked of energy and awake as a morning robin. It's alright, I'm okay, it's gonna be... okay? His thoughts trail off from him, he finds himself having to catch up to them they're darting so fast this way and that. Then why do I feel... no, stop thinking about it. He sits. He gets up. Goes to the other room. Goes back to the bedroom. He lights his Palo Santo. Holding on to – what? There's nothing there.

At a certain juncture in the night, whatever night it is or was – certainly in March – in that time of backward stillness, a day, a night, those last of March. Hard stones to be carried up dark steep pathways. Heavy loads to be hauled along dim passageways. You have no idea why, you keep standing holding these packages you don't recall taking up – okay I'll carry them you say, as if to a doctor, a father, or police officer. I'll do what you say. I'll take up what you say.

"Paul... Paul... you're a failure. Look at you, you're a fuckin' failure."
He spins, affixed. Waiting.
"You blew it man. All those wasted years. All the chances you never took. What was it all for? You've done nothing with them. NOTHING! No house, no career, no family. NO CHILDREN! For chrissake what kind of man has no children, no legacy? Loser!! Illegal immigrants have two or three and you couldn't have *one*? You don't have a wife—not even a girlfriend! You blew it man, what a waste."

Like neon, **FAILURE** FAILURE **FAILURE**, flickering on, flickering off. He doesn't believe in this thing, is it possible that he— his heart racing his mind racing his chest tightening—and he mocked it, said it was bullshit, a fake yet now he was - maybe he was wrong, of course you were wrong when weren't you *wrong*? The years are going by on the spinning wall and they all have a message for Paul. Wrong wrong failure failure. Blew it. Missed out. Gone.

Are you praying Paul? Asking for help? What about the people you hurt, the ruins you've left behind? Remember those? Your parents who tried to help you in every possible way? The girlfriends you betrayed or ignored or closed off from? Yeah. I - okay. The kid you and your friends humiliated, stole money from in camp? I forgot about that. Remember these other things? Here, I'll show you... Remember their tears, their anger, their hurt?

Paul is saying things in a low voice. No he won't die like this a stupid victim of a phony pandemic. But the tachycardia, should he go to Emergency? Counting out his losses. No they'll keep me, I'll never leave the fucking place. You blew it. Failure. Alone. Fifty-two. Just getting by. What... a... waste...

I'm watching myself through these windows she thinks, twenty years of surrounding myself by and watching myself through windows. Looking out at what? My fading destiny. As everydays shrink into everynights swallowed by more of those daynights, daynights, daynights.

Stop it. She opens the back door. Lights a Marlboro light. Two drags - yuck. What's the point? I'm not sixteen anymore. Was I ever? Crushes it out. Shuts the door. It was always myself wasn't it, she says to nothing save the room's revolving walls, wasn't it me myself and I that I was searching for all the days I was waiting and gazing out for my husband to come home for Paul to signal he's alive for something out there to appear and tutor me how to – how I should – how I can *see* and know myself?

She opens the door again – whom did I think I was waiting for? A man named Daniel? A baby? Someone to tell me I'm okay? I shoulda rode horses that's how I always felt, shoulda learned how to care for and raise horses. That all is gone, galloped away, never rose forth from dull ideas and lame aspirations. Ordinary, you're ORDINARY Mary. Face it, you aging wench. You don't want to face it? You soon to be crone. Yeah Danny loves your ass *now*, how about in five years? Ten years. You'll be alone you ordinary hag living on a divorce settlement and – stop. She puts her hands up to petition the wind to subside. Seeing her years collide with defeat her prize a boy and girl whom she loves like a grandmother, not – jesus – a mother. That never – hit her before. Now she knew. As she knew her old life – old self was gone when she stopped bleeding. Washed from her. She thought it'd mean freedom—it meant irritation. Abashment.

She spans her candlelit kitchen for what she knows is not there. Who cares? She, one small person, one small life, a woman, one out of uncountable. On a tiny planet. In the middle of nowhere. That's my problem. I always had big thoughts. Deep thoughts. My deep thoughts never led anywhere to anything. Ordinary. I'm so ordinary it's extraordinary. I don't care if I die of this fucking corona virus bullshit go ahead God. Go ahead virus. Don't spare me. It's all a spaghetti western and we all get shot in the end. Covid Nineteen! You piece of absolute horseshit. Go ahead. Kill me.

It seems it'll never stop for her this movement without moving. I was born tired, not ready, I've grown *more* tired, less ready. I lost my screwdriver. Can't fix a thing. ORDINARY, flicker, ordinary womb for ordinary reproduction. What happened to my orgasms? Flicker, **ORDINARY**, flicker. She views it, herself there...

The night peels apart like an orange. Mary sits in its core observing it split founder and sink, a dying star's last show. Seeing it on candle-reflecting windows—witnessing herself in the core, exploding upward... Sinking, down, again.

Phillip? She pours herself a glass of vodka, a hit of OJ. She actually called his name aloud. "Here's to you Phil, hope you're enjoying your lovely family. And the coronavirus pandemic!" She lifts the glass hears the ice knock and roar – holds it a moment under the skylights of her four hundred square foot living room. The sky is slate-black no stars or any lights shine. Brings the arm down, drinks. Immediately she feels guilty as though she'd wished Covid-19 on the man who broke her heart and his family, his wife Melinda, his daughter Melora or whatever her name is. Does Melinda let you do it like *that*, Phillip? She asked him once. He wouldn't answer. It hurt Jill. Her pain took away his pleasure he said. Perhaps if I'd learned, tried harder, we'd be together now, going through this thing.

You'll always be alone. Loneliness is your best friend. You know that. The mind veers as the air rushes in to trap her in the floors of the room. Loneliness yes was a presence with me as a girl I could actually – talk to it. I shouldn't be drinking I should be taking vitamins like Mary said. My mother is old. I should be there helping her. Why, was she there for me? Physically, mostly... what else? Taking me to the church to imbibe guilt and hell, all that disgusting—no it was—she did the best she could now she's old... My god, alone in this house. It's here, it's still here—loneliness a lover who won't leave. Who can't.

Jill? "What?" she asks aloud. "Yes?" She's sure she's heard a call, a call to her. No. Nothing's calling her. I've clung to this absent lover, this stone in my heart for almost fifty years. It's still here.

She goes from room to room, a doe in the woods looking for mother across every bent branch, startling at the slightest sound. Jumpy at the birds who disturb small leaves. Same room, same woods, same face across every mirror. It's Jill, the girl no one thinks is Italian, the redhead no one deems very appealing.

She's above the world now and it's small. As small as the glass of vodka she holds. She's running over the world, small as the town she grew up in. The town is in the glass and she drinks from it. Swallowing it down she runs over the world. Jill! She trips and falls. She doesn't answer it this time. Her mother flies by, Phillip flies by. Her father, always a ghost, flitters by. Faces she could never understand. Inside her glass. She lives, moves, unmoving. Waiting. Waiting for Jill, herself, to call and answer – in the same soft, clear, harmonious girl voice.

Golden boy. Where had he heard that? Law school. Accusations, angry outburst. Yes, that guy his name was... He said I had everything handed to me on a silver platter, I had to strive for nothing. I was the golden boy to whom everything came, floated to, was the word...he used. Floated to without any effort on my part. It was in a bar, a group of them, law students, drinking, chilling out, and the guy— SAM... Sam... Nafto...Naftal... Naphtali! Sam had been a friend. That night he played an enemy. Something, the booze, frustration with the studies, not getting laid, opened a venomous wound spewing out against Daniel.

Everyone was shocked. They sat while Sam unloaded on him. Someone tried to calm him, he shouted her down, the other patrons got quiet. Then he was gone and they all started talking again, eventually joking. The others told Daniel that Sam was "a little off." Sam called the next day and apologized, briefly, no feeling behind it. Daniel said "accepted." Sam didn't return the following year.

Golden boy with silver hair and lines under the eyes. And indigestion. Sorry to disappoint you, Sam.

He was right. That's why I said nothing in the bar. I took his fusillade. In a way I deserved it. It all came too easy. The place, the parents. The brains, the luck. The looks. Nothing had to be done.

Sammy became a pianist or tried to. Didn't really go anywhere. While I went everywhere. Around the world a hundred times. What was the world and what did I see?

Dan sits in his office, taking swigs off a pint scotch bottle. Yeah, life is great Sam. I've seen the world. I can't see my son, my daughter, especially my wife who sees me all too well. That bitch! No—*witch*. It's dark Sam I can't see well at all. I wonder what you see tonight—what you're thinking. Or drinking.

It's an elegant turning because that's Dan and his "circle." Bespoke suits, cocktails, hors d'oeuvres, expensive everything. He hears himself in a large conference room. Laying it down, the codes, the transgressions, the compromise, to here—*and no more*. The deal. The slaughter bathed in politesse, in international statutes. Forty thousand feet in the air. The arrogance which melded to you without heeding, the years doing it slowly, the phony lack of awareness— Dan? Or is it Daniel? Danny doesn't really fit, does it? *Does* it, you statue? Or is it *statute*? You simulacrum of a husband and fath—Whoa! I'm not that bad he tells the walls as they fling him around his business class cabin all the legroom in the world champagne caviar anything else Monsieur Fox?

It was all someone else, it's all been someone else hasn't it—all that time, all those Boeing seven forty whatevers, displaying his passport hearing it stamped, ushered into another air-conditioned black car office bedroom ballroom bar? Click goes the briefcase again. It was Monsieur Fox, Sam, not me, not Danny the Golden Boy, the kid who aced the exams on torts and contracts. It was never really me – was it – Sam ?

Endings. Endings for him were always epilogues of dramas he had already written, victories of games in his mind already decided in his favor. In the end he'd rise and bow, slip one suit button in its slit, and deposit his papers in his briefcase. The click of it closed, then casually, a champion boxer heading back to his dressing room, exiting.

Nobody really likes me Sam. You were right. Okay? I'm golden it's night and the shine is gone my friend. It was too easy. That's hard. Sam, it is. Is your night turning Sam, is it as dark?

The scotch. Hand shakes. In a small room. I never really won.

VIII

Messages

C'mon Paul—pick up. Mary's called him three times, left a message. Where the hell are you. Texts him. Nothing. She'll go see him. No, it's late. She taps another text:

> Mary: Hey you okay? Been texting
> I left a voicemail
> Let me know

Then adds:

> Please!

She'd met with Jill that day. A text came in the morning:

> Jill: Em do you have a few
> minutes to stop by?
> Really could use a talk
> IN PERSON

The capital letters did it—she went over in the afternoon. Jill tried to hide it but wasn't doing well – you can't hide from Mary. "Em, look at me," displaying the glass, "drinking wine and it's two-thirty. I'm supposed to be working!" Mary told her she and everyone they knew was going through it. A glass of wine is okay. She held out her hand. Squeeze it Jill, she commanded. She needed it as much as Jill. "Take a hot bath when you're finished with work. Relax. No TV tonight. Go to bed early." "Thank you, doctor." They hug. She left, in the car thinking of – Paul, blank – Jessie, reticent – Toby, lonely – her sister Tallie in Boulder, detached – her parents, old and isolated. Daniel, absent mostly.

> Mary: How u feeling hon?
> Jill: Oh better thanks Em
> Mary: You resting? No TV?
> Jill: Yeah and the bath helped
> a lot 🖤
> Mary: I had one too
> Jill: Now if I could only stop my
> mind from going!
> Mary: I know
> Try soft music
> Jill: Sounds good, I will
> Mary: Deep slow breathing
> Jill: Yes
> You're the best Em
> Mary: Sweet dreams

If I could only stop *my* mind from going. Bath, music, breathing. Stay away from the news. Did they work for Mary? Play a game with Toby. Take a walk. Repeat. Why don't you call me back, Paul? Text me. Something. Stop my mind from going.

"Mare, hey."

"Paul, I've been calling you—"

"Yeah, sorry, I—I was up real late and have been sleeping—on and off. Shut off the phone."

"Are you okay? Anything wrong?"

"No, no, I'm tired is all. I had a rough couple of days."

"I knew it. I felt it."

"Yeah?" He chuckles.

"Yes. What is it?"

"I don't know...insomnia? I had this sorta..."

"What?"

"Like a fast heartbeat thing."

"Oh, no."

"Yeah. Then it would slow. And start again."

"How long?"

"One night. It went away, finally."

"Any chest pain or—"

"Not really. A little."

"How little?"

"Not pain...tightness."

"How do you feel now?"

"Better after sleep. A lot better."

"No more racing heart?"

"No, it stopped." He laughs, "I hope it didn't *stop*. You know what I mean."

"I'm glad. Do you need anything?"

"No, I think I'm – overtired, probably nerves...the whole thing...."

"You have to rest, Paul. Turn off the computer. Don't overload yourself."

"You're right. It's beginning to sink in, Mare."

"Don't forget to take the C and D."

"Yes, I will. I mean, no I won't. Oh, I got that Astra something."

"Astragalus. It'll clean anything bad out."

"Yeah? Even memories?"

"Maybe—let's see."

"How 'bout you, Mare. You hangin' in?"

"I'll get you Elderberry gummies. I'm okay. I was concerned. I hadn't heard from you."

"I appreciate it. But you need to take care of yourself."

"I am."

"Don't forget about you. In all this...whatever it is."

"I won't, Paul."

"Come visit me one of these days."

"Soon as I can. But please—stay in touch."

"I'm okay, just...rough seas there a bit."

"I know, honey."

"Honey— that's good for you, right?"

"Oh, for su—" she pauses—and they laugh. "You got me."

"Least I have somebody."

"Listen, when you get a chance—give Jill a call. She'd be glad to hear from you."

"Is she okay?"

"Yes. Call her. Or email, whatever."

"I'll reach out."

"Today if you can. Take care of yourself. Call me if – you need me?"

Hi Jill,

I wanted to see how you're doing.
It's not easy to be living alone
during this time. So we share that,
right? Yeah. Sometimes you need
someone to talk to.

I've been trying to be creative during
these weeks, writing poems,

planning new projects. I'm also doing research on this covid 19 thing they tell us is so dangerous and threatening. I'm not a scientist, but from what I gather, it's not what they're saying it is. I'll link to a few videos which have helped me—and reassured me—to understand what's going on, from a wider viewpoint.

If you'd like to talk – or get together – I'm up for it. Nobody seems to want to meet. Why that is I don't know :) I'm not afraid of being near people, hangin' out, whatever. Every day I'm in town, wandering, doing laundry (a luxury now), whatever. I hardly see anyone around. Worthington is mine! That's how it feels, in a way. King of the hill. Ha-ha. And the parking is a snap... One great perk—for a king.

I'm linking below to special music, it's called Solfeggio. Very soothing, the tones or frequencies. Give it a try. It helped me.

Hope to see you soon Jill.

Peace,
Paul

IX

Interval for Time

Time seemed to be moving from them. Backing off and suspending them. They all had trouble remembering what day it was. They had difficulty remembering what their responsibilities were on any given day, and what lay ahead in the days to come.

In a way they felt abandoned, the children of the pandemic. In a sense they were all children now, waiting for the orders and the guidance of Mama Doctor Papa Governor Grandpa Health Official. Some of them, freed of time's constraints felt ill at ease. Working from home they had a constant nervous feeling as if they were doing something wrong and would be caught and punished. Others, laid off or "furloughed," having nowhere to go and nothing to do, had to either face themselves – their families – or both. Or turn away into a screen. Many chose television and internet to fill up time. Many chose alcohol and or drugs to avoid their encounters with time-lossness. Some pretended, probably got through the least scathed, or appeared that way. Pretended days contained the same amount of hours and the hours were experienced as in pre-shutdown. Those with young children could do this rather easily. They put time onto their kids, followed the hours attached to them and assumed—hoped—they hadn't become lost, only temporarily displaced. A regularity could be seen in the children's activities. They saw their teacher on screen. They had assignments to complete. Meals, bathing, bedtimes. The parents anchored themselves in this.

Some felt they were in a kind of experiment. That they were Subjects in it. Theories spoken of online along this track were usually subsumed in discussions of control and subjugation. Those new to these ideas found it problematic verbalizing what something inside was prodding them to see. Often, their families and friends would listen and – "Hm" and – "Who knows." Change the subject.

Time doesn't just disappear. If it feels gone, it's been removed. It's been *taken*. When something more powerful than you—whether a kidnapper or a World Health Organization—suspends your life, cuts you off from what you do, how you live, leaves you floating in the unknown— have they not stolen your time from you? Plundered part of your *life* from you? Are you then able to retrieve it, to be made whole again? Is anyone, any Body, held accountable for this theft? What recourse is there for the pilfering of days, months of your life when the forces perpetrating such larceny claim it in the name of collective safety and health?

The children of the pandemic, eight, forty-eight, seventy-eight, couldn't answer these questions. Could barely form the questions. Everything was necessary. Isolating your mother in a nursing home and keeping you away from her for six, seven months—perfectly reasonable. For her health, for yours. For unnamed others. Letting your father die alone in a hospital with no one who loves him by his side. How it has to be. They know what's right and they know how to take. The children may not have had all the right words, the perfectly formed questions and arguments but they knew, deep inside they knew what was being taken. They, they – were being taken.

X

Lake Country

Paul came upon information about the test in widespread use for the virus – RT-PCR – Reverse Transcription Polymerase Chain Reaction. According to Jon Rappoport, and others, there were serious problems with this method: *"The so-called PCR test ... takes a tiny, tiny sample of what might be a virus from a patient, and blows it up many, many times so it can be observed.... The PCR test says nothing reliable about quantity of virus in a person. Therefore, even when these tests are done on suspected cases of the coronavirus, they do not result in accurate knowledge about illness and disease...."*

Celia Farber, another seasoned investigative journalist, knew the inventor of PCR, Kari Mullis:

"PCR, simply put, is a thermal cycling method used to make up to billions of copies of a specific DNA sample, making it large enough to study.... PCR is a needle in a haystack technology that can be extremely misleading in 'the diagnosis of infectious diseases.' The first conflict between this revolutionary technology and human life happened on the battlefield of AIDS, and Mullis himself came to the front line

arguing against *PCR as diagnostic tool.... PCR is really a manufacturing* technique...."

Paul posted this on the main covid thread at the Project NSight forum. He hoped it might change some minds on the legitimacy of the pandemic as presented by the WHO and the CDC. Not really. Irv Myre was steering the NSight ship with a tight grip. He believed Covid-19 was a bioweapon deliberately released by a deep state agency, "probably in the U.S." The virus was mutating and new strains might be, or were, still being released. Devastation was certain for the United States—and much of the world.

Paul wasn't buying it. It all seemed too slick, like a spy-disaster page-turner. In his last rebuttal to Myre he wrote—

"So your position is Covid-19 is not an issue anymore. Maybe never was. This 'thing' is a bioweapon and it's mutating. So how can the #s of people they're saying have 'it' be trusted? If it's not what they're saying *it* is? How do you ascertain what's really happening? Whose #s do you trust? People going to doctors or hospitals could have the flu, coronavirus, bioweapon sickness, psychosomatic responses... almost anything."

"At some point," Myre responded, "we need to accept there are things out there that are true, that are *real*. It's about the weight of evidence. Or, we can forget it, we're floating over Flat Earth, gone. Then we might as well question that Mumbai or Prague exist since we've never stepped foot in those places."

Irv was growing strident with whoever challenged *his* version of what was "real." Paul saw others on the forum caught up in a feverish flood of words, assertions, arguments. Frazzled, he recoiled from the vicious circle. He forgot why he was there. So he split.

He ascends to the surface awhile, catching his breath. There was still a lot of work to do, since as the poet said, "We shall not cease from exploration." Paul was game for it, even if at the end he'd "arrive where we started and know the place for the first time." Better to know *something*, if briefly.

There was a lake country—as he envisioned it—where he decided to spend time. He named the lakes: Lake Rappoport, Lake Icke, Lake Kaufman. There were smaller bodies too, ponds and tributaries he found and explored. Sources of water to garner, return from, and hopefully share.

This lake has an ancient quality to it. A biblical-prophetic quality you might say. Affable, humorous, but careful—it'll drown you if you ignore its potential hazards. Respect its wisdom, it'll reward you in untold ways.

Jon Rappoport worked mostly with the written word, publishing several articles weekly on his own blog. His investigative focus for thirty-five years had been what he called **The Medical Cartel**. This encompassed doctors, public health agencies, the pharmaceutical industry, hospitals, and all of their minions. The Medical Cartel was "impartial." It presented "scientific truths," findings from "scientific research," data gathered from "scientific studies." It was immune from criticism and questions surrounding its actions and motives.

Jon was a literary detective who used words to slam perps against the wall, splattering their stories, their myths, till their cores are exposed as hollow once the lies are emptied out:

"You have to understand: most people don't want to hear this. It's rather astonishing. Most people feel compelled to believe in the virus, believe it's dangerous, it's a killer, it's real,

it's a global threat. Pro-vaccine people, anti-vaccine people, it doesn't matter. They salute THE VIRUS....

I started writing about viruses that were never proved to cause human illness—or weren't even there to begin with—in 1987. All these years later, I find myself still doing it. Why?

BECAUSE 'THE VIRUS' IS THE GREATEST COVER STORY ON THE PLANET. IT ATTRACTS BELIEVERS FROM WALL TO WALL.

... The real problem, the one serious problem, you see, is: THE VIRUS.

Sure. Pump up that story to the max, get medical testimony, research money, the whole insane apparatus, and paint over what is actually happening there, and you're in. You're in control. You're king.

Believe in the virus. Pray to the virus. Fear the virus."

He knew how these things were built, he saw beyond the building fronts, past flimsy materials and shoddy workmanship, into the innards:

When I say control of information, I mean disinformation. That's what the EIS is for. [CDC's Epidemic Intelligence Service] *They've never met a virus they didn't love, and if they couldn't find one, they pretended they did.*

They front for the medical cartel. And they provide cover for the crimes of mega-corporations. There's a town where poverty-stricken people are dying, because horrendous pesticides are running into the water supply and soil? No, it's a virus. There's a hotel where the plumbing is broken and human waste is getting into all the bathrooms, and they want this hotel to be the epicenter of a new epidemic? No, it isn't the plumbing, it's a novel virus never seen before by man. There's a section of a city where the industrial pollution is driving people over the edge into immune-system failure? No, it's a virus...

... Psy-op and propaganda begin with the virus hunters of the EIS. They control and own the chokepoint of disease research. They blow up their scanty findings into ex-cathedra pronouncements."

These were waters with unpredictable currents. You needed strength and commitment to withstand the changes, the frigidity, the fire that flew from the deep.

"There is no doubt that this insanity can continue, regardless of the facts: who cares whether researchers ever really discovered the COV virus; who cares that diagnostic tests are worthless for defining a case of COV; who cares that case numbers can be inflated without evidence; who cares that environmental factors in China (deadly air pollution, 5G technology rollout) can explain why people there are falling ill."

Paul did his best to stay afloat. He'd be going back there. To assimilate. Yes, to get the water into his bones.

A lake that is wholly itself, no matter who flies over it, no matter who rows, swims or pisses on its surface. This lake has a depth no one's assessed. Go ahead, it invites you. Come in. Nothing to fear. Unless you prefer illusions.

David Icke. Throw everything you think you know out the window. Jettison it all and read one of his books. Listen to him with an open mind.

His enemies attack him with every trick in the book. He endured universal ridicule in his home country, England. It didn't deter him from moving forward with his legendary lectures and books, packed with dizzying amounts of sometimes shocking information. He'd been at this for thirty years when the pandemic came around. What kind of knowledge did Icke transmit—at first to audiences of thirty, then twenty-five years later to thousands at Wembley

Stadium? Revelations pertaining to the highest levels of power on this planet—and beyond. As world events began to reflect the ideas he'd been discoursing on for so long, he grew stronger and more assured. People noticed and were listening.

He would do a series of three live-streamed interviews—watched by millions—with Brian Rose on his program London Real. In March 2020 Icke was agnostic about the existence of the virus. He viewed the unfolding restrictions on freedom, ostensibly to protect the public from an epidemic, as part of the playbook he knew backwards and forwards. Problem...Reaction...Solution. The power structures seize upon a problem—real or made up—observe its effects—then "devise" a solution which appeases the public and feeds them more control.

David named them "The Cult," those actually in charge, above and beyond governments and elected officials. He saw the coronavirus pandemic as another series of moves in the Totalitarian Tiptoe – the Cult's step by step usurpation and consolidation of authority. Now we were witnessing an acceleration of those moves. He spoke of the Hunger Games Society, vis-a-vis the movie which portrayed a tiny minority dominating those in complete deprivation. "The coronavirus hysteria ticks every box off towards that goal." Event 201, "a global pandemic exercise" held in October 2019, gathered "experts" to exchange ideas, quite conveniently, on how to handle a pandemic. Leading this were the Bill & Melinda Gates Foundation, Johns Hopkins Center For Health Security and the World Economic Forum. Bill Gates would be on TV like clockwork during the shutdown as if he were a medical expert, touting the soon-to-come Covid vaccine. Johns Hopkins would be keeping the count of U.S. covid "case numbers."

"If you want to know what's coming, look at China now," Icke went on, with their technological tyranny of facial recognition cameras and social credit system. The Chinese "technocratic model" is what they foresee for the whole world. He stressed that *unelected officials* (WHO, CDC, etc.) were in charge of this "virus show" and that is the plan for the future.

Icke had been "devouring information," he told Rose at the start of the second talk in early April. He'd seen Dr. Kaufman's presentations on the absence of proof for the "novel coronavirus". "There *is no* Covid-19," he declared. "It doesn't exist...." He lambasted the "Imperial College Model," contrived by "that prat" Neal Ferguson, which claimed there would be at least 500,000 deaths in the UK and 2,000,000 in the U.S. This was the model which led to the lockdowns in both countries. "In a matter of weeks, we have entered into a state of global fascism and tyranny." The WHO unofficially led by Bill Gates, a technocrat and its greatest financial contributor after the United States, "is driving the whole plan."

"During the runup to the virus," he continued, "more and more places saw the introduction on a large scale of 5G," including Wuhan, China the supposed ground zero of the pandemic, where it was massively rolled out in October 2019. Doctors in forty-one countries have urged a halt to the deployment of 5G until it has been properly evaluated and tested.

A doctor in New York had made a video appeal to his colleagues to help him interpret what he was encountering in his hospital: "He's never seen any respiratory illness like this," comparing it to high altitude sickness. 5G, Icke elaborated, at the higher end of its frequencies poisons the cells, hinders the blood from absorbing oxygen, potentially causing the symptoms witnessed in those patients. "The more impact 5G has on the population," he predicts, "the more it can be attributed to Covid—perpetuating lockdowns, and all the other draconian measures."

He expands his vision of the immediate situation to address the planned "technological sub-reality." Elon Musk has already sent up over a thousand satellites into low altitude above the earth, vexing astronomers who accuse their brightness of blocking out the stars. His aim is to put up forty thousand satellites, "beaming down 5G and connecting to the *one million* ground antennae" the FCC has granted him permission for. This Wi-Fi field will surround the planet.

Bill Gates, dedicated to population reduction, has been in charge of the world vaccine program, in collaboration with the WHO. It has caused vast and underreported harm such as paralysis and female sterilization in India and parts of Africa. Gates is financing the development of Covid-19 vaccines through multiple pharmaceutical companies. These experimental mRNA injections may contain nanobots, enabling human brains to be directly influenced by the 5G field. Microsoft and the Gavi Alliance, a vaccine group run by the Bill & Melinda Gates Foundation, conceived and promoted ID 2020, a digital ID— and they intend to utilize a version of the technology to prove one has taken the coming vaccine—a below-the-skin "quantum tattoo." Making us, Icke challenges, "nothing more than computer terminals."

He ends with an appeal and encouragement—

"We are at a pivotal point in the history of the human race—literally. 'Cause there *will be no human race* as we know it if we don't get our asses in gear—worldwide."

We got into this mess ... "acquiescing to the Cult's illusion of power." The only way out is to stop acquiescing.

Something had changed these past few weeks: "The spell has been broken...the Cult has broken cover—it's walked into the room where we can see it—and the door has clicked behind it. We're now in a different game."

David capped these meetings expressing that we are all "points of attention in the stream of infinite consciousness... They try to keep us in a bubble of small-self identities to prevent us from opening to ourselves beyond fear... Their biggest fear is humanity awakening to what the freakin' hell is really going on and who is really in control... Put aside fear, stop asking about consequences and we'll see where the real power is."

A half hour after this conversation was posted it was deleted. Within forty-eight hours Icke's channel was wiped from YouTube.

A lake can revivify a whole life. A plunge, a dive into its water can reveal you—change you. Cleanse your eyes.

There are lakes that look ordinary on the surface. They appear to offer nothing special. You might dip your feet in and feel no need to submerge. You don't take the chance to discern what might be gained by waiting.

A doctor in his fifties, a psychiatrist who's studied microbiology and mainstream medicine—and taught it; who's done medical research, invented a medical device. An M.D. exploring alternative treatments.

Dr. Andrew Kaufman will be remembered. Because of this historical moment, the bespectacled, plainspoken man will be honored by those who cherish the truth. For those to whom truth is a trivial matter, Kaufman will be a footnote, another kook perhaps, a publicity-seeking conspiracy theorist.

But it will be hard to deny by anyone aware of his involvement in Pandemic 2020 that Andrew Kaufman created a rupture in the Covid-19 narrative. By means of his words and delivery came a breaking open of the pandemic story being told, and through this opening those who desired could behold both shadows and light—which exposed gargantuan lies. It was disturbing and many ignored it. When light enters a scene things change.

He created a video in March 2020 on his YouTube channel, **Humanity Is Not A Virus**. He opened with how it had been determined that the respiratory illnesses breaking out in Wuhan, China were viral infections. They collected lung fluid specimens from seven patients. They didn't attempt to find and isolate a virus—the first thing they did was separate genetic material, RNA. They worked out the sequence of this material, the "code," and rushed into developing a test using RT-PCR technology, which Dr. Kaufman underscored as a highly questionable method to diagnose disease.

He then introduced a biological term: **Exosomes** occur naturally in the body. They are *membrane-bound extracellular vesicles*. Cells release them on a day to day basis, for various reasons. They are targeted to different parts of the body, depending on what kind of cells release them.

Dual images are brought up on the screen. On the left an exosome that emerged from a cell and was spherical in shape. On its periphery are circles or dots. On the right an image of the alleged Covid-19 virus (SARS-CoV-2). It seems, as Kaufman says, to show "vesicles butting out of a cell in a circular shape with globular dots on the periphery. So, essentially it's the same thing." Images of exosomes and SARS-CoV-2 particles are displayed *inside* a cell. "Once again, same thing, both about 500 nanometers in diameter."

Besides being compatible in range of size, exosomes and the SARS-CoV-2 particle both have the ACE-2 receptor, used to target cells. Both contain genetic material, RNA only. Both structures are found in lung fluid.

He follows with a slide of a petri dish from a study on the functions of exosomes in removing toxins. Exosomes are surrounding and swallowing up bacterial particles. If the cells in the petri dish released them, they survived. If they did not, the cells died.

His next video a few weeks later, was entitled **Koch's Postulates: Have They Been Proven for Viruses or (The Rooster in the River of Rats)**. In this slide presentation the doctor challenges the papers proclaiming discovery of the novel coronavirus, in relation to Rivers' Criteria (a later version of Koch's Postulates) which are supposed to be met in order to prove a new virus.

The first paper from China did not isolate a virus, only genetic material, did not cultivate in host cells ("cells from the person who is ill or the source of the virus"), but in monkey kidney and other cells, and from *one* out of seven patients. And it did not prove filterability.

In their conclusions they wrote: "The study provides ... evidence of an *association* between the disease and this virus. However, there are still many urgent questions to be answered. We need more clinical data and samples to confirm if this virus is indeed the etiology [causal] agent for this epidemic."

It's clear the Canadian team from McMaster University did not isolate a virus, only genetic material and did not cultivate in pure culture cells, but used unspecified mammalian cells. Astonishingly, they introduce their article with— "The emergence of a new coronavirus in a market in Wuhan,

China in December 2019 *set in motion* the pandemic we are now witnessing in 160 countries around the world."

The Kim paper out of Korea began with the statement, "Following the outbreaks of unexplained pneumonia in Wuhan, China, in late 2019, a new coronavirus was identified as the causative agent in January 2020." That statement is referenced to another 2020 article, which was not a study attempting to isolate and identify a new virus; it looks at the genetic sequence of Covid-19 and examines it from an evolutionary perspective. This second article says nothing about *causation* and concludes, "The unique genetic features of 2019-nCoV and their potential association with virus characteristics and virulence in humans remains to be elucidated."

Andrew Kaufman finalizes— "None of the Rivers' Criteria were met for Covid-19.... Rumors and lies placed Covid-19 as the cause of a pandemic with no proof. No proof whatsoever."

The doctor would reiterate those words in numerous interviews through spring and summer 2020, ceaselessly pointing at a naked emperor.

Some lakes will not alter your state of mind—immediately. After a quiet swim when you're sitting in the sun and you go in for a drink – you bring it to your lips and you don't drop the glass... but it shatters.

Are you shivering yet? Are you shouting out to someone, somewhere? Are you wondering?

Paul was wondering. The Covid thing – it was everywhere. It couldn't touch the lakes though. Shelter was there. Shelter of an endless sky.

XI

Ask Alice

He decides to chance it, what the heck, she'll tell him if she's busy. It's been over a week since Paul's seen Mary and that rarely happens now. He gets out early for him, drives to the higher taxed part of town. They usually meet in Starbucks or at the park. Today Paul wouldn't mind relaxing with a cup of joe in Mary's spacious light-filled living room – sinking into her super-supportive leather couch.

He walks to the left-rear. She's usually in the kitchen at that time, drinking coffee, reading, emailing. He peeks through the window—no one on the other side. After a minute he can hear voices he confirms are Mary's and Toby's coming from the dining room. They're talking about math. Mary the math teacher. Math had always made him feel helpless. She drifts in the kitchen, "Well try it, don't use the converter this time, try it by yourself, you can do it..." Putting plates in the dishwasher she pauses to listen to Toby complaining and gazes ahead at the wall—her face a sad drained surrender to reality. Paul, watching a very private and ephemeral transformation, almost moves to go – she turns and sees him, doesn't show surprise, doesn't hide what's exposed there at the dishwasher, plate in hand dripping. She looks at him. He wants to vanish. He tries a smile to convey, "Hey… it's okay." Her eyes open to him and they hold it a moment. She can tell him more with a look than all the words he can conjure. Toby's voice again, Mary bends, putting the plate in the machine, answering him patiently. She gestures Paul to go to the backyard.

"Hey," she waves like a kid.

"Hey. How are – How's it—"

"Listen, I'm sorry I haven't come by or we haven't—"

"It's okay, I under—"

"No, it's not, especially now when we should be—you know."

"I see you're pretty busy…"

"No. No, Paul, Toby can do his lessons by himself for a while. I may be a teacher. I'm not a babysitter. Coffee?"

"Sure."

"Two minutes. Sit." He does. With her foot holding the door open—"Don't you escape Wilmer!"

No, I won't – where can I go anyway in the pandem…onic. Pandem…oronic. Pandem-onium-ic. Pandem…alefic. He's still fabricating variations when she's in front of him – mugs and a bunch of things – he has to focus on them – books, notepads, newspapers, plate of cookies, cell phone.

"Gee Mare, you forgot the kitchen sink."

"That's rather unoriginal coming from you—I'd have thought you'd say, I don't know, 'the attic's insulation.' Something off-beat."

"Catch me a break would you sunshine? I'm not original till at least one in the afternoon. Or is it morning?"

"Okay, I will," she leans on the table. "Oh, by the way, I have news." She eyes him expectantly— he's hoping she'll ask him into the house—the *couch*.

"Yeah? I could use some news that doesn't come from faceless voices on TV. Or is it voiceless faces?"

"I'm pregnant."

The patio table splits—crumples. Of course it doesn't. "You're...?"

"April Fooooooolllsss!" she almost shouts. Could it be *April first*? Had they escaped from March? How had he not noticed the emergence? No victory parade?

"Relax, it was just a goof."

"Oh... no. I was thinking about...something." April Fools. Why would she say 'I'm pregnant'? He's drifting on that thought...

"Coffee alright?"

He lifts it to his lips, "Yeah, fine."

"Speaking of fools..." she sorts her things, newspapers, books, etc.

"You still get the Times delivered?"

"Yeah, we do. Dan's the one who reads it. Lately I've been – glancing at it."

He takes up the main section, notes the date, March 31, Mary's red stars and circles throughout the lead article.

"Looks like you've been doing a lot more than glancing."

"Yeah, maybe." She reaches for the paper—

"Hold a sec, Mare." He reads the headline: "**Coronavirus May Kill 100,000 to 240,000 in U.S. Despite Actions, Officials Say**." She'd underlined *Despite Actions* three times. "Despite, huh?"

"Yes, very hopeful."

He reads aloud: " '*The top government scientists battling the coronavirus estimated on Tuesday that the deadly pathogen could kill 100,000 to 240,000 Americans as it ravages the country despite social distancing measures that have closed schools, banned large gatherings, limited travel and forced people to stay in their homes.'* 240,000... Not much of a pandemic, doctors."

"Paul. That's a lot of people."

"Is it?"

"Yeah, of cour—what do you—"

He continues, " *'Dr. Anthony S. Fauci, the nation's leading infectious disease expert, and Dr. Deborah L. Birx, who is coordinating the coronavirus response, displayed that grim projection at a White House briefing, calling it "our real number" but pledging to do everything possible to reduce it.'* How reassuring! They're 'pledging to do everything possible.' Don't you feel at ease my dear?"

"Yeah, I'm delighted."

"You must be. You've covered this thing in your lovely magic marker. Adding your own magic to Birx's and Fauci's?"

She smiles and drinks her coffee. He reads:

" *'As dire as those predictions are, Dr. Fauci and Dr. Birx said the number of deaths could be much higher if Americans did not follow the strict guidelines vital to keeping the virus from spreading. The White House models they displayed showed that more than 2.2 million people could have died in the United States if nothing were done.'*

"Oh, now I'm totally at ease. I'll have a bath and take a nap. If not for their 'strict guidelines,' like – collapsing the economy? – we would have had—*will* have had—over two million deaths. So, they prevented a mass die-off—we'll never know for sure will we. Just trust the great experts."

"Yeah, but—"

"The great doctors."

"I know you don't have confidence in the—"

"*Confidence?*"

"Don't you think these measures might have – forget it." He answers only with a sour expression. "What were they supposed to do?"

He drinks. "How about follow science and not quarantine healthy people? Let them make a living?"

"They're saying asymptomatic people can—transmit this thing."

"A...symptomatic. Meaning we're all *patients* now? Including healthy people! Only a matter of time until we transfer this thing to our – Mother? Baker? Candlestick mak—"

"Okay, okay," she titters. "I don't know."

"Someone knows. Theater of the absurd."

Mary cracks a cookie. "No one does, yet." Paul ruefully grins.

"I do feel, in a way, for Trump."

"Why's that? You're not exactly a MAGA guy."

"Because. At first he had the intuition to resist the whole shutdown thing. Then gradually you could see...they were getting to him. Mr. President...do you want to be held—to be accused of responsibility—for thousands, maybe *millions* of deaths? Can't you hear the conversation, Mare? How do you resist that? He caved, plain and simple."

"It does sound like an impossible position to be put in. How could he know? He *has to* depend on them. You don't think this shutdown is helping to – slow this – thing down?"

"Haven't you been watching any of the videos I've sent you?"

"Yeah, I actually have—"

"Or reading the articles?"

"I have, and I want to discuss with you."

"I'm listening."

"There's a lot to digest, Paul."

"Heck of a lot."

"Don't forget—I have them home, all the time. I'm *teaching* one."

"And Dan, he's at Lions Pride?"

"It's too loud and chaotic here – he claims."

"For him. Not for you?"

"I don't fit into the equation."

"Mm-hm. And all this?" he tilts to her pile of things.

"Yes." She's deliberating. The door flies open and Toby sticks his light brown head into daylight—

"Mommm?"

"What? Don't yell I'm right here."

"Hey Tobias."

"Mom, Dad's on the phone. Wants to speak to you."

"Toby, didn't you hear Paul greet you?"

"Yeah. Sorry. Hi Paul."

"Hello Tobe."

"Tell him to call me on my cell."

He's gone.

"It's a cliché—it never stops." Then as an aside—"But what in my life isn't a cliché?"

Her phone vibrates. She taps it. "Hi. Yeah, fine. Same thing they always are, Dan. Schoolwork. Nothing. Yes, he is. Yeah, we're—yes, out back. I said yes, Dan. Look, call me later, I'm busy. Bye." The phone clatters, she blows curls off her face.

"Hey, you good?"

"Yeah, I'm – I'm fine. Sorry 'bout that. And for sitting out here."

"I don't mind, it's mild today."

"Mm. He doesn't want anyone... in the house. He made me cancel the cleaning ladies."

"I should have brought my Windex."

"It's stupid and un—"

"Whatever, I don't care."

"I do, though. You're my oldest... I'm not going to let his paranoia dominate our—" pointing at the house—"lives 'cause he's...freaked out or... I'm gonna talk to him."

"Okay, hon."

"It pisses me off."

"Alright, forget it.

"I'm trying to—"

"What was it you—"

"Oh! Finally, yes. No more interruptions or divagations."

"I promise neither to interrupt or – divagate – if you tell me what divagate means!"

"I promise I will once you stop interrupting me." Their laughter is easy, their flow natural.

"Give it to me!"

"Okay..." excitement lights her up. "I was thinking one night about the name you know, 'Covid...Nineteen.' I started scribbling notes on these napkins." She comes around and stands by him. "I'll attempt to decipher for you." She arranges the napkins juxtaposed like mascara-stained jigsaw puzzle pieces. "Here you have Co which is *together*. We're talking roots. Latin or whatever."

"Okay."

"Co is together or with. Vid is *to see* or to view."

"Got it."

"Then the number 19. I'm not getting into numerology, don't worry." Paul chuckles. "Nineteen—last year. Or 'the past'."

"Mm-hm."

"So there's – Together see last year. Or the past. I dropped 'We' in—Together *we* see the past. I asked myself, what is it 'we' might see in the past? You with me?"

He looks up – "Yes."

"We are seeing...*Ourselves*." Simultaneous chills. "Yes. Together – We – See – *Ourselves* – in Nineteen."

"The past."

"Why do we see ourselves last year?" She sinks next to him. "Because—we're watching ourselves...go backwards."

"Backwards!"

"We see ourselves going into the past."

"Hm... Interesting, Mare."

"But why, Paul? Why?"

"Why...?"

"Why are we watching ourselves going into the past? What does it mean?" She holds up the napkins— "Getting *stuck*. Being stuck."

"Stuck."

"That's what...came to me." Mary shrugs.

"Okay," he tracks, "let me... We watch ourselves...going backwards..."

"Mm."

"Into the past and...getting stuck."

"Basically what I've come to."

"It's a code you're – unveiling?"

"Guess so."

"That's expressing—*concealing*—something about—"

"What our situation really is?"

"Keeping us stuck in the past. 2019. Covid...nineteen. Shut...down."

"Mm, yes. No movement."

"Well... backwards movement."

"Yes, it's a paradox."

"It's into the past—no *real* movement at all."

"Stuck." She locks eyes with him.

"Going nowhere."

"Watching ourselves." She caps it.

They sit a moment. Looking ahead. Listening to the common grackles.

"Shit," he whispers.

"What?"

"It's...compelling."

"Yeah? I'm not crazy? This isn't nuts?"

"Hm?" He's skating in his head around it. "Not at all. Too sane, maybe."

"Can that be? They're purposely – and they're telling us—"

"Purposely keeping us stuck in the past? And telling us—in the name of the disease?" He consults the grass, the trees. "Fucked up, right?"

The coffee bolsters them.

"Are you ready for another one?"

"You've got more?"

"The last one for today."

"I'm still absorbing that one."

"You can only blame yourself. You're my catalyst."

"Uh-huh."

"I'm just an ordinary suburban housewife." He busts out laughing. "What's funny?"

Her cell phone vibrates. A text. She looks at it.

"See? My dear hubby requests me to attend to a certain matter. Guess I'd better attend," she rises.

"Later—housewife 'ordinaire'."

"Hey," she plunks down—"watch it, pal."

"Let me have it." He opens his arms to receive.

She holds up a hardcover volume.

"**Alice in Wonderland**! Gorgeous edition." He flips the pages.

"My parents gave me that for my eleventh birthday."

"These illustrations are amazing. Such detail."

"I remember poring over them for hours. Lying on my bed."

"Is there another code you've discovered—Sibyl?"

"Ha-ha." She takes in her new moniker. "Funny. Yes, discovered it back in Delphi. I had an urge to read it again – when this thing started."

"You quoted it at Jill's dinner—'Do cats eat bats'. "

"Yes. Bats, cats... do they eat each other... It's in the beginning. Bizarre. I read through the whole book and put it down. I picked it up two days ago, reread some sections. And I was like – *huh!*"

"Share Sibyl, share."

"You never called me that before." She's touched and a bit awed.

"You've never been an oracle during a pandemic before. Or have you?"

"Not that I recall. You remember the Mad Tea Party chapter?"

He squints, "The Hatter...The Hare... Alice. The empty chairs."

"Yes, the March Hare, he's called. And the Dormouse."

"Of course, the dormouse. Grace Slick's friend."

"Ha, yes. In this chapter they talk about time—with a capital T. The Hatter tells Alice that in the past Time would do anything for him, arrange the hours any way he desired. But—they had quarreled. Let me read you this passage: *The Hatter shook his head mournfully. 'Not I,' he replied. 'We quarreled last March—just before he went mad, you know' (pointing with his teaspoon at the March Hare)—'it was at the great concert given by the Queen of Hearts, and I had to sing: Twinkle, twinkle, little bat! How I wonder what you're at!'* "

"What!? That's in there—'Twinkle twinkle little *bat*'?"

"Yes. That's not all. He goes on — *"'Well, I'd hardly finished the first verse,' said the Hatter, 'when the Queen bawled out, 'He's murdering the time! Off with his head!' 'How dreadfully savage!' exclaimed Alice. 'And ever since that,' the Hatter went on in a mournful tone, 'he won't do a thing I ask! It's always six o'clock now.' "* Alice, being a bright girl asks him, *"'Is that the reason so many tea things are put out here?'"* He answers, *"'Yes, that's it, it's always teatime, and we've not time to wash the things betweenwhiles.' 'Then you keep moving around, I suppose,' said Alice. 'Exactly so,' said the Hatter, 'as the things get used up.' 'But when you come to the beginning again?' Alice ventured to ask."* Now, interestingly, Mary explains, the March Hare pipes in here— *"'Suppose we change the subject,' the March Hare interrupted, yawning. 'I'm getting tired of this.'" "*

"Am I feeling a connection in this to your 'being stuck in the past' idea?"

"Stay with me. There's a late chapter called Who Stole the Tarts. It's a trial and the Knave is accused, etc. The Hatter is called as a witness. He excuses himself to The King of Hearts, as he *"came in with a teacup in one hand, and a piece of bread and butter in the other. 'I beg pardon, your Majesty,' he began, 'for bringing these in, but I hadn't quite finished my tea when I was sent for.' 'You ought to have finished,' said the King. 'When did you begin?' The Hatter looked at the March Hare, who had followed him into the court, arm in arm with the Dormouse. 'Fourteenth of March, I* **think** *it was,' he said. 'Fifteenth,' said the March Hare. 'Sixteenth,' added the Dormouse."* The King of Hearts goes on questioning the Hatter who becomes totally confused and flustered and says in a trembling voice, *'It* **began** *with the tea...'" "*

A breeze had picked up, neither has noticed. Mary had been animated while reading. Paul's eyes were gleaming. He stands and she follows him on the lawn.

"I'll review," she digs in. "Alice stumbles on these three – the Hatter, the March Hare, note the month in his name, and the Dormouse. Though the table is set for many guests, they're all scrunched together."

"Yes."

"The Hatter explains to Alice his relationship with Time had soured and now Time won't do a thing he asks. It's always six o'clock."

"Stuck in time."

"Yes. After upsetting the Queen of Hearts because his *timing* was off – he was 'murdering the time.' And the song he was butchering was 'Twinkle twinkle little bat how I wonder what you're at.' "

"How I wonder...what you're at. Wuhan. You're at Wuhan, aren't you little bat?"

She knows he's getting it—goes in for the coup de grâce—

"They're in this tea party that never ends. Never can end. They keep moving around the table—"

"As if to accommodate guests who never appear—"

"Yes, *simulating* time is moving, that there's a progression when—"

"—They're actually getting nowhere."

"Bingo Paul! You've got it!"

"No, you got it, Mare."

"One more thing on the tea party..."

He's on tenterhooks, they're pacing like boxers under the lofty multi-branched elm.

"Recall the Hatter said he'd quarreled with Time, last *March*—'just before *he* went mad, you know'—referring to the March Hare."

"Right, go on..."

"The Hatter enters that trial eating and drinking his tea as he must since he can't depart the tea party. The King asks him, "*When did you begin?*"' And what are the answers?"

"The fourteenth of March?"

"That's what he says. Then the March Hare says, 'The fifteenth.' And the Dormouse adds—'The sixteenth."

He stops. She stops.

"The sixteenth of – *sixteenth*...of March." Hand to his forehead. "That's when the March Hare went mad. And when all this shit..." he flings his arm over their world—

"Began?" Mary drives it –"Jill's party was on the thirteenth, remember?"

"That's right..."

"Then that Monday, the sixteenth—"

"The beginning of the madness."

It's like a silent explosion. He goes to the table. She gives him a moment.

"Sit." She's nervous. He takes her hand. Kisses her on the cheek. "I'm proud of you. That's breathtaking."

"Yeah? Truly?"

"I don't know how or what exactly but to me, it's – undeniable – it's there. You illuminated something. Stunning."

She blushes, giggles. "Thanks." She leans her head on his shoulder. "Thanks."

"I need to ponder it."

"Permission to ponder."

"Seriously. I'm getting chills."

"Ooh. When Paul gets chills..."

She puts her arm around him and they reverberate. She feels the house tugging, has to return to the students. Knows he needs her also.

"How *are* you?"

"Me, I'm – I'm okay. Not bad."

"I'm concerned about you. Have you been alone this past— You look tired, honey."

"Alone?" He hadn't considered it. "I go out. I – it's funny you say that, though. None of my friends want to meet. I even promised them proper distancing. None."

"Including me, huh?"

"No, I didn't mean—"

"I'm sorry. I haven't been avoiding you."

"I know that. You're full up with things."

"You need to rest, Paul. Are you taking the vitamins?"

"Yes, every day. Promise."

"Still at the research?"

"Yeah...I am. I did pull away a little. Not as...frantic."

"Remember, balance."

"Yes. I've put it on my wall, Mare. But, it's strange..."

"What?"

He stands, stretches his back. "I uh—maybe I should have expected it. I was sending a bunch of friends links to the stuff I was finding."

"What happened?"

"Nothing. Almost nothing. Either total indifference or weird hostility."

"Nothing between?"

"Not really. 'I totally disagree with this video. Covid is not a made-up disease, I know someone, my sister knows someone...' Or, 'The hospitals are like war zones.' I try to reason with them. I send more evidence that it's not how the media is making it seem. Then—no response at all. Or, 'Stop sending me stuff.' They don't want to look into it."

"Not everyone's like you, Paul. They're just trying to get through their lives."

"Me too. But the truth is – important."

"Sad to say dear—very few people are interested in it. Don't you know that by now?"

"I suppose not. I'm no longer sending things. They can reach out to me if..."

"Fine, that's a better approach. But don't stop sending to me, okay?"

"I will. I mean, I won't."

"I like that Dr. Kaufman fella by the way."

"Oh, you watched his presentations?"

"Yes—not all. I have to take time to understand."

"Please do, Mare. It's important."

"Now *I* promise. I need to—"

"Find more time?"

"Yes. Speaking of which—" she thumbs toward the house.

"Time?"

"Time. We don't want a quarrel," she winks.

"It's not six o'clock is it?"

"Not yet. Not always yet."

"Okay, Sibyl."

She takes his hand.

Her touch, he feels it. She leads him to the edge of the fence near the driveway.

"Call me anytime. If you need me, I'll do my best to..."

"I know that Mary."

She brings him to her, hugging him. What *was* it – about him? She whispers, "Thanks for listening to my – ideas."

"My pleasure."

She kisses him lightly on the lips. They go in again for a kiss—surprised. It lasts a moment.

She breaks it, murmurs, "Okay." He's opening the fence. "Paul." He turns—he's a still life, poised, hand on the gate latch. Watching her. She waves – "Don't forget your writing, sweetheart."

He nods. My *writing*.

Waves. Goes.

April.

XII

Anomalies

Paul had the film The Day of the Dolphin on his mind.

Paul Sorvino playing a spy from an unidentified agency, is telling marine biologists "Ma and Pa" George C. Scott and Trish Vandevere, about a group of rogue agents who intend to use their dolphin subjects for their own villainous aims. Scott questions the spy about whom he works for and is given an ambiguous answer – he gets paid to watch the people that are watching them.

Trish Vandevere tells him that among all the watchers they, the marine biologists, are at the end of the line. No, the spy corrects her – You're watching the dolphins.

Who was *he* watching? Paul asked himself.

He goes for a hike in the afternoon in the woods nearby. When he gets back to the parking lot he checks his phone, sees the sign for a voice mail.

"Hi um Paul? It's Jill. Um… Give me a call when you have a chance. You should have my number. It's Jill. Bye."

He listens again. Can't detect anything in it. He calls when he arrives home.

"Hi, Paul."

"Hi, Jill. How's it going?"

"Oh, not bad."

"Yeah. Strange time."

"It is. How are you?"

"Not bad. Trying to stay creative."

"Of course. Listen, I'm sorry I haven't responded to your email."

"Oh, that's okay. Join the club." He laughs, she doesn't.

"No, I should have, it was – nice of you to reach out."

"Mm. Well I—"

"Listen would you like to – stop by for a cup of – tea?"

"What time were you thinking?"

"How's eight-thirty?"

"That's fine. See you then."

She lets him in and he hesitates, the door closing behind them. She looks like a pinball ricocheting around in this big machine of a house.

"Coming, Paul?"

"Yeah, Yeah."

She's set up at the kitchen island – her MacBook, her wine, her snacks in pretty bowls. The TV is talking down at them from the wall above.

"I have a glass of wine I've been nursing. Would you prefer wine or a cocktail – or tea?"

"Tea's fine. Earl Grey?"

"On the way. Hey—I rhymed."

"You don't say."

"Maybe I'm a poet. Or is it poetess."

He wants to say poet-ass. "I don't doubt it."

Jill's in jeans and a brown sweater, which works well off her red hair. Only socks, pink. The kitchen was larger than his whole apartment. He could tell she lived here, it had her touches everywhere, the pastel colors, the nature paintings, the photos, knickknacks. Yet she resembled—a visitor. She sits one moment, then stands, turns up the TV, then down, puts something away, takes things out, talking all the while. Paul hms and yeahs to her monologue. She's talking he gathers, about working from home, her once a day—or week— Zoom video conference, how the hours drag on, no one to talk to, the coffee break she has alone now, the projects her boss has created for her since work has been trickling in, her colleagues who text her that their kids are "stealing" all their time. I could use such a distraction, she tells him. He hears the TV discussing how the pandemic is raging, they're setting up a temporary hospital in Central Park. How strange waking to joggers outside your tent...birds flapping in and out...

"What do you think, Paul?"

"You're—doing the best you can. Working from home is...challenging."

"I was talking about the pandemic." She gestures towards the television.

"Sorry Jill, I was thinking about what you said befo—"

"I was asking if you heard what happened yesterday."

"What happened yesterday?"

"You didn't hear?"

"There are so many things that are apparently happening, it's hard to keep track."

"They said there were thirty-two thousand new cases yesterday."

"Worldwide or—"

"No, the U.S."

"Hm."

"It's a new record for daily cases."

"A new record, huh?"

"That's what they said."

Anderson Cooper is looking out from the screen at them with his blank pseudo-concerned face. Numbers are displayed on his right. Or their right. Hard to say. Covid numbers. He's talking to a doctor, no two, specialists in determining what was right and what was wrong. They mention the daily American record, the *million* global cases. The deaths worldwide exceed fifty thousand. From this virus. Then there's the lack of medical equipment and who is responsible for shipping all the masks to other countries. Of course measures are being taken... Jill talks in between whatever they're telling them from the screen, she knows someone who knows someone who is very sick. "Sorry to hear." She goes on with words like ventilators, war zone, personal protective equipment. He's drinking his tea, it's good, which tells him something is still good. He feels they're barely in the same house. That he's against a wall, she's against an opposite wall and they're staring at the television. Talking between the blather from the TV. Why is he sitting in the kitchen with Jill watching Anderson Cooper or is it Chris Cuomo now? Face of grave concern. He'll finish his tea and go back to *his* kitchen, no his apartment. He hears something Cooper says – focuses up at them – the sheer audacity of actors playing real people —

"Paul?"

"Yeah?"

"Nothing, you're quiet is all."

"No, I'm—I was listening."

"I'm a little surprised."

"At what?"

"Usually you have strong opinions to express. I figured with everyth—"

"Jill?"

"Yes?"

"Are you listening to this bullshit?"

"What? What bullshit?"

He points at the TV.

"What about it is—"

"They just said a tiger—a *tiger*—at the Bronx Zoo tested positive for the coronavirus."

"Yes, I heard earlier today. Nadia is her name."

"Nadia the tiger? You know the tiger's name?"

"They said it on the news. They say she probably got it from an asymptomatic Zoo employee."

"An asymptomatic... Jesus." He wants to throw his teacup at the screen. Which wouldn't exactly deliver another invitation.

"What?"

"Jill are you..." He's tongue-tied. "Nothing. A tiger?"

"What's the big deal? A tiger tested positive."

"I don't know what to say to that. A tiger. Tested positive. For Covid-19."

"Paul, ten thousand people have died of this virus already—in this country alone. In only what, five or six weeks? And you're talking about tigers. I don't get it. What's the big deal?" She goes to the counter for more wine.

"Me neither. I must be... Please pour me some—of the red."

She hands him the wine.

"Thanks."

"It's a pandemic. Nobody knows what's going on...yet."

"You should stop watching TV."

"Mary told me the same thing."

"Did you watch any of the videos I sent you?"

"I haven't had time."

"But you have time to watch this garbage?"

"It's not garbage. And I'm working, remember? I'm working."

"Forget it. I – I must be tired. I don't understand what's happening all around me."

"As I said, nobody does, we're all in the dark, even Doctor Birx and Doctor Fauci say they're going day to day—"

"Birx and Fauci! The ones who shut down the world with their little coronavirus switch. The big switch flipped by the WHO—the little one the CDC flicks off. Bye-bye world."

"Paul – we're all under pressure… Are you hungry? I'll fix you something to—"

"No. I'm tired. Not hungry. I sleep and I'm still tired. I feel like I'm slipping into a nightmare and I don't see the end."

"I'm nervous too. My nails are all gone. Every time I go out I feel…on edge. Jumpy. Even when I'm home. They'll find a cure or a vaccine to stop this, they're already saying—"

"That's what I'm genuinely scared of – their cures. Their vaccines. They'll be worse than whatever this is. Whatever they say it is. Bill Gates—and his wife!"

"You don't believe anything anyone tells you. Do you?"

"Not from that thing," pointing to the screen.

"When did you get so cynical?"

"When I was born. When did you get so gullible, Jill? When did you become a sheep who—"

"That's *not* nice—"

"—moves wherever they tell you to move and to baa when—"

"That's *hurtful*, Paul. Not fair!"

"I may be cynical but at least I'm not a slave to whatev— hey come on we're *talking*. Jill! We're just… talking."

She's gone, her footsteps bang on the stairs. Great, I've made her cry. I shouldn't have come. I've been alone too much, buried in all this— I couldn't keep my mouth shut, as usual. I'll go. I'll leave a note.

He takes a pad from the counter.

Dear Jill, I screwed up. I'm sorry. I didn't mean the things I said about your being a sheep or any other hurtful things I said. I hope you'll invite me again

The minutes go by. He turns off the TV. Finds brandy, pours a small glass. Why doesn't she come back? He'll say it to her. No, it's better if he leaves. He'll finish the note.

Jill, I

Jill, I

He puts the pen down. He can hear water running upstairs. Holding the pen again –

Was it stones

you left on the

side of the road?

Who saw them?

Who knew?

Who captured lilies

in a time when

Pauses the pen above the –

to see could be a crime

to know would be seen

to be false pantomime

Puts it down. He's about to tear it from the pad, to crumple and toss it when he hears footsteps. She's there.

"Look, I don't know who you think you are. This is my—"

"I'm sorry. "

"What?"

"I'm sorry for the way I spoke to you. If you want me to, I'll leave. It was wrong."

She looks away. He hears her breathe. "Okay."

"It wasn't right to unload on you...whatever I'm going through... Sorry, Jill."

"Okay, you're sorry."

"Should I go?"

She changed. Stretch pants and a camouflage shirt.

"Let's sit in the den. It'll be better in there."

They take their drinks, she brings popcorn. They walk awkwardly in the hall toward the den.

"Remember at the dinner party you played music? Could you..."

Jill retrieves her iPad, puts it on shuffle. Soft voices and guitars come forth.

"Good?"

"Yeah, thanks."

"I know you think I'm a dummy when it comes to all this stuff. I'm a country hick..."

She's cute in the new get-up. Paul stares a moment—

"I don't think you're a country hick, far from it."

"I am though. From a town you wouldn't notice passing through."

"That's what I like about you. You come from a real place."

"You mean a real *small* place."

"A town—with people. Not automatons in cars or on a train with a million others. People who try to—live their lives. With dignity."

"A little uh, romantic... but I accept. I guess you're a romantic though, eh Paul?"

In the low lights of the den she's softened. Her legs curled under her on the burgundy couch. It's better with the music.

"I'm willing to learn. Don't think I – I'm not open."

"No. I won't, Jill."

"Here's your chance. Tell me a couple of things."

"Now?

"Yes."

"I'll tell you... three things, no great detail. The basics."

"Agreed. I can go deeper later on."

 "Dr. Andrew Kaufman. He's from upstate New York."

"No wonder he seems like a decent man."

"You watched his—"

"Briefly."

"Kaufman is saying the virus they're calling SARS-CoV-2 – was never properly, uh, isolated, run through all the steps, the processes normally done to prove a new virus."

"How did he conclude this?"

"He's studied all the papers that came out of China and Korea – determined they haven't proved causation between a 'novel' virus—and the reputed outbreak of Covid-19. If you read them carefully, they actually state it. Also, they haven't fulfilled Koch's Postulates."

"Koch's what?"

"The procedures to prove a new virus. The second thing is Event 201."

"Event..."

"Two Zero One. Event 201 was a... simulation. An exercise. It took place *this* past October. It involved Johns Hopkins, U.S. government agencies, and of course the Bill & Melinda Gates Foundation."

"Why do you say 'of course' the Bill and whatever Gates...?"

"Because Gates has his fingerprints on every inch of this thing. He's a vaccine maniac. He's frantic to inject the whole world with a vaccine they're cooking up in six months."

"He's been on TV a lot. I didn't realize the guy was a health expert."

"This is what I mean, Jill. Bill Gates, software developer, multi-billionaire is suddenly the world spokesman on health? Three months before an 'actual' one breaks out, they get together to pretend there's a pandemic going on. Military, doctors, health agencies rehearsing their plans. That was Event 201."

"I don't see what's so strange—or nefarious—about such a gathering..."

"They're showing us their plans. They've never been so blatant."

"So that's evidence of what plan?"

"We're witnessing it unfold."

"I'll admit it's – odd they'd do such a – what is it called?"

"Simulation."

"Simulation, so – *soon* before...the actual..."

"For sure."

"What's the third? You said three things."

"Let's leave it, for now. It's the test for the virus. Called PCR. It was never meant to diagnose disease."

"Then why are they using it?"

"Many people are asking that question. I'll send you—"

"You have quite a lot of knowledge."

"Some."

"You've done the work, Paul."

Dylan comes out of the speakers, singing Lay Lady Lay.

"I didn't know you were a Dylan fan."

"There's a lot you don't..."

"Why'd you stop?"

"Because it sounded like a cliché." Jill unfolds her legs, rubbing them.

"You could have..."

"What?"

"Made it ironic."

"Hm." She's never been good with irony. She reaches for her wine. "You're much better at – that kind of thing. I never really...developed a capacity."

"And yet—you're one of the most articulate people I've ever met."

She blushes. Is that a cliché too, Jill? If so, I'm fond of that kind of cliché, Paul tells himself.

"I'll accept the compliment."

"Where did it come from?"

She reflects quickly on her past. "Partly from my mother. She was—you see, I was very shy. I had no siblings and my mother felt – I was too caught up in my own world. In my own head."

"Were you?"

"Yeah. She pushed me to get out of myself. Talk more. Play with kids my age. It mortified me but also helped me."

"And the other part?"

"Oh... A teacher I had. Seventh grade English teacher. She made us read aloud a lot – and try to express yourself. Your opinions. It gave me confidence."

"She must have been a wonderful teacher."

"Yes. I still keep in contact with her.

"Wow."

"Marian Mulvaney. Her maiden name. She's seventy-five."

"Do you read aloud to her?"

"No, Paul. She's been a mentor to me. She's in Michigan near her daughter."

"Did you ever consider becoming a teacher?"

"There was a brief time when I... gave education a long thought. I chose accounting though."

"You'd have made a great teacher."

Is it true? Would that have fulfilled me?

"Well, anyway," she raises her glass, "here's to Ms. Mulvaney." He flops onto the love seat nearer her, leans in and they clink.

"Did you ever notice Jill... everyone wants to get to the end of... the thing they're doing?"

"No. How?"

"Anything they're doing. Singing a song. Listening to a song. Watching a movie. Having a chat. Making love. They can't wait for the end. Why is that I wonder?"

She waits for him to answer his own question.

"Maybe it's what Freud said. About the death wish."

"You mean, the death *instinct*?"

"Yeah, instinct. Built—or programmed—into us. We want it to be over. When you're at work you want to be home when you're at home you want to be at the park or the bar. When you're playing a song you want to hit the climax and... fade out."

"That sounds...nihilistic."

"We want the effort to be over. Then you're resting and you want the rest to be over."

"So you can't win. Don't the Zen people talk about this? Being in the moment? Accepting the moment?"

Paul smiles. She's a little box of ... "You're right. They do." ...surprises.

"I'll grant you're a deep thinker. A little crazy but you have – original ideas."

"Maybe original copies." He bursts into a giggle and she follows him with hers. "You're very nice."

"Not too sheep-like?"

"Oh, come on, I said I was saw-wy." He makes her laugh again.

"You're nice also."

"You know what we are, Jill?" He doesn't wait— "We're anomalies."

"Meaning?"

"Something which doesn't jibe with—"

"I know the word. How are we anomalies?"

"Sorry. I mean... I just realized it. Sitting here. In the nineteen covid plague."

"Paul—I don't like that."

"Sorry. I keep saying that. Sorry." Another giggle-burst. "We don't fit in anywhere."

"That's not true. For me, anyway."

"Yes, maybe for a short time. There's always – something – that tells us? – we aren't where we should be."

"We're misfits? Is that what you—"

"Sorta. No, rather—anomalies. It's spicier."

Jill fixes on her painting on the wall. A path through a park by a pond. "It's not a very good feeling. Doesn't quite boost your self-esteem, does it?"

"Well it's not necessarily—"

"Besides, I don't see myself that way. I've always had friends. Mary's a close friend. Others."

"Okay. Excuse me." He heads to the bathroom. She can hear him singing. He comes back, it's her turn. No singing. When she returns he's on the end of the couch. She sits at the other end.

"I do though," he grins.

"What? Are you still on the anomaly thing? How 'bout switching?"

Marvin Gaye is singing What's Going On.

"You're proving what I said – everyone desiring an end to things."

She looks up – chuckles at his clever parry.

"I see us both that way. You here in this house. Do you feel right?" She doesn't answer. "Have you ever felt *really* right—living here?"

"Not every moment, no."

"Being married to—"

"Phillip."

"To Phillip. Was that—"

"What? Let's hear it, what?"

"Fitting? Comfortable?"

"I don't have to justify… We had a good marriage—for a time."

"A time."

"Yes. It was fine. For a – time."

He takes a hit of the brandy. She mirrors him with her wine.

"You've never felt at home anywhere?"

"No. And neither have you."

"That's ridiculous, Paul, it really—"

"Your childhood?"

"You're psychoanalyzing me now?"

"You said you were often mortified."

"I said I was occasionally embarrassed because of shyness."

"How often did you feel…out of place?"

"Sometimes. Okay?"

"How often have you felt totally at—"

"Who ever feels totally *anything*?"

"How often have you felt *mostly*—at home? At ease."

Jill's not comfortable in this area. She's danced around it with a therapist (or three) who kept trying to steer her there.

"There have been times."

"Times. Occasions. Anomalous occasions."

"You make me sound like—"

"*Us* sound like—"

"Total *freaks*! There's your total!"

"Beautiful…anomalies."

"You're obsessed. You've never fit in anywhere?"

"I've thought I have – not for long."

"So there's no – home for us – in this world?"

"I wouldn't say that, Jill. Not at all."

Her silence is her child self.

"It sounds very...lonely."

"No, come on, it's not..." Her brown eyes are getting to him. Again, he had to be the clever idiot. He's regretful for pushing her. He truly hoped it would...bring them closer. "Forget it, I'm... Listen, it's a silly idea. It's cockeyed. Let's change the – let's forget about it. Okay?"

"It's okay," she says quietly. "It made me ponder."

"Jill, I didn't mean for you to... Hello. I'm Ineptitude. Nice to meet you."

She glances sidewise at him, can't help but feel sympathy.

"I admire your eclectic taste in music. And your paintings here—they're vibrant. I find them soothing."

This guy, she muses... He doesn't realize how charming he can be.

He can almost smell her. Does she want me to stay? Or go? I'm ruining this here by talking—

"You separate us out— what about Mary? Isn't she one?"

"No." Paul swivels towards her. "Mary is a chameleon. She's more malleable than us. Doors open more easily for our friend Mary. You and I—"

"Can't find the doorknobs?"

"Haha! Touché..."

"If only life were like a movie, Paul."

"Where did that come from?"

"The magic. You always exit a movie – and your life is – as it had been. My father never went to the movies. It was my mom who took me. 'Why go to a movie,' he'd say. 'It's all lies.' "

"That's wise."

"Maybe. It didn't exactly bring us – all together."

"No. I imagine not." He slides in a few inches. "What's your favorite movie?"

"Favorite... I'd say... Jaws."

"Why Jaws?"

"Not sure. It might have been my first one—in a theater. The excitement stayed with me."

"Why don't we pretend...outside that window is the ocean off our boat. And I'm a captain protecting you, my passenger, from the savage shark that's darting all around us..."

She laughs at him. "You're not serious?"

"Forget it. No, let's try it. Why not?"

"Oka-a-y... Go ahead."

He hasn't got a clue how to start. He rises, moves to the window, peering as if with binoculars. "All clear ahead crew." Looks over shoulder – "I'm going starboard side." He shifts left. "That's port side." "Thanks—uh, thank you my passenger." He returns to the right. "Captain—I'm your First Mate." Jill's on her feet. "Yes. Of course you are." He gazes out. "All clear. Why don't you—First Mate—check the um—" he indicates the left side of the 'boat'—"Port side?" "Aye-aye, Captain." "Ouch!" Jill bumps into a chair. "Careful, sailor. Mind the rigging." "Damn." Paul bends down, rubs her shin. "Thank you—sir." They stand. "What do you see?" he motions outward— "All's well, Captain." "No sharks? Or dangerous— anything—out there?" "No. No, sir. Clear."

"Good work, sailor."

"Thank you. Captain." She's enjoying the game.

"I believe we're steady – for the nonce. I won't say we're safe—no, not yet."

"For how long, Paul? Uh, Captain?"

"If we can—get to the morning, we can signal for help. As of now we—"

"We must remain vigilant."

"Absolutely. Good call, First Mate."

"Thank you, Captain."

She's smiling up at him, his tone alters—

"We'll need to depend on—"

"Each other?"

He comes closer.

"No question about it."

"Captain, what about…you know, sir. Social – distancing, uh – protocols?"

"For now we may – dispense with those."

"Yes?"

"Right now it – would assuredly be our ruin."

"I will be guided by you, Captain."

Paul meets Jill's lips. She takes him – he takes – to touch and kiss.

"Paul. Why haven't you kissed me before?"

"Tonight?"

"No. When we went out. Before."

"I don't know." He kisses her, the ocean surrounding them. "Maybe I needed to save you first."

XIII

Jill – Levitation

She wakes up running and says "I'm going to be late, I'm going to be late, Mother," her mother's not there – neither then seven years old or now forty-nine. She wakes up sweating she's going to be late she'll be in trouble once again receive another note to take home to her parents who are not there. She has to choose a dress as Mommy forgot to lay it out for her the socks the undies and her shoes are smeared what can she do with so much snow slush and rain. She looks at the time she's late and will not make the bell that says they should be sitting in their seats. Washes her face brushes her teeth quickly she has to ask herself later did she do it? Mom left a brown bag with a sandwich an apple two cookies. On the kitchen table and it must be peanut butter jelly that's what it is three times per week she's tired of peanut butter jelly but turkey or chicken is expensive she says. Daddy is not home from his job working nights in the factory. He's never happy when he comes home so it's better she leave anyway she's going to be late. She snatches her heavy coat, oh no! it's still damp from the snow yesterday oh well she only has that one and her mittens and wool hat her boots dry shoes in her bag with books she puts it on her back goes out the side door puts the key in her inside coat pocket zips it up and she starts to run where she can where the paths have been cleared of snow cutting through backyards for a shortcut. She's nervous going to be late doesn't want to slip on the snow or ice her mother told her not to run after it's snowed 'cause she could crack her skull open she must this morning many mornings like this one when Mommy didn't wake her up and she skips and jumps over piles of snow it's very cold and goes through her the coat isn't really good enough she forgot to put on the second sweater she usually wears her mittens are bright orange and purple she loves them and the sun is out she almost feels she can fly a little bit soar above the street and whiteness there on her way to school where the teacher is waiting will probably be upset with her for being late again it's so good to skip along like that in the cold which tells her she's alive a girl alive in the world she knows it's a world because Ms. Lavely showed them where they are on the globe in the classroom. She's in a small part of a big world that is round sort of and has many different kinds of people in it. She pictures herself skipping along above the globe in the cold air above the world she laughs it's not true funny just the same and Mommy and Daddy are not there in the morning and sometimes she's alone after school what can she do she has to cut through backyards if she's to appear only a bit late and she often wakes up like this out of breath from running to school in New York upstate a seven-year-old girl named Jill who comprehends where she is on the globe though cannot locate herself anywhere else not in her father's and mother's house not in her classroom or the lunchroom but here on the wet precariously tempting sidewalks and gutters of her black brown grey town she finds her self in a running figure alone out of breath out of reasons out of words something in her knows how it feels to rise above the hardness of ice concrete and snow packed as tight as the tension between her parents most days and there she goes off the ground no one sees except her self who wakes up breathless nervous throwing off bedcovers quickly confusedly and saying "Mother, Mother, I'm going to be late – Mother? I'm going to be…" stands a moment in her adult night dress touching snow hearing wind rush by the ears of a girl and that feeling once again ascends an unknown calendar page returning out of nowhere she's late she's going to be late she's flying and moving in icicles she's standing in the cold of a room in morning a woman alive to what it's like to wear damp coats in frozen mornings to leave a house alone and yet forget forget everything at the touch of the morning air upon a young thing's body as it runs and says I'm sorry Miss for being late please— is interrupted told to sit down— I'm sorry Miss and sits down quietly panting the others looking at her whispering as she removes the cold coat sits breathing listening listening to the way she knew she was alive there for a moment or two or Yes Miss I'm listening I have my homework right here.

He stayed for coffee the next morning. She had to be on a conference call at nine sharp, the time on the oven read 8:40. She had said – "Finish inside me…" He paused, she whispered, "It's okay…I promise," and he did, gladly. Coffee and a laugh or two then Paul says "Well…" She follows him in the hallway, slides her hand in his and at the door before opening he stoops to kiss—he wants to embrace her against the wall and so does she. One more kiss. Only. Then one more.

On the verge of getting left back, was it fourth into fifth grade? She was late all the time. Her test scores were abysmal. Her homework was often half-completed. Why, her teacher asked, when she had started the year off so well. Now, in February, it was crumbling. And her clothes were dirty. At first they sent her to the school psychologist. Her mother was opposed to it, interrogated her when she came home. She didn't know what to tell her, what to say to the bald guy in his office who had a weird way of staring. Everything okay at home? Do mom and dad get along? Oh yeah, they can't get enough of each other. If they didn't grunt or snarl they wouldn't communicate at all. Not that she told him this. They get along okay. They work a lot is what she says. She doesn't say dad hardly comes home. She doesn't say mom often sleeps downstairs with the TV on. She answers her mother, I didn't tell him nothing – said yes or no. There's a meeting with the teacher, the psychologist and someone else—the principal, maybe. Something's wrong, Jill won't talk to the shrink. Please Mrs. Merigeli, help us to help you…. By the way, where is your husband? He works nights. That's all she said. Jill felt her life slipping away. She, slipping away from her life. Nobody cared, however much they all pretended. It was their job, she intuited. Her mother also. It was someone else named Jill they were talking about, someone who didn't matter. She saw the bland green paint on the wall and felt the same. "Look," Mom said, smoking—you could smoke inside in those days—"my daughter may have been a little preocu—distracted the past few months—it's gonna change, I'll make sure of it." We hope Mrs. Merigeli, she'll do better next year. "Oh, she will. I'll say *one thing*—you are not, most definitely *not*, holding her back a year. She's going on to the next grade with her classmates." They didn't 'appreciate' her tone, they couldn't possibly see how…at this stage in the year… You can't come in here and… "Jill, go outside in the hall and wait for me." She can recall the posters on the peeling white walls, an ugly deformed lady holding a cigarette, "Isn't smoking glamorous?" it said. Another of two girls hugging, "Friends are better than candy." The drawings and collages the students had done were up there and she saw her own, on farmers in France. Or was it Belgium? Buttons and cut-out pictures glued on awkwardly. "Remember what I said," she hears her mother as the door is opening squeakily, taking her hand, yanking her down the hall. "Mom, Mom." She keeps pulling her away from the office. "Mom! Mommy!" "*What*, Jill?" "My bag— it's—on the bench." "Go get it, I'll wait for you here." She runs around two long hallways a short third her bag is there—they're all, all three of them out in front talking, gesticulating, folding arms on their chests. Jill stops running – they notice her. The principal realizes, he takes her bag off the bench, walks over, bends, "Here, Jill." "Thank you, sir." "You're welcome." She turns to go, to run again, out of there, run from who they think she is and what her mother said to them. For a moment she weighs heading to a different hallway out another door into another parking lot maybe a new mommy'll be there arms out smiling waiting for her with a beautiful car like her friend Lorraine's mom and she'll bring her to a house up a hill make her hot chocolate with sugar cookies they'll watch a color TV not an old black and white and she'll sleep in a big—when she hears her mother's voice yelling—Jill? Jii-ii-ll? It echoed through the empty school she blushed they were back there talking about who they thought she was and how could they know that when even she didn't— "Where have you been? I've been waiting." "Nothing, I …got my book-bag." Her mother pushes open the heavy door lights a cigarette she'll smoke on the drive home.

When they arrive she's eager to jump out, her mother stops her. "Listen, don't you worry about those—all them at the school. They heard me and you can believe it—you can bet on it—you'll be going on to fifth grade in September." "Okay, Mom." Her mother nodded fiercely, hint of a smile. She didn't pat her on the cheek or chin as Jill hoped. She waited as her mother took a last puff and squashed the cigarette out on the driveway underfoot—then stared at the house a moment. Jill viewed her from the cracked porch steps. It was freezing, as usual. The moment froze there.

He became a regular at her restaurant. The tall preppy guy who came in with his friends, sat at the bar and started coming in alone, asking to be seated in "that area," observing where Jill had been assigned. She had no time for dating or socializing. After her classes at University of California Berkeley, she went to the restaurant, waited tables till ten or eleven, studied for an hour and slept. She waited on him four or five times before he asked her out. She knew he was from New York, *downstate* as she emphasized. He was studying business at University of San Francisco. He'd taken a year off, did his freshman year in New York and had transferred out there for his sophomore—quite similar to Jill's trajectory. She couldn't grasp why he kept crossing the bridge to Berkeley every few days. Was the food that good at the Italian joint she slung Veal Piccata and Spaghetti Bolognese in? She finally asked him point blank – *Why*? "Why do you think?" he stared, holding the check folder, his credit card sticking through. "Can't stay away from the antipasto? Or is it the espresso? You do order one every time you—" "The petite redhead waitresses. That's the draw for me." He called the restaurant the next night as she was prepping her shift and asked her out. Her heart was beating fast, she was going to refuse, stopped herself, said "Why not, Phillip Chambers." It's on the credit card. He told her he'd pick her up the next night, no she was working, the subsequent night, at her home. He took her to a restaurant in town where Phillip spoke French fluently. No big deal, he assured her, his mother was a native. It was a big deal to her. She'd barely passed high school Spanish, which he *also* spoke, semi-fluently. She knew this was a boy who'd come from a different world than she. She figured they'd go out, she'd reveal her background and he'd drop her. Following the lovely meal on their first date she didn't hear from him for a week. When he called claiming he'd been "very busy" at school, she balked. Stopped answering. He showed up at the restaurant—in the parking lot as she was leaving. It made her nervous. She didn't like guys stalking her, no matter how wealthy and refined they were. "Why haven't you returned my calls? I left you several messages on your answering machine." She usually rides the bus home or gets a lift from a colleague. "I'll take you home," he says.

That was the first time they had sex. It hadn't been a proper date – and it was their *second* date. He came in to her apartment, a room and a half with a dwarfish bathroom. She poured him a beer and soon they were going at it on the bed which only just fit them both on it. He was very persuasive Phillip, no surprise that he became a successful financial whatever. When he put his long fingers under her skirt, Jill forfeited any resistance. His handsome face, besides his family wealth and connections, told her he could have anyone, so why *her* was the continual question. He removed her soiled waitress uniform, his slacks and shirt. She gasped when he put it in—he was bigger than anyone she'd been with, anyone she would be with. She told him she wasn't on the pill. He reluctantly took a condom out of his wallet. She said "Wait," did something she'd learned and he went "Oh!... Whoa!!" He'd always say her mouth was "an automatic orgasm." She sat atop him and that's how their second date went, he came first, then she, trailing him as would often occur. Walking, screwing, deciding. They did it again that night.

Why she ever expected it would last—when he kept retreating from her—finally saying "have to marry you...won't be with anyone else"—she could never understand. Others were interested in her during the time in Berkeley when Phillip regularly stopped calling. She knew he was seeing other women. She dated other boys—young men, Psych. or English majors, budding writers who blabbered about Kerouac and Ginsberg. Jill listened, read some of "the beats." No one, in her mind, touched Dickens for depth of humanity and beauty of prose. She indulged them, laughed, drank with them, read their own work which she gently—astutely—critiqued. When Phillip came around again it was hard to compare them. He was somewhat old-world in manners and bearing. Not a snob, it wasn't a pose. His mother's family had been gentry—fallen on hard times—into ordinary wealth. Nothing could mar his abilities, his knowledge, his position.

It was all a fairy tale. She knew it would end as most fairy tales—not Disney versions, the originals—humdrum girl reverts to accustomed life, shaking pixie dust from her hair.

She's in the room upstairs she uses to relax. No TV in there, no computers. She turns on the clock radio. "The United States has surpassed Italy for the most confirmed Covid-19 mortalities in the world.... Over 550 crew members aboard the USS Theodore Roosevelt have tested positive for coronavirus...." What was he famous for saying? Speak softly and carry...something. Calendar on the wall. This year she'll be fifty years old. It's late afternoon. She pictures people in the hospitals laid out with this China virus as Trump calls it. Her colleague's husband is sick. Fifty-six. He's lost smell and taste. That's now a symptom. A friend's father, in a long-term care facility, tested positive. She can't get in to see him, those places and the hospitals are closed off to visitors, immediate family included. People dying alone no comfort from someone who loves them. It's not right. To separate them. She writes it on the pad in front of her – `it's not proper to let people die alone with no one — no one present who` – dragging ink along the `page`_______________________________ `no one who — goddamn it!! loves them`. Crying silently.

What the hell is all this? she whispers to the room.

They say they don't know when it'll end. She saw Bill Gates on TV last night. "Only a vaccine could bring the country—" no, he said *world*—"back to a state resembling normalcy." She'd never paid him any attention. Now he's sitting there talking, *glee* on his face—about injecting people with a new vaccine, implying it's up to him to decide when the world can reopen. A computer salesman.

She calls her mother every night.

She was in San Francisco when she got the call. Engaged to Phillip, living with him in Pacific Heights. "What, Mom? What is it?" "Jill, honey..." "Just say it, please." She was already crying, she knew it was horrible. "Mom. Please." "Jill, I'm sorry. He's gone. Your father. He died."

Her father. "He died." Two words and that was it. Father gone. Father gone for a long time. Yeah, when she started junior high. He stopped coming home. One day her mother said to her at the dinner table, they were divorced. "We're finished. Your father and I." She pointed to papers on the table near the corn. She understood. "He's still your father. Of course." That made her nauseous. She excused herself, went to her room. He's still my father. She lies on her bed ready to puke. He's my—he used to hold my hand. Then he became a man living in the house who argued with Mommy. When I walked in the room and he was watching the game he'd smile and I would smile. Once in a while I'd sprawl along the wall playing. He'd drink beer and smoke a cigar. I'd cough and talk to the dolls. His gaze on me—sadness in his eyes. When it got too smoky I vanished.

"They found him in his place, his friend or girlfriend." He died alone in the dark with his bottle his cigars and his television. She remembers him at her high school graduation. Wearing an old suit, cleaned up. She saw him arrive, walking stiffly. He was alone and sat in the bleachers. When they called her name she saw – he clapped for her – he waved. She had to beg him to go out to lunch. Her mom's boyfriend Jim, friends of hers, their parents. He hardly said anything during the meal as everyone joked and told stories. "I'm proud of you Jill," he told her. He handed her an envelope and put a bill under his plate. He rose and left, nodding to his ex-wife. For years she fantasizes she rushed out—halted him on the street, saying, "Thanks for coming Daddy, I love you," embracing him. It didn't happen. She went to the bathroom and looked in the envelope at the two hundred dollars – in twenties – and cried in front of the mirror.

Paul asks her, "What was your father's name?" They're on a walk in a park. She slows. "My father?" She stops, admiring the trees— "People called him Bill. He preferred William." She strolls in the April sunshine, Paul beside, his coat slung over a shoulder. "Your mother's name is Sylvia?" "Yeah. My mother's name is Sylvia."

Sylvia Tulino whose family came from somewhere around Naples in the Campania region. William, whose father chose Guglielmo, whose mother prevailed, calling him Billy. Whose roots were farther south in Calabria.

When Phillip took her to Italy for their honeymoon she tried to get information from her mother on her genealogy. Nothing came of it. She played tourist. Fucked him in expensive hotels. Mrs. Chambers, she was called. It sounded—inapt.

Sylvia Merigeli became Sylvia Tulino again six months after the divorce. Jill was angry when she showed her the new driver's license. Dazed. Smacked.

She never told William about Sylvia's name reversion. She watched him—helped him—rebuild his life—and watched him—imploring him—undermine it. It was a cycle. "Please Dad, don't drink during the week. Or have a beer or two. You need to keep this new job." "I promise Jill, this time..." "Please Dad, don't date that woman. She's bad news, will only encourage more of, you know, bad...activity." "She likes me, Jill. She seems to care for me." She couldn't argue against that. She was sixteen and also needed someone to care for her. "Daddy, be careful."

Her memories of leaving his apartment. Then his trailer she decorated and cleaned every week or two. Put up art posters. Plants she watered. For a while. And started again. He waved to her from his window. She waved back, she always returned. Cleaning. Shopping. Cooking dinner for him. Not many words. There with him.

He said to her, when she was going to California, "You Jill—only you—never gave up on me." He was happy for her new life. All she could think was—who's going to watch over him?

She asked her mother, in her late teens, "Did you ever love my father? Because I can't remember any real times of love, or tenderness, between you." Her mother took a long time to answer. "Jill, the love we had is here – in front of me. It's you." Which was a *no*—"Why did you stay together so long? Why live – why make a loveless house?" "You're right. I—we waited too long. It wasn't fair."

After the funeral they went to her mom's house. Sylvia put food out for the small group. Cold cuts with mayo or mustard. They drank wine, whiskey and soda. Fizzing of seltzer, ice cubes, awkward conversation. Laughter, cut off. That's how it always is, she thought—embarrassed laughter. Phillip was with her and was kind. When everyone left she saw her mother in the kitchen putting dishes in the sink. She paused, water running, looking out the window. Jill read her mind – *What happened – What did it mean*? "Oh!" She flinched, Jill's hand on her neck. "Mom..." She shuts the tap. "Mommy..." "I know, baby." Nestles her daughter like she's still a girl.

I'm going to change my name, she mulls, walking with Paul. I haven't been Chambers for a long time. "Paul, my real—my maiden name—is Merigeli." "It's pretty," he says, taking her hand. An older couple coming towards them make an obvious point of distancing from them. Paul stops, calls out, "I'm fairly healthy, I promise." "Paul." "What?"

"Ignore them. Let's walk." He was going to kiss Ms. Merigeli. Once more this *thing* ruins a beautiful moment.

She keeps wanting to go somewhere. She should be going. There's somewhere to be. It's an itch she cannot reach to scratch that there's a movie she should see, a friend upstate or in the city to meet. Who needs her. No one calls to say that. She should be getting in the car to go somewhere, getting dressed putting on earrings perfume to go to a play a restaurant or maybe a mini vacation. Nothing's open except Rite-Aid. There's nowhere to vacation. It's all closed. Everyone's gathered at the TV waiting for something to happen. Her wish is to dress and stand by the door in the moment of anticipation on a night out. There are no nights out anymore no nights period. Just periods of darkness. She can't shake the feeling holds on because if she loses it she'll lose part of herself that breathes in her and has life. They are choking the life out – she will not probe it. She can hear it pass through the house. Its annoying presence stripping her peace. She can't find it to still it.

"My father's in the hospital."
He says it with the flatness she'd come to recognize, no matter what was happening in his life. Calls her in the middle of the day.
"Hi, it's Phil."
"Phil. How are you?"
"How are things – going? During this weird um time?"
"It is weird, that's true. I'm okay, working from home."
"Right, us uh, me too."
"Uh-huh. How's the little one?"
"Yeah, Melora's good – she's doing the online school thing. Whatever it is."

"Yes, I've heard." What was the call for?

"Jill, we talked about putting the house on the market... You can understand, at this point...it's not...feasible."

"Well yeah, of course I can."

"I – wanted to – make sure we both...saw eye to eye on it."

"Phillip, what's going on? Is something – what's going on?"

"My father's in the hospital. Yeah, the corona thing, covid, whatever it is. He was sick, his physician examined him at home. His heart might be an issue, he's had heart problems. They checked him in. A couple days ago."

"I'm so sorry to hear that." She couldn't recall one in-depth conversation with Simon his father, in all the years they were together.

"In Palm Beach. Melinda says it's futile to fly down—I've cancelled three flights. They're not letting anyone in. It's fucked up."

"Yes. Very frustrating. I'm sorry. I truly hope he gets better soon."

"I'd like you to know that I really appreciate... your kind words. Thank you, Jill." It was strange to her. Was he thanking her for something in the past?

"You're welcome. If you – if you ever ne—want to talk – you can call me."

"Oh yeah? Well, that's great," he chuckled. Was he drunk? Or dazed with anxiety? "I will, I'll do that. I appreci—thank you, Jill. We'll settle the house when things are... how they were. Before."

"Keep me posted. Okay?"

"I sure will."

"Goodbye, Phillip."

"Bye, Jill." He wasn't drunk, she realized. He was dealing with lack of control. Unfamiliar. She nearly felt sorry for him. No, she did.

In the park that day she took Paul behind a tree in a deserted area. His back against the trunk kissed him put her hand on it rubbed and said "Let's go" and they did, to the car the road the house.

The first night when he rescued her from sharks something changed in her. They were naked quickly in the den she made the moves he heeds and she told him "Yes, fuck me Paul," he was thrown by her language, she said "Don't pull out I don't care how fast you—" she was upon him they went ahead like charging forms in a forest when she said again "Fuck me Paul!" and "Stay *in* me" bounded upon him and he fled into her it was a scratch screech and pop her nails his sweating and falling off a wall together. Breathing not separating. She kisses. He's ready again. In her hand. She takes him to go upstairs he stops her on the steps kisses her a different movie now a movie of two people sailing away alone. She took him.

He tried to confirm it—the great night he had—on the phone she's distant. Worried about the corona monster. He tells her he's driven by Worthington Hospital recently, hardly any activity. "No sirens, no ambulances." "Well, you don't know what's happening inside." "I asked people out there—security. They said they're not overwhelmed." "Security? Come on...things are getting worse." "No, they *seem* to be getting worse. The picture is worse than the reality." "Alright. Thanks, Paul."

Maybe there are tigers he can save her from—"I want to see you again, Jill." "Yes. I'll call you—we will." Later that week she calls, let's go for a walk. The connection again, her long red hair on his chest his back pressed to an oak tree. Her oval sexy mouth fresh breath. Her house again in approaching twilight. A glass of chilled white wine—cool falling rain—god it tastes *good*. She's trembling—they both wonder why. He holds her in the hallway—a long moment. She remembers what she felt as they went to the bedroom after the first time. Something *new* she hadn't even felt with Phillip. It was Paul and it was her, he was touching it. She had to hold in emotion Paul could sense tried to ease it out of her. This something new like the feeling of moving through the backyards the alleyways that what was in there promised inside of that on frigid mornings dancing on around over the ice puddles caressing her breast under a painting of a mountain naked both of them in the hallway she lifts a moment it is me there and she points with her mind at the girl climbing a fence effortlessly she's laughing there dropping on snow with her mittens pink fingers running her face moving against all resistance moving through walls of wind and his hands are moving down his lips on her face tender and she sees her in leaps across gulfs of sidewalks into streets herself there in this new feeling like a tiny bird on her shoulder she can barely conceive all the same had reasons to fly abilities to rise into the air above them.

XIV

Paul – Fade appear

She doesn't remind him of anyone. Maybe that's why he could never get a read on her. What astounds him is her softness—totally unfabricated, totally real and he doesn't know what to do with it. "Jill." He says it, sitting in his room. It's in her name, too.

He doesn't go anywhere so it's not such a big deal to him. At first. Then he starts to miss the libraries. The windows front onto green lawns that let him daydream when his brain gets blocked or clogged with the words crashing in front of him he can't coalesce. The way he'd break every couple of hours, chew an apple, walk the outside perimeter. Buy a bad coffee from the machine, peel the creamer, sip it strolling the essay stacks. Lonely rarely checked-out books of giants – Mencken, Twain, Emerson, Fuller, Mailer, Vidal, Hardwicke. Paul would crack them open, let the words flood his mind.

He missed that. His own laboratory in the libraries. His own office, of sorts. His own place. To create. They were locked.

This sinking feeling that no matter what he does—or has done—he's always failing. He's always losing ground. Behind somehow. No matter the efforts he's made over a given period. He drifts from the momentum, it's as if all progress is lost, all striving was for naught. He's unaware of how he picked it up. Deeply embedded. A tick. A twitch of the psyche. Like the beast—sheared, gutted, cut, prepared, feasted upon – who pops up the next day, blood and guts on your kitchen floor. Too obvious that metaphor, for Paul. He's a subtle kind of guy. So subtle in fact no one's aware of his presence. His siblings often forget him, his old friends are so "old" he can't remember their names, almost, his solitude is indistinguishable from his social life. Everything slips through his fingers—it feels that way. He says he doesn't mind. Those acquainted with him – landlords, neighbors, faces in the park he hellos to—find him curious. Not strange, not weird, if a man were a question mark Paul would be its manifestation. He's not a bohemian, not a mystic, not a forlorn lover, not a bitter bachelor, not a resigned "middle-aged dude who's kinda cool." They don't wonder about him, though they'll give a second look. He sees time going by – is both benumbed and consternated. He's not that age, that number can't be, another cliché he tells himself. But it's true—it feels wrong. He's lucky he never became an alcoholic or drug addict. Why not drink every day? Why not get "fucked up" and forget everything? Why stop at a drink or two why not get blitzed, numb, untouchable? It's the same with suicide. He ruminates on it—at intervals—how easy it would be to exit, to disappear. Burn his identity papers, destroy his cell phone, depart unnoticed, fall down a mountain into nowhere where snakes and eagles will witness his fading flesh. He's spiritually dumb enough or smart enough to intuit he'll probably have to come back, struggle through another womb, play little league, impress Sally, learn chemistry and algebra again, eat bread crackers butter meat, then shit and slaughter the beast again. Suicide, he surmises, is temporary, bodies are a dime a dozen in this universe. He'd like to be drunk or high on grass all the time, he'd like to choose to end his life when *he* wants to end it, and... yet... He'll go on taking the looks of the neighbors, not unkind, the unstated questions from landlady, the mornings of circling the block of his landlocked mind. He used to wake up confused who was waking up. Now he knows—but doesn't know why.

She's the one who believes in him. Who ever did, really. She goes where he is. California, upstate New York, New Mexico. She read his work, criticized it, often brilliantly, telling him he was creating something new, "only a matter of time" before it is recognized... Yes, he said to himself, it's a matter, only, of time. And matter is finite, there's only so much you can work with. Even tailors get tired and have to go home. He actually wrote that to her. She didn't understand it, Mary. He'd stop writing, avoid her. She felt like an accusation, a debt he'd never repay. She gave him space, then drew close—because—he knew—she needed him also. He was the one who never "gave in," who never compromised. She didn't realize it wasn't a choice of his, wasn't a heroic stance on some far-off lonely planet, it was just the color of his eyes or the way he tried to listen as no one he knew listened. Where did it come from? He laughed when others were serious and cried when they were jubilant. He found it hilarious people still saw rebels and anti-heroes where he knew the silence in a room after dusk when darkness is giving you a chance to breathe beyond your name and wallet. She treasured it, his indomitable non-concomitance, his unmusical musicality. He couldn't explain it.

Why weren't they ever *together*. He couldn't answer that either. It was the way words fell both in silence and in speaking and she turned away, he was gone, there were others in the place, where they had been once – . It was bodies probably, wasn't it always, money and bodies money and bodies money and... The world in a shell made of nuts cracking open. To reveal what? Bodies. And money. This is where his head goes. Why they glance at him and wonder since he's half faded already while holding on to a dream of beauty. Beauty has no weight so he looks fat and thin at the same time. No one is clear what to call him or how to call him or what to say. So they don't say. His solitude tells him Mary is his bride who never said I do and he's the groom who forgot to appear, therefore friendship holds the cards. Mary always had them in her hands and her love is the thing which sustains, the force that remained over years that saw him moving in circles both passing and being possessed by her gaze that knows him and has never known his unseen passage.

He sends query letters/emails to literary agents, parts of his stories, pasted into the message, or a Word doc. How they instruct to send it. Most never respond.

Meticulously refined. Each sentence.

His manuscripts. His words. Piling up on digital files, on drives, laptops, portables. Paper, in drawers, boxes.

"Why don't you self-publish?" he asks himself. Yeah, why don't I? he answers himself.

On a drive. A drive that doesn't move. Abandoned vehicles.

He realizes, the first night with Jill...he had been alone too long. Trying to connect to her, to ease her anxiety, he was missing every time. His attempts at commonality came out as insults, his efforts to draw nearer were pushing her away. Feeling it ruin, instead of leaving he goes headlong into it. He had no gauge and relied on unpracticed skills, rusted instincts.

Wet markets reopen in Wuhan, China. April twelve, 2020.

They show you pictures—the struggle to breathe—tube in the throat—life draining out. Hospitals are full, overflowing. Ambulances moaning down city streets. They tell you. The fear of losing the ability to breathe. They tell you. It will take your breath away, your smell and taste, this monster Dr. Kaufman said had not been proved to exist.

"SARS-CoV-2 is experiencing an existential crisis, ladies and gentleman. It is consulting psychoanalysts. It is staring into the mirror. It is visiting psychics. It is in discussion with its team of New York attorneys. It is mounting a defense for its life—yea, its very existence." That can't be found on the news. The virus hunting for its own identity. They show you pictures, exhausted nurses and doctors faces marked by days of masks attached, refrigerated trucks waiting outside for the bodies. The numbers on the screen escalating every hour. They are saying, "We have to flatten the curve" to revert to a semblance of normality. For a "true" normal you must inject your bodies with a vaccine, a technological concoction, poison to fight poison. The body is a field for forces to clash and intervene with each other upon. We don't even own our body. That's the news, Paul realizes. That's the *real* news.

In Prague a few years post-Velvet Revolution—he's teaching English. Twenty-six years old. Living with a strawberry blonde Czech girl in the city where Kafka made words sing in chaos and defiance. Beer gardens, laughter, sun on ancient buildings, learning the language. They were one pair of lips and eyes. In the mountains she brought him on her favorite trails. He'd never been that high up—or nervous—in nature. She was at ease, self-assured on the ice and snow, he fell into her rhythm. Madlenka, Lenka her friends called her. For him she was Leni, with a long e. They argued over minor things. They'd exchange barbs, she'd pout, he'd split, come back with beer, make love. The routine brought them closer—for a time. Sitting outside a café, his teacher friends, her university friends, envisioning the possibilities after the Wall had come down and necessity hadn't set life into patterns. Now his Leni had three children. What pushed him to buy the ticket home? She made him feel it was he who upset their scale. Something changed. What was it? Who were they together? One night exiting the cinema—they loved going to movies—they met a group of free spirits and were swept up by them to a party with fun, eclectic people. At home later, stoned, they sat on the floor, connecting deeply. She was immature, sexy, innocent, knowing. She'd whisper his name sometimes. He didn't understand what he had.

A winter when he had turned thirty and was again on the island, at his parents' home. They were mostly tolerant of his strange hours and the untold places he went and came from. What he was doing in his room. That was the winter of "the word" for Paul, the "alchemy" of the **Word**. He started to get what Rimbaud was talking about, the search for a poetic language to transform reality. He wandered the streets of his hometown in sharply cold days, sitting on benches, slurping coffee, toking weed, going into diners and pool halls for warmth, poring over his books and notebooks. His folks assumed he was riding the train into the city to apply for jobs. He was only miles away, contemplating the mystery of language. Deceiving his parents was nothing new. Shirking responsibility was second nature. Diving into activities that don't bear fruit, modus operandi for the poet of dreary suburbia. All the study could have gone towards something…with a decent return on investment. He wasn't twenty anymore, sniffing after the secret of life. When he looks back he sees a man seeking illumination, revolving in almost complete darkness.

Mid-April. Twenty-two million Americans have filed for unemployment insurance during the previous four weeks.

Paul is out every day. He walks the streets of Worthington. The pizza places are open. Starbucks is closed. Take-out food, supermarkets yes, cafés no. Liquor stores yes, other stores no. The strangeness, the self-quarantining, the shutting down of businesses. The obedient acceptance of it all. *There's nobody there.* This was the land of Samuel Adams and Paul Revere? What would they say about hiding inside from a virus?

He goes to the park, walks around the pond, up among the trees. The playground is sealed off by yellow police tape. The pandemic days of April were mild and pleasant, optimal for strolling. Scarcely any took advantage of the oxygen the massive pines and oaks kindly put forth. As days went by he began to recognize the smattering of people who *did* venture to the park. They'd nod and smile as they passed, winding the bend, sharing the best things—sunlight, movement and oxygen. Paul spoke briefly to them— "Where is everybody? Anybody?" "Yeah, right, uh…" "They're afraid, you think?" Nobody answered. They'd tip the hat and keep going, round the pond. Mallards. Canada geese.

Thousands in the houses shunning sun and air. Following voices from the screens. He kept walking.

Then he – one hazy day – he used to go – close by. Exits his car, walks into the large meadow that leads into the trails. Dogs and their people scamper. Climbing into shadowed leaves and muddy soil he gives a silent "ahhh," breathes in and out – the body remembers. The brain catches up. His legs lead him around, under—yes, a stable a couple of miles down, riders canter horses over these muddy rocks. Usually more poop piles, maybe they're in corral-quarantine watching CNN. Now he's alone. He's not alone, he hears them—underfoot, in the trees. Definitely not alone.

There *was* a sign. That winter in the late '90s when he rode on wind and trampled concrete. One snowy day he was doing his usual peregrinating and ended up at the town's raised railroad platform. He was forlorn, verging on nihilistic when he ascended and stood under the thick falling flakes. How's he going to get home? Walk three miles in this wet and freezing? Nothing made any sense. He watched trains come in and go out as the city commuters made their ways, gingerly, towards the stairs, their patient cars, home to wives husbands and televisions. Paul knew they weren't reading Rimbaud and cared nothing for the alchemy of words. He didn't care, much, for it either anymore. It's the end it's the beginning yet again he thought without thinking. Trains coming in trains going out. Home work home work. That's why they gave us homework in school, to get us ready for this. He tries flirting with the women who either completely ignore and brush by him or smile indulgently as if a poodle pissed on their path. One day these people would be washing their hands thirty times a day, scrubbing their counters and floors of marauding viruses while they lose their jobs but for now it was a-ok and driving home in the snow waking in the dark falling asleep and rushing off as their stops are called, "annnnnnddddd Babyyy*lonn!*" And they're home. Nobody used hand sanitizer in those days.

He's about to leave, make his own way home through snow and low visibilities. Train doors open, forms emerge, female and male, he pronounces stale jokes, tame insults, lame challenges, to them, nothing lands they're impervious, they deserve a soft pillow, a beer and scotch, meat and ketchup. One guy fortyish, mustachioed, holding a briefcase, shuffling by and Paul stationary says out of the nowhere of a white grey afternoon doors closing as he passes him on the platform, "Does it matter? *Does it*?" The man turns – regards him intently, keeps stepping, descends the staircase. Paul shambles on the white wet concrete, decides—that's it, his last train to Clarksville has arrived and he is on the brink of descending when he spots that man walking back in his direction. Oh boy, here we go, I pissed off the wrong guy, he's got a knife or a – shit did I need to do this today when the weather is crap and I'm cold, damp and on foot – Paul moderately wards him off – "Hey listen man, I didn't—I wasn't—" he approaches – interrupts—"What did you say to me a minute ago?" "N-nothin', I was just messin' around." "You said something, tell me what it was. I want to hear it again." He's four feet away headphone wires dangling on his coat. Probably not psychotic, Paul evaluates split-secondly. "I said," he gives in, " 'Does it matter?' " The guy's nodding, half astounded, grinning, "I *thought* you said that! Wow…" Paul has no idea where this is going. "Why did you say that to me?" he asks him earnestly. "I really don't know. Look I didn't mean to – if I offen—" "No, I – found it amazing...I was walking down the stairs, asking, 'Did I hear the question correctly?' " "Oh, yeah? Why—uh, why's that?" "Because, I was on the train a minute ago listening to the word." Paul's not sure he hears him right. "Listening to what?" "The Word of God." "Ahh..." Paul takes it in, then sighs, seeing and feeling the cold and snow in a new way. "Yes, a sermon recorded by my pastor." What the sermon dealt with he may have said, Paul didn't hold on to it. The man was happy. He was happy too. A burden felt gone from him.

To the man with the mustache it was a sign. His path was righteous. He was open, listening, receiving confirmation in random comments from strangers on train platforms. Was it a sign to Paul? That *his* search, his call for wisdom and understanding was being acknowledged? That he wasn't going down quickly like snowflakes, had a little more resilience, perhaps meaning, connection to – something? "I was listening to the Word." This sentence stayed with him.

Two days before Jill's dinner party in March Paul attends a meeting of Worthington Citizens For 5G Awareness. He learns that two hundred "small cell" poles had been installed in town. They were not yet transmitting 5G. But it was coming soon, the group informs. This new wireless technology is on a far higher frequency than 3G and 4G which utilize microwave frequencies from 800 Megahertz to 6 Gigahertz. 5G runs on *millimeter* waves occupying the spectrum from 30 to 300 Gigahertz. The cellular phone companies and internet and television providers could operate their new systems in the 54-67 GHz spectrum. Because these "short" waves are easily blocked by trees and houses and can't travel far in open air, they plan on—already are—installing poles every twenty to thirty feet, often in residential areas. Paul listened as women talked about the poles outside their children's bedrooms. He finds out 60 GHz is the frequency at which oxygen molecules oscillate. At 60 GHz, 98% of transmitted 5G energy will be absorbed by atmospheric oxygen—including human oxygen.

The United States Department of Defense developed and first deployed, in Afghanistan, a "non-lethal" crowd control device using the same millimeter wave technology the 5G systems use. It directs a beam of 95 GHz frequency waves. Anyone in the target area will feel their skin is being burned.

He's hiking in the woods. The white sand of the path winds. A man in the distance who nods as he passes him. Then he's alone. Branches and leaves. He doesn't have his mistakes. He's here to balance the world with – the air the ground what crawls and flies there. They try to poison you with images. With narratives. Instinctively you go to the trees plants dirt and sky yes the sky endlessly above to poultice the wound they offer you. The wound they purvey in the guise of true information fades out. Forgotten.

He stands – off the trail now – motionless, listening. Watching play of light on branch and spaces between leaves. He *knows* them. He wants to run to them—into the reaching arms the diaphanous forms green brown vertical older and younger beings without words— run through there ignoring bones blood body that keeps him apart from the real—this is real life. Without words images warnings. Without subtle tyranny inherent in shapes and explanations. Don't touch. Don't come near. Don't get close don't speak when all the heart seeks is to get close. They can *kill* you. You can kill them. When what the heart desires is to approach.

He touches the trunks, inhales, presses against, the smell of spring on the advent. A limbo space. It's where he lives. It's real. He moves in and out. He goes back to his small flat is still in the woods that heal. In the woods with the swallows who shake leaf squirrels who tunnel ground and upwards in air chasing sparks of sunlight. Lying down, he's there. It's in his room when he arrives, on the walls as hidden darkness emerges to say "It's night again." It's in the food he heats, forks out into a bowl it's in his water that fills his brain opens him up to a sky he can't remember—can't forget. He's as large as a tree in a wood which encompasses and becomes his rooms it's there when he wakes in confusion it's earth the mother who gives him breath and stone dirt and love diffusing even the ugly malformation of words into stories. It's in his computer he probes like a penitent on the path towards the shining city, digging for the *other story*, the one telling him we cannot countenance chains boundaries narrow bands to live and die within. The plants struggle to grow forth out of his computer to expose roots that are strong have meaning have life nourished and granted via mysteries in the dark-light in the water and drying. It penetrates the covid thing, the word they gave to cling and confine, it clears it, opens a seeing, past the screen into a wood a sky without bound.

The stillness – standing off the path where the horses trod – he becomes it, for a moment. The *moment* is good, enough. It carries him across the corridor where the pathways are delineated and set, the walls, floors of doubt and anxiety, of precarious waking sleeping. And touching, yes touching for yes, the computer, the food, hand, mouth, is touched and touching. The trunk gnarled hard whole giving of the oak, pine, elm, magnolia. He's alone in a shadow, he's not alone. Walking on the path in a day and another a new one, he's being carried on a huge but gentle wave an ocean of green-brownness soft and hard, in a time of raining complexity. Carrying between air and soil over the warning of those who want to be killers. Those who want to die. Beyond their stories.

He tries to apologize to her. His attempts to help her have merely harmed him. When you have a bandage on all the time, you forget it's not part of your body. He *sees* her at one point in the night—has a hunger to discover her.

Paul had nothing going on in his life, he was twenty-two or three, living at his parents'. One day he scribbles a note saying he'll be in contact. Visits a friend in Chicago, she's not welcoming. He moves on, buses, trains. Makes it out to southern California, the Valley, a friend. Nothing happens for him, without a car you're lost in L.A. Money gone, his friend takes him out to the highway, he sticks his thumb in the air. Dangers and adventures on the road. Sprinkling postcards to his folks. He arrives at the island, thousands of miles and months have passed, at their door on a Sunday morning. He's exhausted. Knocks on the door. It's early. It's cold. The tired, lined face of his mother appears in the opening. **Mom**. In her robe. "Hi Ma," Paul says softly. His rag and bone bag at his feet. She gazes at him a minute. Opens the door wider. "Well…?" looks him in the eyes—"You're not going to kiss me?"

He kisses her.

His father said to him, several times in his last years—"It's like a dream. That's how it feels. Like it's all been a dream, the whole thing."

They went within six months of each other. Paul feared they'd break apart when he was a kid, the cracks were palpable. Nearly sixty years they stayed together. He dropped by to repair things if he could. Assist when they had "computer issues." They had never refused him help. He spoke with them as friends, asked questions about their lives. Recorded their conversations.

He was half relieved. They'd gone through enough. If home waits for us, they were there.

Sitting against the wall in his room. Evening coming on. He heard someone say, the silver lining of the pandemic was giving you time—to evaluate your life.

I mixed the spiritual and the worldly too much. It's been my major problem. I became like a car I've stripped wheels off believing it would be better able to fly without them.

Is truth always the best thing? Or could it be as destructive as lies? And is destruction always the worst thing?

Mary came to see him when he lived in Mendocino. He introduced her to his friends at the food co-op where he and his girlfriend, Melody, were working. Patchouli, weed, trail mix, hallelujah. Paul took her to the cliffs over the Pacific. Rough surf day. They both knew the timing was off—neither would remain in California. Nor would they leave—together. She put her arm on him as the spray flew and they watched boats going out past the horizon. Melody and company frolicked in to the house they shared and they made a spaghetti-veggie-meatball dinner, drank wine and sang songs. The next day Mary heads south to San Francisco where Daniel was working.

She gifted him an elegant leather journal the next morning. A letter inside with her beautiful thoughts—and three hundred-dollar bills.

They went out on the porch after dinner. Mary had a smoke and Paul saw a praying mantis on the boards below them. "Mare, a praying mantis." She tossed her cigarette, "Oh, Paul! Let's pray. Close your eyes." They stood holding hands in the misty night hearing the crickets. He felt her breath, smelled her tobacco. He prayed to be near her. She prayed for his talent to be received. Then she kissed him and left. She slept and took off.

Years are moving. His manuscripts...are motionless. He hears others being hailed, feted. Is his work less...what? Valuable? Impactful? He knows the Word—he falls back on it. What else can he do.

He figured he'll comfort her, she'll resist him, he'll go home. He'd hardly seen her until the dinner party on March thirteenth.

Had he ever assisted a lost child? Paul is bending, asking it for Mommy's phone number. A child in a shopping mall. He takes it to the security desk or wherever lost children go. "I'll stay with you, don't worry," he tells the child. "Until your mommy comes."

In the fantasy on the ten minute ride to Jill's house, he was the child—and the adult helping. The child's emotions were his. I want mommy—I *don't* want mommy. My love for mommy isn't pure—mommy isn't pure. They feel what we feel.

He arrived and Jill with the door open, was waiting. Straightaway, though ignored in greeting and acclimating, he knew they would never be acquaintances again. He'd have to go through whatever it was tonight, the stumbling, the abasement, apology, abusing her almost involuntarily, because somehow they were trapped in something seeking a way out hoping the other would help – extend a hand. Paul was a painting on her wall. He admired it—the way he *could* look. It was a park or a pond and turned inside out it was him emerging from the wall. She was the image on his screen when he finally logged off took a breath and it was late it was early he was so tired of knowing and not knowing what there was to find know and find out. It was she her red hair tied then falling on shoulders he saw when the dark faded out in his room before dawn and his aloneness could not be more together alone. He had to make a story for her, you see, a story they could breathe within and see, finally, for a moment, themselves, in each other's reflections. Moving together made sense when it was released from their hands and minds, the other stories the words, he said her name, as softly as she was, "Jill," he knew what it meant now when he heard his name long ago spoken for no reason in the darkness. He spoke Jill anew and she said "Yes. Yes, Paul."

XV

Mary & Paul in the Stars

It was a Wednesday—or a Thursday—in mid-April. Mary had finished the kids' dinner, finished cleaning their dishes, finished putting the leftovers into the refrigerator, finished unloading the washer and loading the dryer, couldn't find anything else to finish. Daniel was working at his hotel room, had said he probably wouldn't be home. Mary pushed on the dishwasher and made a decision. She headed upstairs and knocked on her daughter's bedroom door. "Jessica?" As much as the door itself the dumb volume of what she and her friends called music, was an obstructing field. She knocks louder—turns the knob, the door swings in, halfway. "Open it," she commands, which Jessie obeys, speaking low into the cell phone at her ear, "Hold a sec." On her desk the sound blares from her laptop. "What?" she mouths to her mother, implying the impossibility of dealing with another irrelevant distraction.

"Put the phone down."

"Mom, I just—"

"Put that phone down for a minute Jessica."

"I'll call you right back," she says. She lowers the device to her hip. "What?" Mary stares at her a moment. "Yes, Mom, what?"

"I'm going out for an hour or so."

"Where?"

"To Jill's. I want you to keep an eye—and an ear—on Toby."

"No problem." She moves to close the door.

"Don't close the door in my face."

"I wasn't cl—"

"You were. Keep it open. *Open*. Music low. Please."

"Okay, Mom."

"Call me if anything…"

"I will."

She goes to Toby's room, tells him she's going out, his sister will be in to check on him. He's rolling on the floor with blocks he's smashing together. Mary smiles at the boyish mush lifting whatever's at hand and dropping it to see what happens. She throws a kiss to his upside down cheeks.

She goes to her bedroom, shuts the door, tosses off the housedress she's been in all day. Rummages her walk-in closet…nope, not there. She rifles through her dresser, finds it neatly tucked away. Those old worn-out jeans, lived-in tears and holes. Will they fit? She squeezes them up her shapely legs, pulls them over her admittedly widened hips. Slight struggle getting them buttoned, she sucks in her belly. She takes out a burgundy top, throws it over her strong, curving back. A dash into the bathroom for a pee and a mirror glance. Rouge? A touch. Lipstick? A smear of lip balm. A brush through her intractable curls. She's locking the front door, asking herself if she has her phone. It's in there.

Mary drives to Jill's house, stops. Lights flickering from the TV giving off its shadowy images. She's alone. Alone with the coronavirus people. I'm alone too.

She crosses into the village. Seven-thirty on a warm spring evening. Hardly a body to be seen. Dark stores, solitary streetlamps. She turns into narrower streets, checks the license plate on an older model Nissan. It's his. She parks. Should she? A minute. Why not, what's the...? Two minutes. Now. She waits. —Grabs her things off the seat and gets out.

She's on the side of the house. More alive suddenly. Rings the bell.

"Well, hello," Paul's tired face says, smiling. "What a surprise."

He's got black sandals on no socks. T-shirt. Sweat pants.

"Hey, Paul. Thought you might want dessert?" Mary holds her bag of goodies up.

"How 'bout dinner first? Yeah, sounds good to me." He swings the door open.

"If you're busy..."

"I'm never busy and always busy. Especially lately."

His place is small, spare. The boxes are gone. The books are mostly on a shelf, refugees on the floor and tables.

"You've been cleaning."

"Yes. You noticed."

"Good job. You could use a larger bookshelf and an actual kitchen table."

"Don't rush me, dear."

"No, you've only been here, what, two years?"

"Two and a half."

She espies his open laptop, numerous tabs open on his browser. A video on pause. Notebooks all around, scribbled post-its on the wall.

"Knee deep in your pandemic research?"

"Almost thigh. Scamdemic, you mean?"

"Is that your new term?"

"I didn't coin it. The names are proliferating. As are the lies and bullshit. Hard to keep pace. Bobby Kennedy Jr.'s been doing some terrific exposing of Bill Gates and his—"

"Let's ease into it. Okay?"

"Of course."

"It's been non-stop anoroc."

"Ano what?"

"Anoroc...suriv. Corona...virus."

Paul cracks up. "I love it. Ano-roc-suriv."

"Every channel—Anorocsuriv—and its child. Divoc 91."

He laughs louder—"Continuing your breakdown of the codes?"

"Didn't you tell me Burroughs said language itself is a virus?"

"Yes, from outer space. That led him to his cut-up method. Liberating grammar and patterns. Maybe you can help people loosen the hold of the words on their minds."

"I have my doubts. Anoroc all the time."

"Of course. Gotta ramp the fear—more fear, more obedience."

"Mm..." Mary agrees, walking

"I'm impressed, yet again."

She peeps into the bathroom and bedroom. Neat. Clean.

"*I'm* impressed. You worked hard on this."

"Vacuumed, mopped. Dusted, scrubbed. Worked up a sweat."

"A pandemic workout?"

He goes to the table. "I have a hard time with...objects. Little things that—" he picks up papers, clips, business cards, pens, pads—"can't be quite identified—placed somewhere definite."

"I use plastic boxes to keep that stuff in."

"It's a constant battle I'm constantly losing." He stares woefully at the pile. "Plastic what?"

"Boxes. Dump it all in, deal with it as needed."

"*That's* what I need. Plastic boxes!"

"Yes, it's what you've been missing, Paul. Your entire life on this spinning ball. The plastic boxes."

"Where have they been all my life? What have you got in your magical brown bag?"

"Here," she holds it open.

Paul peeks inside, takes a whiff – "Ooh, lucky me. Coookkkkiiiieees...." he groans.

He goes to the cabinet for a bowl, dumps them in. "What a variety. Did you make all these?"

"Toby and I went on a baking spree the last couple of days."

"A good use of your time," he mutters between bites of a chocolate chip. "And a good education for the lad. Ah, gingerbread."

"It helped pass the time. Toby's very bored."

"Of course he is. Can he play with his pals?"

"There's one mother who'll let them. Not every day of course."

"Jeez. They're scared to let the kids play together?"

"They're afraid the kids'll pass on to them what the parents have or... I don't know... I can't keep track of their logical pretzels."

"When all this ends we'll open a store with that name. Would you care for some rational mustard with your logical pretzel?"

"They won't see me, they won't let the kids meet."

"Freaked out by the 'invisible enemy' as Trump calls it. Absolutely fucking nuts. It's a fear parade. A brass band playing—"

"And never stopping." They laugh. "And the playgrounds are closed. Taped off like a crime scene."

"He must be lonely."

"He is, poor tyke. Hence, the cookies. I'm...trying."

Paul breaks off a half moon, offers half to Mary. Chewing in contentment.

"You both did great."

"He did. Me, eh."

"Tea?"

"Sure."

"Green, Lemon, Earl Gray, Constant...something. Comfort."

"Comfort?"

"*Comment*, I meant." Holding the reddish box. "Constant Comment."

"What's that again?"

"It's black tea with what, orange and spices..."

"Yeah I love that."

"Comin' up."

The water heats. The night is quiet, birds give forth final chirps, codas to their day-songs. Birds singing during a pandemic. Paul listens. He turns on a floor lamp to the first setting. Lights a fat blue candle.

"Sit." He points to the couch. "Something stronger?" He gestures at a pint bottle on the chipped coffee table.

"Scotch?"

"Bourbon."

"Let's see."

He puts the teacups and cookie bowl down, pulls over an old wooden chair. They reach for the cups, steam rising. It's a strange little moment they recognize. Like they've lived it before.

"Here's looking at you, kid." She watches him a moment. What's she looking at? he thinks. Yet he knows.

"We still have Paris, right?" she answers. They sip, hot spicy and orangey.

"How's everything Paul, with..."

"I'm okay. For now. I've got savings from the last job. I'll get the twelve hundred bucks from my buddy Trump."

"The stimulus check."

"I applied for unemployment insurance. Alongside seventeen million other people. Who by the way are all in that room, there—"

"All of 'em? All seventeen mil—"

"Yes. They're all crashing here till the unemployment checks kick in."

"You're very charitable."

"Thank you. I should share these lovely cookies with them."

He stands, grasping the cookie bowl—"Guys, how 'bout some of Tobias' and Mary's cookies...?"

She's gazing at him.

"What?"

"Nothing."

"Come on, Mare."

"What you did there was...how I remember you. How you used to be."

He's not sure how to respond—opts for play—

"Lotta tea—and boibun—under dem bridges, eh?"

She grins at his un-clichéd cliché. He tips his glass.

"Sip?"

"Boibun?"

"Yup."

She takes it. Lets the dark liquid pour into her. Winces. Again, swallows. Chases it with tea.

"Constant Comfort, indeed," she grunts, adjusting to the sharp sensation.

His turn to grin.

"Why'd you come back, Paul?"

"How's everyone faring, Mare? Your folks? Your sister Tallie in Boulder? In these wild days of 'the new normal.' Gad, I find that phrase particularly disgusting. 'We're all in this together' comes in a very close second."

"Why, Paul?"

"Come back here? In general?"

"In whatever. Your family's around but you're not close to them."

"Hm." He'd rather talk about his pandemic research. "In the mood to challenge me tonight?"

"No, forget it..."

"Hang on. Let me cerebrate to some music."

He picks up a cassette from a stack on the floor. Flips the cover on his boom box. Hits "Play." Piano notes tinkle out a pattern. Bass comes in—Da-doo, da-doo, da-doo, da-doo, da-dooby..." Piano and horns respond: "Ba-DA!" Paul snaps his fingers—So What, Miles Davis.

"Still a jazz head, huh?"

He listens, standing in the gathering shadow, bent and taut, as Miles' horn comes on smooth, subtle, undeniable.

"Only boy I knew in high school—or college for that matter—who was into jazz. You used to play this."

She reaches for the glass, Paul for the bottle, he trickles out more as Coltrane comes on strong as a January wind. I AM HERE he says—Listen to me Now, I'm laying it down for all time. Trane blows out into the ethers. Cannonball

Adderley takes the baton, singingly delicately extending the story...

"Sipping bourbon listening to jazz. Not a bad way to spend a 'pandemic evening,' " Mary says. Mary sips, Mary smiles. Mary listens.

"Yeah." He nudges the volume down a notch or two. "Why'd I return? Why did I back-come? You really want to talk about this Mary-Mary?"

"Why not, Paul-Paul?"

That was her—to play his games with him. To respond.

"Sure you don't want to talk about anorocsur—"

"No thanks. Got my daily dose courtesy of CNN ABC MSNBC and Fox."

"A Fox watching Fox, huh?"

"Very funny. It's not my name, in truth."

"You took it, didn't you, Mary Wellner?"

"It's Dan's name.

"Okay. You were saying?"

"Divoc all the time."

"Of course. The more afraid people are, the easier to control them."

"Yes, you told me that ten minutes ago."

"Whoops."

"And you told me that last week."

"Right."

"And in your daily emails."

"Yeah."

"And texts."

"Alright Mare, I got it."

"Which I love. By the way."

"You do?"

"Yes. You have—a searching mind."

"Ha."

"You do. A curious...spirit. Which I've always...appreciated."

"Thanks, um, Mare. Even if Dan considers me a – what'd he call me? Conspiracy nut?"

"Whatever, Paul. Dan's... *Daniel*."

"Hm."

"Is that rain?" she perks. They listen.

"I'll check." He moves to the sliding glass door. Pulls it aside. The soft ssshhh of a shower comes in the room. "Good call, I didn't hear it."

"It's nice." It did sound nice. Soft. Cleansing April rain. Paul turns his chair around, sits and leans over it.

"Why did I come back?" He hangs his head a long moment. She watches him, deciphering the man from the boy she'd known—and the young man from the middle-aged man four feet from her now.

"When did we meet?"

"When did—" he's slightly startled. "The first time? We were what, six, seven years old? The playground?"

"Yes. Nineteen seventy...four." Mary sighs, spreading her arms along the couch.

"Was it really Seventy-four?"

"Yup."

"A different world altogether."

"I know. Long time ago."

Reflecting. The rain comes on harder, accentuating the mystery of time.

"Then we met again."

"Junior high. Seventy-nine."

"You were skinny with braces," he laughs silently.

"You were very blond—with a fresh mouth!"

"Mean fresh or—"

"Sometimes quite mean. But—"

"Sorry for that."

"You were also – quite... *forgivable*."

"Oh, good. *Forty* years ago? Wow. "

"Yeah, wow."

The music tinkles on. Bill Evans playing to the knowledge of escaping time... Blue in Green.

"And here we are now. In *fresh* Paul's apartment."

"With *not-so-skinny*-anymore Mary."

"With sweet Mary, his old buddy."

"Yeah. Have a cookie."

"Oatmeal raisin. Delish."

"I'm glad."

They listen to the rain or the music. Not sure which is which.

"I came back because...because... I didn't know where else to go. What else...to do. And there's something..." He falters.

"What? Tell me."

"Every ten years or so, I— I get this— this sense of being— lost. Totally lost in this world. And – when it sets in, when you can really *feel* it —"

"Yes..."

"It's like nothing else."

"Describe it."

"You feel – you've changed. Like you're not the person you were. They say every six years your body – what's the term?"

"Develops new cells?"

"Yes, exactly. Except this is...a mental thing. Or spiritual. I'm not sure. You question yourself. What's happening? After a while— after it happens a few times—you say shit, this again. You—recognize it. Remem—"

"Does that make it easier?"

"To deal with?" He ponders— "Not...much. It's an

upheaval. You try to run from it. I pack a bag and go."

"Why here now—not home exactly—but close?"

"Yeah." He says the word as if saying it for the first time. He speaks it to the ceiling. The sky. "Yeah… Why here this time?"

Mary's leaned into the dark blue cushions of the old couch.

"Maybe because it's where I started from. This thing that happens— this time it was—it felt more difficult than usual. Maybe it was turning fifty."

"Forty was hard enough."

"It jangled me—'I'm fifty and this is *still* happening to me?' "

"Did coming home help?"

His eyes meet hers. "Being near you helps."

"You never told me. Why?"

"Am I crazy, Mary?"

"No, Paul." She brushes his cheek.

"I've wanted to—I tried to write you a few times about it. I couldn't get the words."

"When did you first…"

"Early twenties."

"Any drugs involved?"

"No. In fact, I was hardly partying."

"Any idea what - could have brought it on?"

"None. I went to a shrink. Several. It didn't go anywhere. I read books, but…nothing satisfied me."

"You know what I think?" He wants to.

"It's… what makes you *you*. Hard as it is to go through - maybe you wouldn't—think and feel the things you do. Write the things you write. Receive the inspiration to… be as you are."

Paul just misses a collision with the freight train of Mary's words.

"Mare, I'm... gobsmacked. I uh..."

She's pleased. "I gobsmacked Paul Wilmer? Well shiver me timbers!"

Tension cut, smiles. Mary gets up to pee, Paul puts on Waiting for the Sun. She returns as the gentle Love Street begins.

"Mr. Mojo Risin'?"

"Thought it was a good moment."

"Let's sit down. Here, on the sofa."

He sinks near her on the cushions. They listen to Ray Manzarek's piano mingle with Jim Morrison's hesitant declaration of commitment.

"Paul, remember...how much...how *intensely* we were into the music?"

"Absolutely."

"Every concert, if we could scrape up the bucks between us—"

"We were there."

"We collected albums, shared them—"

"The Stones, Beatles—Zeppelin."

"You were always a Doors freak!"

"Can't deny it."

"Oh man," Mary intones, "it's flooding in... Donna Donna on WLIR spinning all the New Wave cuts."

The cars. The parking lots.

"Tears For Fears, Psychedelic Furs, The Clash..." she chants.

The basements. The beaches.

"The English Beat, Blondie, Talking Heads..." he echoes.

Cassette tapes changing hands.

"The Cure!"

"Your favorite."

"My number one," she coos. "Robert Smith stole my heart at fourteen."

"Didn't we see Iggy Pop?"

"Malibu, at Long Beach?"

"Holy moly."

"Punk rock and bodily fluids."

"The Who at Shea Stadium. The Clash opened for them." He scans memory—"Eighty...two, was it?"

"Yes. We went to *two* of those shows that week! Could it have been 1982?"

"I believe it was."

"Fifteen years old. Can it actually *be*, Paul?"

"I think it happened, Mary."

They drink a bit of tea. A pinch of whiskey.

"Some of the shit we did..."

"Yeah..." he chuckles breathily.

"...Was crazy."

"True."

"I mean—really crazy."

"I can't argue with you on that."

"Shea fucking Stadium? Fifteen years old? Out of our minds on who knows what, riding the trains late at night?"

"We were incorrigible."

"Going to bars at sixteen," she breezes on, "parties with twenty-year-olds? The stuff we took—no questions asked?"

"Mm. We certainly took our chances."

"Can you imagine if our parents had known—mine sorta suspected—*half* of what we got involved in?"

"The little my parents found out almost landed me in a teenage druggie facility."

"Mine were always freaked out about my lifestyle. Nothing could control us, Paul."

"Control is what we—"

"Were throwing off."

"Running from."

"I had massively mixed feelings when Jessica hit that age. I wanted her to have fun...but I was..."

"Nervous."

"I feel kinda dumb saying it. I was... outright scared."

"It's not dumb, it's your kid. Ironic, perhaps—" he smiles.

"I looked back on us and—the world is different now, I—"

"I get it, you didn't—"

"I didn't want her to take the chances we did."

"Sure. Things are different now. I suppose."

They sift through the here and the then.

"Undeniably," he steers, "we were—"

"Wild?"

"Wild. And...curious. I can remember feeling this...thing inside – this *yearning* thing—"

"God, yes," she splutters, "same here!"

Mary explodes in sound, in laughter. They both do. The room becomes shimmering colorful --- ---

"It was passion. That's what made us...seek to discover. To experience."

"It *was* passion." She pauses—stares— he shivers—

"What, Mare?"

"You were the most passionate."

"Was I – really?"

"It poured out of you, day and night." She takes a breath—"You used to quote William Blake to me." She throws her head in a guffaw—or is it a cry, a mixture of joy and sorrow? "Yeah! Sixteen years old. Blake..."

"Wow. I guess I did. Was it pretentious?"

"Far from it. We were in awe of you. You lit up our lives, Paul." Now her throat does catch.

"Mary..."

"Yeah. I'm fine." She leans forward, collects. "Then you started to write your own poems. You gave some to me."

"I remember."

"In our way we were... as free as the hippies."

"We certainly tried."

"No cell phones. No computers."

"Nothing to track us. Or distract us from—"

"Being—who we were."

"Being."

"Nothing burdening us. Except—school and parents. As we perceived."

"Yeah," he whispers.

"That passion was where we lived. Where you lived."

"I wasn't alone. You were with me."

"Yes, but your, how can I put it – sort of wild uh sense of or *quest*, yes quest for freedom, for a new feeling—was like our beacon. We all moved towards that."

Paul quakes inside.

"You never told me this before."

"It's been buried a long time."

"I've forgotten also."

"You've held on Paul! You're the one who's tried to hold on!"

"Maybe. But did I peak too soon? If at sixteen I was reaching for – the moon – by thirty-five did I touch... disillusionment?"

"No! If you touched disillusionment it didn't—" she turns away—

"Hey. Hon..."

"It didn't touch *you*. You still have it."

Paul half-smiles at Mary. Overwhelmed. Looks to the rain.

"You're the only one of my friends—challenging this whole—the whole story they've been telling us—for weeks now. You've always been like that."

He pours them more. Listening to the rain, sharing tea, bourbon and cookies.

"There's something else I've been...considering."

"What's that?"

"It's related to what we've been...discussing. Then I should go."

"The vampires ain't even up yet."

"They found a way to stay up. As you showed me."

"You're showing me. So, spill."

"I'm not clear why—I've been getting flashes of this memory... or... cluster of memories."

"Pretty please, tell me it's positive?"

"It is. Scout's honor." She bites a cherry-centered cookie. "Maybe it's having you here. Or time to daydream."

"Things churning?"

"I'm almost - afraid to speak about it. Not afraid... I don't want it - to dissipate."

"Gotcha." He rises— "Well, let me shut the door—"

"We won't hear the rain—"

"—So it won't escape."

She giggles.

"I'll hold my invisible butterfly net at the ready in case this gem of a memory—attempts to flee from my Mary."

" 'My' Mary?"

"Hm? Did I say that?"

"Okay, let me try." She pushes the coffee table. "Do you recall the laser shows we attended at the planetarium?"

"Oh yeah, the Hayden Planetarium."

"Sounds right."

"In the Museum of Natural History. The dinosaurs, the floating whale. The laser shows. Sure."

"You do. They had Led Zeppelin, Pink Floyd—"

"Dark Side of the Moon laser show!"

"U2 and one or two others. We hit the Zeppelin and Floyd shows multiple times."

"Did we? How many?"

"I don't know exactly, Paul. Quite a few."

"It's a wee bit blurry. Let's see—We're...sitting—in the darkness, comfortable seats—staring up at a dome scattered with stars... waiting for the blast of music to start the show and all those... dancing colored-light images come exploding out towards us."

"You got it."

"Great time, Mare. Does Jessie attend?"

"I don't think they do them anymore."

"Pity."

"We'd go in with a bunch of us, all piling onto the Railroad."

"Yeah, the whole gang."

"Occasionally it would be a few...of us."

"Mm-hm."

"This one time – it was early spring, cool, fresh, like tonight. It was you, me, Laura and—"

"Laura Unsler!?"

"Yes. Laura and her boyfriend—from Brooklyn. His name was Bobby."

"Bobby. Of course." Paul peers at the glass door and the outside space. The subtle lines of rain coming down. "I can picture him—dark hair piled high, real thin—and platinum-haired Laura, together."

"Yeah, cool couple. We didn't take the train, Bobby drove us into the city."

"In an old...baby-blue...Cadillac!"

"Wow, how'd you—"

"It's coming back."

"Great catch."

"Gorgeous set of wheels."

"It was the Floyd show that night. We parked in a garage. Then we got our tickets and hung out in the park there."

"Yes, surrounding the Museum. Did we toke up?"

"When didn't we toke up?"

"True."

"But you had something special for us that night."

"I did, huh?"

"You sure did."

"Pray tell—what was I holding that spring evening at the Planetarium?"

"Your magical little purple dots."

"Purple...dots." Paul's head swivels—"Ah! Mescaline."

"Yes."

"Those...purple dots. Hmm..."

He inches forward on the couch, leveling himself with Mary.

"It's funny. I can summon where I used to cop the mescaline. A certain street. Near a store. Adjacent to a park. At certain days and times." He glances at his palm, and looks up, his eyes gleaming. "They'd come in lozenge containers."

"We went to a secluded area. You held it out in your hand." He raises his hand. "Yes, that one, probably."

That hand. That time. Not now – That night. Holding it. The purple... Thirty-six years. Holding it. This hand.

"Some good candy from the candy man." Says the man who—held out his hand.

"*Strong* candy. And we dropped them. All of us."

"Yes. You're making me *see* it, Mare."

"Good." She gets up, paces. She leans against the humming refrigerator—which stops its hum.

"Then we went into the laser show?"

"Yes."

"I can see the four of us in those high cushioned black seats!"

"Ha-ha! Me too."

Paul gets up, faces Mary.

"Laura and Bobby and Mary and me! These totally open astonished looks on our faces—"

"Staring up there, sometimes turning to each other—"

"Smiling and—"

"Bumping against each other."

"Yeah," Paul raves, "this crazy enjoyment bubbling out of us!"

"Yes," Mary spirals the air, expressive fingers, "that was the feeling of it!"

"What a night. You've revived it for me..."

He's bopping up and down, she's sparkling—

"Yes, incredible night."

"And then?" he speaks low.

She retreats a few feet to find that night on his ceiling.

"Then... Oh—at the end of the show we felt...kind of shell-shocked. We walked awhile. Wandered."

"Were we stoked?"

"Yes. But we were high, Paul. *Very*."

"Yeah. We were tripping balls."

"We started to peak. Needed to...find a spot to chill."

"We stayed in the park."

"We found a quiet corner, a bench, and...went through it."

"It wasn't *too* heavy."

"No. Just...intense."

Paul starts— face lighting— "You and Laura—were singing songs."

"My god—you remember that."

"I do. Now." He drops on a wooden chair. She pulls another near him. "You uh...you were sitting together on the grass. Under a tree. You were...singing."

She can see the memory actually come into his body, out through his eyes, his cheeks, expression in his mouth, sound of his voice.

"It was... nursery rhymes, children's songs. *How* am I recalling this?"

"You're right, Paul. We were singing whatever came into our heads, rhyming random things and howling in laughter..."

"I can hear the *cackling*!"

"And we started playing pat-a-cake, pat-a-cake."

"Slapping hands."

"Ha-ha. Bobby—was standing there watching us."

"Yes! For a long time. I finally went over to him and said, 'You good, Bobby?' "

"Did he—"

"You know what he said? He was focused on you both – he had a glow – he said— 'It's *so*—beautiful.' "

They steep in it.

"From there," she says, "we played together, the four of us. Like children. For hours."

"Singing and skipping."

"Running. Climbing."

"Giggling like lunatics."

Mary has the glow now. "People thought we *were* mad."

"Yeah, nuts," he snickers with her. "And the night seemed—unending."

"We saw the dawn come. We really saw each other, didn't we."

"Yes, we... How could I have forgotten?" he asks the floor, the walls. "How, Mare?"

She inhales, taking in that night and this one, making those two skies one, those two springs one, those two darks one.

"At one point late in the night, on the down side of the trip...we stopped. Everything. We were—standing in a - in a - sort of circle. It felt - Laura told me also - like we were slowly rotating in that circle under the spring stars - in the freshness of the air—"

"Touching our faces."

"The smell of the flowers."

"And the trees."

"Yes, and we reached out—"

"As we stood there—"

"Took each other's hands—"

"Watching one another—"

"That moment, Paul, I swear—" he moves to Mary's chair, kneels at her feet—"that moment seemed to - stop." Her eyes glitter. "Or it—went on - and filled—"

"Yes."

"Every other moment."

"Into forever?"

"Yes. We were standing together in the - movement - the ongoing movement."

"Seeing each other."

"Yes, yes." Mary flows to him on the floor.

"It's here." He takes her hands. "You've brought it back and it is *still here*."

"What was it, Paul? What is it?"

"It's where we are. Where we live."

"You mean it?"

Had he ever been asked a true question before that moment?

"I mean it."

"Can we sit here looking at each other forever?"

"Yes."

"That night."

"Yes."

"And this one."

"Yes."

"What's happened?"

He understands.

"Nothing has."

"No?"

"Nothing."

The rain goes on.

XVI

Daniel – Landing

Caroline. She was the afternoon-evening chambermaid. The deaf one. He'd met her his first day after checking in.

He had asked for a quiet room at Lions Pride Inn and been given one. They were happy to have guests at all as most of the rooms had been vacated and snowbirds in all likelihood wouldn't arrive this year. Besides Daniel there were a couple of dozen guests. He hardly heard or saw anyone, which was exactly what he wanted. The windows in the front room faced a courtyard. This is where the desk was, where he set up his computer, two monitors, folders, files. He asked them to bring in another desk for him, which was no problem, especially since the staff realized "Fox in 224" was a generous tipper. They connected them and Daniel stacked his accordion folders and his documents—began to ply his trade.

The younger lawyers in the firm spoke among themselves about "Dan Fox" – would query his team—secretaries and paralegals. What were his work habits? They were mostly tight-lipped, loyal to their boss. "He works hard—smart." "Very concentrated... In the zone..." What else? "Good sense of humor... Likes a good joke..." Any particular books he reads? They shrugged. "Legal journals, the newsletters..." One requests information on Dan's diet. They don't bother answering. Alcohol consumption? "Social." Drugs? They pshaw at that.

The earliest memory he has—which comes to him at unpredictable moments—is in his childhood home lying on his belly on the carpet. He's trying to find something. He's peering under the couch through the dark opening—sticking his arm under—reaching—in to grasp it. He can't make it out. Or reach it.

He's in the suite five miles from his family on a Wednesday in late March—stops and thinks—I haven't been on this island on a weekday afternoon in years. He's usually high in the air, thirty stories or thirty-nine thousand feet. Sitting at his desk he's looking out the window to the courtyard below, baskets of flowers hung along the perimeter. One floor up. How strange. He's never given it much thought. He'd gotten used to feeling normal at high altitudes.

Each new group seeks the lowdown on "that Fox guy." How can he not be a *partner*? No one knows. He doesn't socialize often. Puts in an appearance at company functions—lunches, holiday parties—and is soon gone. "Well he has a family... He's a private man, but friendly..." What kind of music does he listen to? "He prefers classical... Beethoven..." Ah, a clue at last. So they listen to Beethoven in their earbuds. One of his paralegals told Dan – Finally! he said, I'm having a salutary effect on the next generation. "How does he get it all done—in at eight thirty out by six!"

Attorneys in rival firms discussed "Danny Fox." He catches it in their eyes as they shake hands after a deal, when a case is settled. Sometimes they'd invite him to lunch or dinner. He rarely accepted since it became a surreptitious staring contest. He had no idea what they were probing for. "It's uncanny—the way he knows what to say, gestures, facial expressions!" He tried to help the kids when they came to him – his door was open to them – usually they went to other associates or partners. When they did, he gave his time generously, directed them on the best course of action. He would tell them – "Wait and see." "Do nothing." "Thank them for their cooperation." Those words meant little to the cub lawyers and nothing to the experienced ones—who consistently deleted what Dan had told them, advising detailed actions. It was all he had to teach them.

Doing nothing was sometimes the best thing to do. Corporate lawyers were notorious for—skimming—Sun Tzu's Art of War. They disregarded *Lao Tzu*, of course. Daniel didn't pretend an understanding of Lao Tzu and the Tao or Way. He picked up a few things. Life—and work is part of life—was give and take, energy exchanges. One needn't extensively strategize, employing guile and "ambushes." Maybe it's why he was highly valued and generally marginalized. You couldn't teach what he did, though the more plain he was the more others accused him, behind his back, of obfuscating.

It was petty. He persisted in what he did, aiming to enjoy his work. One thing he found especially childish—and amusing—was how it was noticed that occasionally he'd be gone when no appointment was on his schedule. Which should have been private. Where was he going in the middle of the day? Hookers? Crack binges? Smack on the Lower East Side?

This is what he couldn't share—wouldn't, if he could.

He didn't go anywhere during those "absences." He was walking or drinking java in a coffee shop. Window glancing at antiques on Third Avenue. It was time going somewhere, not him. He was going into time, with time.

He hailed a cab. Got out wherever. Didn't think of litigation. It was life happening, always. He was there and so were the others... They thought it was a ten or twelve hour day they worked. When it was life that was always happening why separate work from life? You're going along in it. Leaving the office he observed, listened. Walked.

It wasn't mystical really, or a thing you could write in a book. He was trying to tell the newbies, *don't concern yourselves* with success and they couldn't hear. It would have sounded daft if he actually said those words. He used others to barely any effect. They wondered how he accomplished so much in that "limited" time. It was funny to him. And wistful. This is the part of him Mary loved and married. If he had creativity it lay in this area. It was something about time.

Boris Johnson, UK Prime Minister, is in the hospital. He's got it, they say.

Eleven thirty in the morning. Daniel hits send on an email to his secretary. Switches on the TV behind him. The talking heads tell of massively rising unemployment insurance applications. Shutdown... construction and manufacturing halted... factories closing, production slowed... air travel nullified... And the real estate markets? Trump put in place an eviction moratorium. Will it snowball? Empty buildings? Unpaid mortgages, defaulted loans—another 2009? Fire sale devouring by BlackRock and Goldman Sachs? And how is Main Street going to survive?

He couldn't help chuckling bitterly. As he worked on property disputes for a multinational company.

"Do you want me to make your lunch in the morning? Or will you do take-out?"

Mary spoke to him from her bathroom naked – as they got ready for sleep. She was still beautiful. He smirks – she turns away. He does his own wash-up, lies down, switches off the TV. She gets in next to him.

"Goodnight, Dan." Her nightgown brushes him...he smells her soap. Twenty years next to her.

"I'd like that."

"Hm? Like what?"

"For you to make my lunch. To take to my—the room."

"Oh. Okay."

"I'd really like you to do it." He turns on his side to her. Lying with her in the dark he invariably feels needy, hoping to please her.

"Okay, Danny. I'll make you lunch," she says faintly.

She hardly ever calls me Danny.

"Good. Thank you. Thank you, dear." Was she sleeping?

Last thoughts. I won't always be here. Next to her while she falls asleep.

An image of a plane against a pure blue sky—then gone. He's sleeping.

Some days he takes his brown-bag lunch onto the golf course behind the Inn which now, without players, is a bumpy meadow with holes and sand. A place on the grass. He eats the sandwich and fruit she's prepared. Afterwards lies back, views the sky. Closes his eyes.

He hasn't heard or seen many ambulances. It never stops on the news. Neither he nor Mary know anyone who's been afflicted. Everyone they know seems to know someone who knows someone. Some of the stories are horrific. Mary urges him to examine what Paul sends. "Okay," to placate her, "I promise to check it out." He dips a toe in—hesitates to advance. The trains are running. The station parking lots are empty.

"How does Fox use his time?" You don't use time. You're walking in it, breathing in it. You either resist it—or you flow with it, let it take you. It's moving and you are whether you're aware or not. Time "Management" was a puddle children splashed in. Living in a narrow corridor when a mansion is on the other side of the wall. A waste of energy to go against time. As if you could. The best you could do with that tension was "get things done." How does he explain it—when you can't explain music. You either go as it goes or you fight the inevitable. Which is fighting forces we can't understand.

He did what they gave him at Roxwell Hearns Somers – Mergers/Acquisitions, Energy, Intellectual Property, Global Disputes. He made his reputation doing the first, his career eventually centering on the last. RHS dealt with medium-sized players. The trickiest part was learning to talk to boards of directors. When to speak, when to listen. How to convince them to leap. He assimilated from Ron Hearns for whom corporate governance practices and tax law were breakfast and lunch. The curve for Dan was the financing of deals in the multi-millions. He studied. He scaled it. Clients grumbled about his "strange ways of doing things." Then lauded his ability to close deals in "unexpected fashions." They didn't know what to do with him. They gave him complicated cases. A back-corner office. They assigned to him the older support staff or the inexperienced. He used their strengths. It either clicked or it didn't. Whoever worked for him was intensely loyal or asked to be transferred. No one ever said a bad word regarding his interpersonal style.

Beginning of April he leaves his Lions Pride suite, Mary's brown bag and thermos, goes to his area on the golf course. Puts the phone on airplane mode. Sinks and stretches under the mild spring sky. Closing his eyes another sky remembering where blue met another blue on the horizon. The Algarve, Portugal. He surprised Mary with a trip after she told him they were expecting their second—Toby. Spontaneously he books a room at the secluded resort his accountant recommended. The firm is cold about his short notice for time off. He'd already been looking elsewhere.

He'd lie on the smooth as baby skin sand, she beside him smelling of lotions, beads clanking and he nearly slipped into a real sense of peace, forgetting. He hoped his touch would fill in for the absence of his words.

He thought the surrounding beauty would merge them. In paradise he was failing. They stroll through the town, enjoy delicious meals, local wine, the music. He beams, confident his wife was the most magnetic—the other couples gawking in their direction. Every night as they glided on the placid air in the winding alleys to their stone villa by the sea, all he could focus on was – we have another child coming and I'm not sure she wants to be with me. Maybe it's a mistake. Every night they lose themselves in each other's bodies. He looks for words. I love you... No one else for me... That's all he finds. And another day on the sand, she becomes quiet takes a walk by herself, he drinks at the bar by the pool talks too much and rum-drunk goes to their room, lies down waiting. The TV on the air conditioner buzzing waits for her reclining and the opening door she kicks off her sandals strips heads to the shower. He feels as he had eleven years before—listening to her bathe after they'd made love—he'll never know her. Inside. She won't show him.

He wakes on the grass. The light has changed. His mouth is dry, ants are exercising on his arm. He reaches for his phone, the clock says 4:04. He'd fallen into a heavy sleep. Two hours. In his room he's in a daze, can't shake it. He logs off, packs, and leaves. As he shuts the door he spots Caroline the maid, three rooms down. He waves to her. "Can I..." she says in distorted tones, pointing at his room and her cleaning cart. "Oh yes, yes, of course. Thank you." He's taking her in for the first time. She's not a maid, or a "deaf maid." She's a woman. She replenishes her cart, he remains, probably making her uncomfortable but he can't stop looking—she's alive in a light he hadn't noticed—or known— What...is it? She's *shining*. Chunky and her hair unkempt she's filled with – grace – is the word. She peers again, he tries to play cool, checks his briefcase. He meets her eyes and they smile a moment. *Graceful* is on her whole being. He backs away, takes the stairs to the parking lot, tilts up—she's pushing the cart toward his room. Caroline who shines.

Eating with his family that night – out of courtesy she waits till he goes to clean his Lions Pride room – "You okay, Dan? You don't like the pasta?" "No, I do—it's very good, Mary."

Learning and making money and being away from home—he knew she wasn't exactly happy. They had never discussed having children in depth. He assumed. He was mistaken. When she told him she was pregnant he ran to embrace her. All he felt from her was detachment. "You're not happy?" She wouldn't answer, buttered his toast. He stared at her, in shorts and t-shirt, morning-wild hair in the cluttered kitchen they'd been in for three months. Who did I marry here? He left the house for work. It was always up, down or sideways with her.

An email from one of his paralegals: Tony Levi is in Mt. Sinai. Respiratory issues. They think it's Covid. No one can get in—not even his wife. Dan's secretary calls his wife, asks if there's anything she needs. He sends her a note, flowers – the appropriate words. Not a bad guy Tony, overall.

Disputes practice. Global disputes. Dan disputes.
To engage in argument or debate; to argue vehemently; wrangle or quarrel; discuss; call in question.
He saw himself in the first and last parts of the definition. He highlighted things, inconsistencies, falsities, contradictions. He questioned. He became recognized for astute handling of "disputes," particularly in construction and mining projects. He never undertook to destroy his opposition. If work was to continue fruitfully there's no reason to leave the opponent on the ground bleeding. They'd like to hate him but he made that difficult too.

He was sought after for Post-Merger and Acquisition disputes. A new family. Mom's kids grab all the good blankets. Dad's won't give up any playground turf. Knees are skinned, lips bruised, egos clamor. Until he gets them all in a room he has no idea how to proceed. He listens to all the sides, the "arguments." If there has to be hurt—he makes it quick and limited—and moves on.

More recently, getting them in a "room" meant faces on screens. It made it arduous to feel what was happening. What was *wanted*. He adapts, slowly.

She sticks Post-its on his sandwich bags.

> **Dr. Andrew Kaufman. Jon Rappoport.**
> **Dr. Tom Cowan. Max Igan. Amazing**
> **Polly. Spiro Skouras. Event 201.**

Every few days, a new name or idea to explore.

They had offered him China and he declined. The facial recognition cameras, the constant surveillance. The social credit scores. Maybe it's headed everywhere. He couldn't pretend it was okay to profit off of it.

Singapore starts to implement it. Almost omnipresent surveillance cameras. London's had them up for years. Now New York. After 9-11 they habituated everyone to the body scanners in the airports. Always, for your *protection*. Dan's an "enrolled traveler" in most of the airports. He can usually avoid the body scanners and the fingerprinting—which is required at Singapore's Changi Airport. They already *have* his prints and photos on file. (Soon to be replaced by facial biometric and iris scans). Quick scan of his passport on the glass, the AI tells the humans "Okay," and on he goes, into the dripping wet city. Don't forget your umbrella.

He watched it being built year after year, step by step. First the fear, then the precautions, then the new technology. Each time more invasive. Each year normalizing the previously unacceptable. He's a miniscule part of the machine they're building. He doesn't know why they're building it.

Sitting at his desk he wanders, gazing at the sky above the Lions Pride courtyard. He'd been true as they say, for...nine years? Well, a blow-job or two. One at his buddy Frank's bachelor party. And his old girlfriend at the high school reunion. They got each other off in her car. That was all. Until the traveling.

Until Katherine. Toby was toddling. He'd play with him when he came home. Jessie would join him for dessert and tell him about her day. He suspected Mary was involved with someone. One morning as he's leaving on a trip to San Francisco—"Tell me something, Mar." "What, Dan?" "Tell me you're not sleeping with someone else." So quicky and casually—as if asking to have his dry cleaning collected. She pauses – picks up a dish – wishes him safe travels. "Right," he says and stoops to kiss Toby, on the floor in the hallway.

In San Francisco he visits his client, a big developer, his wife Kathy and some friends at their estate overlooking the city. There's a lot of wine and inside jokes. Kathy, as Jack the client calls her, is not participating much. She prefers *Katherine*, he'll discover. Dan mentions he'll be free the next day and Jack suggests Kathy take him around—her favorites.

On a windy day they're entering the regal archway of the Legion of Honor Museum. "Vertigo was shot here—remember?" He hadn't seen the film, only images of Jimmy Stewart and Kim Novak viewing the painting. "Yes," he says. She's plain and thin. Her hair, long and brunette, is lovely. A tranquility exudes from her. When she smiles he tingles. As they move through the day, the tingle stays. They lunch in the museum cafe. Dan talks about his children – Katherine was childless "for now" – "It's *wonderful* how they come out with the unvarnished truth," she says with an irresistible innocence. "Like you." "Hm?" "Wonderful." "Ah, Mr. Fox, you're..." and she taps his bare upper arm. At the Presidio, strolling in the proximate crash of the Pacific, she tells him a story of when her grandparents took her there and she ran and hid, terribly upsetting them. She still convinced them to buy her an ice cream. He suggests going to the beach, "Oh sure, I'll show you Baker Beach," and they're on the sand, the Golden Gate Bridge suspended in sunlight before them. He has a camera, she takes a pic of him and he asks a man to snap one of them together – "No, no Daniel," "Come on Katherine, just one." They walk the beach, silent awhile. She says out of nowhere, "I'm not happy." "I'm not happy either," is his reply. "I'm...afraid to be alone," and after she says it they stop, he lightly touches her wrist. Over her shoulder he sees a man with a cooler who shouts, "Ice Cream Sandwiches, Popsicles, Creamsicles..." They run to him, tear off the plastic, tasting their ice cream where the ocean draws near.

She drops him in a cab at his hotel, and he lies down, thinking about her – the phone rings. "Daniel? It's Katherine." "Katherine...hello." "Dan?" "Yes, Katherine?" "I'm here." "Where? Where are you Kath—" "Downstairs." "Oh, you're—" "Dan?" "Yes, I'm here—" "Do you want me to come up?" Oh, please do, and bring the beach and the water and the ice cream man and his cooler. I'll fit them all in here. "Yes. Yes, I do." "What's the number? Your room."

She's at the door her long hair and all he desires is to tell her he wants her to be happy and to give her happiness. You plain gorgeous girl I found by the ocean, no you found me. Touches her hand pink nails long fingers she skates hers on his that *thrill* my god he says her name the sun going down over Frisco she pulls the blinds a trickle of light comes she takes off her things he watches she says "Go ahead, Dan," and he undresses lies beside her in the king bed. Before they lay naked she kissed him by the door he fell against the wall her hot mouth breathing his name in the kiss. There by the door kissing his neck and ears he's holding on to her cascading hair she puts one hand under his shirt on his back runs up and down. Tickling. Scratching. She goes to the window draws the blinds extending her arm to him – they're swimming in a pool pretending to reach the end when all they aspire to is playing. She tells him in no words to promise her, he can feel it in her movement. Be as wild with me as you—there'd better be love in all of it. Her mouth was sour and sweet, sad happiness, she didn't withhold a thing, bad good in between. I promise he told her in the breath on her neck – and she kissed him —

He stayed an extra day and a half. For her. As he had a hunch Mary was involved, Mary had the same. He flew to San Francisco every month, several trips on his own dime and time. She came to Manhattan. They drove the hairpin road to Big Sur. The cliffs and forest. The ocean. "I want to have a baby with you, " she tells him softly, naked to naked bodies. Their cozy room in the bed and breakfast. "I love you, Daniel. You should feel it, by now." He felt it there in the Santa Lucia mountains.

At home, Mary was paying attention – reeling him in – saying in her idiom, "Okay, Dan, let's come back to each other." Katherine died a few years after that. Though it finished slowly, he wounded her. *He* was wounded. She wrote him a letter he received after – her best friend sent it and attached a note – "She <u>truly</u> <u>loved</u> you, Daniel." He dreams and dreams and daydreams Katherine.

As he moves into April, Dan feels unmoored. He goes into "work," five mornings per week at his Lions Pride Inn room, thermos of coffee, brown bag lunch. "Thorny" negotiations he'd hoped to have resolved; a new case out of Manila on mineral rights; details of international trade agreements recently amended. There's an unreality to it all. Emails go unanswered—from opposing counsel and his own clients. It takes days or weeks for basic information on matters which last month were stamped urgent. Singapore and Australia are under lockdown measures. Communication and responsiveness is spotty. His staff have children and spouses at home.

He goes on YouTube to browse things Mary had sent him. He had a pretty good idea of how power was wielded in the world but he's never examined it from the points of view of these people, it was like another language: purposeful manipulations, distortions of truth—including the medical issues confronting all of them—if not outright lies. He doesn't know whether he can trust this new language—and learn it, let alone use it.

He's drifting. His sense of time—is loosening.

He begins taking his lunch to the courtyard and eating on a bench. No one else there except the maids darting in and out. No one chats or stops to meet new people. He has nothing to read except his NY Times. It's all "panic and propaganda," as Mary terms it. After a while, he'll close his eyes, April light penetrating his tired brain. One day heading into the room he sees Caroline's cart and hears her scrubbing in the bathroom. She hums to herself. He listens, smiling. Can she hear herself somehow? She comes out holding a toilet brush, sees him— "Oh, excuse—" "No, no, I'm sorry, please continue," making sure she can read his lips. On a whim he lifts his hand to his head—sends it quickly to the right—saying HELLO—in American Sign Language. Her face illumines – a thick "AH!" comes forth and the same greeting. He tries one more, bringing his right hand up to his chin, tapping it, lowering it to the left palm— for "Good." Then flipping the left palm he brings the right hand over it twice, like pushing air —for "Afternoon." She laughs with delighted surprise, reciprocating the sign and asking him—hands together fingers curled and folded outward—"How are—" points an index finger at him— "You?" He answers with another "Good" and repeats the question – "Good," she signs. "That's all I've got," he says, shrugging. "No, it's gwate, reawy gwate." "Thanks. I watched a video." "But—why?" "I wanted to communicate with you." She blushes—doesn't hide it, doesn't look away. She touches her chest, takes two fingers from the right hand and taps two from the left saying aloud, "My name is..." and signs the letters for "Caroline." She points at him—"What is your—" taps the fingers together again, asking him. He follows her, tapping "My name is..." and says, "Daniel." "Ah," she grins, rapidly forms the letters of his name. "I haven't learned the letters yet," he admits. " 'at's okay," she says, ready to go – "Uh, Caroline—would you like a water?" He pulls out two bottles from the fridge. "Than' you...Danel." He gestures her to sit, which she does, opening the water and swallowing large gulps. Sweat glints on her brow, in drops. He passes her a box of tissues.

She asks him about his work and he explains it, slowly enunciates, and she nods, glancing at his scattered folders, legal pads filled with asymmetrical notes. They chuckle at his inability to keep them ordered. "Oh," he says, jumping up and spinning, remembering he has to face her—"I'll show you where I travel for my work. Well, where I used to..." He types Singapore into Google Maps on his laptop. He points to it, she bends – "Vewy lon' trip?" "A whole day from here... to there..." he taps the screen. Her eyes widen, he notes the arch of her back—full-bodied, she carries it well. "I went here too"—he drags the screen to the left to expose Australia. She straightens, appraising him—"You reawy get aroun' Danel," flickering D-A-N-I-E-L – smiling. Shining.

The next morning all of his folders are ordered, one atop the other; accordions side by side along the wall; his stacks of papers collated. All of it neat and easy to locate. Caroline came in after he'd left.

She goes into his room to clean in the afternoon while he eats lunch and when he returns he offers new signs and she corrects and adds to them. Before he leaves they speak a bit more—she's applied lipstick, her hair's been brushed. And they say— hand tapping chin, touching other hand, then making a diving motion— "Good night."

One day he forgets his lunch and Mary texts him saying she'll deliver it. He waits in the courtyard. Caroline emerges on the corridor and they have a signing conversation – sunny warm day, she rests on the rail amending his attempts, he's absorbed in her laughter, unaware that Mary's arrived and is watching from the courtyard door – "I messed it up." – "It's okay Danel, you're doin' good."

"Good afternoon," Mary says to him, then waves up at the maid, who waves and pushes her cart down the hall into a room.

She extends the brown bag.

"Thanks, Mar. I appreciate it." His heart is running. She sits next to him on the bench.

"Nice place."

"Would you like to share my lunch?"

"Not hungry."

"See my room?" He points.

"I can't, Dan. I told Toby I'd take him to East Nook. The one friend whose mother will allow them to play together will be there. We hope."

"The beach, huh? Sounds like fun."

"Is fun allowed during a—plandemic?"

"Clever."

"Did you look into Event 201?"

"Event...no. Not yet. I've watched some...and read articles—you sent me."

"And the verdict?"

"Interesting content. Some of it."

"You can thank Paul."

"I will."

"He's the diver."

"He's what?"

"Anyone you like in particular?"

"Like?"

"Appreciate?"

"I find Jon..."

"Rappoport?"

"—an intelligent man. What he has to say related to the medical..."

"Cartel?"

"Yes. Cartel. Intriguing. He's got knowledge. On a deeper level."

Pretty rare—smacks of a compliment.

"I figured he might appeal to your—perspective on things."

"Sure you won't check out my room?"

"No time, cowboy."

"Too bad."

"I'll see you," she shifts, rising. "Enjoy your roasted red pepper romaine carrots artichokes and pineapple slices."

"I will. Thank you."

She dallies a moment in her torn and tight jeans he hasn't seen her wear in a long time. "Since when do you know sign language?"

"Oh, that," he chokes on a laugh. He stands, speaks low. "She's a nice lady and I thought I'd learn a few phrases since – she cleans my...room."

"Uh-huh," she pivots, pauses—"Why are you whispering?"

"Hm? Oh, yes...silly."

"Seems you learned more than a few phrases." She leans in and kisses him – "Later, alligator."

Alone in the courtyard holding the bag. The hummus sandwich he had forgotten.

He tells Mary he's willing to stay home one day during the week and take care of Toby. Mary says – "Thanks." She lets him have her in her bathroom on the make-up table threatening to crumble with their grappling, her bottles tumbling. Caroline subtly enters his rhythms. Mary's wondering if the hotel in Westchester has travelers during this fucking thing. Everything slides.

His father was dying in the hospital. His brother and sister were saying goodbyes. Dan was in the doorway. They gape at him, Come on, it's your turn. He went in, his father unconscious. Stood dumbfounded, empty in the head. He bent, touched his arm. Mumbled something. Lingered a moment. Retreated. Mary came down the hallway in disarray, she says her goodbye. Tears on all their cheeks. Dan is dry. No one looks askance. He asks Mary in the bedroom, late at night—Why didn't I cry Mary—Why can't I cry *now*? Embraces him on the bed. She's crying, giving him her tears. Mary... it's my father... my father.

Months later in a hotel room at night in Boston. "Oh God," he tells the ceiling as it bleeds out of him, "Why am I crying for my father in a hotel room?" He calls her. "Mary, I can't stop crying." "Danny, let it come. It needs to come out." He'll walk the streets. But snow is piling on the ground. Damn. Drinks something strong. It doesn't stop. Mary calls a last time. And sleep.

Caroline comes in one afternoon as he's reading an email from Tony Levi's wife. "It's not good. I can't get in to comfort my dying husband!!"

"I wish I could help her, Caroline. He's my boss. He's alone in the hospital. They don't let anybody in. She's freaking out."

"I heard about tha'." She – and then Dan – smile at the verb. "I read it."

They're sitting by his desk. He looks in her eyes.

"I don't know. It's all hitting me now. My kids at home, me here, normal life gone. People kept apart from loved ones in hospitals, nursing homes. It's inhumane. I think about my kids—yours—"

"Yes, Danel."

They'd shared pictures of the kids. Caroline's seven-year-old, Tatiana. Tani. Her father had disappeared.

"What do you think, Caroline—is all this real—this covid thing?"

"I don't – reawy know Dan. They say it's a pandemic. People are sick. Dying."

"People get sick, right?"

"They do."

"And die? All the time." She moves her hand lightly over his. "I have a friend who says – " he makes a 'who knows' face – "it's mostly bullshit. That there's a plan – an *agenda* behind the whole thing."

"Hm, reawy? Wow. It *is* vewy stwange, Dan. The whole wold…cwosed…suddenly. No custmers." She smiles – "Well, awmos' none." He puts his hand on hers. "Maybe your fwend is – onto somethin'?"

"Could be." They're communicating with touching.

"Danel…" she *signs* – "You," pointing at him – "Have," fingers curled into her chest – "Good," hands intertwined circling her chest – "Heart." She lays them over his heart. It's hot in the room. Her hair is down— her hands are moving on his chest in circles.

"I guess I'm a little – afraid," he says to her eyes. Leaning forward into a kiss now inevitable and it's her laughter he wants, it's her blush he craves, her acceptance of herself and himself he needs. She wants his heart covered by years of what is foreign to her. She leads him into the next room to the bed whose sheets she'd carefully replaced. "Oh...Danel," she hums thrillingly in his ear and he whispers, "Carol...ine," into her eyes and it's her pillows they sink into, the ones she brought for him. They remember nothing for a time.

All she wants is being seen for things illuminating her. All he wants is no words to speak.

XVII

Mary – Above & Below

She starts writing in her journal every day. It's a small thick spiral notebook. She puts down sentences which look to her like childish rubbish. Her thoughts on Alice in Wonderland and the endless tea party. Lists of vitamins, minerals, what to send to whom. That's what she focuses on – serving. She sends things out you can hold. She sits in her backyard, eyes closed—sending things you can't.

She's a sentence you can't finish. There's no accurate way to describe herself. "Are we all essentially tongue-tied and gasping for straws?" she writes.

She left out the R after the G in the word. Fitting, she thinks.

For twenty years, ever since the life in her belly became her daughter, distant and sullen in the bedroom fifty feet away, her surrounding circle has been her children. What she wakes to every day. They expect her to tell them things, to instruct. She won't do that. If they can't apprehend what she's giving them otherwise, only then she'll give them words. She provides in touch, gestures, expressions. She doesn't give what's not hers, though she used to when they were young. It drained her. It taught her that to lie to children by magnifying your own knowledge or wisdom or emotions is to plant destructive seeds in their brains. She was a full time mother and didn't pretend confidence in what she was doing. The other mothers talked of her behind her back as "not attentive enough," "not mirroring enough." Let them tie their nots. They thought she was a parent, no. She had kids. That was all.

Sometimes she felt equivalent to a woman sometimes a man. Usually neither. She tried to tell her mother once and Mom changed the subject. She tried to tell her older sister Tallie who asked Mary if she was stoned. She wasn't uncomfortable in her body, she was... puzzled. When they showed them the pictures of all the bodily organs she burst out screeching laughing and couldn't contain it despite being rebuked by the Health teacher. The more she pointed at "This is the liver," "This is the pancreas," her giggles got louder and uncontrollable. Her classmates laughed along with her, then at her, then they tapered off uncomfortably as the peculiar river flowed out of her—slowed down—*roared*, insuppressible. She was told to leave the room and go to the Assistant Principal's office—erupting in hilarity as she left. For twenty minutes she couldn't stop laughing. When she finally did, it started again when the guy in the ugly red tie asked her what she had found so funny in a lesson on human anatomy. They called her mother and she didn't ask any questions, drove her home, put her in a hot bath then to bed. "What was funny, what made you laugh, sweetheart?" her dad asks in the evening, leaning against her dresser. "I'm not sure, Dad. I – I knew, I guess, we had organs – in our body. Seeing them for the first time colored pink and whitish and like, purple...

it...seemed...so bizarre to me. We're...loaded with all that. Just to stay alive." She's cackling, can't prevent—embarrassed, near to horrified at this point. Her folks sat by her on the bed – held her, her mom whispering "It's okay Mary, my dear, it's okay baby. Let it out, let it come out." Her father had her taking deep breaths. In a while she fell asleep. They watched her in the following days.

She was able to control herself. Those impulses faded. Tallie got a kick reminding her of it every few years, telling new friends. Mary didn't find it humorous. She never—quite—"lost it" again when viewing images of human insides. Something about the whole design—bags and tubes inside us like an old TV or a vacuum cleaner—disturbed her. All that blood, tissue, muscle and shit. Giving birth teaches you shit happens. A lot of it from these bundles of shit—er, joy. When she really considered it, or her sister reminded her, she couldn't help think – it's a shitty deal....

She should have moved to New Mexico when Tallie was living out there and invited her. "We'll get a place together. Why live in crowded Manhattan?" Paul was in Santa Fe that year. It would have changed her life. The whole thing.

On Facebook she talks to the other mothers. The online school thing happening. They trade ideas on how to keep the kids productive. Some rarely go out. They order their food in through the supermarkets off their websites. They post the latest pronouncements of King Fauci and Queen Birx. Where to buy sanitary wipes. The best cleaners to use to kill "the corona." *Stay safe.* The new mantra. *Stay home.* Mary almost posted, "Yeah, I'm sure being at home is great for spousal and child abuse victims." *Wash your hands* they repeated constantly. Maintain distance, stay home "unless you're essential." Yeah, Mary thinks, out at the supermarket, these clerks and cashiers here—are they essential? How do they "stay safe"? They weren't wearing masks till late April in the shops. She wanted to offer compassion, not hollow words on Facebook from a sanitized kitchen. Her friends who had parents in nursing homes had no access to them—besides a voice on a phone. She's relieved her parents live independently. Alone in such a residence you're lost. Cut off. One more stop on the medication merry-go-round. A payment coming in from Medicare. In hospitals they're dying alone, old and young.

How do you condone that? Mary asks the dawn light: Is it a crime?

Being depended upon lends you a false sense of significance. That's why many doctors are hollow and have huge egos. You get authority, dim to your own blind spots and vulnerabilities. You don't know you've slipped away until you're out on the ocean, floating. Pretending.

Becoming a parent is similar. You can barely tie your shoes, suddenly you know everything. Mostly, she felt fake. She was fine with the baby part. By age five or six—she'd emptied. All she had was the same kiss and hug. Her guilt and love was mixed for her daughter. As if feeding her spoonfuls of honey and garbage.

Daniel outside the bar on Third Avenue where they'd meet. She was having a smoke on the sidewalk as the Thursday night parade went by. He was with his friends. She doesn't pay them any mind, converses with a woman, lights her cigarette. One of the boys—that's what they were to her—beams his energy at her. Lanky, tall. She glares— WHAT? He doesn't look away.

Something spun in her. A revolution – a literal one – happened inside her… to do with her future… her sexuality – her desire – what she found – easy life – a glide rather than the hard choreography of a map written as you move. It stirred a life in her womb, she groaned, turning to face her reflection in the glass of the bar. People beyond were laughing and gesturing. She turned, he was gone. He was inside. Last drag of the butt, she drops it, lets it burn out on its own. If it's gonna burn, stepping in her expensive boots to know this boy, let it….

The two towers were standing then. Third Avenue that humid evening in May, 2000.

When this thing is done, this pandemic hogwash, I'm going. Toby can come. Or remain with his father. I'm leaving. There's still time for me to screw up my life. The way *I* want to screw it up. Live in small motels, rent a house by the month. Disappear again. Fuck men *and* women. Be celibate. Keep ten books. Or eleven. Give them away, get ten more. Paul will go with me. I'll support him, I don't care, it's my money after so long. We went in opposite directions. Danny traveled to Asia, I to Mars. I traveled cheaply, on a budget. Round and round. My down-market Mars inside this house circling the sun of the big apple. Sparkling with rotten beauty faded. My toilette mirror where I saw the universe be born and die, in the far off reflection of my make-up tubes and perfume bottles. Glinting with contumely and obedience. There I went, my luggage made of televisions turning off, of music fading out…toys coming to a final rest… There we voyaged my companions and I into the ethers of a trip Dan never knew and couldn't possibly understand as children slept in shadows and lawyers took casual blow jobs. Where he saw sunsets I had the most gorgeous red dawns. There at the top of the stairs I learned how civilizations form, order themselves, eventually become enslaved, over and over. On the landing I met new friends, night-lights glowed, we conferred in the living room as Brahms sang of empires expiring. Yeah, I was, Daniel, a traveler also. I was a desired partner in the art of taking one step then another step. You didn't catch my moving, my lift-off and touch-down. You had your talents – I had mine. I knew when not to stop. The ceiling of puce never halted me nor did ephemeral pantries or a garage where gathered the remnants we cast away. Time wanted me. I only gave it what I had to—I'm leaving you boy outside the bar when the clock strikes and the tea party is finally over. Watch me leave. I'll evade the trial. I have no opinion on missing tarts. I'm a tart who's found who's gone and saw the sky from above the sky and the houses all looked the same. It's amazing how little love I encountered—visioning down through the kitchen windows at 6:15 p.m. between fried chicken cartoons and something giving birth to something dying—I'm the tart who stands naked in the doorway watching it.

She thought she was an eccentric soul who'd lost a child and came to the playground to grieve. It was untrue yet not without substance. She sat by herself. Jill wasn't akin to the people Mary had grown up with. Unaffected. No pretense. Difficult to believe she'd been in Worthington for years. Now she realized why they'd never met. No kids. Separated, soon to be divorced. They didn't speak for two weeks. One afternoon she complimented her on how cute Tobias was in his blue winter coat. They shared smiles shielding their eyes from the sun. Her voice did something to Mary this first day – and thereafter. It was a girl's – not in timbre or pitch – in its openness. Children said things only to say them – it was Jill's voice and why she fell slowly in love with her. Mary felt she'd been waiting for her a long time. She didn't rush or push, she let their friendship flower naturally. She let Jill know, as with her children, by her presence, she would do anything for her.

Food banks. On the news. The cars lining highways for miles, thousands of people. Hungry people. People with no work. People unable to receive unemployment insurance. People whose kids ate at school and now there was no school. They waited for hours on the roads. Driving up to volunteers where they'd be given a basket to last a week, canned things, bread, soup, fruit, veggies. "Thank you so much," "You're lifesavers," "God bless you all!" Mary is crying, angry. This is her country.

Jessie and Toby should see it. She calls to them— hold on. They're hungry also—for their lives, friends, routines... Jess in her room, alone with her gadgets. Her professors and classmates on a screen. Toby playing video games in his room alone.

"What, Mom?" "Yeah?" From upstairs. "Nothing. I... I found it."

Her eyes close. It's *off*. Something way off with all this... People sick, some dying, the answer is collapse the lives of everyone?

She hears Paul— Mare, stop trying to find sense in it.

She was thirty, past thirty and you can't stop it, you deal with it. Working as a nondescript secretary in a "financial services" firm. Sharing a rent-controlled apartment with a flight attendant gone half the month. She listened to her Walkman, typed on the computer. Lunch hour she walked to Bryant Park, falafel and tahini on the grass. Dickens or a

Bronte. Minimal makeup, hair tied back, bland colors. Men were indifferent. How she wanted it. A direct-deposited check, vodka martini at 5:30. Younger ones in her department asking her out for Thursday happy hours. Drawn to her no bullshit attitude. She admired their endless energy for partying. She met them one night at a dive bar on Third Avenue in the Fifties. She got on the Six train and rode underground. Her mother asked if she's dating. Her parents wondering why she's not married. Even her hippie sister is engaged—and pregnant. She's riding a train under a city after typing up clumped together mortgages to create a new "financial instrument." It was messed up but what could she do? Morality? People had to eat. Tell it to Charlotte or Charles. Pages turning. People had to plunder. This was the 21st century, soon we'll all be half machine anyway, right? Her stop. Shriek of brakes. Steps up and out—night air, warm. Dark.

I gave him a chance, the lawyer kid—nothing there. Chinese dinner and drink put her in a cab kissed her quickly. Now his mouth on her mind constantly. Debating his three voice messages. He made her laugh, she let down her guard during the second bottle of Tsing Tao. The lawyers she had met seemed miserable, this one's enthusiastic about his new career. "Yeah, give it a few years." He told her how he saw creativity in it as she had in Matisse and Picasso—and who was the gal you mentioned? Berthe Morisot, 1841-1895. She didn't buy his comparing legal work to artistic creation. She respected his energy and his mischief had smile in it – his mouth made her breathe faster.

She told him "Okay." She could use a lay, then she'll cut it off. She howls at her "sharp" wit, pressing lips to lipstick in the mirror. She changed her bra to a loose one and deliquesced downstairs.

He dives in for a kiss on the stoop of her walk-up. She pulls away.

"What's that you've got?" It was in cardboard, rectangular. Just like a man, no matter how young they beguile you with their presents and before you know you're sucking on their—"Come up a minute, I can't carry it with me, right?"

He peruses her apartment as she removes the brown wrapping. "This guy..." she whispers under-breath, recognizing from half the face, **Portrait of Julie**, 1889. Julie was Berthe Morisot's daughter. She was eleven or twelve in the painting. Her candid, tender round face fills nearly the whole frame. Two pink flowers shine from her light brown hair. The girl's dress, and the background, are a yellowish white. It's the face, so full of openness, which draws the eyes in.

"Thank you, Daniel. That was—very—thoughtful."

"I'm glad you like it."

"Yes." She told him she'd decide on a good position for the print. She was walking to the couch for her bag, he blocked her, she had no defense to stop the kiss, the mouth she'd fantasized was on hers, the tongue meeting hers, the warmth building in her belly, he was growing and it was now or—"Daniel...why don't we go out...and..." She takes her bag and unlocks the door.

She recollects how he had bypassed the many impressions the Morisot image had evoked in her. He determined what would move her but he couldn't *receive*—what it brought *out* of her. Damn it, she spoke aloud ten years later in therapy, why hadn't she seen it – that night she'd have halted and changed course. "Why do you think you didn't allow yourself to see it?" The therapist evasion as usual. "Why am I here?"

she sat up. "You tell me, Mary, why do you feel you're here?" Such predictable garbage. She reached for her handbag, wrote him a check, said "I'm not coming back. Don't try to convince me. It's finished." If she didn't end her marriage at least she'd save a hundred-fifty a week severing this farce.

The problem was she'd married a penis, not a man. A mouth not a mate. No one affected her erotically as Danny did. Then or since. Sex was how he gave himself. She couldn't resist it, twenty years down the road from the two-bedroom off Sixth Avenue where they spent weekends ordering takeout. Traversing each other's bodies. Nobody caressed, nobody kissed, like him, the way he used his thing in her was a revelation. When he did it to her something healed in her, her sense of absence, of being divided, when he moved in her, stabbed her with it, a light shone, a goodness filled her, she felt even, she shook, writhed – for once she accepted domination because she heard bells that told her life was not inane walking down idiotic streets endlessly and stroking him ass balls back chest it wasn't a man it was a reason steel like river like at once his kiss was flowers his kiss was chocolate his kiss was killing saving he moved in her for hours till it was liquid between them she was a goo of tears and surrender and washing or eating naked a graze on her breast was yet another promise of sliding away from the dark and from the light. Their love was built around those days joining in pleasure that always mounted, promised more. Their life formed out of those early ways they got close and made their foundation. Touches, kisses...glimpses. Inhaling—imbibing—each other in a bed.

Then it happens. Like everything happens. They can't keep apart so they get married. Her parents are overjoyed at last and a lawyer! Grandchildren to dote upon!

She rebounds to the island where she told herself she wouldn't return. A house. Decorations, beds, appliances. She's pregnant surprise surprise. Oh, it happened, she stood sat and lay watched it swell inside her and her name was Mary she reminded herself in the back of her mind this is not the life I foresaw and every time she talks about it she can't stop herself from breaking up. It pours out unavoidably with Tallie's questions on her state of mind. "Mary..." she says in a serious tone—"are you all right, babe?" "I'm okay—." "You were doing that weird giggling, it reminded me—" "Yeah, Tallie, the Health class, I know." "Yes. Well...at least the sex is good." "Yeah Tal, the sex is good. Was good."

She puked in every bathroom of the new house. Dan arrived home late each night. She rebuffed him when he tried to initiate sex. She left, sojourned at her parents until she invited him for dinner. They were rubbing under the table. I love you Mary come home. She relented, thought she could go ahead, it would all be normal. Days will flow one into the next. At intervals they did. When the girl was growing inside her at five months the terror set in, she saw she'd have to talk to this becoming girl person for the next fifty sixty years tell her things let it suck the life from her breasts dress her feed her say two plus two equals be nice and I love you how many times and the bedtime the fears how about *her* fears who would soothe hers when she has to climb the stairs alone it never stops growing in you then you feel it there's a point when it's unmistakably talking to you Mother it's saying mama and mother I am here are you THERE? It's actually saying it in a breathing moving kind of way Are you *there Mama*, Mary didn't know how to answer maybe if she doesn't answer it'll go away or at least stop asking but it didn't it carried on moving knocking and in the night she could hear it scared tired with asking breathing its meager life through her mouth and nose could feel her there gaping at her in the mirror Mother ARE YOU THERE? Are you *there* – for ME? asking her.

On a day of rotten rain and TV sadness she shuts it all off walks outside goes down the street in her nightgown like a lunatic in a movie scene she's fully sane finally and puts her hands her hands she's given to the girl person inside her who keeps asking and with her hands underneath her dress on her bursting skin at six and a half months in the middle of the street in drenching rain she tells it I AM HERE FOR YOU GIRL I am here. WILL BE HERE. You won't be alone. I am here. Falling rain on both of them running and leaving down the sewer. The asking stopped the breathing grew steadier there was a lull a sigh she found a name in her mind at night wrote it on a pad in the morning Jessica she told Daniel Jessica and he lit up his breath touched hers she felt love with him she lifted the days were lighter because Jessica her small asker was coming through a garden wall towards her and she wouldn't let her alone she'd be there waiting and wasn't she?

The travel ban has been extended. Immigration has halted, so they say. 3.24 million tests have been conducted in the U.S.—"indicating" 20% have tested positive for coronavirus.

Mary takes a drive one afternoon, eastbound on the Expressway. There's nowhere to go. Signs above in Electronic letters tell her:

STAY HOME   SAVE LIVES
FLATTEN THE CURVE
Everywhere, the park, the supermarket, the drugstore, signs tell you stay six feet apart, flatten the curve, go home, stay home. Paul said the masks were coming—a matter of time. People around her "stayed safe," kept their kids inside or in the backyard. She kept her own counsel.

Jessica punished her with sixteen hours. Why, 'cause I waited to tell you? Did you punish me for that? I should call you Ruth. An agony of ninety minutes at the end, here she comes, primal scream two-thirty in the morning, greeting a chirping sparrow. Mary pants and blinks at her in her lap. "See the tears you gave Mommy? How you came into the world my Jessica, making a mess of your mother?" Everyone sighs laughingly, Daniel, his parents, hers. The girl's eyes open clearly, gazing at her mother—recognizing her. Straight in, girl to girl. "Oh you want *more* tears, huh, little girl?" Mary was there.

She floated through those early years of Jessica, wraith and human combined. Sleep, feed, clean, diaper, wash. Daniel helped, Daniel was absent. Coming home in darkness most of the year. Sending her cute emails during the day. She loses track of days, months. Forgets to read her books, neglects her painters. Tallie blazes in for a week or two. A blur. She's wading across milky waters in the bliss of a life depending on hers, learning everything from her hands, voice and face. Her milk runs forth, she swims in it with the girl, pushes her down the street singing songs to her. Carriage on the sidewalk, she fantasizes thumbing a ride and getting gone. She promised her. She who needs only her pool to float in. She's not the only one depending. Her new hips make him full of hands when she bends or reaches. "What do you want?" she challenges, his breath on her neck. He won't take no for an answer, tickling. Jessica's gurgling in the crib. "I'm beat, Dan. She drains me." He'll get up tonight and soothe her, he promises. "Oh, you'll feed her?" "Yes, if you have a bottle, I will." No, it's her body or nothing. Okay, husband, here I am, supine. Milky and misty, pawing and thrusting, she can't feel a thing. He says her name, calls her "baby." He presumes her chuckling is from pleasure. She gives in, half asleep.

Paul was away longer after her marriage. He still wrote, then emailed. She visits if she's free. When he's in the city, she's euphoric. Forty miles. They'll be as before. What's strange is, they're not. Perhaps he sensed my loss of energy. Does he believe I've trapped myself – mother, wife? They talk and drink. Shaky. A screw or two has fallen from the works.

She sends him a card.

"Paul. Nothing will ever separate us. No matter what happens and how things go I'll be here for you however you need me. You mean more to me than I can say or write. Your recent poems are gorgeous. Preserve your fire. I'm never far from you."

Encloses cash: "For healthy things to eat."

He calls her. "Mary, Mary, you...darling." He misses her. "Time is going by, you know?" She knows.

Most of the dreams she remembers are related to him. They're sixteen laughing. Challenging each other. Doing something crazy. Rolling up a hill. Running with their pals – through walls – across windows. Sharing colorful tablets. Doors of perception. Seeing new things. His friendship, his heart. He revealed a mode of seeing for her. "You scare me when you look at me like that," she told him, one night towards the end of high school. As if they weren't separate. He smiled. "Doesn't mean you should stop." He never stopped.

They hold hands when they're together, often. They talk or text once a day, at least. Mary values her. Jill is delighted by her. Mary is the strength saying it'll all work out. Jill is the innocence and presentness making life fun.

She falls ill when she hears Phillip's girlfriend had the baby. Her pregnancy was what led to the finale of the marriage. She can't work, stays in bed. Mary gets her up, into the shower, helps her dress. Feeds her. Her thin body getting thinner. Chooses a therapist and drives her. Daniel starts to complain and the kids miss their mom. "Oh give me a break, I help a friend and you can't handle me being gone a bit? Why can't you pitch in?" "I'm working, remember?" "Yeah, how could I forget," as he packs to go on a trip. "Don't tell me what I can and cannot do for – with – *my* friends, Dan." He lays off. Mary hires sitters. She's not going to abandon her. One night she's leaving her and hugs her extra long. Jill groans.

"Sorry, did it hurt?"

"No, not at all, dear Mary. You give me so much energy." Faces close she smells Jill's breath, remembers her at the playground saying her name—

"Yes, well... You deserve it."

"You're so good to me. You're my best friend in the world. I don't deserve you."

That's how Mary had seen *herself* in relation to Jill.

"You're beautiful, Jill. Inside and outside." She was caressing her cheek. "You deserve wonderful things, sweetheart." Mary felt she could do anything with her. Jill blushes, hugs her, to avoid her eyes.

"Oh, Mary. You're so good."

Not quite true. Uplifting all the same. She releases into the hug and thoughts dissolve. They're in the hallway, cheeks, love-pecks, quick soft lip-kisses making them giggle. Then a real one, their mouths open. Their arms are around each other. "Mary," Jill whispers. They clutch there kissing for a while. They release, and she goes.

She feigns home demands a day or two, texting to confirm she's okay. Then goes to the big house, to the petite red-headed woman, bringing vitamins and homemade lentil soup.

"Mary," Jill tells her directly, "I'm okay with what happened between us. I – want you to know."

"I'm glad you said that. I'm fine also." Jill pours tea and they sit on the couch. She tells Mary about her child years, her parents and being alone. She's drawing broken shadows. Mary follows them, holds her hand. She can lose everything for this girl—this woman—and be aloof to the consequences. She'd had an affair with a woman. A teacher's assistant in her Renaissance Art class, sophomore year Cornell. She noticed Mary's passion, *Darlene*, for Carpaccio, invited her for a drink and a lot more. She was angular, buxom. Low-key persuasive. Her lack of inhibitions accelerated something nascent in Mary. She learned how a woman can give—be—what a man is unaware of. In between somewhere. Darlene was a lesbian, she said, how she was born. For Mary it wasn't about being a lesbian. Or anything. It didn't matter what the name was. The equipment. She made love with her *self*, not from between the legs.

That day she held Jill—a child. Jill kissed her—a woman. Mary was wet, couldn't go on unless they *went* on, as Jill was starting in on her neck, a hand circling her breast over her sweater. "Okay, babe... Let's stop for now." Jill's mouth on hers hungry. "Okay," she concedes.

Mary goes home and to bed early. Ruminates. Prays. The redhead who's melting inside her. Dan comes to bed, isn't in the mood. She would have refused him. Ah, Jill. Falls asleep.

The next day Jill is happier than she's been in months. That alone is reward for Mary. "I'm so glad you're here." They go to the den. Jill gushes over a new knitting supply store in town. She's going to improve. To make a sweater "for you." Heat burns in her—this is my *lover* speaking—when Jill kisses her she freezes—

"What is it? Did I—was that not—"

"No, nothing honey. Nothing." Mary kisses her. "I'm so happy – I'm so relieved you're feeling better." She hugs her a long moment.

"Honey."

"Yes, Em?"

"I was thinking last night...a lot."

"So was I. I couldn't wait to see you."

Jill's fingers slide on her thigh. Mary's in a skirt, a current shoots through her. She takes her hand, holding it. "Jill, I'm going to tell you exactly what's in my mind. It's—either we have to stop these making out sessions—or we go all the way." Jill hears the tension in her voice. "And if we go...I don't know how it's going to—where it'll end up."

"I'm not sure why you—"

"Let me finish." She rises, steps around the coffee table. "I could fall in love...with you. I *am* in love with you. I always was. She sits near her. "I mean—really fall in love."

"Wow. You're so intense, Em. You're everything I want...to be."

"That it!" Mary stands. Sits. Sighs.

"What, sweetie, what?"

She almost cries out the words— "That's how I feel...about *you*."

"Then why—"

"Because once we do everything, and it's wonderful, we'll want *that*—over and over. I will. We'll – get lost in it."

"Hm. Do you think so?" Such a timid innocent question. Don't do this to me Jill.

"It's... very possible."

"But what's so – wrong with it, Em? Isn't that what lovers..."

"Yes, I suppose. Then—what happens to – Jill, what'll happen to... It's hard to put into—"

"Do you mean who we—what we mean—to each other?"

"Yes, yes! outside of the—hunger."

Jill blushes, shifts in her seat.

"It's a very sweet hunger, Mary."

"Yes. I don't have the answer, Jill."

"Well, what if – what if we were to – try it one time – see how it – "

"How it ... what?"

"Maybe it would – go out of our systems?"

"Our systems?"

"Oh not that I *want* it to go out—"

"I understand."

"I just—"

"Jill... Won't 'trying it' – put it deeper into our systems? That's what—"

"I think—"

"Could change us. Our...connection. It's what concerns me. Disturbs me, actually."

"Me too, Em."

"If we – start and then stop – that's like – breaking up. I can't—break up with you."

"No, I... can't either."

Mary's already lamenting. She aches to touch her but any contact might collapse her reasoning. "Look at me." She flashes her eyes on Mary's. "I feel...the same – as you. You know what I'm hesitant of – fearful of – don't you?" She almost said 'baby.'

"I do. I understand what you're—yes." She reflects a long moment. "It *could* change us. Even if we – tried – not to."

Mary is familiar with sexual obsession. The rise and fall of feelings. The jealousies. Sex becomes the dominant force between you. Jill is aware the wonderful delicate balance between them could be threatened.

They sat with the day fading. Mary left when it was dusk in the room. She kissed her and said, "I'm closer to you than my own sister. Than my husband."

She hadn't been faithful. Nor had Daniel. A hotel in Westchester. She books a room for the weekend, twice a year. Goes down in a short skirt to the bar. Allows herself to be seduced. To let a man—clean, clear eyed, gentle—take her to his room. She told them – "If you rush things – I'm leaving." She had to reassure the younger ones. The nervous ones. Teach some. Most were nervous in their own ways. Why wasn't she? Because love wasn't involved. Intimacy, need, yes. Porn wasn't enough. Sometimes a session lasted hours. She was abandoned, astounded them. She never exchanged numbers, never saw them again. Except for one, inadvertently. An Australian guy. Had he and Dan crossed in the air? He was smooth, cute, his accent aroused her. She broke her rule. In the morning he begged for her information as she dressed. She contemplated giving it. Afterward, in her room, she sat at the bathroom mirror, mascara in a rivulet. Her name, as he remembered and whispered, was Sophia.

She said the name aloud. That was it, she decided—for Sophia and the hotel in Westchester. "Farewell, Sophia."

There was one who persisted. Jill was dating Brendan and they threw an end-of-summer barbecue at her house. She went alone. Brought her "famous potato salad." She met Brendan's friend Cal, whose wife sat quietly chatting. Cal was funny and ribald, they all joked and Mary vaguely felt they'd grown up together. His wife observes them—as he flipped a burger onto Mary's bun they exploded laughing. I had better be careful here, she reminded herself—he was attractive. When she left he shook her hand. A note was in it – "Call me." She didn't. They cross paths at a Halloween party in the neighborhood, she dressed as Jane and Dan as George, meet the Jetsons – Cal was Ed Norton from the Honeymooners— his wife wasn't there. He leers in her face roguishly. Dan came and handed her a champagne. She was waiting for the bathroom upstairs. Cal popped out of it, they grinned, shrugged and did the "Oh, excuse me" routine. He pulled her in without resistance, kissed her amidst the bright wallpaper, she said Stop and he did. She asked him to leave and he didn't. "Why did you come as Norton? Isn't he a bumbling ne'er-do-well?" "Yeah, he is," Cal answered. "But he's *really trying*." She paused—laughs from the throat—laughs from the belly—he kisses her, tongues her, lifts up her purple flared Jane-skirt, she says No and brings it down. She lets him kiss her, they grind, she slips his belt open, unbuttons slacks, there it goes—space-age Jetsons lands in kitchen-sink Honeymooners in modern renovated suburbia. Ass sliding on sink. Head trembling against mirror. "Shh!" Porkpie hat drops to floor. Faucet runs. Lather and rinse....

He despised his wife who was chronically depressed. And *resentful* of his good moods. They had fun. Neither Cal nor Mary was serious concerning a way out, so he went in to her, now and then, over a year. Jill knew and respected her choice. Sneaking around, Mary and Cal got tired. They had one last go in a bathroom at a holiday party synched to their initial night.

"Let's go out with a bang," she told him. "Merry Christmas Cal," holding mistletoe above his head, undoing his pants and guiding him. Repeat... Cal was game for anything.

Seeking an ending all she finds is a yet again beginning. She can't say why she stopped taking it a psychoanalyst might say she actually wanted a baby or a pregnancy to trigger an end to her marriage she couldn't remember when she stopped she felt better without them more like herself and Dan wasn't fucking her anyway he started to sleep in the other room when they were cold and saying no words. It must have been a night when she needed it, went to his room, and he woke to her stiff in seconds. That was the night.

She'll go in one afternoon when he's crossing a time zone. It would be taken from her so nothing could tear their asunder apart after she walks out the door and tries to leave a house that's not in flames. She's the one in flames. She longs to move through the door she's filled with what he put in her that night and she'll go there one afternoon lie down have them take it final remnant of a strange union. Maybe it'll come out in the bathroom and she won't one night Tobias was vomiting and she sat on the floor in the bathroom he looked up at her dripping puke said "Mom— why is it so hard?" She had no answer for him. She wiped his face.

All she asked was a good orgasm why did she forget why now when all she wanted was to walk away lift off into her own – maybe it was secretly to tarry there another thing growing inside her so she could name it watch it search for itself in the shape of her breasts the smell of her hair the shift of her eyes. Maybe she desired only to burst open again a flower with sudden light and a voice and a reason push out in the world a running repository of possibility.

She neglects to go in the days passed and it grew she told him he was ecstatic took her to a beautiful warm place to celebrate. She sought a mirror but couldn't find one and gave up. She let it grow one day found a name and wrote it down. She tells Toby it gets easier the puking stops and it's all going to be okay. Puts him to bed, looks out the windows—feels ashamed. The moon there above. She lied to him. She was tired. She needed more time now to prepare. For what – she didn't know.

Paul wrote her after settling in Worthington. Ten minutes from her. Sent a card. A white horse on the front running—leaping.

"Mary, for me omnipresent, one drop of the sea all nourishing, bitter in beautiful truth, beloved for who you are and what you will be."

He always had a surprise.

XVIII

Triads

I

There's a knock, at first he thinks it's Jill and his heart jumps, he throws on the t-shirt and sweatpants he's changing into. Hides the sweaty things behind the bedroom door. Peeps into the bathroom mirror, wets his hair. The best he can do...

"Oh, Mary, hey."

"Hey yourself. May I come in, Paul?"

"Of course, sorry."

"Ah, return of the disordered poet." She steps over some books.

"Yeah, it's gotten away from me again—but I'll reconquer it."

"I can help—if you like?"

"No, no, it's not as bad as it looks. You sit, I'll make tea. Green, okay?"

"Fine."

"Did you watch the vid I sent you a couple days ago?"

"Which one?

"Sara Cunial, the Italian congresswoman speaking on the congress floor -denouncing the shutdowns, the lies about mortalities, the crimes of Bill Gates—"

"I haven't watched it yet."

"It's inspiring."

"I could use inspiration. Where were you? I stopped by earlier."

"You did?"

The kettle whistles.

Mary's in a long black skirt, a red blouse. Paul notes her knee-length boots. He hands her the tea. He can smell her, some cinnamon thing.

"I took a walk at the County park. You know those horse trails?"

"Oh, yeah. You're there often?"

"Lately I seem to be. I go where nature is—the most real thing now."

"M-hm." She blows on the steamy cup— "And I?"

"Meaning? Where you should go?"

"No. Am I real?"

"Yes. The most real th—"

"I am... I was wondering." She strolls the room, picking up things, hangs his jacket on a hook over hers, crosses to the bookshelf. She plucks a volume out—"Mina Loy. I've been wanting to read this poet. Her poems are very—erotic. Are they not—Paul?"

"True, they are. Borrow it."

She sits, the book in her lap, on the couch. Her skirt goes above her knees. "You see, Paul, I'm a mother, I'm a cook, now I'm a maid and a teacher. My role has vastly expanded. But my pay hasn't."

"Dan's not helping you?"

"He's been charitable to grant me one day free per week. Which I usually of course... spend at home."

"Why not go somewhere?"

" 'Cause I'm waiting dodo-head. For my husband. But my husband—speaking of maids—is I'm quite sure boffing the maid who cleans his hotel room slash office."

"You serious?"

"Quite. Mina would probably write a poem describing such a scenario—" she flips the pages. "I've seen them together. They're either doing it or about to be."

"That's—I'm sorry." He pulls a chair near the couch.

"It's alright. It's not our first go round the hotel room bend. I'm not that bothered by it. She's deaf by the way. Maybe he prefers not being heard—or answered." She laughs at her witticism. Paul smiles, cautiously.

"And you, Paul? Is it just books for you—or have you found a maid also?"

Has Jill told her? They stare at each other a long moment. Everything about her is gorgeous.

"Me and Jill... we kinda got together, Mare. She told you?"

"Kinda got together. Is that like my husband is 'kinda' banging his deaf maid in a hotel room while I do fractions and spelling tests in the middle of the day?"

"You're upset we—?"

"And no she didn't tell me. I *knew*. Okay. I knew you were doing it. My best friends who kept their thing a secret from me."

"Come on, it wasn't a secr—"

"For weeks I had a – strong suspicion. I hardly heard from either of you."

"Well you admit you've been—"

"When I couldn't deny it anymore, I went to her."

"And?"

"She was nervous. Coy. 'Yeah, we kinda,' same bullshit 'kinda' and 'sorta' thing. Tell me, I said. 'It just happened.' 'I haven't been hiding it, Mary,' she says. Really? Why haven't you told me? Why wouldn't you? 'Don't press me like this.' I wasn't pressing her. Then she actually says, 'I was afraid to tell you. I didn't want to hurt you.' No—'disappoint' was the word she used. My best friends are sleeping together, I told her, and I feel – maybe I'm wrong – that I shouldn't be kept in the dark."

He and Jill had discussed it and arrived at no agreement on revealing it to Mary.

"Someone should have told you, Mare. It wasn't—"

"Someone? How about, um—you. Does that ring a bell? You, Jill, you... let's see, who else?"

"I thought Jill would have told you. I didn't know if it was...my place to tell you."

"A month goes by—not a word from either of you. You didn't think I'd care to—"

"It's not a month—"

"Whatever it is. It feels crappy to be in the dark when the people you most care about...start fucking and leave you ou—not leave—you know what I mean. Why, Paul?"

"I'm sorry. It wasn't intentional. Maybe we—weren't sure how you'd..."

"What? React? To my closest friends hiding their affair from me?"

"No, not that—to our – being together."

"Oh, please. What am I, three years old? That's why you're hiding this from me?"

"I'm not hiding it."

"Tell me then – if you and she were not hiding it – why do I feel betrayed?"

"*Betrayed*?" His mind hits pause. "I'm gonna get a beer."

He takes two out, snaps the tops. She's gone, in the bathroom. Minutes go by. Sound of water. She comes out, damp, hair hanging down her back. She grabs the beer and passes him.

"Why do you feel betrayed?"

"You became lovers and you hid it from me."

He understands her being upset for concealing it. Why the betrayal?

"Look Mary, I—"

"You were right."

"About what?"

"She said 'I wasn't sure how you'd react—I know how much you—' "

She lets it hang in the air between them.

"Finish it."

" 'Love him.' Okay? She said she was hesitant because she knows – how much I love you." Paul is mesmerized. Mary goes to the table, sets the beer. "Forget it. I don't know why I came. Just forget it, we're all—adults, so—" She takes her jacket down, hugs it to her chest.

"Wait, Mare. Can you sit a minute?" She shrugs, flops on the couch.

"How did you—respond to her when—"

"That's when I left."

"I didn't want to keep anything from you. Or hurt you. You encouraged me to pursue—"

"I did. Yeah..."

"Mary, try to understand. I'm – I'm not sure if I did wrong or – . You know how I feel..."

"Do I?" She trains her gaze directly at him. Her denuding profile.

"Don't you?" She doesn't stir. "You're my oldest—my dearest —"

"Yeah. I get it Paul. Your friend. Your pal. Your buddy."

It's quite dark now in the room. One floor lamp on.

"No, that's not—come on, you know what I—"

"Do I?"

He's never seen that look on her towards him. Her face is still beautiful but—disappointed. He's in a cul-de-sac.

"Let me ask you something. Why didn't we make love that night—when I was here," she touches the sofa, sweeps out into the room.

"That night..."

"When I was *here*. When we talked about—everything."

"The planetarium?"

"Yes, the planetarium... and everything." They peer in front of them at the floor where they'd merged.

"Why didn't we make love?"

"Yes."

"*Didn't* we make love that night?"

"What! What are you—"

"To me, what happened between us was beyond 'making love.' I felt no distance between us."

She puts her hand on his. "I understand, Paul. We were closer than we've ever been. I'm wondering why...it didn't go to its logical conclusion. Why did we stop?"

He doesn't think they 'stopped.'

"That's what it was. What the moment was..."

"I don't mean to pressure you. I—"

"What?"

"I—nothing." She sighs, shifts her legs out in front. His focus travels from the silver boots—to her hazel eyes. "Tell me this—in all the years—you never wanted me?"

"It was always—you were dating someone or I was—our relationship became..."

"Yeah, drug buddies."

"Come on, not only drugs... and not 'buddies' ...soulmates is what I'd say."

"Yeah. I don't get why we never—"

"You may have forgotten – we did try once."

"We did?"

"Yeah." He laughs, half bitterly. "You really forgot, didn't you? End of senior year. We were at your house, everyone was out. We'd come from some all night festivities... we woke up and... went at it. Tried to. I couldn't do it. I was impotent." She gapes at him. "You have no recollection?"

"I...really don't. I must have shut it out or—"

"I wish I had."

"We never tried again."

"No."

"Was it because—"

"No... It didn't bother me. *That* much."

"I'm sorry, Paul."

"Mary, it was – thirty something years ago."

"I wish we'd – tried again."

'Tried.' Now she won't forget it.

"We were usually—seeing other people. You always had a steady thing."

"And you always messed around. You didn't care whom with, did you?" She swings a leg up on the couch.

"Did I care? Yes and no. We were kids. They were your friends also. We enjoyed each other's company."

"But not...me."

"You were dating *other people*—exclusively. It was your m.o. That guy Adam? A year older? Then Don what's his—"

"Sorenson. Donnie."

"There you go. Donnie. Why are we—"

"Rehashing the past?"

"I never think about those things."

"About me?"

"I don't have to. You're in my life."

"Just not like that. You've never thought of me as a woman.

"I've always thought of you as – a woman."

"Someone to desire."

She's pinning him to the wall.

"You've been married for what, twenty years?"

"I've had affairs, Paul."

"You haven't told me your... history." He'd strongly suspected. "All I knew is—you're married. And you never..."

"What?"

"Never...made it clear that..."

"How much clearer could I make it?"

"I'm dense then."

"Have I ever said no to you? Have I ever not been there for you?"

"No. Of course not. I've become used to who we are to each other. Who we've been."

"You can't envision me as a lover."

She's breaking me down. She's cracking something open in me. Jill is my aim now. Mary is in a soul place. Comfort. Connection. Now she and her full expressive mouth her flowing hair her red shirt that hides the bosomy skin within arm's reach. That skirt. Her thighs...sticking out. Why *didn't he*... Timing. Not only... What's the difference, she's my best friend on the whole planet. Sitting there now—*bursting* out at me three feet away—she wants me. Now. Not thirty years ago.

"Mary, you're a beautif—you're very beautiful. You're fasc – a fascinating – woman. I'm... Didn't you intend for me and Jill to—"

"Yes. I did. Can't I feel two ways? Or three?"

She checkmates him.

"Jill and I..."

"She knows, Paul. I told her I want you."

"You said that—to her?"

"Two days ago."

"And she—"

" 'I know,' she said. 'There's nothing I can do about it.' "

Paul stands and goes to the refrigerator for a beer, pops it, swigs. Mary follows him, reaches for the bottle, tips it to her throat. She's innocent and tainted. That's her allure. She's making no sense to him. All he knows is he can smell her, her raw attitude has a scent, it always did – something untold, green, straight, brown, bending. A forest. A fire. She's dangerous. He'll back away slowly.

"Do you want me to go?"

"Yeah," he says, startled, a pounding inside him saying *No.*

She steps towards the door. She turns, locks into Paul like she never looked at a person.

"What?" He's parched. "What's that *look*?" Waiting. Staring. "You gonna say something?"

She breaks, faces the window. She's utterly beautiful, a Greek statue. Carved out of cool shadows. Clothed yet already naked in front of him. She drops the coat and lifts her hands to him.

"Paul?"

"Yes?"

"If you don't make love to me tonight I... I don't know what I'm going to do." Her hands come down.

"Why don't we – talk in there." He means the bedroom.

She goes up against him—a child without decorum. Her breath is on his chin, in his nose, she kisses him once and whispers – "Let's go."

She's naked to her panties in ten seconds. He's in undershirt and briefs. She removes the shirt crushes her breasts to his chest. "Paul. That feels good, baby."

"Listen."

"What?"

"If you're used to your lovers rock-hard immediately—" She shushes him, lays one of his hands on her breasts the other on her back. Listens to his heart. Kisses him over and over, she's dominating and surrendering, he's forgetting everything. "I think you like it," taking down his shorts, "I really think you do, Paul."

They fall.

"You're the diver, aren't you? Isn't that who you are? Go ahead—deep as you want."

"Mary. Mary."

"Mm?"

"It's late. Should you go?"

"I texted him. I'm staying at a friend's."

Lying next to each other in the dark. She wipes herself, she wipes him—his face, chest, belly. She craves to kiss and they kiss and a question rises in his body but she caresses it away and it's them there as kids again in the park at dusk running over and under objects throwing balls dodging broken branches and her kisses take them through autumns of developing wind which shudders stops and shakes you unawares gasping in sudden late light. Takes them through and around winters where sunshine deceives the eye and air encoats the body with familiar shocking chill and then laughter as the liquid steamily enters the mouth two young faces giggling, again. His kisses are summer and promises of music and lassitude and attitude and dropped pretenses in quiet humid-heavy evenings of beer bottles and moth-light and then spring with the release of all of it and memory too is a song that fades...pure sensation becomes awareness... Oh Paul, she says eight years old waiting for him to throw the ball because it's getting late....

"Oh, Paul..."

He feels a sadness in her hands and lips.

"Mm."

"Paul... Why weren't we together..."

"Mm..."

"Why didn't we have babies... together..."

Her breath on him in the dark she puts their question. He asks the dark and the light – can't hear an answer. All he can do is meld with her.

"They'd be miracle children... Wonders..."

He won't look at them in a field somewhere calling out their names.

"I know, Mary."

"Oh, Paul." She makes night morning in lieu of legacies unknown. She makes magic in the absence of who they were and why they become.

In the morning showered wet hair she embraces him: "I love you." Switches to his other ear—"Promise me not to—break—*her*—from me." He doesn't understand the request. But he nods. And she's gone.

∎

I need to see you. He texts and calls her. She doesn't answer. One morning she asks him to come to her at noon.

"Sorry I'm empty-handed Jill, you need a genie now to conjure up a bagel and—" she goes back into the house, barely a hello.

She pours him a cup of coffee, sits at the kitchen table, flips open a women's magazine.

"How are you, Paul," with indifference.

"I've missed you. You didn't return my messages."

"Didn't I?"

"Well—." He sits across from her. "What's happening?"

"I got fired." She's looking at the drug advertisements.

"Really?"

"Or laid off. Take your pick."

"When?"

"Two days ago. On Zoom. Isn't that nice? Well hey, it's a pandemic. Anything goes."

"I'm sorry, Jill. I wish you'd let me know."

"I thought you'd be busy."

"Why?" She riffles pages. "Have you applied—"

"Unemployment? Done."

"Did they give a—"

"Slowed way down. They may rehire when this thing..."

"It might start to diminish. June, July."

Now she looks up. "You really believe that, Paul?"

He smiles and stretches to touch her. "Flattening the curve and all..."

She begins to form a smile to match his. She gently pulls away for more coffee. "It wasn't just me—there were six others."

"Is it – a comfort?"

"No. I'm sad for them. My friend Sandy, she's been supporting two kids on her job."

He gets up, when she turns he leans down to take her in for a hug. "This will be the start of something better." She lets him comfort her. "I missed you. Why didn't you reach—"

"What about you? How've you been?"

"Plandemic research. Writing. Hiking."

"Uh-huh. Any visitors?"

"Not really, besides the landlord for the rent."

"Let's sit down."

She pushes a plate of cookies to him.

"Mm. Did you ma—"

"Target. Aisle twenty-seven."

"Good memory," spewing crumbs of dough and fudge.

"Anything to tell me?" He stops chewing.

Here it is. She suspects—never wants to see me again. She's scrutinizing him with a disarming patience.

"Jill, I need to... I have to tell you—"

"I knew it." She clamps shut the magazine. Sits back. Glowers.

"You did?"

"When?" She bites her lips.

"A few days ago."

"So fucking predictable."

"Jill. I don't want this to ruin things between us."

"Hm." Her mouth is pursed, her arms crossed, he's off balance.

"I mean it. I—Jill, this wasn't planned."

"Oh, not by you!"

"I had no idea it would—happen."

"No, no of course you didn't, Paul. In a way—and this is what's lovable about you—you are *so* clueless." Stings him. "It *had*—" she bangs on the magazine— "to happen didn't it.

Mary had to have Paul didn't she and Mary and Paul had to take that final plunge since for – whatever reason they never fucked – in thirty or whatever years." He'd never seen her angry. "So this had to happen." He's immobile. "Had to." Now her eyes show wetness. "The had to only came of course after Mary found out Jill and Paul have been fucking themselves. Not themselves—you know what I— suddenly Mary had to make sure she stakes her 'claim' – she uses finger quotes – "on 'her' Paul – " now the tears come down and the words surging out coldly. "She had to run to take you as if I could ever take Paul away from 'his' Mary – like it's some world-quaking thing she has to run to seduce you – for what – " Jill's standing, wiping the counter – "to prove that you love her?" She stops, twining the cloth around her wrist. "A small bit of happiness comes and...why does it..."

"What, Jill?"

"Get...crushed. Like a can in the street."

"Jill, listen to me," going to her. "I know you probably don't feel as I do, you don't seem to. Anyway – I'm in love with you." She whirls to him. "What happened isn't fair—not to you, not really to me, either. What I have with her is different from what I could have with you." She slips by, opens the side door, light streams in. "I didn't think it was possible between us. I've opened up to who you are. And I want more."

She says simply, "It's not over. Is it."

"Jill, I don't see it lasting. It can't."

She takes it in. He watches her carefully. Any wrong move will bust it between them. Red hair messy no makeup pastel green blouse—she's fragilely beautiful to him in the light of early afternoon.

"I saw it coming. She's wanted it for years, Paul."

"Apparently I'm blind."

"I'm almost—it's crazy—glad for her. She's like that—" snaps her fingers— "spins you... Hard to withstand. Trust me, I *know*." Eye-pinning him as she finishes.

"Did you – and her—?"

A hundred pages of thoughts and feelings in flight through her mind—in six seconds. "No...not... no. I should be angry...er."

"You're not?"

"I'm a lot of things." He approaches, she puts up her hand, quietly says—

"Don't let her...drift. Away from me."

He can't help bursting out in laughter. "That's the second time I'm hearing that—in three days."

She smiles, "Do you feel left out, Paul?"

"I'm not sure—what I feel."

She tiptoes for a kiss on his lips.

"Did you feel it?"

"A little—try again." She tongue teases him. "Okay, I promise—if it's in my power."

"Now what?"

He grins.

"No. Not now."

"Well, then... back to the pandemic." He tickles her.

"Stop it, you! You're in your element, aren't you? All your 'research'."

"I don't know abou—"

"Something in all this—stop!—gets you going—creatively."

"You get me going."

"Seriously. You're a detective in a way. Always sniffing around."

"Getting laid—off—sharpens your wits."

"I'm gonna give you a punch. First I'll give you lunch—then you can do— whatever you do, Paul. Knock on doors...look into windows..."

If she asks me to, I'll stay. If she even hints.

She's slicing a tomato... Mashing tuna. "Okay, Jill. Feed me."

III

She calls him the night before. "Pack a change of clothes and your toothbrush. Ten a.m. Be ready."

She's there. He's not ready. She waits, drinking her coffee. "I have coffee for you." He's searching for a notebook. He forgets his toothbrush.

They're on the road entering the expressway eastbound. Mary at the wheel of her cream-colored RAV4. Paul eyes half-shut, surrendering to her inscrutable ways.

Above the expressway a sign blinks:

STAY HOME   STOP THE SPREAD SAVE LIVES

"You see that, Mare?" "Yeah, I saw it. Fuck them and the curve they rode in on." Paul smirks. It's not funny. The sun on her face, tired, softly smiling. "Hey..." "What?" "You're a real beauty." Glances to him, she flushes—changes lanes. Morrison on the stereo singing about changelings and the Western dream and cold girls in darkened rooms. Hills filled with fire.

"The Doors are perfect for this time," Paul observes. "This strange pseudo-apocalyptic time."

"Yes!" She taps the steering wheel in time to L'America. "I took a trip..."

Daniel shaves in his hotel suite bathroom. She leaves him little things, Caroline – candies, mints, soaps. Lotion. After he leaves she goes in and makes the place smell sweet. He's preparing a surprise and can't wait to tell her. They have to be careful for a half hour in the afternoons. She's nervous her boss will come looking for her—and did one day. Knocked on Daniel's door when they were in bed. Her cart was outside. He cordially told the man, standing the prescribed six feet distance away—yes, he'd seen the maid, "Caroline, correct?—she mentioned she'd be back in a short while." He points to the far end of the hallway as the direction she'd gone. The manager begs pardon for disturbing him, babbles about a room requiring immediate attention. "Of course," Daniel assents. "Oh, and sir," he stops him, "Caroline does excellent work. My room is very well taken care of." "I'm glad you're pleased with the service, sir. Good day."

Caroline is already dressed. He signals her "be calm," tells her which way the manager went. "Don't worry, he wants a room cleaned. Relax and push the cart down the hall." She's rushing. "Oh, I told him how great—" he signs, palms elevated pushing outward—"you are at your job." She laughs, looking up at him as she zips her dress. He finishes the zipping.

The manager suspected nothing. She was nervous, on the lookout since then. She started bringing her cart into his room. By 2:00 he hears her vacuum downstairs and his heart leaps as he's drafting a document on a case between an energy company and the Malaysian government. He hits "Save."

She's bending over, humming. He flips the door stopper and steps out. There are cameras in the courtyard, he's discreet. He signs "Good afternoon," she signs "Hello, handsome." "I have good news for you," he mouths. Oh? her eyes ask.

"Please drop off towels when you get a chance? Thank you."
He walks into his room, closing the blinds. She knocks, he
tosses the things she's brought, covering her in hands,
mouth, breath. In a moment they're on the bed—

"I'm going to have a *whole day and night* free tomorrow."

"I'm off tomorrow, Danel..."

"I know. Could I come to you? Meet your daughter?"

"Oh... And your..." she signs 'wife,' clapping one hand
over the other, and speaks, "She's—"

"Gone. A couple days. I'd really like to meet Tatiana."

"Me too, Dan. We'll... we'll figur it out." She rises, he
enfolds her. Releases. She goes. He lies on the bed. The world
moving on another plane he can sense but no longer engage
directly.

This is travel—being where you are—*right here*. The
ceiling above him recedes.

Paul wakes when they're on a two lane road.

"You don't know where we are, do you?"

He squints sleepily. "No, do you?"

"I'm taking you to the end, Paul. The end of the night.
The end of the island. Beyond, it's sailors and dolphins."

"Who's watching the dolphins."

She stops at a small market and pops out. Returns with
beer, wine and snacks.

"Is that our meal plan you've got, Mare?"

"All children get thirsty. Forgot cups—no, no need."

She pulls up to a building, tells him to wait.

"I'll check us in."

She wasn't kidding—it wasn't far from island's end. On
the ocean. A breezy May day, warming. People exit and enter
the hotel, a few wearing masks. Here we go. A tide coming
in. Only the beginning. Paul gets a shiver.

"All set." She parks on the side of the building. They remove their bags. Mary slides the magnetic-striped card in the side door and they go towards the elevator.

"It's clean and comfortable enough. I found out it wasn't crowded."

"How crowded is it?"

"They said half full. Escapees from the city..."

The elevator dings and opens... Paul looks at Mary picking up her things— *What am I doing here...* He presses the open button. She smiles, passes him. He hesitates—he could let go and disappear. Hitchhike back or keep going. A couple enters, says "Two, please." He enters. Mary presses the buttons.

It's a big room, kitchenette, desk, armchairs. King bed. Balcony. "Expensive..." he mumbles.

"Not compared to the famous place down the road."

They put their things down, the drinks into the refrigerator. The bed is piled with thick pillows and a golden fresh-looking bedspread. The room is in blues and light greys— murmuring, "Relax... chill out..."

Paul tests the television remote. "Two White House staff members have tested positive for Covid-19. The global total of cases has reached four million." He switches it off.

"Thank you," Mary sighs, taking clothes out of her bag, folding them into the dresser. Paul looks at his duffel bag, same one he's had for—twenty years? He left his laptop home. "Paul, I'm gonna—I'll be right back and we'll—how 'bout a walk on the beach?" She's already in the bathroom, he can hear the fan. "Yeah, that's..." "Then we'll get lunch... Check out the balcony."

He takes a beer from the fridge, pops the cap. Raises the blinds. The day is hazy. Mary comes out, an iridescent blue dress casually draped around her.

"Lovely," Paul slants his bottle. "Suits you well."

"Yes, much better. Thanks. Starting without me?"

"No, I...yeah, I guess so."

"Would you like to walk? We don't have to, we can relax." She joins him near the windows, takes his beer.

"Sure. We can do that."

"Which one?" Mary chuckles, gulps some Becks.

"Oh uh...walk?"

"What's up, Paul? Are you doing okay?"

"Yeah, I'm good. Just tired is all."

"I hoped you'd rest here."

"It'd be nice."

"You're chewing over something. Is it Jill?"

"No." He swallows the beer. His brain tingles. "It's me. I was 'chewing over' myself."

"Tell me." She sits near him on the side of the bed.

He looks out to the Atlantic Ocean. He hears it faintly. "Same old thing. It's—absurd. I don't know where my life is going. I'm gonna be fifty-three in a few months. My life has gone by and I missed it. I took notes maybe but...I can't find them."

"Paul, that's not—true and—"

"I have no home, no family, no money, no recognition. No nothing."

"No, you have—"

"I have my work? My writing?"

"I was going to say you have me!"

"Do I have you?"

"Of course you—"

"I don't, though. This will be great, this one or two days together. Then you go back to your family. I go to whatever...I have. Let's cast illusions aside. That's the one thing I've depended on you for. You haven't let me down."

"Alright, Paul. I won't let you down."

"I know."

She can hear it now, the ocean.

"Talk to me?"

"Nothing... Lost as ever. I look to ground myself in something and as usual—it feels—like quicksand, eventually. I've spent what, nine, ten weeks in the underbelly of probing this covid thing, gathering information, listening, watching, digging, connecting dots, day, night, trying to figure out what's really going on."

"And it is amazing. The way you gather it, shape it into your own interpretation. Your own vision."

"Yes, but what for? Where is my own life in this? What fruit do I bear from it? Am I helping anybody from all this immersing? Am I helping myself? Or is it more of the same slog through words, images, on and on, for what, I can't remember." She's uncertain how to speak, to comfort. He glances at the silent TV, constantly covid-ready. He imagines it as a ticker on a building unspooling without end.

"I'm out of ideas, babe. I can see the picture and know what it says – how to tell others I have no idea. I don't have the language."

"You'll find a way. You'll find a form to express what you've seen and gathered."

"Before this started I was...floundering. Finally I had some time and I—*knew* I was squandering it."

"No, Paul, you were searching for the inspiration that would have found you – had this thing not—collided with all of us."

"My god..."

"What?"

"I think I'm lost *now*. If you weren't in my life I'd be... dead in a gutter. Drunk in a cheap motel. Or worse, working in a fucking bank."

They laugh, scraping the ice inside them.

"You don't realize what you have. That's your only real liability."

"You're my most precious asset. That I know."

"Second-most. You're the primary—you, for yourself."

They drink the beer. Tally up feelings and thoughts in silence. The ocean touches the end of the island where they met.

"Mary, whatever I...do or don't do—our lives will not be the same. Their plan is our lives never going back to before the tea party began, as you say, in March."

"I can feel it. Pushing us to some brave new world of distances – spaces between us. Fear climbing into every aspect of our lives. I don't know what to tell the kids. Especially Jessica. She won't talk much to me but she can't hide a thing from me, I can practically read her soul. She's terrified of what's coming."

"They're wearing masks now. I saw some here—and at East Nook Beach last week."

"Walking around with masks?"

He crawls against the headboard. "Will it matter—if almost everyone accepts all of it—as their new reality? I do all this research, gather information. I told you, few are interested. Others aligned with us are scattered—online, the chat forums. We're all preaching to the choir."

"Paul, you're a searcher. You're obsessed with truth."

"Which truth? And how obtained? Truth can be its own trap. The *search* for truth. Is it the truth I crave—or—what I get hunting for it? Do you follow me?"

"Yes. Go on." She leans next to him.

"Eighteen, nineteen years ago I didn't give a shit about computers. I had my books, notebooks, I was afraid to get involved in the whole machine world. My mother kept telling me, 'Paul, you *have to learn*, it's the future. You'll be left behind.' So I did. I had no idea how seductive the internet would be. I discovered it. Fell down its hole. Not the porn—a problem at times—the real issue is the information itself. Sometimes it's hard to shut down. To get off the freakin' thing. It clings to you. Strangely magnetic. One more site...one more video. They say the Internet will develop its own self...awareness? What if it already has? Is that what I'm feeling? This AI pseudo-consciousness?"

"Creepy. And familiar. The...hanging on. Like it's 'never enough.' I couldn't put that into words. Wow..."

"It's endless, Mary. You never really get anywhere, though you think you have. Some of it is valuable. You think you'll create something with what you learn or collect... yet it's just... more. Is that what this is – another addiction? An addiction for losers."

He moves—

"Wait." She brushes a hand through his hair.

"You are the farthest thing from a loser. You're a seeker. You follow trails...for gold to bring back from journeys. You go overboard, yes. Then you collect yourself, attain the balance necessary...for creativity."

"I wish I had it. Balance must be the key."

"That desire alone will create it. I see you lessening the need for those...ways of information. Others will open for you."

He goes to the sink, splashes water on his face and neck. Returns, drops on the carpet.

"Mare—it's a mystery—you always make me feel better."

She sits across from him.

"Paul, this 'trap of information' as you call it—is still fairly new. *No one* knows how to wrestle it. Or dance with it. The big It. You're a pioneer. You've looked in the many rooms. You've explored the alternate views, the spaces. You've tracked what power—and *deception*—have done, are doing—"she points outward—"on the planet. I said you're a beacon. You must believe me. Before we leave here."

He embraces her. "You restore me, Mare. You re-make me."

"And you astonish me."

"Why does it seem – it's all slipping away from me?"

"It's slipping away from all of us. There's no gauge, no measure, Paul. No finish line. Who says we should hold on? It's all in here," she palms his heart. "Let's walk now. Move the energy."

"Good. Breathe the ocean."

He arrives at eleven a.m. She has the upstairs of a house fifteen minutes from Lions Pride Inn. Mary had left early. He made breakfast for the kids, of course Jessica was sulking because she had to stay around for Tobias. She didn't mind really, Mary had given her lots of leeway and little hassle since this thing began, let her have friends visit. Daniel left Jessie cash, told her to order in lunch and dinner. Toby approved. They both had schoolwork, online classes. "I'll help you tomorrow with anything you don't get," he told Toby. "Call me if anything—if you need me." He was making an effort, devoting one day a week to him—and Jessie, if she cared to spend time. He told them in the evening there would be overseas video calls at his office. "You mean your 'hotel suite,' Dad?" Jessie archly implies—something. "My office. For the moment." "Uh-huh..." "It's quiet, I can work unimpeded. But you knew that already, my dear Jess." He poke-tickles her, she giggles, slapping his arm. "Freak!" she calls him. He *is* a freak, kind of, ignoring the mirror in the foyer, exiting. Lying for love is still lying—does she see through him? Lying and longing to reconnect with them.

He texts her when he's downstairs. Waits with the briefcase she'd instructed him to carry. Then she's descending, her open smile, blonde hair swirling, in a pretty scarlet dress. "Hello," they mouth and sign, "Good morning," and Dan signs – "You – look – lovely," running his hand in front of his face and exploding it out, as a chef does for an exquisite flavor. He'd practiced it. "Thank you, Danel," bringing her hand to her mouth and downward. He follows her upstairs.

In her small kitchen she pours him a glass of lemonade. The living room had a beige-colored couch, love seat, comfortable chairs. The walls were light blue. The kitchen area cheerful pink. "So," he says, making sure she can read him—"when do I get to meet Tani?"

"Dan – I thought it ould be better if – not today. My motha picked her up – little while ago."

"Oh… That's…okay." He had brought the briefcase to pose as a lawyer to justify his presence when Grandma comes. He hasn't asked her why they had to pretend—was it covid? Or his marital status?

"Danel, don' be…disppoin'ed." She signs the word, he fixates on the motion, her index finger darting from her belly to her chin—

"No, no, I'm not disappointed," he apes her motions. "I'll meet her another time." He is, actually. He really looked forward to meeting Caroline's child. "Guess I don't need this?" he raps the case, and they laugh.

"Maybe you need this" – placing his hand on her breast. "Oh. Yes."

"We have time, Danel?"
"All day and night, Caroline."
She walks to the couch, sits. Beckons him.

The beach at the end of the island wasn't crowded but people were out enjoying a pause in their pandemic. Thirty percent, or so, had masks on.
"Man, it's freaky," Mary mutters, unfastening her sandals. "Paul, take your sneakers off, the sand is soft." He does, she leads along the shore.
"At least the children aren't wearing them."
"I'm not ready for that."
"I saw them with masks on last week."
Paul doesn't catch it— Mary halts—whips around—
"No—"
"What?"
Now he sees.
Stepping from the road a family all masked. Small children among them.
"No!" she yells, stamping her foot, spraying sand, raising heads.
"Mare!"
"Shit... Shit," she says, calmer, kicking sand.
"Hey, c'mon now." He pats her back.
"That was a sucker punch. To the gut."
"Yes, it's – quite a sight."
"Is this the 'new normal'? Children in masks? Toby? Jessie? In *schools*? And people everywhere—in fucking masks?"
Paul, Mary, the ocean. Voices of gulls, voices of people, masked, un-masked, fly above, fade.
"Come on let's walk," he dispels. They do, the white bubbles rushing in, flecking on their feet, rushing out.
"It's cool."

"Yeah, and the breeze ain't so bad either, eh?" He gets a smile out of her.

"Sorry 'bout that. It was... whoa. To see it on a beach is a bit of a shock."

"I know, it was for me too," Paul consoles. "It's going to be hairy for a while. The election coming up, the maniacs pushing those vaccines."

"I was reading there are at least a dozen in development."

"They can't wait to start jabbing us with their gene therapy. Who knows what'll be in it."

"Now Trump is pushing it with his Operation Warp Speed. They want to roll this out—a *new vaccine*—in six months!"

"Donald," Paul mock-yells out to sea—"listen to Bobby Kennedy, Jr. You should have listened to him befooooore...." They make a way to humor.

"Let's sit...there," she points. Mary takes a sheet from her bag, they spread it, jamming shoes on the corners, flop down. She produces a bottle of Chardonnay and plucks out the cork.

"I admire your style Mary Wellner... called just prior to Paul Wilmer in homeroom."

"And I yours Mr. Wilmer, who tugged at my hair and..." she pours into the hotel cups, "...passed me dirty notes."

"Hm... Are you sure it was me?"

They drink.

He takes her to the famous beach on the south shore of the island. It's a windy day. Caroline signs-speaks to Daniel, "Stwange to see people—wearing masks." "Very strange," he agrees, carrying Caroline's basket. They walk down onto the sand, choose a spot where they can lay their blanket. Daniel digs his shoes into the corners. Caroline unwraps the sandwiches she made and opens containers with coleslaw and potato salad. "Hope you like these Dan—turkey, Swiss cheese... mustard and ketchup in here."

"You thought of everything, didn't you."

Her eyes are bluer. She's different—absent her maid's uniform and cart—sensuous, a whole woman, not a 'working woman.' She slides her hand under his pants cuff, tickling skin and hair on his calf. He opens mini bottles of rosé.

"Mm, terrific," he says between bites of rye and turkey.

"Tell me, Dan," meeting his eyes. "Why...me? Us?"

He tastes the wine, surveys the beach and the ocean. Gulls, strolling people, ships on the horizon. It's hard for him to believe a pandemic's happening—that his boss might check out at any time.

"Mary and I were never an ideal match. She's a unique person. I respect her. We've been married now... twenty years. I told you I travel often. I'm ending that. It caused a lot of damage to the relationship. Which already had been...*hadn't* been real great." She nods, reading him. "She's never been – " he wavers – "very happy. With me, our marriage, with herself, I think. We've had affairs, come back to each other...never really sorted much out. Now I don't know what we are to each other. And when *we* met," his face relaxes, "I started to have this... It's hard to explain, but I'll try," making the sign that resembles revving a motorcycle. "Whenever I see you—everything is new again. I can be renewed."

"Reawy, Danel?"

"Really, Caroline. Even my relationships with my kids are promising. For the first time in so long I can...start over. There's an open road ahead of me."

It's rare someone says the words you've dreamed of hearing.

"Mare, I think about all the people in apartments in the cities, no nature around them, in small rooms, buildings, concrete—how are they dealing with all of this?"

"Absolutely. There's been a steep increase in suicides."

"Depression, booze, drugs..."

"Lost jobs...businesses. Income."

"We're lucky to be close to nature."

"I pray for them."

"Pray for all of us." He smiles. He's not joking.

The gulls are scrounging the garbage cans. Half the wine is gone. The sun is dropping.

"Are you hungry, my dear?"

"These snack bars help..."

"We'll go soon. Let's lie down a bit."

They breathe in the end-of-island breeze and exhale a restful relief. From out of silence Mary speaks, eyes closed.

"When I met Daniel I was – pretty lost. I had turned thirty, working a blah job, staying out late. I had never met anyone so interested in *me*. So passionate, focused, on me. It was intoxicating."

"Natural high."

"He was this young guy, ambitious, talented, funny and – he made it no secret he wanted me—in every way. It became very hard to evade his..."

"Charms?"

"Relentless charms. It felt completely – inexplicably – inevitable to me, this was the man, the *person*, I had to spend my life with."

"He put a spell on you?"

"It's strange you say that... I think he may have. Or the universe did. I fell for it. I couldn't resist, Paul."

"It's not easy."

"I blame myself. Not blame – I wish I'd had the strength to... hit the brakes. To see it was the wrong path."

"You regret all of it?"

"The kids are my own self in a way. I can't disown that. I don't know anymore how I feel towards Danny. Kinda sorry, mostly. The time we both wasted."

"By staying together?"

"Yes."

She gathers sand in one hand, lifts his shirt—trickles it onto his belly. He giggles. She blows it away and lies back.

"I always had this – odd relationship to my body. The thing that happened to me in health class. The anatomy lesson?"

"Tallie always enjoyed—"

"Telling everyone. That's my sis. After making two bodies of my own it still seems bizarre to me."

"It is kinda strange."

"When I discovered sex, touching myself... then kissing – 'practicing' with girls, then boys and... putting it inside me... something finally made sense to me. Those body feelings – that disconnection... subsided. I felt whole for a time."

"Having sex."

"Mm. When I met Dan he was confident, he – had a hunger for me and knew how to press my buttons. Like me he was using—"

"Sex—"

"To free ourselves." She props on her elbows gazing at the ocean. "Maybe it's what kept us together. For an hour we become – complete? We push each other, take each other to a place where it – where everything stops. You were speaking of the internet and information. With porn...I felt myself getting sucked in. No pun intended. My god, the endless combinations. Anything. I was aware of the compulsion in me. Developing, building. Internet porn is treacherous. A blur...of tongues, mouths, fingers. Hips, asses, dicks. Pussies. Lots of pussies." She sighs, watching the sky.

"All going toward a fixed end. Every time. You know what the ending is. I'd fantasize...these girls leaving the – houses or wherever they had worked, going food shopping, pushing a cart with eggs, apples, carrots and – cookies – driving home, bitching out loud at the traffic. Do they have boyfriends? Cook for them? I imagined it...How was your day honey? Planning, thinking, tomorrow a lesbian scene in the morning and an office scenario fuck at two-thirty. And your lover...does he or she want sex? Of course. Is he wondering if you're picturing the guy or girl you mixed fluids with today for three hours? Or the others, last week? All these thoughts... And all I am – all we millions are – is hand on mouse, clicking and clicking till we find that one clip, one forty second section making the other hand get interested, go faster, till the brain flickers and gasps, till something cracks, you're there now, broken free of the banality, the crusts of all the videos you shuddered to previously – holy moly – the dozens you've just rejected and you've got the forty seconds and rewind it five, ten, twenty times, focusing on the ass, the fingers, the expression on her face, a gaping mouth, his animal motion, a kiss, and something in you, a free little remnant appears, you smell it and rub towards it, eyes on screen, rewinding a last time and ... there ... there ... you go. You go.

"I feel sorry for them. Maybe they had an orgasm, maybe not. Going home to an apartment. A burrito in the microwave. Check Facebook. I feel sorry for me. Wipe myself. Millions, wiping themselves. Deleting internet history, as though that'll squelch the compulsion. It's perpetual stasis, porn. Constant losing and constantly – accruing. Like a marriage you stay in.

Because, isn't there a balance? No, it's...nothing. Getting nowhere.

"As with my other vices—I got out. Eventually. My carpal tunnel really thanked me."

Paul inhales. Takes a moment to catch her humor.

"Sex is what's tied Dan and me. It's the bond between us. It doesn't free him or me. I no longer think it can. I knew, Paul, it would be something else with you. Ours is... meeting. Not getting there and disappearing. Being together there."

Her eyes locking on his. He hears the ocean. She's waiting for him. "Thank you, Mary, for telling me. All of it."

"Are you ready? We'll order some good seafood. I have a place." She corks the wine.

She's wonderful – imagination couldn't make her.

"Yes." He relaxes and lets go, holding her. "I'm ready."

They stand kissing on the beach, sun setting. Their bodies are loosening in the breeze.

"Tani is staying at my mother's tonight."

"I told the kids not to wait up for me."

They walk the beach to the boardwalk, slowly, basking in the sky colors, glancing over shoulders... In the parking lot Daniel whips the blanket, where masked people are drifting and driving away. She watches him – his back expresses somehow, 'I don't know what's going to happen either.' A last snap – folding it – 'I'll never wittingly hurt you.' He opens the passenger door for her.

She kisses him—wet, seductive, giving. He could slip down her panties, unbuckle and up against the door. Move in rhythm with her, in the parking lot. He puts his lips on her neck, Mary flashes inside him, the burning need for her. Was it love or biology he asked himself, so many times the concept wore itself out. With Katherine there'd been a difference. Not fevered or desperate. Caroline's cheeks and lips tender on his, fingers down his sides. She's not shy, she enjoys all of it. It's her heart. Inviting his to be open. Less need, more desire. To reveal what each one touches and responds to in the other. He's sorry he never had it with Mary.

"You're wonderful," he says to Caroline, holding her at arm's length. He blends in it, her laughter, her shine. Knows himself in it.

"I have a surprise for you, Dan. Wait one minute." She leaves him in the living room. Caroline's presence is all throughout the peacefulness of the space. He inspects Tatiana's drawings taped along the walls. Skies, fields, birds, animals, children running. She must be a joyful one. He thinks of Jessica, all he missed--a week here, week there. Days of her changes. He'd come home and she'd present herself to him—a difference in her—secret to her. The bookshelf is interesting – he plucks out The Fields of Kilimanjaro, Don't Sweat the Small Stuff, Selected Poems of Robert Frost and—Tao Te Ching!

"Here I am..."

He turns to the voice, drops the Tao, fumbling for it. She's changed...into pink fitted pants, a white t-shirt, dark-blue hooded sweatshirt. Furry slippers on her feet.

"I thought I'd get comfortable?" She signs and speaks.

"Gorgeous!" he signs, "Surprise, indeed."

"Oh, no, no," she giggles, "it was – I have something nice to eat." She takes a tray from the refrigerator. "Do you like blintzes?"

"Oh...very much." Dan's glued on the pink pants.

"My Russian mama makes them. Traditional." She slides them into the oven. "We get them every week."

"Lucky you, to have a blintz-making Russian mama." He can't keep apart from her. "I know," she says into his ear, her breath arousing him – "Me too, Danel" – and her buzzy voice. She chops a salad. Dan sets the table.

They're giving off heat, the blintzes. He sits next to her. He wants her and the blintzes and this apartment and the drawings on the wall. Does he fear being in her house? Does she fear him being where her mother comes, her daughter sleeps? That something will spread to—and from them? If others choose to have that—God bless them. And keep it away.

"Here's Mom's special sour cherry sauce. May I?" She dollops it for him, sauce dancing over the artfully folded floury creations, and observing her a wave of sweet energy crosses his chest, sweeps his skull, tasting extends the sensation, his pleasure received in her silence, 'What is he laughing about?' swallowing and chewing, more blintzes please, laughing, he's not sure why and she rubs his back, laughs with him, feeding him, "It's so good Caroline, mmm, delicious, it's really the best I've ever had...."

They're in the room, showered, robed, the ocean tumbling outside. The bags of food delivered and waiting, redolently on the table.

"It's a shack on a side road, Paul, but great food."

Crab cake sandwiches. Fish tacos. Chips cut thick and glistening. Creamed spinach.

"You're weren't kidding – this crab is incredible!"

"I'm glad you like it."

They eat, dripping sauce, to the clock radio playing oldies. Carly Simon. Bob Welch. Seals and Croft. Cat Stevens. "This music," Mary winks. Coke and ginger ale slosh in their plastic cups. 'Summer Breeze.' Simple contentment. Paul stops eating, stares off.

"Should I change the station?"

"Oh, no, it's fine...I was..."

"What?"

"I don't know, Mare. Transistor radios."

"You getting nostalgic on me?"

"Nostalgia, the last refuge of a ... someone ..."

She rolls the dial to a classical station. "Let's change the mood, eh?"

"I'm game."

She rises to make coffee from the brewer on the counter.

"Do you love her?" She's sifting powder into the filter.

He's gathering cans, containers—wasn't expecting that. Tosses them in the wastebasket.

"She kinda got inside me."

"You do."

He'd texted Jill when Mary was in the shower – 'Hey. I took off for a day or two. Out east. Thinking of you. Missing you.' She responded, 'Call me when you get back. Be careful.'

He lets Mary's words hang in the air. He goes to his bag in the corner, takes off the robe, putting on sweat pants and t-shirt.

"You've got a cute behind, you know that?"

"Thanks."

"Does Jill squeeze it? I love to."

As usual, he can't see where she's going. She pours him a coffee.

"I saw her yest—the day before. She knew, Mare. About us."

"Yes. Was she angry?"

"Upset. She feels she's...being cheated. Not cheated on, cheated *out of*...something."

"She wrote me a short email saying as much."

"It's really remarkable though."

"Why?"

"In the end she was most concerned about you—losing you." Mary has to suppress a flinch. Paul marks the effect. "Does it sound familiar, Mary?" She sips the coffee. "What happened between you?"

She comes over, perches on the bed, her cup on the night table.

"Love, Paul. Real love. I'd had things with girls. Not this. Not love. We didn't—consummate. Believe me we..."

"Wanted to."

She gives him a Mary stare. "Sometimes I still do. Our deeper connection could... ruin." She's mournful.

"And this," he signals the room, "won't ruin *our* friendship?"

"If I thought—no. No. It can't." Her head quivers in certitude.

"How can you be—"

"Because I am. Jill and I—that's something life presented. To us. That came out of a thing we both needed. You and I Paul," she glances at the darkened beach, "is fate. A given."

"Like a tree that has—"

"Been there forever." She loosens her robe. "You want to be here?"

"You're asking me?"

"And telling."

"I don't have a clever answer."

"Good. Then...maybe you...want to hold me?"

IV

She sits alone in the dark musing. As the hours fade from sun to springtime shadows. She no longer buys the covid tales they peddle day and night. The TV is not on. She has cold vodka in a glass, potato chips in a bowl, sits on the expensive sectional couch she'd purchased a day before the papers were signed severing her marriage to Phillip. Under the skylights. He emailed her – his father's in his final hours – he flew down. None of them can get in to see him. Now Phillip will run the company, effectively alone. After they sell the house, she'll rarely if ever hear from him. She's sorry for Phillip's mother. His father is old and had cancer, fortunate to buy more time. With the help of Sloan Kettering and their potions. A 'debonair' man, adept at the proper approach to any situation. Jill spotted it immediately, despite her country upbringing. Calculating, rapacious and—no, no—she mentally toasts him with her vodka. He once told her at a party he 'fancied' the skirt she had on. Undressing later, it hit her – he meant what the skirt was hiding. She lifts the physical glass and gulps the cool sharp river of forgetting.

She's not eclectic or spontaneous like Mary, can't talk politics and current events like Daniel or share ideas on literature and art like Paul. Why does Mary feel such affection and – yes, ardor – for her? She was never very pretty, her body was average, petite. Mary could have had a lesbian tryst with some other friend—suburbanly gorgeous, busty, possibly bisexual. But Mary didn't just want her ass—she said she loved her. And she felt it, the way she eyes her sometimes, how they greeted and parted, silently regretting their almost affair. Why had Paul fallen for her? 'Cause she was the only woman available during a pandemic? Until, that is, his platonic goddess stepped forth? 'Cause his life wasn't exactly full of sunshine and roses? Paul wasn't a schlump, gone to seed, living out his days in a blandness of could have beens and we'll see maybes. She's been reading his stuff—he gave her a folder of poems and stories. His talent was unmistakable. She didn't read widely but she intuited he was practicing – albeit without a discernible audience – at a high level. There was a flair, a crackle to the way he used words, in poems and prose fiction as well. She couldn't say what it was exactly, a kind of knowing, not a 'posturing,' as some writers affect. It appeared he casually tossed words out and let them land wherever, no, he aimed where they should go, like placing wild animals in his preserve. She hadn't told him any of these thoughts and maybe she wouldn't the bastard, screwing Mary as she knew he was right then, she's got the manuscripts in front of her on the table and when she looks at them, thinks of them, of *him* her heart aches. It's not fair he slipped through the cracks and might never emerge to be welcomed for his gift. His offering. It aches and angers her. All lights on the invisible destroyer, their virus. While artists struggle in darkness. Their work could be healing in ways these witch doctors in death-bungalows couldn't dream of. She's heard about the ninety percent death rate for those put on ventilators. She's thinking like him now – she had, even as a girl, a mind which quickly absorbed what it found compelling. He was compelling. She knew why Mary couldn't let him go – because there was nothing to let go of. He was a movement of words that went through you and was always changing. He didn't know how to stop changing. His beauty was in his living within that. She saw him the night by the window, when she feared the world coming apart. Felt him. He hid nothing. When he made love to you you faced yourself in him—and you unfolded. That's not it but it's close. I can see him now, perhaps as well or better than Mary can. She drinks the nearly gelatinous frozen-flowing vodka. Oh, that's good, *so good* ...Yes, more of that. The liquor stores have been open every day, thank heavens. All she has to do is wait. He'll come back. They both will. She doesn't know why.

∨

She leaves a bedside lamp on if he has to say anything important. He should have learned sign language a long time ago. What was there to say really? How many ways could you say, I'm angry at you, disappointed in you, for not being there when I needed you. There wasn't much to say and he was tired of hearing it. In the air, in the boardrooms, the bedroom. In his own head.

She tells him she's not expecting anything from him. "You have a family. It comes first. That's all I'll say, Danel." After dinner he takes her to the bookcase, pulls the Tao Te Ching. "Yes Dan, it's splendid... Vewy deep," she signs, one hand finger-pointed shooting down past the other bent inward, "and simple," one hand over the other as if striking a match, "at the same time." They leaf the book, he grows animated, expressing himself. She takes him in – "It means a lot to you, doesn' it?" "Yes, it does."

Caroline puts dishes in the sink and lowers the lights. On the couch they pass a bottle of Heineken in between smooching.

"I know you're tired, Dan...of all you've been involved in. Of moving on the map."

"Yes, Caroline. It's true. It's pleasant to be still."

"Find something light." He clicks the channels, they've got hundreds. They're lying in bed, one warm body beside the other. He stops on the sound of four familiar "golden" ladies, who break up the audience (or the laugh track) with sassy exchanges. "Leave this, Paul."

"Are you cold?" she asks, her eyes on the TV. "No, I'm okay." They enjoy the show, commenting and chuckling. Another impression enters the room, unsaid between them. They're viewing a program from a world they knew once, fairly recently, but it's losing its visual coherence, its shape. They are people – actors, audience, all of them in 'there' – who believed in the basic stories which formed daily life— being cared for, taken into consideration by systems making enormous decisions regarding their lives. As Paul and Mary watch, sharing unspoken references to that world, it's not possible to ignore the way the broadcast seems to be receding... gradually... until its images and sound are almost... imperceivable.

He can't whisper to her in the dark. He lets his body tell her things. How he feels being with her. Caroline shows him no defenses, no pretenses. He was alarmed by it, weeks ago. She wouldn't hurt me in return. It's completely unfamiliar. She's not someone to say no to love. Listening to herself inside when being around him. Sitting at home when Tani's in bed and he's gone to his home, as she knows he does. They could give each other something. A realization as clear as sunlight through the window she dusts above his desk. Something they both terribly needed.

"Beethoven," he said when she asked what he was listening to. In his Lions Pride room in March. "Ah, Bethoben..." She gestures, he lifts the speaker, she presses it to her chest. "Turn up the volume, please." "It's the seventh symphony." Her mother taught her to do this. Dan's talking, her eyes are closed, for a moment he forgets she can't... The third movement, he sways as it jumps along... At school they told her this man became deaf and was a great composer. Pushed them all against the speakers. She was thrilled feeling the vibrations. Music was real to her now. Beethoven was deaf like them and did that. His wild hair, intense glare in the paintings. An angel of possibility to her. She opens her eyes puts the speaker down. Daniel is listening. When she watches someone listening to music intently she imagines the notes floating in the air.

She didn't care about stations, status. She never learned to divide. She's too sincere for me, Dan thinks, overwhelmed, holding her naked body. Yet she wants me. He smiles, it grows until she feels him shaking... "What, what, Danel?" Oh, it's laughter – "What's funny?" She twists to face him – "I'm..." he tells her eyes, flinging his hand repeatedly from his bare chest, signing "Happy... Happy..."

They go in and out of sleep, in and out of loving.

Hot then cold, wet and dry, he's impelled by her will and desire. "Sibyl," he whispers as she tells him stories in her sighs and surrenders.

"Let's stay another night. We'll rest. Sleep." He agrees. She calls the front desk, hooks the Do Not Disturb on the doorknob. Stands a moment in the shadow. Paul lying motionless in moonlight. Jessie and Toby alone in the house. She'd called, texted. Dan will be home soon. She slithers under the covers.

"I discovered this video on YouTube." Mary's voice in the dark quiet room is soothing. "She calls herself Saratoga Ocean. She's speaking – channeling – in the voice of Archangel Michael."

"What does the protector angel say?"

"That Earth has been a slave planet for a long time. Under the control of – off-planet... whatever they are. 'Entities.' And now there's a – she calls it an 'ascension process' – going on."

"I've heard the term 'ascension.' A sort of ramping-up of energies?"

"Frequencies, yes. Available to us now. And the controllers are making a last ditch attempt for total permanent control over us."

He tugs at the blanket. "And the pandemic is a pivotal part—"

"Of this attempt. Many people are feeling that things don't make sense. He urges us—it sounds flaky..."

"Everything sounds flaky at this point."

"To raise our vibration." She reads from her notebook – " 'You must get out of fear—into love. Pure love and confidence of being who you truly are.' "

"I'll drink to that."

" 'Tell yourself—I am more powerful than this situation.' "

"The plandemic."

"The whole thing." She turns a page, reading, " 'You are a creator... Come into your true power as an infinite being...' "

"Infinite... Do you really think we are, Mare?"

"Maybe it's time we believed it."

"So he's saying it's fear that keeps us trapped?"

"Fear. Despair. Even anger. 'Don't take the bait' he says."

"Don't play into their game."

"Mm." She kisses him.

"It's empowering. Whoever it comes from. Are we in an 'ascension process,' Ms. Wellner?"

"I'll say...yes!"

"I'll say..." he sits up, back straight, eyes narrowed, chants, "Ooommmm... Ooommmm... Ooommmmayyybeee..."

They crack up, tangling together.

VI

Light starting to break. He pins on her refrigerator—**You Are <u>Beautiful</u> Caroline**.

No one else on the road. He used to feel awful after being with another.

Daniel lets the kids take the day off from school. Toby invites a friend, thrilled to have company. Jessie's boyfriend Todd comes from Connecticut. He orders in lunch for them. Plays ball with the boys in the yard. She asks him if Todd can stay the night. They set him up in a spare room. He knows what that leads to. Mary will be taken aback at his tolerance. He lays off work, sitting in the sun, being with his children. They make dinner as a group, listening to music. He lets them drink wine.

Is this our honeymoon, Paul thinks, the one we'll never have? They sleep half the day, eat a lazy brunch. Have a bath together. It's magical. At night they walk the deserted town, stumble on a sort-of open ice cream shop. They lick their cones rambling the sea-spray street, an empty store's awning to sit under. Enjoy the silence. The moment. Will they ever be this way—again? In a May with quiet emptiness and a breeze that makes her beauty charming, consuming?

"Paul – you don't have to do everything yourself. Alone. You're not responsible for finding out what's really going on…telling everyone. It's enough if you are able to use it. Even then, darling—you can't know everything. Or solve everything."

"This butter pecan is scrumptious. How's your rocky road?"

"Extra delicious because you're here, my poet."

They trade cones. They lick and kiss the stains from their mouths, chins.

"Mare—sometimes I want to know nothing. Anymore. Forget it all. Get away from this noise, this *information*.... Not look anymore. I'd like to disappear into the woods. Can I?"

"Maybe, Paul. Anything is possible. Right?" She stretches her arms wide then crunches her sugar cone.

The evening lets them be... lets ... them ... be...

In their room, by the window. Her back to him. The curtain frames them. The ocean facing them. She cracks the balcony door and they hear it rumbling towards them, sliding away, locked one to another. "Go ahead Paul—push me into the ocean. Yeah..." She's pulling him, wants him to move and lift them into flying over the spray the needles of coldness that make up the water white grey and oily brown. She pauses, he, then in harmony and for a moment the window blows away the night draws out their joined forms, takes them, up, above sand, over swirling tides towards stars and dancing on air she turns to him with her ecstasy and before they fall they flower in tangles of light, water, unsolidity.

They're parked near his place. They can't say goodbye. They sit in the car, silent, exhaling. It's twilight. Mary's kids are waiting.

"Let's disappear in the woods, Paul."

"Let's go."

"I'm serious."

"You are?" She really is. "And Tobias? Jessica?"

"They have a father. Let him parent. Don't I have time for living?"

"You're brave, Mary even to—"

"I'm not—"

"—Think like that."

"—Brave. I'm – just – getting older. Aren't we?"

He looks from her to the street through the windshield.

"I know you're in love with Jill – or something close to it."

"Yes. There's Jill."

"This is – our only chance. To be together. Isn't it now or – "

"Never."

"What's left? Twenty—thirty? Maybe?"

"Years... I don't know what the word means anymore." Her eyes are replete with something, everything. "What'll we do?"

"Be with each other."

"And Jill?"

"Can that work? A triad?"

"No? Yes?"

"Isn't it intense enough – the two of us?"

"Aren't *you* in love with her?"

"She can't be our little lover, our pet. Can we be all equals? We're not twenty-five."

"You told me not to – break you apart. Remember?"

She looks to the darkening street. "Someone gets hurt. If I thought there was a way..."

"And Daniel?"

"I gave him twenty years."

"Didn't he give?"

"We gave. Enough."

"And I? I'll be—"

"You'll be you. I'll be me. You need someone, Paul. The world is changing, fast, as you've been warning. It's not good to be alone. Anymore."

"This won't go away tomorrow? This talk, these ideas."

"No."

He's transfixed—she's a girl and a woman simultaneously.

"We'll awake and it'll be real?"

"Yes."

"More real than anything?"

"Than all of it. All. Okay?" She's soft and serious. Her whole way about her is tugging at his heart.

"Be careful, Mary. You'll make me fall in love with you."

"Fat chance." He can't resist, kisses her.

"I don't know... how to proceed."

"It'll be messy. For a while. I told you I want to live *too*. You can sit there watching the clocks tick and the sun move across the lawns – only so long. Till you desiccate. Moving in place."

"Everything. Your will, your heart. Your balls."

"This is it. One last go."

"I'm – Mare, I..."

"Say it, sweetheart."

"I'm afraid." She runs a finger on his forearm.

"So am I. That's why I've always loved you. You value truth above all. That's...rare. I'll never find anyone close."

"And you Sibyl – you make the fire and the water – don't you?"

"If I'm lucky. Sometimes only instant coffee and crackers."

"*You...*" He gets out, goes to her side, helps her out. She leans against the car, his hands on her waist. He can't let go.

"Doesn't it feel – *well*?" she semi-whispers.

"Hold me," he answers. "Then you can drop me off."

She can hear him breathing, his heart beating. "You need to tell me something, Paul?"

"A lot. And I will, Mary. I will."

XIX

Pandemic Thoughts out of Season

In late August 2020, the NY Times publishes an article on the RT-PCR Test used worldwide to diagnose cases of Covid-19. The article admits the test is highly unreliable in detecting *quantities* of coronavirus and depending on what laboratory is processing the test, amplification of the genetic (RNA) materials can vary wildly. Millions of people who've tested "positive" for Covid-19 may have had such small amounts of what is being called viral material—that to say they have the illness is highly misleading.

That same week in August, the CDC releases a report on Covid-19 mortalities. For 6 percent of the deaths, Covid was the only cause mentioned. For 94 percent, on average there were 2.6 *additional conditions or causes* per death.

In May, David Icke makes his third London Real appearance. He speaks to Brian Rose about how all perceptions must be controlled in order to pull off "this virus hoax"...thereby intimidating the masses to relinquish most of their freedoms. It's perception—and fear of consequences— allowing all of this to happen. We are now "living in a global version of Nazi Germany," and this has all been planned by the controllers for a very long time. He focuses on the willful destruction of people's livelihoods leading to dependence on the State, thus consolidating its control. He sees the West "becoming more and more like China," stressing the rising censorship of the major internet players—Facebook, Google, Twitter—who've decreed any information contrary to what the WHO is putting out will be challenged or deleted. He rails against Neil Ferguson with his absurd "computer models," against Bill Gates whose tentacles reach into every corner—from the WHO to Imperial College to the vaccines in development. Hospitals in the UK and around the world are empty and nurses have been laid off. The imminent rollout of 5G and its effects on human health will be called Covid-19 cases. He goes into the development of AI and the plan for humans to be connected to it directly – "AI will be thinking for us... They're preparing people psychologically to be fused with machines." The push for mask wearing is to breed human alienation, erasure of identity. The coming "vaccine" will contain nanobots that can change the structure of our DNA—"furthering a synthetic merger of human and machine." Icke emphasizes the way out of all this – *Do not acquiesce*. We must live from here—placing his hands over his *heart*—and opening them outward into the world.

In mid-April 2020, Dr. Scott Jensen a physician and Minnesota state Senator, is interviewed on Fox News. He holds up new CDC Death Certificate Guidelines explaining that doctors are being told to use Covid-19 as cause of death even if there are underlying conditions involved—such as cancer or heart disease. In addition, they should use the Covid designation if the decedent *hasn't been tested* for Covid-19, but is *presumed* to have had the virus. Dr. Jensen details the financial incentives for hospitals which diagnose and treat it under the Medicare program. If a patient is diagnosed with pneumonia or influenza the standard payment is $4,600. If diagnosed with Covid they receive $13,000. If a patient is put on a ventilator, payment will be $39,000.

Soon after this interview, a study was released showing a nearly 90% mortality rate for those placed on ventilators in New York City area hospitals.

By the beginning of September 2020, the state of Victoria in Australia, is under a de facto police state. 8 p.m. curfew. People are beaten by police in the streets for not wearing masks. A pregnant woman is arrested in her home in front of her children because of a Facebook post inviting fellow citizens to a peaceful protest. Journalists are visited and warned they are being "put on a list" for being present at and reporting on an anti-lockdown protest. A video circulates of a man talking to police from his window regarding another Facebook post. He tries to reason with them until they break down his front door, enter and wrestle him to the floor, restraining him.

Since the May 25, 2020 death of George Floyd during an arrest in Minneapolis, Minnesota, demonstrations—some peaceful, many involving rioting and looting—have exploded across the United States. In Portland, Oregon by September the police will have been battling Antifa, a self-proclaimed anti-fascist group, for over one hundred nights.

Black Lives Matter has taken the lead in these demonstrations. At first there is sympathy and support for their movement but as the summer goes on and violence and chaos permeate the cities, it largely fades. In some cities BLM has blended with

Antifa groups. There is growing disillusionment and anger among the general populace still unable to attend churches or schools, gyms or clubs – all the while watching thousands of people march with impunity, often causing property destruction and disruptions to traffic flows and the daily lives of citizens.

CDC survey data of June 2020 states that one in four young adults between eighteen and twenty-four considered suicide in the previous month. The data exposes a massive increase in anxiety and substance abuse in this age group, with 40 percent disclosing "mental or behavioral health conditions connected to the Covid-19 emergency."

In late May, six hundred U.S. doctors sign a letter to President Trump urging him to end the "national shutdown," to avert what they see as a coming nationwide health catastrophe: "We are alarmed at what appears to be the lack of consideration for the future health of our patients," the doctors write. "The downstream health effects ... are being massively underestimated and under-reported. This is an order of magnitude error.... The millions of casualties of a continued shutdown will be hiding in plain sight, but they will be called alcoholism, homelessness, suicide, heart attack, stroke, or kidney failure. In youths it will be called financial instability, unemployment, despair, drug addiction, unplanned pregnancies, poverty, and abuse. Because the harm is diffuse, there are those who hold that it does not exist. We, the undersigned, know otherwise."

In April 2020, Lady Gaga and Global Citizen produce a program titled One World: Together At Home, featuring pop and classical stars performing from their homes, including

The Rolling Stones, Eddie Vedder, Celine Dion, Paul McCartney, Andrea Bocelli.

"Today I'm so happy that we are one world, together at home. I feel very honored to be a part of the World Health Organization and Global Citizen in the fight against Covid-19 and raising money for the Solidarity Response Fund," Lady Gaga announces. She then performs the song *Smile*.

During the broadcast Bill and Melinda Gates are interviewed by talk show host Stephen Colbert. "The eventual end," Gates tells viewers, "comes when we get a vaccine that protects all of us, not just in the U.S., in the entire world. There's a lot of vaccine candidates that we're backing, and I'm optimistic by late next year, one of those will come out and we need to make sure—" he breaks into a grin— "that gets out to everyone in the world."

Also in April, Moderna, Inc. is given a U.S. government grant of $483 million to develop a Covid-19 vaccine. They are aiming to create the first vaccine to utilize mRNA technology, which some researchers say has the potential to alter human DNA.

A spike protein sequence is duplicated from the purported SARS-CoV-2 virus, reverse-transcribed into a segment of mRNA, and injected into the cells. It's then "read" by ribosomes which produce the spike protein molecules that leave the cells and enter the system, theoretically triggering an immune response against this protein sequence.

There are serious concerns about this never-utilized-on-humans technology:

What prevents the mRNA from continuing to produce the protein molecules in cells?

If these "RNA sequences" are patented by the vaccine companies, could they claim ongoing *ownership* of the RNA material—now fused with human cells?

What will the "delivery system" of this new vaccine be? The manufacturers, Moderna and Pfizer, are not forthcoming with this information. One possibility came from researchers at MIT who "created a microneedle platform using fluorescent microparticles called quantum dots (QD), which can deliver vaccines and at the same time invisibly encode vaccination history directly in the skin. The quantum dots are composed of nanocrystals, which emit near-infrared (NIR) light that can be detected by a specially equipped smartphone."

There is speculation that the new vaccines may include hydrogel, developed at the Pentagon's Defense Advanced Research Projects Agency (DARPA). Hydrogel can carry nanobots that assemble, disassemble and reassemble. This technology could conceivably connect or respond to exterior devices.

In January 2021, Moderna publishes information about its vaccine technology: "**Our Operating System**... Recognizing the broad potential of mRNA science, we set out to create an mRNA technology platform that functions very much like an operating system on a computer. It is designed so that it can plug and play interchangeably with different programs. In our case, the 'program' or 'app' is our mRNA drug – the unique mRNA sequence that codes for a protein."

Prior to this so-called vaccine, Moderna had never brought any product to market.

President Trump, after withdrawing funds from the World Health Organization to the acclaim of its myriad critics, pledges $1.16 billion to Gavi, the Global Alliance

Vaccine Initiative. Gavi is run by the Bill and Melinda Gates Foundation, now the largest funder of the WHO.

At a rally in Trafalgar Square London on August 29, 2020, attended by over thirty-five thousand people, David Icke gives an impassioned speech, urging non-compliance "to the psychopaths" and their plans. At the end of his address he roars out — FREEEDOMMMM!!" to the crowd—which responds in kind.

In late summer 2020, colleges announce their fall classes will be either completely online—or a small percentage of students will be allowed to learn in person. Similarly, grade schools and high schools around the U.S. will be a mixture of in-school and at-home education.

Restaurants in American cities reopen in restricted ways throughout summer, 2020.

In mid-September, a federal judge decided on a lawsuit brought by four Pennsylvania counties and several Republican state lawmakers, challenging the coronavirus-related shutdown imposed by Governor Tom Wolf.

Judge William Stickman IV ruled that limits on gatherings of twenty-five people indoors and 250 outdoors—and stay-at-home and business shutdown orders—were all *unconstitutional*. The Governor and his team are appealing the decision.

On September 1, 2020, a lawsuit was filed by attorney Thomas Renz and his colleagues in the Northern District of Ohio Federal Court to remove Governor Mike DeWine's emergency order:

"We believe that the response to Covid-19 has been the greatest fraud ever perpetrated on the American public," Renz said. "The objective of this legal action is to force the state to honor the Constitution and to stop the lies, manipulation and fear-mongering intentionally being promoted by public health officials and elected officials.... There is zero basis for a state of emergency. Based on what we know about the consequences the emergency order has caused to the physical, financial, and mental well-being of Ohioans, and the vitality of Ohio communities, this is truly a crime against humanity, and it must not be allowed to continue."

In Berlin, Germany on the same day that David Icke inspires the London rally, Robert F. Kennedy, Jr. speaks to a huge crowd of protesters. He praises their unity and passion for freedom. Fifty-seven years previous, his uncle President John F. Kennedy, told assembled Berliners: "All free men, wherever they may live, are citizens of Berlin. And therefore, as a free man I take pride in the words: Ich bin ein Berliner."

"Governments love pandemics," RFK tells them. "They love pandemics for the same reason they love war. Because it gives them the ability to impose controls on the population that the population would otherwise never accept. To create institutions and mechanisms for orchestrating and imposing obedience."

XX

Housekeeping

Jill 'attended' Simon Chambers' funeral on Zoom. Someone at the grave site—she guessed Phillip's sister Trish—held a device and the audio came through to her and dozens of others, named and unnamed, whom she could see listed on the screen. The minister was quoting bible verses and he added personal reminiscences of Phil's father. His older sister spoke, his younger brother, then he – stammering words – bicycle riding instruction, trips abroad, wisdom imparted in brandy and cigar sessions. Jill sat in the den of the house they'd shared for eight years with a candle burning on the table in a late May afternoon. She was dressed all in black. There was no need, it would be audio only. She heard his throat catch in the middle, he gathered himself, pushing on to the finish. Melinda at his side, her hand on his long back clothed in a dark suit.

Trish thanked everyone for joining them, she'd look forward to when they could have a "proper memorial for the man we all love." The transmission ended. What was happening now? She'd seen it many times. Her grandparents. Her uncles, her aunt. Her father, on a cold sleety day. She'd lived what was happening now.

May 27. "Coronavirus deaths in the United States exceed 100,000." Has the curve been flattened? "We're not there yet." They call for more testing. More and more swabs up the nose.

Dan gets the text at night. Mary's sleeping next to him. Tony Levi is gone. Passed that evening. He was okay, Tony. He let Dan be as he was. Didn't lean into him when clients got antsy with his tactics. He believed in me. He wants to talk, almost stirs Mary. Refrains. He's staring into the dark – sad, angry, the old lion didn't have to die alone. He lies awake watching Tony recede. Each hour a little more.

Paul takes his walks in the woods. He goes to his writing, his notebooks and words. Information piles upon itself... It's beginning to look the same to him. He's waiting for a mode or means to use it.

Mary rings his bell. She's sorry for not being there sooner. She's scattered, hair wild. "I missed you," she whispers. Her mouth is warm. It's familiar now. She's attuned to his body. What'd he want to ask her? Oh, yes... *What is happening between them?*

"I can't stay long. Things are changing. For the better. Believe me, I miss you—and this. Do you?"

"Believe you?"

"No, miss me."

"Yes."

"And you believe me?"

"Should I?"

She unzips him, laughing. "Okay, but we have to be quick."

They're on the couch he found on Craigslist. It's in decent condition, if a little lumpy. She does things with her hips and her heat and hands and they accelerate chemistries. Unreleased releasing, neither satisfied. In fifteen minutes they're at the door. She takes hold of him in a gentleness which makes him gasp.

Paul is left on the couch.

She called him after the funeral. She hadn't seen him since he'd been away with Mary. She lit candles in the den. Poured brandy. Paul expressed condolences. They sat in silence.

"They said it was covid."

"Hm? Oh. Mm-hm."

"You don't believe it exists."

How should he interpret? It wasn't the time to get into it.

"I don't know, Jill."

"Do you or don't you?" Quietly, pointedly.

"We don't need to—"

"Yes, I need to, Paul."

He's gotta tread carefully, he fears a trap being laid. Funerals swerve people unpredictably.

"I think they make it exist. Like dyeing a white blanket purple. The whole thing takes on the color purple. That's a bad metaph—"

"No. It's... it's okay."

She's mute. He daydreams. Why did she invite him?

"Do you want to go up?"

"Up? The living room?"

"To bed." It was spoken softly, he wasn't sure if he imagined it.

"Oh. Uh...if you want to, Jill."

She starts moving—stops by the stairs. "What are you waiting for?"

"Oh, okay..." he bangs his knee on the table. "Shit!" rubbing it. "Ow!"

"Are you all right?"

"Yeah." It smarts. "I will be."

"Be careful. It's dark."

"Should I blow out—" she's already up the stairs. He's hovering in the shadow of the candlelight—they're in a glass container. He stops on the stairs—a moment. Then follows her.

"Maybe we should consider a separation."

They'd never said those words to each other but to Mary it was as if they'd discussed them a hundred times. They were walking through the neighborhood in early evening. Daniel had stopped after saying the words and she had kept going, thinking *wasn't their whole marriage basically a separation* of one kind or another and this is just another one of the games they play. She no longer wants to play them. She doesn't look at him thirty feet behind her.

"Well—you coming? Do we have to separate right here? Or do we finish our attempt at exercise?"

He catches up to his wife.

"What is it, Dan? Fallen in love again?"

"Don't mock, Mary. Aren't we past that by now?"

"I'm serious. Is it the deaf maid?"

His body freezes, not from surprise—from her audacity to name without hesitation what she suspects with seemingly no emotion.

"I saw you together, remember?"

"Her name is Caroline."

"The deaf maid, Caroline. There was another time. One day I came to Lions Pride. I stopped at the door to the courtyard. You were – hands flying up and down – with her. Giggling. You looked happier than I've seen you Danny in... Maybe ever."

"You didn't come through?"

"I left. I saw you didn't need me." She slows her pace.

"You want to be with her, Dan?"

She's watching him for any ounce of lying. She feels like a good friend, abruptly, walking beside him. Or a good enemy. Pungent, reliable, to waken you to what's really going on.

"You can tell me."

He stops—eyes blurring off a bend in the street, the green lawns leaf-blown into ear-splitting evenness—he sees his boyhood, school days, relationships... years spent building an identity based on what his parents chose in him, friends and teachers approved in him, piece on piece until he can't remember the first one. Or the last.

"She makes me feel...myself. No pretend. No struggle. I'm happy around her." He's almost stopped breathing.

Standing on the concrete experiencing his handsome, worn face, it sinks in. He's been inside her so many times. And now, no more. He moves on, she trails, towards their home.

Paul awakes, it's morning, alone, Jill's funeral attire on the chair. The smell of coffee draws him into a shower. He dresses and goes down.

She hands him a cup and drops a plate of toast and eggs. They eat. She looks preoccupied. Shouldn't they be snuggling? Instead it's pass the salt pass the pepper please.

"How do you feel, Jill?"

"Pretty good. How about you?"

"I always feel good after – when we're together."

A fleeting smile and she butters her toast.

"I'm gonna get some air. Care to join me?"

"Not now, maybe in a bit."

He hesitates then takes his mug through the glass doors into the backyard. Amongst the warmth and bird songs words— lines— come into his head— *In single file, in simple rapture, the spent light and sorted feeling, the mindless genius the heartless glory, to watch them is to learn what it is to be a child of the earth, shorn of laughter, stripped of memory, jumped of unity, jumbled with...* He's knocked over the mug, his head's on the table, the coffee is a rivulet...

The birds are still singing. He feels like going back to sleep, how long had it been? He gets up slowly, forgets his mug on the table.

Jill's not in the kitchen. She's gone, he thinks. They're all gone. They've all died of Covid-19. The whole world. It's only me who's left to fend for myself. Every room is empty, every voice has closed.

Is she for me? Am I for her? What am I doing here? I should be in my room, writing. He looks down the empty hallway where no one is. Is the other one for me? That beauty my old friend? Is anyone? Or am I destined to be alone, in the desert, searching for a cure to a disease I can't name. They love me and I love them..."

"Paul?" She's calling him. From where? Nowhere? "I'm in here." He follows the voice. He enters the living room, she's there on the couch thumbing through a magazine. Nothing's the same, he can feel it. Or was he recognizing the feeling that was always there?

He stands near the couch. "Why don't you sit?" She finally looks up.

"I don't feel like... I'm stiff, fell asleep outside."

"Okay, whatever you want."

"I think I'll go, I don't think you—"

"Mary came to see me yesterday."

"Yeah? And?"

"She said—"

"Look Jill, I don't think I want to – maybe I should go."

"You don't want to hear—wait a minute."

He feels exhausted, like he's still in the dream state.

"What'd she say?"

"She's sorry about what's happened. She never meant to hurt me or to damage our ... friendship. 'It just happened,' she said. And, oh, she said she loves you but if – I truly am in love with you – she wouldn't hesitate to disappear."

"Disappear? That's the word she used?"

"Yes. Disappear."

Jill stands up, facing him, her hands on the leather cushions. What's the difference? Hasn't everyone already disappeared?

"Okay. Well. That's interesting, I must say."

"That's not all."

"Oh, there's more? After she's disappeared?"

"Very funny, Paul. She also said that—let me see if I remember it correctly." She reaches for her mauve coffee mug and drinks. "She said... 'Paul is a moon and I'm a sun'. Was it the reverse? No, that was it. And she added, 'One without the other is an imbalance.' Something like that."

"I gotta go, Jill."

"What do you think of that?"

"Of what, which part?"

"All of it."

Which one was I? Moon or sun? Can't even remember my birth sign. And I'm a middle-aged man, tired and confused, with callouses on my feet. And a sensitive stomach.

"It's fine, it's...interesting. Sounds like her. But what do *you* think, Jill?"

"I don't...I don't really know, Paul. It was nice of her to say that. That first part."

"Yes, it was."

"And – it's confusing. What's happened between us. The three of us."

"Yes, it is. I had a good time last night. You're very sexy."

She blushes and whispers, "Thank you."

"I wish I knew how to proceed. But I don't. I keep going round and round in my head about it...all."

"I know the feeling."

"I'm not sure what you want, Jill."

"Are you sure what *you* want?"

He's sure he wants to go at that moment or thinks he is.

"You're not, are you?" she softly challenges.

"No."

"At least you're honest. Kinda cute, too."

She takes his hand and they walk to the door.

"What are you working on?"

"A story about a man alone in a desert."

"That's all?"

"It's a beginning."

"Seems... insular."

"Maybe he looks up at the stars. Or something. Finds a mirage or two."

They smile at each other at the open door. She looks out at the sunlight – "Nothing makes much sense does it? These days."

"You startle me sometimes with your – insights."

"Do you give me enough credit, Paul?"

"More than you know, Jill."

He watches her. The sun covering her freckles. I want more time with her. I want more time to get to know her.

"I'll call you," he touches her cheek.

"Okay," she turns to him. "Call me."

I'd like some more time with him. He's moving down the walk. More time.

She hears his voice from behind the door, peeps through the hole, yeah it's all six foot three of him in his dark suit and pocket handkerchief.

"Jill, are you there? It's Phil."

She'd been in a bath twenty minutes before. Her hair was wet. In t-shirt and sweats.

"Uh, one, one, minute..." She backs against the wall. Why did I speak, I could have feigned absence! Her heart running, respiration sped up. What does he...want?

She'd dreamed him for years afterwards. Waking in bed with him sleeping, his body commanding the full length of the mattress. She'd wake up in real life reaching for him, feel foolish. She hadn't noticed it had ended, the dreams. Now what could he – for a moment she imagines he's there to ask for her back – it's impossible...

Her clammy unsteady hand on the doorknob, stops, darts to the mirror—she sees her age in the light streaming through in the face with lines without makeup. Rapping, "Jill, you there?" "Yeah, I'm here," falling to the dizziness of years she's forgotten into the mirror brushing her long damp hair over her— "Coming!"

"Phillip, hi, what uh, what's—"

"Thank you for the beautiful card you sent."

"I was so – sorry to hear about your father." She leads him into the den. He sits on the couch they picked out together. Briefcase at his side. "Can I get you—"

"No, nothing, thanks. I haven't got much time, I'm afraid."

"Oh. Okay." She hesitates, off balance, till he glances at her. She sits across from him.

"What's goi—"

"Jill, I—"

They smile. She gestures him to continue.

"Your words mean a lot. They're consoling. My dad was fond of you – he was sorry when – he often asked after you." She smiles politely wishing she had a glass to grasp. "These past couple of months I've...had some time to think. When all this... and when Dad took ill it – put me into a state of mind – new for me. I'm not a reflective person. But you already knew that." She smiles again. "I've been forced into reflection." He pauses, clicks the briefcase open. Lifts the lid, focusing on her intently— "I wasn't a very good husband."

"Phillip, you— Is this the right time to—"

"It's true. Our happiest, our best...period—was San Francisco."

"Yes. San Francisco was...special."

"Idyllic. When we came here and got the house—it changed between us."

"You were busy, you had responsibilities."

"That's kind. I disconnected from you. Myself too. I thought we were both drifting from each other. I'm not saying it was a merely one-sided thing—"

"No, it never—"

"But I didn't do the work I needed to. Our marriage needed. The truth is—I didn't try enough." He's getting emotional, sucks at his breath, she flies to him.

"Phillip. Honey." Touches him. His wrist. His shoulder.

"I – thanks. I... threw it away."

"I'll get some water," she whips to the kitchen. Pouring the shaky pitcher into a glass. Staring a moment at the granite counter she had built for him.

She takes a seat opposite, he drinks.

"I appreciate your – expressing that. We were young, we... made mistakes."

"I want you to know I've realized my missteps. I wasn't able to...meet you. Where you were. I'm sorry for it."

Her jaw won't move, she squeaks out, "It's ... okay."

"Well..." He takes out papers from the case. "We talked, weeks ago about the house and eventually proceeding to sell it. In brief, Jill, I've made the decision to sign it—" he grins the way that used to make her into mush—"over to you." She blinks, nodding. "Do you...understand me?"

"You're signing – the house – *this* house – over to – "

"To you, yes. In full."

"Wait, am I – hearing this correctly? You're—"

"Yes, it's yours. Think of it as a way of...atoning? Is that the word? Forget it. Would you sign here, please." She does. "And here. And...there. Good. I'll have it properly stamped and sent to you. In your name, solely."

"Solely," she repeats.

"It's yours—to do with as you wish. Happy?" He rises, gathering his things.

"I'm flabbergasted. It's – generous. Incredibly generous."

"I want you to be happy." He leads her to the entrance, opens the door. "Goodbye, Jill. And thank you."

"For what, Phillip?"

"For the years we shared." He bends, kisses her on the lips.

She watches him stride to the curb and his Mercedes. Case in, body in, engine on, and gone.

She closes it. Her house. She looks up into the corners, down the molding, swirls the wallpaper. The long walls. The spotless tiles below her. The mirrors. Up, down, through, all of it. It's hers.

XXI

Eternity in an Hour

And he causeth all, both small and great, rich and poor, free and bond, to receive a mark in their right hand, or in their foreheads: And that no man might buy or sell, save he that had the mark, or the name of the beast, or the number of his name.

These verses from the Book of Revelation circulate as the propaganda for Vaccine-as-panacea grows strident through the summer, 2020.

They say we were born... on the beach. That it begins and ends there, the proving ground for life to emerge, to compete, to struggle. We came out of the ocean, bed of life, gasping for air and a place to stay. To call our own. A tribe scuttling the shore. Looking for, finding, joining. Will they accept me? And what is me? A thing hopping along, from you to you. This is where We is formed, battling together to trek from the brackish lip upwards, without sizzling in the sunlight, without squelching under fang, claw, exhaustion, surrender.

In these small packs we climbed to the dunes where we could organize. Build a fire. Take a breather. Make a plan. For movement, gathering supplies, for a raid. Protection.

Hierarchies. Strong, weak, in-between. Alliances. Sun down, sun up. You barely recollect where you came from. How you emerged, searching for a taste of sustenance, a sign of a friend. You lie on the beach and can't explain why it feels like home. Why you hesitate to leave at sunset, pack your stuff, fold the sheet. In the parking lot as you bend into the car seat you glance back. Fire. Shadow. Light. Darkness. Fear. Relief. You hear terns and gulls—warnings, invitations. You get in. Stare a moment through the windshield. Foot on the brake, you release, turn, steer. You accelerate, in the rear view mirror the birds and fading light you left behind.

In the summer messages flash repeatedly above the highways:

Covid is still a risk. Wear a mask.

And—

Wash hands. Wear a mask. Social distance.

In August, Jon Rappoport writes: *Save the virus. Save THE STORY ABOUT THE VIRUS. Keep it going. Don't let it slip away.*

George Floyd declared, moments before dying, "I can't breathe... I can't breathe." This is written on signs and chanted at protests in the days and nights of spring-summer, 2020.

Towards the end of spring Paul can almost feel the way it's constructed, the invisible filaments of the Narrative. They were living in the story they were being told. They slept and woke in it. It seeped through the walls, came out of the taps. They breathed it in the air in closed or open spaces. It was a word—a code. The core of it, as usual, was fear. Fear of death, fear of pain, fear of irretrievable loss. Fear of being singled out; fear of losing livelihood; fear of being taken away and punished. A narrative invariably had a counter-narrative. It winnows the nay-sayers, those who sow doubt. It's an outlet for the pent-up anger of those who stay in line. It spotlights the abhorrent attitudes of those who would mock the dead and the suffering. It shows what it is to become perverse, anti-scientific. To have lost all reason.

You were either with *them* or you were with the lunatics. The conspiracy mongers. You either take your place in the story—dutiful listener and repeater—or you tread water in a vile, unthinkable pool. Filled with lonely swimmers.

They talk, the bright Medical lights, of "the second wave." No doubt there'll be another wave of Coronavirus. Only a matter of when the tsunami will subsume the beach, again.

Picture millions of people watching thousands of people shout, march, loot, smash, set fire to buildings, destroy businesses, dance and sing, break windows, scream at and confront police, throw Molotov cocktails at police, demand police kneel, attempt to wound and kill police, sit in silent tribute, form friendships, feel they're contributing to something worthwhile, express their anger and pain, topple statues both of defamed and revered historical figures, arrogate lawless "autonomous zones" in major cities, insist diners at restaurants say "the name"—and that *certain* lives matter.

Picture millions of people watching thousands of people, week after week as the temperature rises and the pandemic rumbles on, sitting in rooms watching it all unfold night after night via smart phones, tablets, laptops or televisions.

That's late spring and summer 2020.

Picture a whole society made to wear masks because of a supposed virus already run its course, not only inside public buildings, but outside. Picture these people living their lives day after day, children included, breathing through face coverings. Maybe you were one of them?

Summer, 2020.

And picture this – information censored, videos removed, ideas erased, lives and careers CANCELLED – for tweets, blog posts or comments construed or misconstrued, words unacceptable to the new doctrinaire lines of the correct and the anathema, propagating around them.

Retired policeman David Dorn shot and killed in St. Louis by a looter breaking into the shop he'd been guarding. Federal officer Dave Patrick Underwood killed while on duty in Oakland. Italia Marie Kelly, twenty-two years old killed by a randomly shot bullet as she left a protest in Davenport, Iowa. Jessica Doty Whitaker, a twenty-four-year-old mother shot and killed in Indianapolis after uttering "All lives matter."

And others—following the death of George Floyd in police custody in late May on the streets of Minneapolis. George Floyd, symbol of the pandemic summer.

The curve was flattened, case numbers were dropping. And in June the masks were everywhere.

> Jill: My god Em, what the fuck
> is GOING ON in our country?
> Mary: I know darlin'
> It's totally fucking crazy
> Jill: Everyone's gone mad
> Mary: Yeah
> Maybe WE have

> Jill: Are you as worried as
> I am?
> Mary: I'm very concerned
> Something feels OFF
> Jill: It's scary
> Mary: Remember hon--
> This too shall pass

She doesn't know what else to say to her friend. She looks at the images on TV and online and the ground splits beneath her. "Keep it together," she orders herself, "for the kids." It's early June and Jessica's en route to a Black Lives Matter protest in Brooklyn. Dan is working and Mary can't stop her. "Please use your head, Jessica." Her friends beeping at the curb for her. "Bear in mind where there's an exit, a *way out*. And don't hesitate to go." "I'll be okay Mom, I promise. I'll be aware of my surroundings." She opens the door, moves down the walk—"Wait!" —Mary thrusts a plastic bag with water bottles and snack bars in her hands. "Don't resist the police if they stop you or—" "I won't." "And don't talk back to them, don't be – " "I won't, Mom." She hugs the girl. "Text me, Jess." "I will. Let me go, Mom." She releases her.

All night she's collecting her fingernails, pouring red wine into herself. In return to her texts she gets – "I'm ok" and "Good." She plays games with Toby who cheers her up with songs and cartoon characters, chomping pepperoni pizza. Daniel calls, "Everything okay?" "Yeah, fine. Jessie went out." "Into the city? I heard there's craziness in Brooklyn tonight." "I don't think so..." "You're not sure?" "I can't put a chain on a nineteen year old - woman." "She's not exactly a seasoned—" "She lived alone in Spain last year, remember?" "Yes, with a family. The angry crowds out there has me jumpy. It's volatile and she could get caught—" "She texted me. She said she's...fine." Dan yields. Mary feels guilty, letting her go, lying to him.

She calls Paul—

"She went in tonight? The march in Brooklyn?"

"Paul, I'm – "

"Nervous?"

"Yeah, what does she know about this? A kid from the suburbs."

"A lot of them are young. From everywhere."

"She's a little thing. What if—"

"She'll be okay, Mare. She'll march, shout, lose her voice."

"It's nuts out there. The cops are on edge, everyone's losing it."

"She's smart, she's been—"

"She's not *street* smart."

"You sure 'bout that?" Mary breathes into the phone. "Would you like me to call or text her?"

"Would you? Oh, that'd be so cool. I'm sending you her number. Thanks, honey."

> Jess, it's Paul, your mom's
> friend
> She mentioned you're at a
> protest
> Be cool okay?
> Don't antagonize the cops
> Or anyone
> GET AWAY if it's heating up
> Stay hydrated
> Stay COOL
> Good luck

He calls Mary. "I sent something."

"Thank you. Let me know if she—" He checks—

"She answered— 'Thanks Paul, I will.' With a smiley face."

" 'I will' what? She will what?"

"I told her to be alert and a couple other things. She's okay. Oh, another one – 'Tell my mom Don't worry,' ha-ha..."

"You've calmed me, as usual. I'm gonna put Toby to bed. I'll see you tomorrow."

"You will?"

"Yes. I miss you."

"Me too."

"Say it."

"I, Paul Wilmer, sincerely—"

"Just say it. Please."

"I miss you."

"Thanks. À demain."

"Ciao."

One morning Tobias catches his father leaving the spare bedroom, wearing pajamas.

"Dad, how come you sleep in there now?"

"Oh, hey, 'morning. I uh... I work late sometimes, Tobe. I don't want to bother Mom when she's already asleep. So I work in this room and then... go to sleep."

"Oh, okay, Dad." He skips on into his day. He'll have to be told. They'll all sit down some afternoon— Toby ducks his head out. "Dad? Will you be home for dinner?" "Yes. I'll be here."

An old man in a room on an estate in a secluded suburb. Walls, gates, security circumscribe him. He's wizened, saurian. Screens are arrayed, printers eject data. Land lines and old and new style cell phones. Yellow pads with scribbled notes. A cigar burns in his fat fingers. As a child this man collaborated with the side oppressing his people. He went on to manipulate levers that collapsed the bottom from the currencies of nations. His foundation has an inviting name. It gives money to organizations and influential people. Politicians. District Attorneys. Money moves people, induces them to say and do things they wouldn't ordinarily. Some assert he funds groups advocating, ostensibly, for "anti-fascism."

He won't be operative much longer. But his sons will. They know the family business.

Offices start to reopen in New York and other cities.

Nicholson Maxwell Levi sets up a staggered schedule for their employees, two days on site, three at home.

The suite at Lions Pride is paid till August. Daniel sends a letter to Darren Maxwell requesting approval to rent an office nearby. It'll be less expensive than the suite. He needs to be close to home.

Caroline invites him for dinner and he meets her daughter, Tani. He's fascinated watching her conduct a lightning fast signing conversation with her mom. The eight-year-old girl doesn't shy from candor. When Caroline exits the room he asks her a question about school – she ignores it, shoots point-blank, "Do you like my mom, Daniel?" "I do, Tatiana." "Do you—*really* like her?" There's steel in the unflinching stare. Enigmatic girl, he thinks. A hardness which comes from protecting the vulnerable. He smiles at her—and her absent mother. "Very much." She seems satisfied with his answer, softens the glare.

He wants Caroline on the stairs but there's a little girl above and a landlord on the other side of the wall. She gently detaches, her mouth wet from his mouth. She signs to him— "Dream...about...me." Driving home, he considers the chaos in the world, in his personal life. Why am I not in turmoil? She wants to be in my dreams.

"When will you put it on the market?"

Mary's sipping iced tea in Jill's backyard.

"Probably July, August."

"Quite a thing Phillip did. More than your standard nice gesture, no?"

"For days I felt I'd dreamt the whole thing. He sent the papers – it was real."

"And all yours. Do you have plans?"

She tips the glass, tinkling the ice cubes. "No, Em. First, I'll have to figure out what to do with the furniture. I was researching auctions. I can't take all this with me." She samples the tea, "Needs sugar. I'll visit my mother. When it's done. Then – "

"An escape? Somewhere new?"

Jill's quiet, reflective. The blue jays conversing in the grass and trees.

"You okay, hon?" Mary touches Jill's chin.

"Yeah, yeah, thanks. I'm okay." She sucks on a fragment of ice. The June sun reveals lines under the eyes of the woman Mary cherishes as a girl from the country. "Where is there to escape to? If it's not roving bands of maniacs—and the police—it's the masks they compel you to wear. I thought the curve was flattened or whatever. Now we need to wear a freakin' mask? Forever or what?"

"I think it's a psychological game they're playing with us. *On* us. 'How far can we push them? What *won't* they submit to?' "

"You really think so?"

"They're actively making our lives unlivable."

"Wherever you go it's all this...hassle."

"Convincing us to feel we're all walking patients."

"Yes! That's it, Em. It's so bizarre. What the hell is happening in this world? Does anyone know?"

"Honestly... we're at a crossroads. We either surrender or— "

"What else? How do we fight it?"

"Don't cooperate with the insanity. To begin with. Don't wear the mask. Don't take the vax. Don't let them brainwash us."

"I want to begin."

"Me too." She sticks her pinkie out, Jill giggles, twines her pinkie with Mary's. "Have you seen Paul?"

Brushing hair from her cheek, "Yeah – he came by. We had lunch."

"What'd you have?"

"Oh, um... a salad."

"And Paul?"

"The same thing I—"

"No—did you have Paul?"

"What? You mean..."

"Yes. C'mon—tell me, Jill."

Jill nods. "Do you – mind?"

"No. I don't mind." They take each other's hands across the table. It's lovely, the sun and breeze. Summer's down the block. "Maybe we should."

"Hm?"

"Maybe *we* should." Mary raises her eyebrows, daubing color on Jill's pale cheeks.

"Wow. That came out of nowhere." She considers a moment. Years before she'd been ready to dive into anything with her older friend. "You know Em, I feel ... I could. I wouldn't be able to let you go. You'll wrap me up in you."

"Yeah," Mary throatily laughs. "We'll get lost in each other." She leaps— "I wake up sometimes—" emotional dimensions— "thinking about you."

"You do?" The answer's in the eyes. "So do I," Jill admits."

The ice has melted into the tea. Jill peeks at her empty house. "It's not easy to be without a man."

"Dan's not sleeping with me anymore. He's using the spare."

"How long?"

"Weeks. It's strange. He's there, in the house, comes home at night. I know he's been with another woman. That never stopped us. Something's different now."

"For him or—"

"Both of us."

"You think he loves her?"

"Probably."

"Are you in love?"

Mary wants to evade but can't. Was she in love? Did she know what that meant anymore?

"I suppose I am."

"Suppose?"

"And you?"

"I...do love him."

"But – what?"

"At our age, everything feels different. Like it's shifted in ... the mind. Does that sound—"

"Yeah. Being in love. It doesn't mean what it used to."

"No," Jill agrees. "It's changed. Maybe I don't know what I want. Anyway, it seems like, just personality wise... that you are more suited..."

"He really likes you, Jill. I think he loves you."

"Maybe. But I know he loves you."

"I'm not so sure."

"What?"

"Yeah. We crossed the line we never had and it's... fine. It's lovely. But is that—"

"Enough to make a whole life on?"

"Funny way to put it. We always worked as soul friends. Who knows if it would work... this way. And personalities... That's mostly surface. You feel you're too different from Paul?"

"Sometimes, yes. It's pretty glaring."

"Well, I feel we're too similar. So what's the difference?"

They laugh and throw up hands, drink the tea.

"I want you to be happy. You know I never meant to hurt you?"

"I know, Em. What happened with you two seems – inevitable or—"

"I know you've not been very happy in love."

"I don't think either of us has been happy in love."

Jill didn't pause at all in answering. The truth of it hits Mary hard. She blanches. It rolls over her like an engulfing wave. She almost needs to catch her breath.

"I'm sorry, I – honey are you – you okay?"

Mary nods, tries to compose.

"Yes, I'm okay. I guess it never – struck me before."

"I didn't mean to strike you."

"It's okay, Jill. The truth can be bracing." She covers Jill's hand with hers. "Thank you."

"You're welcome. Not sure for what?"

"You're my best friend. And so is Paul. To me, that's all that really matters."

"Me too, Em."

Jill peers into Mary's eyes. Is the sadness she sees Mary's or hers?

They both have a feeling they're revolving together. Around each other. And away from each other.

Oxygen is critical for cellular respiration in all aerobic organisms.

Oxygen is one of the most essential requirements of life, without which organisms on Earth would not survive.

Improper metabolism weakens the cells and causes them to lose natural immunity, making them susceptible to viruses that may lead to fatal health conditions.

Paul had seen a photo online that lodged deeply in him. Two Portland Oregon police officers lying on the ground outside of their precinct – *gazing at the stars.* They'd been battling, nightly, the gangs who hated them in the summer streets. Instead of going home to booze and oblivion, they lay and watched the heavens.

"What are you working on?" She knew he had a writing project in motion.

"A title came to me: **Children of the Earth.**"

Mary's facing Paul across the fold-up table containing his notebooks and laptop.

"I chanced on a line by Robert Desnos, the French poet. *'When all human decency was imprisoned I was free amongst the masked slaves.'* "

"That's incredibly apropos."

"Isn't it? It stirred something in me. I thought of one free man or woman – among hordes who don't perceive they're enslaved. And I started..." Mary revels in the vivacity in Paul's features "...putting ideas down."

"Poetry? Prose?"

"Prose."

"Narrative or free form?"

"Narrative...ly free. The overall feeling is – the children of the earth groping for their freedom. Their true liberation. The majority's unaware it's what they're reaching for. It's like...holding a flashlight on a pitch black field."

"One man?"

He picks up his coffee. "One is a symbol for a group—of individuals—aware of what's happening."

"In the vanguard."

"Yes." He sits, flips pages in his notebook. "Can't even read my own handwriting."

"What is it? A moment ago you were enthusiastic."

"Maybe it's a dumb idea."

"It's not. You'll follow it."

"It'll fall apart."

"It won't! You'll develop it. It's a wonderful idea, especially since it's real. Transpiring in front of us."

"I hope I can realize it."

"You will. And it'll be a valuable offering. Creative and unexpected."

"You empower me."

She sits. Kisses him. "You saw Jill."

"Mm."

"You had fun?"

"Occasionally I'm fun. Sometimes she's fun. You don't mind?"

"I don't mind."

"It's confusing. At least, I'm confused."

"We all are, Paul. I'm sorry this has gotten so – entangled. I don't have an easy answer. But you know you're...free, of course."

"Am I?" Mary goes to the window. "What's up?"

"It's over."

"Man, I *wish* it was over. No more masks or people yelling at me in supermarkets."

"I mean Dan and me."

"Is it – really?"

"This time…it is. He's in love with the maid at Lions Pride. Who cleans – his room."

"Seriously?" She nods. "He travels the whole world for years and five miles from home—"

"Finds a maid and falls in…"

"How do you feel?"

"I don't know. Pissed, I suppose. But also like my—one of my— roles is being taken away from me."

"That must feel strange.

"It does. I'd anticipated it but I wasn't quite prepared."

"Maybe you don't need it anymore."

"How do you feel?"

"Besides confused? Oh, up in the air."

"What's wrong with that? Don't you enjoy flight?"

"I'm tired of flying solo."

She kneels at his chair. "Me too." She takes his hands.

"Mare, I think I'm going to keep it platonic. Between us. Me and you. Me and Jill. Till something gets—"

"Resolved?"

"Clear."

"Yes. She gets up, plucks a blue Sharpie from his pen holder. "Can I use a piece of that box?" She rips off a section of cardboard, tapes it to a wall lighted by sunshine. Squashes the Sharpie against the cardboard and whirls it quickly—a thick blue circle. She whirls another circle around the first – withdraws – advances… Makes a third circle surrounding the others. She grabs a white-out roller from the table and erases small sections of the inner circle—then does the same, creating openings, in the outer ones. Examines her work. Tosses the Sharpie and white-out.

"You mind interpreting this for me?"

"In time, Paul."

"Alright, mystery lady. Speaking of time, I've been reading Blake again."

She goes to his table and sits, picking up the book. "Yes, I noticed."

He sits across. "I've been thinking about time. Your Alice in Wonderland decoding...inspired me."

"I'm delighted to hear that. And so are, I presume, Alice and Lewis."

"And that video you sent me—on timelines and personal creativity."

"Oh, yes. About focusing on what we truly want to experience – rather than blindly going along with what *they* are pushing us towards."

"It reminded me of what Jane Roberts wrote in her Seth books. That time is never closed – there's always a pathway, a detour you can pursue to another, more favorable outcome."

Mary's getting pumped. "In the video they talk about choosing a higher, more joyous, timeline. You move toward it somehow, from within. Is that possible?"

"It's ancient. Hermetic."

"Oh, yeah – as above so below."

"That's what led me back to Blake. I remembered his deep insight into space and time. 'To see a world in a grain of sand and a heaven in a wild flower... Hold Infinity in the palm of your hand... and Eternity in an hour...'"

"I remember you reading that to me when we were sixteen. My oh my." Paul takes her hand.

"I think I'm finally getting its significance. Somewhat."

"Well, don't hold back."

"They're just some ideas... Let me see if I can put it into words." He stands, picks up the book— "We don't live here – in a room, a house. A place."

"Really. So where do we live?"

"In time. We're not separate from the...flow of events in our lives. They come out of our thoughts, beliefs, emotions. Everything we think and feel, conscious, unconscious... is where we are in time."

"You're saying our inner lives – are manifested out here."

"Is that what I'm—yes. Something like that."

Mary stands, facing him. "Go on."

"We move towards – merge with? – timelines, time-realities, that align with...who we are."

"What we vibrate with."

"It looks like space where we are – but it's time. Where we live in time is where we live in space."

"Write that sentence down. Immediately, Paul."

He laughs, she joins him.

"Either we make it—or it's made for us."

"Someone else controls our time." Mary dovetails. "Our space."

"By controlling the story."

"Covid nineteen. Wear a mask. Take the shot."

"Believe in the virus. A timeline created for us."

"A narrative transformed into a collective reality."

"Yes, Mare. And people go with it – entering it like... a train or something, believing it's the—"

"Only train in town."

"Instead of seeing—we have magnificent vehicles of our own."

"Beautiful ones." They embrace. "We need to remember this, Paul."

"Always."

"Okay guys," Jill's email reads, "I'm breaking July fourth tradition and will have a Sunday dinner – not a barbecue – on the fifth. Weird, yes, but what's *not* weird now?"

The four hadn't been together since Friday, March 13. Just before time stopped. Had it begun again? They didn't know where they were or really going. They put their clothes on as prior, bathed as they had, lay down to sleep as in the past. Was the body the same lying down and fading out – was the mind the same making choices about what to wear and when to turn the water off and on? They'd like to think so. They know the calculations are different. The points of the axis have shifted. They still speak American English but the words sound as if the meaning of many has been altered. They're trying to keep up with changes they can't see and can't name, locate a rhythm to suit the undefined new tempo. Every day they secretly expect to find new clothes in the dresser, an obscure car in the driveway, answers to emails they don't recall sending, a waving neighbor whose face doesn't compute. They brace themselves, subconsciously, for the knock on a door or window they hadn't noticed. A waiting without awareness, an anticipation without precedent. Is it another barbecue and beach season kicking off? It must be, it's hot, sunny, grills are smoking.

"...Here's a fruit salad..." Jill spreads the platters, "...cheese and crackers... vegetables and dip. Beer and wine in the cooler. Yummy lasagnas coming later. Meat *and* veggie. Get your tummies ready."

It takes a couple of drinks and the conversation finds legs.

"I had the world in my hand and I looked over pleasant valleys." They all look at him—

"What's that Paul? Is it from a poem?"

"It popped into my mind, Dan. I voiced it."

"That's Paul," Jill pinches his cheek.

"Jill, may I broach the elephant in the – yard?"

"Please do, Daniel."

"That For Sale sign propped against the house. Will it be in the front yard soon?"

"Yes. August. September."

"Where will you be...going?"

"I haven't decided. I'll go upstate to Mom for a bit – then we'll see."

"*We'll* see?" The attorney follows up.

"It's a figure of speech. Am I right, Jill?"

"Yes, Em, you are."

"I think I know why those lines came into my head," Paul diverts.

"Which?" Mary asks, "I had the world—?"

"—In my hand and I looked over pleasant valleys."

"Well?" Dan is interested.

"It's not something I read. Or wrote. It's this: When you're young and the possibilities lie in front of you there's no end to anything, only endless beginnings. We may not have been young in – March – but there were possibilities. Now look at us—most of us in masks, afraid to shake hands – or come closer to listen. Can't go to the gym, can't see a movie, can't hardly share a meal with a friend."

Dan taps his bottle on the table. "Yes, the world looks far narrower. I ask myself—was it worth it? The shutdown? How many will lose their jobs—businesses?"

"Was it even necessary?" Mary bores in. "People are talking about Sweden. No lockdowns, no masks, no social distancing. They've done better than us and all the European countries."

Jill traces a finger in spilled wine. "The world's changed in...four months. *Four*."

"Paul—was it Rappart? The guy you sent me a link to?"

"Oh, Rappoport? You read his articles, Dan?"

"Incisive. You can tell he's been around. I read some of his pieces and felt like someone threw freezing cold water on my head."

"You didn't mention it to me."

"I did, Mar."

"Yes. The day I brought your lunch."

"What he says about the – 'medical cartel'– quite an eye-opener. I never dealt with the pharmaceutical or medical fields in my work, directly. I didn't know the power they wield. WHO. CDC. Which apparently is a semi-private organization. The thousands who die each year from the drugs and erroneous treatments. The falsified data. The b.s. studies in medical journals. Now I know why," he looks at Mary, "you stopped the vaccines for Jess. And now none for Toby. They've eliminated the religious exemption in New York state schools. Every year they make it harder. Anyway... I was reading about the other 'pandemics.' Swine flu. Sars one. Duds, never went anywhere. It took off this time, didn't it? And the PCR test? Not, apparently, *designed* to diagnose infectious disease..."

"I'm impressed," Mary raises her head, proudly.

"You've done your homework," Paul lifts his glass.

"It's dizzying, at first," he admits. "Some very smart people have a lot of doubts regarding what's going on. We all..."

"What?" Jill prods.

"Need to ask more questions. They've upended millions of lives. It's unprecedented. People have gotten ill, some have died. It's a part of life."

"Something else," Mary underpins, "is going on now. This 'new normal' bullshit. Do they actually believe we're two-year-olds?"

"That's how we've been acting," Dan replies.

"Yes," Jill dips in the cooler for a fresh bottle, "we did exactly what they said, every step of the way. Stay inside. Work at home. Look at us now."

They sense the claws overhead in the shadows lengthening in late afternoon—

"Okay guys, lasagna in twenty, how does that sound?"

—Upon the treetops...

"Sounds good, Jill..."

—The rooftops.

Lasagna's the last things on their minds.

"You know what I think?" Paul says, twirling the wine in his glass.

"Don't tell me," Jill ventures, "You're 'gazing down the mountain' – and the river is... 'revealing its secrets to you'?"

They all crack up. "Nice one!" Mary high-fives her.

"I deserved that," Paul grins. "What I think is—we are in the second wave."

"The second wave?" Jill muses. "Isn't that the resurgence of—"

"Anoroc suriv, yes."

"How dare you mock the *virus,* blasphemer," Mary puts the table in stitches. Paul flagellates himself with an empty bottle.

"They talk of the coming winter," he continues, "on the contrary. The second wave is happening now."

"Care to elaborate?" Mary challenges.

"The riots and looting, defund police, divisions between races, sexes, opinions, suddenly so prominent. We were told a virus was going to kill millions. Now there's another kind –

racial enmity... mixed with woke mentality. And like the insane extreme of isolating healthy people in their homes— we get the insanity of blaming an entire race for the death of a man in police custody. It doesn't negate the heinous treatment George Floyd suffered. But the reaction. Cities on fire, businesses and buildings demolished, sections of cities taken over. Encouraged by politicians. Millions of dollars pouring in from Silicon Valley, big corporations, Hollywood. Alliances with irrational, destructive elements. The sincere are being used like the scientists, doctors and nurses who built the covid story. To keep the "virus" going, the idea spreading. The spaces between us widening."

They breathe ... out. Cicadas buzz peculiar rhythms.

"But what is it all leading to?" Jill nibbles her nails.

"What's the endgame?" Dan seconds.

"The Great Reset," Paul states, stoically.

"Hm? The great – ?"

"World Economic Forum," Mary expands. "From Davos, Switzerland. They're calling for a 'great reset' of the entire world economic and governance systems. Covid as the catalyst."

"And every aspect of our lives," Paul amplifies. "Food, medicine, living places. Work."

"Energy use," Mary adds. "Population, depopulation."

"This is a real thing?" Jill poses to anyone.

"Yeah," Paul and Mary jumble. "It's on their website. Their videos."

"Is it true, Dan?" Jill's dazed.

"I've seen more and more, every year traveling – rules that make no sense. I've concluded they're for one reason – control."

"It reminds me," Mary quietly says, "how you can't recognize an acquaintance on the street with the mask on.

They're making us anonymous. Drifting, unknown, from each other."

The words sink. Twilight's come.

Jill stands, "Guys, it's time for lasagna." They all agree. "Okay, we'll break for ten."

The moon comes out low, and *full*.

In the house Mary discovers a bottle of tequila. Shots poured, a lime cut, lined on the island counter. "C'mon y'all," she drawls. The women are eager, the men reluctant. They all gulp one. She pours again. Gulp. Twisted mouths, laughter. Lasagna oven-mitted on the air. Jill lights citrine candles to scatter flies.

They're not kids anymore. No. It's been a long time but on a summer night, the night after Independence Day, you can graze a remnant of when you were an adventurous kid who didn't give a shit about politics or money or monogamy or the world. All you cared about was the next corner and what might be waiting. Maybe they shouldn't take it all so seriously, they all thought, biting into the steaming chunks of beef, ricotta and saucy noodles, maybe we should take it as it comes, not worry about how our lives feel like they're being slipped into a sluice gate beyond control. Was any adventure left for them? Any adventure, period? Did they want it? Could they find it? Should they forget all of it, the invisible virus, the screaming crowds, the fires and shattering glass, the anger, fear and anxiety, the mind control and mass compliance? They weren't kids anymore on a summer trip to the beach, coming home with sand and sleepiness, thinking only of the plan for that night. Now the world—in twilight— was looming and they couldn't deny it. They had to look into the valley.

"Let's make a li'l Inderpendance Day toast," Mary mumbles, pouring wine for all. "Firs' one is mine. To the full moon—looks pretty damn full to me!" They drink. "And to – Sacagawea..."

"Hear hear—"

"And—Janis Joplin." They touch, drink.

"I've got one," Jill lifts her wine. "To Elizabeth Cady Stanton, Susan B. Anthony... and the suffragettes of upstate New York."

"Hear hear!" Mary shouts, clanging glasses with her female counterpart. "Suffragette city."

"Dan, you got one?" Jill coaxes.

"Okay, here's to – Thomas Jefferson." They noisily concur. "One more. Louis Brandeis—and his 'fact-based evidence.' "

"And here's to a revival of fact-based evidence—damn it!" Paul smacks the table and they burst into laughter.

"Well, Paul?" Mary lures.

"Here's to—Dwight David Eisenhower who warned us to – 'guard against the acquisition of – unwarranted influence, something something, by the military-industrial complex.' " They raise. "One more. Louis Satchmo Armstrong. Oh, and—Carson McCullers."

They drink. They eat lasagna, meat and veggie. Chewing, smiling and almost satisfied.

In a moment between words and silence, a POP! startles them all—they jerk to attention. Another pop! Pop-pop-pop, pop, pop-pop-pop. With one set of eyes they see it—light and color exploding above them, curtaining the white-peachiness of the moon—showers rising, glittering—pinks, purples, reds, blues, whites, golds—booming then popping, sputtering, crackling. A cascade—and bursting—coming out of bursting.

The four friends step from the patio onto the grass closer to where the fireworks are launching. "Is it the street this way?" "No, it's that one—" It doesn't matter, anywhere they look it's up, where they ascend, bloom, fall fluttering and shooming sizzling down and out.

"Isn't that lovely" Jill avers, her eyes fused with the explosions echoing a song about a promising union. All four feel her *lovely* enter them, also a promise, a seed of possibility, something aside from the dwindling light and space. Paul turns to Jill, the lights dance off of her chocolaty eyes. Mary on his other side, borne by the booms and flying colors. Daniel, next to her, mesmerized by the effulgent show. They've forgone everything for the moment except light, sound, color. The desire to connect to the boundless, color-splashing sky.

She picks him up in the RAV4 in late afternoon, first week of September. "Hello sweetie." "Hello pretty lady," he answers. He doesn't inquire where she's taking him, relaxing in the passenger seat.

"How's *Children of the Earth* coming?"

"It's going. Oh, I added a crow who'll be an – alternate narrator."

"Whoa... You're speakin' my language! Forward me pages posthaste."

"Directly, my retainer to yours." She winks at him.

They drive for ten minutes. Mary turns off the road onto a driveway. An old wooden sign: Sandrey Hall.

"Oh yeah..." Paul reflects. "I forgot—"

"This place?"

An old estate converted to county park. Sweet sixteens and weddings celebrated in the ramshackle building. Paul and Mary walk the gravel lot to where the green hill descends. It's warm, still summer, though when September arrives there's change in the air.

"I spoke to Jill this morning," she tells him. "She got an offer on the house."

"Oh, good."

"An 'attractive' one, she said."

He peers at the green and blue expanse stretched before them. "Then she'll take it."

They go where the vista opens widest—Worthington Harbor dark blue rimmed by sandy-mottled beach. The boats, dozens, rocking in the wake of one returning to anchor.

"A grand view. Hm, Paul?"

"The best. Which I also...forgot," he chuckles ruefully.

Dogs bark and play, humans in proximity, obviously excited to be socializing.

"Look Mare—no masks."

"What a refreshing sight," she says with half-irony. Two of the four-leggeds race to them –"They're friendly," someone hollers. They sniff, jump, yap, circle. Mary kneels, petting the larger black dog, "Yes, oh yes, good girl." Paul's not sure what the beige one is, he strokes its back and ears. Tails wagging, barking thank-yous, they dash back.

Paul absorbs the animated bunch—"They can't stop that."

"Not a chance." They head down the hill to the beach.

" 'And we are put on earth a little space that we... may learn to bear the beams of love.' "

"Blake?" she looks sidewise—

"Blake."

The grass is soft and the wind is gentle.
"Will Toby have to wear a mask at school?"
"From what I've heard, yeah."

"Kids don't deserve that."

"None of us do. I can't do that to him."

The grass fades and a dirt path leads to the beach. Couples and families are enjoying the last of the sun.

They walk the beach kicking cracked shells. "Let's take our shoes off."

"Mare, it freakin' hurts!" He submits. Shoes and socks left behind. The sand was rigid, dotted with rocks, shells, pebbles. On bare feet it kept you alert.

"We'll go that way," Mary points to the sun.

They amble, savoring the warmth, sounds of gulls and children playing. She pauses taking the floating colorful assemblage in to herself. A longing inside Mary Wellner. For movement. For journeys. For blooming. The boats bobbing in the water that rolls everywhere.

"I want to leave, Mare. This isn't my place anymore."

Mary remains fixed on the water. The girl from the south shore. With the boy from the playground.

"*Our* place anymore." A hush. "Envision where you might...want to voyage. I'll do the same."

"You will?"

"Imagine it. Our timelines will meet."

They walk in the line of the descending sun, nearly touching the lip of the harbor.

"It's not over. We're not done yet, Paul. We're not done."

He feels her whole being in the day and night hour.

"I was thinking the same thing," he responds, simply.

Her hand is his guide.

"Mare... you never told me—what the circles mean—the ones you drew on my wall."

"Come on..." turning. Enticing him. "Follow me—and I'll tell you."

Their feet skim the rocks, lightly, and they're on the earth, they're in the sky, sun giving off beams of orange, of yellow, of gold.

Michael Schuval writes poems and prose.
This is his first published novel.

Citations and references for material herein
can be found, along with more of his work,
at: https://michaelschuval.substack.com/

Look for more of his books to be following shortly.